Margaret Thornton was born in Blackpool and has lived there all her life. She is a qualified teacher but has retired in order to concentrate on her writing. She has two children and five grandchildren. Her previous Blackpool sagas, *It's a Lovely Day Tomorrow*, *A Pair of Sparkling Eyes*, *How Happy We Shall Be*, *There's a Silver Lining*, *Forgive Our Foolish Ways*, *A Stick of Blackpool Rock* and *Wish Upon a Star*, are also available from Headline and have been highly praised:

'A brilliant read' *Woman's Realm*
'A gentle novel whose lack of noise is a strength' *The Sunday Times*
'Delightful' Netta Martin, *Annabel*

Also by Margaret Thornton

It's a Lovely Day Tomorrow
A Pair of Sparkling Eyes
How Happy We Shall Be
There's a Silver Lining
Forgive Our Foolish Ways
A Stick of Blackpool Rock
Wish Upon a Star

The Sound of her Laughter

Margaret Thornton

HEADLINE

First published in 1999
by HEADLINE BOOK PUBLISHING

First published in paperback in 1999
by HEADLINE BOOK PUBLISHING

10 9 8 7 6 5 4 3 2

ISBN 0 7472 6042 7

Typeset by Avon Dataset Ltd, Bidford-on-Avon, Warks

Printed and bound in France
by Brodard & Taupin.
Reproduced from a previously printed copy.

HEADLINE BOOK PUBLISHING
A division of Hodder Headline
338 Euston Road
London NW1 3BH

www.headline.co.uk
www.hodderheadline.com

For all the teachers with whom I have worked during my years in the profession; especially those with whom I am still in contact, most especially my good friend, Gladys.

The teachers portrayed in this book are fictional characters although, here and there, certain characteristics of teachers I have known have crept in. The schools, however, are based, very largely, on two Blackpool schools in which I have taught, although the names have been changed. Many of the former members of staff – and pupils – may recognise them.

But the incidents that take place in the schools and elsewhere are figments of my imagination.

Chapter 1

'Now you won't forget to write, will you, dear?'

It was the umpteenth time that Alice Rawlinson had asked that question during the ten minutes they had been standing on the platform at Haliford station. But Frances answered her, once again, good-humouredly. 'No, Auntie Alice, I won't forget to write. Don't you worry. I'll let you know how Mum's getting on. And I'll tell you all about my new school.'

Frances had grown very fond of her aunt during the two years she had been living at her home. She knew that she would miss her very much at first, but not nearly so much, Frances guessed, as her aunt would miss her. Alice had come to look upon her as a daughter rather than a niece but it was time now for Frances to go back to Blackpool, to make her home once again with her mother and to continue her teaching career in the town that was really her home.

It was the ruling of the Chief Education Officer for Blackpool that local girls should not be encouraged to apply for posts in their home town until they had taught elsewhere for at least two years. An unfair ruling, many thought. Why should Blackpool be allowed to pick and choose like this whilst other authorities were only too willing to employ probationers? After all, young teachers had to gain their experience – and make their mistakes – somewhere. The rule, admittedly, was relaxed from time to time, usually in extenuating circumstances such as the ill health of a parent. But when Frances had left college in 1956 her mother, Iris Goodwin, had been in reasonably good health and quite happy for her daughter to take a teaching post in Yorkshire, the county where she had done her training. The situation had now changed and Frances knew that she was needed at home.

'Goodness me, I wish that train would hurry up and come.' Frances glanced at her watch. It was only five minutes late, but they seemed to have been standing there for hours, Aunt Alice having insisted, as usual, on getting there with time and enough to spare. Partings were always distressing, and it only prolonged the agony when they dragged on and on.

'Don't worry, love. It'll be here in a minute or two, I dare say,' said Alice, sounding the more relaxed of the two of them at that moment. 'Now, you've got your ticket safe, haven't you? And don't forget to eat those nice sandwiches I've made you. They're beef, off yesterday's joint. I always think it cuts better when it's cold . . . And give my love to yer mam, won't you, dear? I hope she's on the mend. Though I doubt if she'll ever be able to dash around like she used to, not now that blessed "arthuritis" has set in. We're neither of us spring chickens any more, are we, Iris and me? Your Uncle Jack's doing all right, though, for an old 'un, isn't he? Sixty-four next birthday and still working at Hammond's mill. Mind you, I reckon that's what's keeping him going. I don't know whatever he'll do when he has to retire. Me neither, love.' Alice chuckled. 'I can't say as I fancy having him under me feet all day . . .'

Frances smiled, not answering. She had heard the same remarks time and time again and knew that her aunt was chattering so there would not be a silence heavy with the threat of separation. She glanced up now at the view across the railway lines. It was quite a nice day, although it had been a poor sort of summer so far – cold and rainy for most of the time. Frances viewed a pleasing scene: the railway station was in the valley, and the hillside, one of the lower slopes of the Pennines, formed a backdrop to the clusters of grey-stone houses huddled on its slopes. An orange bus, looking at this distance like a child's toy, crawled along the road that snaked round the side of the fell, northwards to Bradford or beyond, and a couple of cars were heading southwards towards Lancashire. Here and there a tall mill chimney belched smoke out into the still blueness of the sky, besmirching the quality of the air and light. There were not so many chimneys now as there had been even a few years ago. The Yorkshire woollen industry, that the mill owners had believed would last for ever, was already in decline.

Haliford had once been one of the main centres of the 'shoddy' industry, the process by which old clothes made of wool were ground into a fibrous mass – shoddy – then mixed with virgin wool and remade into new cloth. Now, with the advent of synthetic fibres, many of these mills had closed down or had been converted into factories producing kitchen furniture or electronic equipment. With the march of progress many mill workers had lost their jobs or had been forced to learn different skills. Jack Rawlinson, however, still held on to his job of warehouseman at Hammond's, where he had been for as long as Frances could remember. Aunt Alice and Uncle Jack never seemed to change and Frances had been glad of their reliability and the welcoming comfort of their home as she settled into the first post of her teaching career.

'It's here now,' said Frances with some relief as the train puffed its way round the corner and into view. She was glad to see it was a corridor train – you never knew who you might end up with when it wasn't – and she quickly bundled her belongings, a suitcase that weighed a ton and two bulging travel bags, into the nearest compartment.

'Oh dear, however will you manage at the other end?' said Alice, worriedly eyeing the mountain of luggage. 'And you've to change, haven't you, at Preston?'

'Don't worry, Auntie; I'll be OK,' said Frances. 'I'll get a taxi, and I dare say I can get a porter to help me at Preston. I'll be fine.' She stood on the step, reaching down to put her arms round the plump little woman, placing a kiss on her rosy cheek. 'Bye, Auntie Alice. Love to Uncle Jack, and to Len and Karen and the girls. Take care of yourself now . . . I'll write . . .'

'Just think on that you do,' said Alice, a tear glistening in her eye as the guard waved his flag and the train pulled away. 'Remember now, give my love to yer mam. And to Josie and the family. Bye, Frances . . . goodbye.'

Frances waved until she saw her aunt turn to leave the platform, then she settled down. She was pleased to have a window seat because the scenery, at least until you reached the border with Lancashire, was quite impressive. She feasted her eyes first of all on the dark grey houses, many of them former mill workers' cottages, and the higgledy-piggledy cluster of mills strung along the valley bottom. Rising above it all was the extravagant folly of an octagonal mill chimney topped with a Renaissance-style pinnacle, erected by a mill owner who believed that even chimneys could be things of beauty. Then the industrial landscape gave way to wild moorland, brown with bracken and purple with heather. Hump-backed bridges spanned the river that had once brought power to the looms and soft water for the washing, carding and combing of the wool. Sheep grazed between the limestone boulders, smoke curled from the chimneys of what must be some of England's loneliest farms, and here and there a waterfall cascaded down between granite rocks.

Frances knew that she would miss the hills of Yorkshire. From her aunt's house on Baldwin Lane, the thoroughfare that climbed steadily out of the valley floor, there was an uninterrupted view across the moors. It could be bleak in winter, especially in a house that was not centrally heated – and few were – although at least her aunt and uncle had finally managed to persuade the landlord that they had to have a bathroom and an inside lavatory. Her mother's little bungalow was not centrally heated either, but there were gas fires and electric radiators; besides, the place was too tiny ever to get really cold.

The train chugged its way over bridges and through tunnels cut through limestone and the darker millstone grit, towards the border with Lancashire, the home of the cotton, not the woollen, industry. Blackburn, Accrington, Burnley, Nelson and Colne. The names of these towns were engraved on Frances's mind and had been ever since she had learned them, by rote, when she was studying for her O level Geography exam. The five main weaving towns . . . or were they the spinning towns? She could never quite remember. No; Bolton, Bury, Rochdale and Oldham – those were the spinning towns.

The train was pulling into Blackburn station now, a huge building that seemed far too big for the amount of traffic passing through it, though once it had been at the very centre of all the industrial hubbub and commerce. Now, though the station was fairly busy, it was mainly with businessmen, shoppers and holiday-makers; there was little sign of the industry which had once been its very life blood.

In Lancashire, as well as in the Yorkshire Frances had just left behind, working 'at t'mill' was no longer the way of life it had once been for countless men and women, Frances's mother, Iris Goodwin, having been one of them. Her mother was very much in Frances's thoughts as the train left Blackburn, heading towards Preston, where she would change for the Blackpool train.

Iris, from being a girl of twelve, had worked long hours in the woollen mill. One of a very large family, she had been sent out to work at an early age. Frances knew from the odd remark her mother had made, or from snippets of conversation she had gleaned from Aunt Alice, that marrying her first husband, Alfred Collier, had been a good step up the social ladder for young Iris, especially as he had been more than twenty years her senior and, when he died, had left her very well heeled. Strictly speaking Iris was not Frances's mother. She was her stepmother, having married Samuel Goodwin soon after Florence Goodwin had died giving birth to Frances; much too soon, many had believed. Iris had been forty-two then, some ten years older than her father, but Frances had never thought of her as old. She was just Mum, the woman who had loved her and cared for her – spoiled her at times, if the truth were told – the only mother Frances had ever known.

Dad was long dead, killed in the war, and now Mum's health was deteriorating. She was becoming more and more incapacitated by rheumatoid arthritis – 'arthuritis', as Aunt

Alice always called it – and it was no longer wise for her to live alone, especially as her heart was not too good either. She had given them quite a scare several years back, when Frances was still at school, when she had suffered a heart attack. This had forced her to give up her boarding house in North Shore and move to a little bungalow in Layton. She had lived there quite happily on her own while Frances was at college, then teaching for two years in Haliford; but now, with the onset of arthritis and a few disturbing warnings from Iris's heart, this was no longer possible.

Which was why Frances Goodwin was on a west-bound train experiencing, if she were honest, very mixed feelings at the thought of living at home again. The last time Frances had seen her, Iris had seemed rather querulous, something she had not previously been, and more demanding. Frances had tried to think, charitably, that it was the pain that was making her so difficult, although Iris, it had to be admitted, had always been a tartar for wanting her own way. But they would learn to adjust to one another again, Frances told herself, and if things proved too difficult her elder sister, Josie, who lived in Blackpool, was always on hand to help.

Having boarded the Blackpool train at Preston, Frances breathed a heartfelt sigh of relief when she had heaved her two heavy bags up on to the luggage rack. Whew! Her Aunt Alice had been right to worry about how she would manage to change trains. There was not a porter in sight when she alighted. Then when she had struggled about fifty yards along the platform, a suitcase in one hand, a travel bag in the other and the remaining bag tucked, somehow, under her arm, one had appeared. Cheerfully he had taken charge of her luggage, heaving it around as though it weighed no more than a few ounces, leading her along the subway and across to platform one where she caught the train with just a few minutes to spare. It had been well worth the shilling tip she had given him, feeling very much a woman of the world and an intrepid traveller to boot.

She stared now at the suitcase on the floor, wondering whether it would be worth the effort of heaving it on to the rack, if, indeed, she could manage to do so. There was only one other passenger in the compartment, a young woman whom Frances had hardly glanced at as she stumbled in, so it wasn't likely the luggage would be in anybody's way. She caught sight of her reflection in the mirror on the wall, which was sandwiched between two sepia photographs, one of Southport and the other of Morecambe. Goodness, what a mess she looked, her fairish hair all over the place, her face red and perspiring freely with her exertions and a black smear of soot on the side of her nose. As she drew her hanky from her cardigan pocket to wipe away the offending smut she saw two blue eyes, paler than her own, staring at her quizzically, reflected in the mirror.

'It is Frances, isn't it?' said the girl uncertainly. 'I thought it was when you came in. Of course I haven't seen you for ages . . .'

Frances turned to look at the young woman. Wispy blonde hair, an earnest little face, pale blue eyes, Yes, Frances remembered those intense eyes which, at times, had seemed to be probing into her very soul.

'Megan . . .' she said, with a glad smile of recognition. 'Megan Ashcroft, isn't it? How nice to see you again.' Frances spoke sincerely. It was good to meet old friends again, although the two of them had never been bosom pals.

'Would you like me to give you a hand with that?' asked Megan, nodding towards the suitcase. 'You seemed to be having rather a struggle. I managed with just the one.' A medium-size case, as neat and unobtrusive-looking as Megan herself, was on the rack above the girl's head. 'But then I've only been away for the weekend. You look as though you've been globetrotting?' Those pale blue eyes beneath politely raised blonde eyebrows were watching Frances intently again.

'No . . . thanks. I think I'll leave it there if it's OK with you,' replied Frances. 'If somebody gets in at Kirkham then I'll think again.' She collapsed gratefully on the opposite seat. 'No, I've not been globetrotting, though it certainly feels like it. I've just come from Yorkshire. I've been teaching there, you see, for the past two years.'

Frances hadn't seen Megan since they'd both left school, Frances to go to teacher training college and Megan to take up a nursing career. She had been keen to work overseas, on the Mission Field, Frances remembered. She was just about to mention this when Megan leaned forward intently and asked, 'You've been teaching in Yorkshire? Why was that? Couldn't you get a job in Blackpool? Or did you want to get away from home?'

'Not exactly,' replied Frances. 'They don't like giving jobs to local girls, you know, not straight away. But I've got a post in Blackpool now and I'm going to live at home again. Mum's not too well, you see. Her heart's not too good and she's got arthritis.'

'Oh dear, I'm sorry to hear that,' said Megan. She did look quite concerned. She had always had a sympathetic nature, Frances recalled, though she could, at times, be rather judgemental. 'And where's your new school?' she went on. 'Is it near where you live?'

'Quite near,' said Frances. 'Not actually in Layton – that's where Mum lives – but it's only a bus ride away, on that big new estate they've built. Wyre Bank, the school's called – not that it's anywhere near the River Wyre, but they've called it after our local river, I suppose.'

'And what age group do you teach?'

'Infants . . . for my sins,' added Frances ruefully, reflecting, when she had said it, that maybe it wasn't the wisest thing to say to Megan Ashcroft. In the old days she and her friend, Janet, had been forever harping on about sin. 'What I mean is . . . I wish sometimes I'd trained for Juniors, not Infants. The young children can be so terribly wearing, especially the Reception class, which is what I've had for the last two years. I'm having a Third Year class, though, at Wyre Bank, six-to-seven-year-olds, so it might be less harassing. I'm hoping there'll be more teaching and less tying shoelaces and mopping up puddles, if you know what I mean.'

'I think so.' Megan smiled politely. 'Where did you live when you were in Yorkshire? Were you in digs?'

'No; I stayed with my aunt and uncle,' replied Frances. 'Our family came from Yorkshire originally, you know.'

'Oh yes, I remember now,' said Megan. 'You're not sand-grown, like me, are you? Your family came to Blackpool during the war, didn't they, to take a boarding house?'

'Yes . . . at least my mother did,' said Frances. 'Dad was killed in the desert war in Africa so Mum brought us to Blackpool, me and my sister and brother. She'd always fancied having a boarding house; well, a private hotel it was, really.'

'But she's not there now?'

'No, she had to give it up when she started to be ill.'

'So you're going home to look after her?'

'Something like that,' said Frances evasively.

'Yes . . . she was quite a lot older than some of our mothers, wasn't she?' said Megan thoughtfully, and not very tactfully, in Frances's view. 'I remember seeing her when we were at school. What about your sister – Josie, isn't it? Does she help to look after your mother?'

What is this? thought Frances, beginning to feel a trifle annoyed. *Twenty Questions* or something? 'Of course she does,' she replied, as evenly as she could. 'Josie does what she can. But she has her own family to see to and she lives right at the other side of Blackpool, in Marton.'

'She married a policeman, didn't she?'

'Yes, that's right; Jimmy Clegg. We don't see very much of my brother, Bertie,' Frances went on before Megan had a chance to ask. 'He's teaching in the Midlands. He married a girl from down there and they don't come up to Blackpool all that often.' She didn't explain that Iris was only a stepmother, albeit a wonderful one, to the three children. Whether Megan was cognisant with this fact Frances wasn't sure, but there was no point in telling her.

Frances smiled in a friendly way at her travelling companion. 'Well, I think that's enough about me, isn't it? What about you? You went in for nursing, did you, like you said you would?'

'Yes, I'm at Victoria Hospital,' said Megan. 'I've been there since I was eighteen. I'm a staff nurse now. And . . .

I'm engaged to one of the doctors there.' She hung her head, blushing slightly and staring down at the solitaire diamond ring on the third finger of her left hand, something which Frances had only just noticed, 'He's a gynaecologist – Dr Conway, Bernard, he's called – and we're getting married next year, we hope.'

'That's wonderful. Congratulations,' said Frances. 'I must say you look very happy.' For Megan was certainly looking radiant now, her pale face flushed and her eyes sparkling with fervour; the way they had used to do, Frances remembered, when the girl spoke about her love for the Lord. 'Let me see . . .' Frances said now, although the last thing she wanted to do was embark on a theological discussion. 'Didn't you think of going overseas at one time? Becoming a missionary?'

'Oh yes, yes I did,' said Megan earnestly. 'I think I would still like to . . . if I hadn't met Bernard.' She twisted her ring round and round on her finger. 'He's convinced me, you see, that there's just as much work to do for the Lord here without going overseas. Bernard has all those babies he's bringing into the world, and I'm doing what I can to help the children who have to stay in hospital. Poor little mites; some of them are so homesick. That's where I am at the moment, on the children's ward, though we get moved around from time to time. Yes, there's plenty of work to be done here in God's name, Frances, without going overseas.'

'Absolutely,' replied Frances, not sure what else to say. 'And what about your fiancé, Bernard? Does he belong to the same church as you? Weren't you a Baptist before you joined that . . . that other group?'

'The Friends of the Carpenter you mean,' said Megan, eyeing her steadily. 'You went there for a while yourself, Frances, when we were at school.'

'Yes . . . so I did,' said Frances, somewhat cagily. Her encounter with the Friends of the Carpenter was something she didn't often think about now. 'What happened to them?' she asked. 'Are they still going strong?'

'No, I'm afraid not. The group folded a couple of years back. Lack of funds mainly, and the numbers were dwindling. Yes . . . as you said, I was a Baptist before that, but not any longer. Bernard is a Catholic and – you may be surprised to hear this, Frances – that's what I'm going to be as well. I'm taking instruction from the priest at Bernard's church. So that we can get married at the high altar. It means a lot to him, you see . . . And what Bernard wants, then I want as well,' she added demurely.

Frances was more than surprised at this news; she was flabbergasted, though she tried not to show it. Megan, who at one time had believed that even Church of England vicars with their elaborate vestments and ceremonial worship, smacked of 'popery', this same Megan was to marry a Roman Catholic?

'Yes, I am rather surprised,' she replied guardedly, 'but I'm very happy for you.'

'Thank you. I am happy as well,' said Megan, once again blushing prettily. 'Meeting Bernard has made such a difference to me, to my outlook . . . and everything. After all, He's the same God, isn't He, for all of us, no matter how we worship. Bernard has made me see that.'

'Absolutely,' said Frances, for the second time. This Bernard must be quite something, she thought as she smiled at her rediscovered friend. What a change in Megan, and all because the young woman had fallen in love, an experience as yet unknown to Frances.

'What about you, Frances? Have you a boyfriend? I can see you're not engaged.' Megan was looking somewhat pityingly at Frances's ringless hand, a tendency Frances had noticed before in newly engaged girls. Megan was certainly inquisitive, but Frances found that she didn't mind. Megan seemed much more human now than the 'holier than thou' young girl that Frances remembered.

'No, I'm quite footloose and fancy-free,' replied Frances, laughing easily. 'And, at twenty-two I've got plenty of time to find the right man. I went out with one or two lads when I was in Haliford, but nothing serious. You don't meet many men in an infant school staffroom. My last school was both infants and juniors, but there were only four of us altogether on the staff, all women. It was just a small village

11

school, less than a hundred children in all.'

'You'll find a big difference at Wyre Bank then,' said Megan. 'It's a vast estate, so I should imagine there'll be hundreds of children in the school, won't there?'

'Yes, about two hundred and fifty in the infant school alone,' replied Frances. 'It should be quite a challenge. I'm looking forward to it.' She was trying to convince herself of this. At times, if she were honest, she felt quite scared at the prospect. A large class, almost twice the size of what she had been used to, and a headmistress who, at the interview, had looked aloof and forbidding.

'That's good,' said Megan. 'It makes all the difference when you find the right vocation in life. I'm so glad I have.' She was looking dreamily again at her little solitaire diamond ring and Frances guessed she was thinking of her forthcoming marriage to the wonderful Bernard rather than her nursing career. Then she looked up, staring intently at Frances. 'Shall we keep in touch, Frances, now we've met up again? I'd like to . . . if you would.'

'Yes, I would like to,' said Frances, finding that she really meant it. She had lost touch with most of her old schoolfriends in Blackpool and her college friends were mainly from Yorkshire or further afield. She would no doubt meet a whole new set of acquaintances – possibly friends – at her new school, but she wasn't going to spurn Megan's offer. She felt, somehow, that the young woman wanted – or more than that, needed – her friendship. 'Yes, I'd like to see you again, Megan. You must be very busy, though, with your nursing . . . and Bernard.'

'Yes, I am, that's true, but I'm sure we can sort something out. Give me your address and I'll give you mine. Is your mother on the phone?'

Iris Goodwin was, but Megan's parents in South Shore were not. The two young women swapped details and Megan said she would ring in a few weeks' time when Frances had settled into her new job and she, Megan, was on a convenient shift.

'Now, let's look out for Blackpool Tower,' said Megan, sounding like an excited little girl. As she peered eagerly through the window she did, in fact, look much younger than her twenty-two years. She was slightly built, with a small face and delicate features, and her pink and white gingham dress, worn with a white woolly cardigan and flat-heeled sandals, only served to make her look more childlike. By comparison, Frances, in her blue rayon costume, recently purchased at Leeds C & A, felt positively sophisticated and quite the height of fashion. 'I always look for Blackpool Tower when I've been away,' Megan explained. 'It's like a "welcome home" sign. Don't you think so?'

'Yes, it certainly is,' said Frances, although she had forgotten about it until Megan reminded her. The silhouette of Blackpool Tower would soon appear on the horizon, just after the next hillock.

'There it is,' they both cried in unison as the tall slender structure, no bigger than their little fingers at this distance, came into view. They burst out laughing. 'Like a couple of kids, aren't we?' said Frances. 'It's a welcome sight, as you say. I remember Josie and Bertie and I looking for it every time we came back from holiday. Where've you been, by the way? You didn't say.'

'Oh, just to visit an aunt in Shropshire,' replied Megan. 'My cousin's just had a baby and I thought it was a good opportunity to see them, especially as Bernard was working this weekend. He often is . . . but I'll see him tonight.' Her eyes were shining at the thought of it. 'I start a week of late shifts tonight.'

'Oh dear. Poor you,' said Frances feelingly.

'Not to worry.' Megan sounded very cheerful. 'There are compensations. A great many of them.' She smiled serenely. All centred around Dr Bernard Conway, unless Frances was very much mistaken.

They fell silent, each wrapped in her own thoughts, as the train stopped first at Poulton-le-Fylde, then at Layton. 'Are you getting off here?' asked Megan. 'Didn't you say your mother lives in Layton?'

'Yes, she does, but it's a long way from the station, and I won't be able to get a taxi here,' said Frances. 'There should be plenty of them at North station.'

'And plenty of holiday-makers to fill them, no doubt,' said Megan. 'There'll probably be a queue a mile long.'

'Job's comforter,' muttered Frances, but she was smiling. Meeting Megan had cheered her up no end, helping her to put to one side her feelings of trepidation at her home-coming. 'I'm so pleased I've met you again,' she said as the train, with a screech of brakes, then a tremendous jolt, pulled into the station. 'And we'll keep in touch. Don't forget to give me a ring.'

Chapter 2

The forecourt of North station was more crowded than Frances had expected, with cars and taxis coming and going, visitors arriving and departing, newspaper sellers, ice-cream vendors, porters pushing trolleys piled high with luggage, and half a dozen small boys offering to 'Carry yer case, missis?' There was a queue, if not a mile long, as Megan had predicted, then certainly a good twenty yards or so, waiting for taxis. Megan, only having one small case, had assisted Frances with her luggage, then hurried away to catch a bus, leaving her friend to tag on to the end of the queue. It was mid-August, the height of the holiday season. Frances had decided not to travel on Saturday when the trains would be extra busy, or on Sunday when they were few and far between, but it seemed as though many visitors had waited until today, Monday, to start their holidays.

In the queue in front of Frances there were a dozen or more children, from various families, jumping up and down with excitement, running the length of the queue and back or banging metal spades on the pavement.

'Give over, our Alfie,' bawled a harassed-looking woman with a red face and a net over her newly permed hair. She made a grab at the boy who had trodden deliberately on his little sister's toes, making her whimper, then danced away. 'If I've told yer once I've told yer twenty times. Leave our Joanie alone. You'll get a good hiding if you make her cry again. Kids! Who'd 'ave 'em, I ask yer?' She cast an imploring look at Frances, who smiled politely then looked away. Children were pretty much the same the world over, she guessed, although she wouldn't fancy a dozen like that one in her class.

It was right in the middle of the school holidays, of course, and many families were taking their annual week's holiday. In addition, it would be the 'Wakes Week' for several of the inland towns. Still, there was nothing Frances could do about the taxi queue but wait. She couldn't attempt a bus journey with all this luggage.

To while away the time she studied the posters on the hoardings, advertising the season shows. Blackpool had certainly got its share of celebrities here this summer. David Whitfield and Arthur Haynes at the Opera House in 'The Big Show of 1958'. The Opera House always liked to boast of the 'big one'. Ken Dodd and Josef Locke at the Central Pier; David Nixon and Joan Regan at the North Pier; Winifred Atwell and Michael Holliday at the Hippodrome . . . It would be nice to take Mum to one of the season shows, Frances mused. They were spoiled for choice with such an array of talent. Frances would have opted for Rawicz and Landauer at the Winter Gardens. She liked listening to good pianists, although she couldn't play herself, but she couldn't stand that awful Hylda Baker who was also in the show. She would just have to let her mother make the choice, provided Iris wanted to go. From what Josie had said, their mother didn't go out much these days.

'Where to, luv?' asked a taxi driver, flinging open the door of a black cab and bringing her out of her reverie. The queue had dispersed much more rapidly than she had expected.

'Oh . . . Layton, please. Near the bowling green,' said Frances, lifting one bag while the driver threw the rest into the back.

'Here on holiday are you, luv?' he asked as he drove away.

'No . . . no, I live here.'

'Coming back from holiday then, are you?' he persisted, looking back over his shoulder and taking one hand off the wheel in an alarming way. 'Where've you been?'

'No, I've not been on holiday either. I've been living in Yorkshire, and now I've come back to live here,' said

16

Frances, wishing that the nosy fellow would shut up and concentrate on his driving. She didn't intend giving him her life history – she'd done that once today already – although she knew he was only trying to be friendly. Most cab drivers in Blackpool were friendly, as were the bus conductors and conductresses. They had a reputation for cheerful banter. It was that sort of a town.

'Oh, I see. I was only going to say I 'ope you 'ave a decent sort of week,' said the taxi driver. 'Although you'll be lucky, I say, you'll be lucky! It's been a bloomin' awful summer so far, it has that, but they still keep on coming. T'visitors, I mean. We had one hell of a storm last night. Thunder and lightning and hailstones and God knows what. T'tramlines were blocked with all t'sand swirling about and t'buses were diverted. Some o' t'roads were like rivers. You should've seen 'em. Like rivers, they were. I've nivver seen owt like it. Some poor beggars were flooded out.' He sounded amazingly cheerful though, as some folk were apt to do at other people's misfortunes.

'Oh dear,' said Frances. 'We've had bad weather in Yorkshire too, but we didn't have a storm like that.' She was hoping that her mother would be all right. Iris had always had an irrational fear of thunderstorms.

'Aye, well, d'you know what I blame it on?' He didn't wait for an answer. 'It'll be all this mucking around with that there atomic energy. And trying to break t'bloomin' sound barrier. That's what it is, you mark my words. Where did you say you wanted to go, luv? Near t'bowling green?'

'Yes, you can turn right here,' said Frances as they passed the laundry on Talbot Road. 'Right . . . then left . . . It's just here. This bungalow, the one with the green gate.'

She paid the taxi driver his fare, plus a shilling tip, and he helped her to carry the bags up the short path to the door.

'Cheerio, luv. Be seeing yer.' He gave a cheery wave then he was off, his mind, no doubt, already on his next fare. 'We have to make our money in the season, you know,' was the familiar cry of not only taxi drivers, but boarding house keepers, stall holders, rock and ice-cream sellers, everyone who was employed in the transitory holiday trade in this, the most famous seaside resort of all.

Frances had half expected her mother to be looking out of the window, waiting for her, but there was no one in sight. The little bungalow looked very neat and well cared for, the green paintwork shining and the lace curtains at the windows crisp and clean. Iris Goodwin, crippled by arthritis as she was, still liked to keep on top of things. Frances knew she had a woman in to help her a few times a week, but she guessed that her mother would still try to do as much as she could herself. The pocket-handkerchief-size lawn was bordered with bedding plants: begonias, clumps of alyssum and aubretia in a cheerful pattern of red, white and blue. The grass had been recently cut, as had the privet hedge. Jim Clegg, Frances's brother-in-law, came every couple of weeks to do that.

Frances lifted the gleaming brass knocker and banged it a couple of times. She didn't have a key, with living away from home, but no doubt her mother would soon provide her with one. Now where on earth was Mum? She knocked again, then, when she was just beginning to feel worried, the door opened.

'Good gracious . . . Frances! You're early, aren't you?' Her mother was peering at her uncertainly. There was not, to the girl's dismay, the welcoming smile she had anticipated on her mother's face, only a look of bewilderment. 'I wasn't expecting you, not yet.'

'No, I don't think I'm early, Mum,' said Frances, trying to smile. 'I told you what time the train got in.'

Iris was rubbing at her eyes, dazedly shaking her head, and Frances guessed that she had just woken up from a doze. She felt concerned. It wasn't like Iris, at least not the Iris she remembered, to sleep during the day. To her relief the confused look soon disappeared and her mother smiled. Her grey eyes, always her best feature, shone with the delight Frances had been looking for as she threw her arms round her daughter, the stick she had been leaning on clattering to the floor.

'Silly me,' she said, kissing Frances on both cheeks.

'What a chump I am, to be sure! I only went and dozed off, didn't I? Fancy me doing that after I'd been looking forward to you coming home. I must have been asleep ages!'

'Are you sure you're all right, Mum?' asked Frances, standing back and taking hold of her mother's shoulders. 'You're not ill, are you, apart from . . . well, you know.' She stooped down to pick up the stick. 'Here you are, Mum. You need this, don't you?'

'Aye, drat it! I need it, more's the pity. No, I'm not ill, love, no more than usual. Just a bit tired, that's all. We had a storm last night. And what a storm! I never remember anything like it. So I didn't get much sleep. You know what I'm like about thunderstorms, love.'

'Yes, the taxi driver told me about the storm,' said Frances. 'Come on, let's get in, then I'll make us a cup of tea and we can tell one another all the news.'

Iris subsided into the armchair at the side of the fire, easing herself in stiffly as though every movement was an effort. Frances eyed her worriedly, although she knew better than to fuss too much, to offer to plump up her cushions or get her a footstool. Iris had never wanted to be treated like an invalid, at least the person Frances remembered had not. But her mother had changed; she could tell that already. Her once-black hair was now almost entirely grey and her once-chubby face had sagged, her cheeks becoming pendulous and her mouth drooping into heavy lines. At one time Iris, in spite of her disability, would have insisted on making the tea; but it was Frances who made it, poured it out, found the sugar and biscuits, and cleared away afterwards. Of course she didn't mind, but she was more than a little dismayed at the lack of interest her mother was showing in what she, Frances, was saying. Iris used to be so eager to hear everybody's news; she had, in truth, been something of a gossip.

'Auntie Alice sends her love,' said Frances. 'And Uncle Jack as well. And Len and Karen and the girls. Susan starts school in September. She'll be five at Christmas . . .'

But Iris merely nodded in an abstracted manner, seemingly not very concerned about the doings of her

Yorkshire in-laws. Strictly speaking they were not her in-laws at all, but those of her husband Samuel. Alice was sister to Frances's real mother, Florence, and Iris and Alice had become quite good friends. But now Iris seemed far more inclined to talk about herself and her own doings, and Frances feared she was becoming more than a little self-centred. This had been apparent, to a certain extent, the last time Frances had been home a few weeks ago, but it was far more obvious now.

'Eliza comes to see me every week, more than once a week sometimes. You remember Eliza Pendleton, don't you, love? They had a hotel in Albert Road, then they moved to Cocker Street. Norman died a few years back and Eliza sold up. She's got a little house near the park . . .

'And our Josie comes round, only once a week, mind. No, I tell a lie; she came twice last week. She always says she's busy, but you'd think she could spare a bit more time for her mam, wouldn't you? She fetched me some new cream, though, that the chemist recommended, to rub into me joints. Can't say it's made a lot of difference though . . . Her Jim's a good lad; I've got to say that. He cut me lawn and hedge on Saturday. Looks nice, doesn't it? And Eliza put them flowers in for me. I can't manage the garden now . . . Frances, would you be a love and go and fetch my library book? I've left it on t' bedside table . . .'

Then it was her cardigan she wanted. She was feeling a bit chilly in spite of the gas fire being turned up high. Then her slippers, then a clean handkerchief. Then some new photos Josie had taken of Valerie, her little daughter. Would Frances go and look for them? They were in the dressing-table drawer, she thought . . . They weren't; they were on the sideboard, hidden behind the cut-glass vases, the fruit bowl and the plethora of silver photograph frames and china ornaments.

When Frances had finished looking at the photos her mother had appeared not to want to talk any more, turning to her library book, one of the latest Agatha Christies. But when she had been reading for a few minutes her head began to nod. Frances stared bemusedly round the small,

20

overheated, overcrowded room. Iris had always loved to be surrounded by her possessions – nests of tables, standard lamps, vases, brassware, velvet cushions, lace-edged covers; all the things she thought made a nice comfy home – but there was really no room for them all in this tiny sitting room. And the dining room across the hall was just as small, filled to bursting point with an immense oak table and six chairs, another sideboard, just as full of knick-knacks as the one in the lounge, and two crowded display cabinets. Iris had moved house many times, particularly when she lived in Yorkshire, and had been loath to part with any of her belongings.

Frances tiptoed out of the lounge and into the minuscule kitchen. She had better see what she could find for their tea. She had only had those beef sandwiches at lunchtime and she was feeling very hungry. There were potatoes in the vegetable rack – but very little else – and bacon and sausages in the fridge. (At least her mother did have a fridge, which was more than Aunt Alice had.) That would do; bacon, sausage and chips. And there might be some cake in the tin . . . There was, but to Frances's disappointment it was shop-bought Swiss roll, not the home baking that Iris had once excelled in. A feeling of depression settled over her as she set to, peeling the potatoes and cutting the rind off the bacon. This wasn't the homecoming she had expected. She had known her mother's health was declining, but she had thought that Iris would still take a lively interest in everything. She hadn't even mentioned Frances's new job. Frances tried to tell herself that Mum was just tired. There had been that awful storm last night and she was now catching up on lost sleep. She would be all right, no doubt, when she had had a rest.

Fortunately Iris did seem to brighten up considerably once they had had their tea and Frances had cleared away and washed up. 'Pull that other chair round and sit down.' Iris was already ensconced in her favourite chair. 'We'll have a see what's on the telly. I think we're just in time for *I Love Lucy.*'

The American comedy show starring the scatter-brained

Lucille Ball was not really to Frances's taste, but she bore with it for her mother's sake, while Iris laughed out loud at the antics of the dizzy star. Television now played a very big part in Iris's life. She had always enjoyed variety shows and visits to the cinema, and now that the entertainment was brought right into your own living room what could be better, especially since her movements were severely hampered?

'She's a caution, isn't she?' she chuckled as the show came to an end. 'Lucy's one of my favourites, but my very favourite programme's on tomorrow: *Emergency Ward Ten*. D'you watch it, love?'

Frances had sometimes watched it with her aunt and uncle; it was a favourite of Aunt Alice's too. They continued to watch the news and a quiz programme, then, later in the evening, switched over to BBC for *The Night and the Music*. Goodness, I'll have square eyes at this rate, thought Frances, fidgeting more than a little at the enforced inactivity. For more than two hours now her mother's eyes had scarcely looked away from the screen. Frances would have preferred to escape to her bedroom to read a book – she had often done so at her aunt's and no one had seemed to mind – but she felt it would be impolite on her first evening at home.

The Night and the Music, a light-hearted programme billed as 'melody, song and dance', was, however, very much up her street, as her mother would say. Frances loved music, especially that of the light classical sort, and Eric Robinson and his orchestra excelled at that. Hungarian dances, Schubert's Serenade, the tranquil strains of Delius; Frances felt the familiar well-loved melodies soothing her feelings of irritability and boredom. The Television Toppers, too, with their smiling faces and highly synchronised movements, long legs kicking and shoulder-length hair bobbing in unison, were a sight worth watching.

'Eeh, aren't they good?' Iris enthused, leaning forward even more eagerly in her chair. 'I never get tired of watching 'em.' She did take her eyes away from the screen at this point to look fondly at Frances. 'D'you know, at one time I thought you might end up on t'stage doing summat like that. Grand little dancer, you were. D'you remember when you were in the Tower Ballet? Stole the show, you did. I were that proud of you. That's when our Josie took that picture.'

Of course Frances remembered. Her mother's 'do you remember' was only a figure of speech. She glanced now at the photograph her mother was indicating, which still had pride of place on the sideboard, of Frances in her ballet dress, lacing up her dancing shoe and at the same time smiling winsomely into the camera. Yes, she remembered how she had loved taking the lead in the Children's Ballet, held each summer in the Tower Ballroom. She recalled, too, that she had been a somewhat precocious little madam at the time, very full of her own importance. How her family had put up with her she couldn't imagine. She also remembered that her mother, despite what she was saying now, had not been impressed at all with Frances's hankering after a stage career; a childish whim as it happened, although she still enjoyed singing and wasn't averse to appearing on a stage.

'Of course I wouldn't really have liked it, you know,' Iris went on to say, as if reading her thoughts, 'if you'd gone on to the stage; properly I mean, for a living, like. I wouldn't've stood in your way, but I don't reckon it's the right life for nice well-brought-up girls. It's all right for such as them.' She nodded towards the line of dancing girls on the screen. Nice well-brought-up girls, most of them, Frances guessed, finding it hard to suppress a grin.

'No, I'm glad you decided to be a teacher,' Iris continued. 'A good steady sort of job, teaching, especially now you've finished your gadding about in Yorkshire. Happen you'll settle down here now.'

Frances cast her eyes towards the ceiling, sighing inwardly, though her mother didn't notice this. It was almost the first reference Iris had made, since her arrival, to teaching or her new post. 'Yes, I'm looking forward to Wyre Bank,' Frances said. 'We've a staff meeting there next week, so I'll be able to tell you more about it when I've met the teachers.'

But Iris had switched off again, it seemed, from the conversation, her eyes once more glued to the screen. Damned television, thought Frances. She had heard it called the most antisocial invention ever conceived and this household was no exception. She went on talking, raising her voice. 'Watching those girls dancing has started me thinking. I wouldn't mind joining a society that puts on shows. A light opera group, singing and dancing and all that – an amateur one, I mean. I expect there are quite a few of them in Blackpool, aren't there, Mum?'

'I'm sure I don't know,' replied Iris, huffily. 'How should I know? But you'll be too busy with your teaching, won't you, without getting mixed up in owt like that?' She gave an audible sniff. 'You'll have to concentrate on your job, Frances. It's what you're getting paid for.'

'Yes . . . I will, Mum,' said Frances, through clenched teeth. 'I've every intention of working hard. But you know what they say about all work and no play. You need another interest, especially when you're a teacher, or you can get too bogged down with it all.'

'Don't see why you should,' said Iris, sniffing again. 'I've just told you, it's what they're paying you for, not for jigging about on a stage, so you'll have to put your back into it.' Her lips closed together momentarily in a stubborn line. 'Of course you'll please yourself no matter what I say. You always do . . . Go and put t'kettle on, will you, love, there's a good lass? Me tongue's hanging out for a cup of tea.'

'Honestly, Josie, she's driving me mad. I don't know how I'm going to stick it. It's fetch me this and carry me that, and just go and answer the door or slip out to the shops. And I've only been home for two days.'

'Precisely! You've only been home for two days and you're grumbling already,' said Josie Clegg, looking point-edly across the room at her sister. 'Don't you think that perhaps Mum deserves a little of your time and attention when you've been away for so long? Don't be so selfish,

Frances. It won't hurt you to run a few errands and wash a few pots. Mum's on her own an awful lot, you know, and you don't seem to realise how crippled she is with this damned arthritis. She has a job to move about at all sometimes.'

'I don't know that she's on her own all that much,' retorted Frances. 'She has a woman in to clean, doesn't she, about three times a week? And Eliza's often there from what I hear, Anyway, if you're all that worried about her being on her own why don't you go round more often? She remarked about it, you know. "You'd think our Josie could spare a bit more time for me." That's what she said.'

'Well, I like that! Of all the cheek! I go round every week – twice last week. Don't you forget I've a little girl to look after and a husband on shifts, and what amounts to a full-time job of my own.' Josie's dark eyes flashed and her heavy brows drew together in a frown. 'What more does she expect? That is, if she said it at all . . . I wouldn't put it past you to make it up.'

'Well, of all the things! Of course I didn't make it up. That's what she said. It's the honest truth. "You'd think our Josie . . .".'

'Girls, girls, please!' Jim, Josie's husband, came in from the kitchen bearing a tray holding three steaming mugs of coffee. 'Give it a rest, can't you? I could hear you right out there, going at it hammer and tongs. I've heard every word you said.' He placed the tray on the table and perched on the arm of his wife's chair. He put an arm round her in a casual manner, fingering the dark shining hair which hung in a page-boy bob almost to her shoulders. 'You've got to admit, Josie, that your mother can be something of a trial.' He looked across at Frances and grinned, his grey eyes twinkling roguishly. 'In fact she can be a pain in the you know what at times. Oh come on, Josie . . .' as his wife opened her mouth to protest. 'You know as well as I do that Iris has become more and more difficult over the last few months. I'm not surprised she's driving you barmy, Frances. We've all suffered, believe you me, in spite of what this one's trying to tell you.' He gave his wife an affectionate squeeze before getting up and handing a mug of coffee to each of the young women.

'I never said she wasn't a bit of a trial,' said Josie, 'I know she is. I'm saying that I don't think she can help it. She's in a lot of pain sometimes and I think Frances ought to be a bit more understanding . . . Oh, I'm sorry, Frances.' She stopped suddenly and grinned at her sister, all traces of her ill-temper fast disappearing. 'I didn't mean to snap at you.' She gave a sigh. 'To tell you the truth I do feel rather guilty that I don't get round more often. And of course I believe you. I know damn well she grumbles. She has a go at me every now and again. But it's very difficult now I'm getting so many engagements. And I won't neglect our Valerie. I always make sure I'm here when she comes home from school. I won't have people accusing me of having a latchkey child. I dare say you've seen enough of those in your job, haven't you, Frances?'

'Yes, quite a few,' agreed Frances. 'It can be a problem now that more women are going out to work. But nobody could accuse you of neglecting Valerie, not either of you.' Josie, Jim and little Valerie Clegg – aged five and now fast asleep in bed – were to Frances the ideally happy family. She was sure they had their ups and downs, as all families did. How could it be otherwise with someone as volatile as Josie? Frances well remembered her sister's frequent changes of mood, but she knew that Jim helped to keep her quick temper in check. He had been a red-haired scamp, the terror of their class in school, when Josie had first known him in the Haliford days. He was now a policeman, a very steady, placid sort of fellow. Although he was often on awkward shifts he certainly pulled his weight in the house and with looking after Valerie, enabling Josie to concentrate more fully on her career as a freelance photographer.

'You say you're getting a lot of engagements?' Frances asked now. 'Weddings and all that?'

'Yes, I must admit I'm doing quite well,' replied Josie. 'Aren't I, Jim?'

Her husband nodded, smiling proudly at his wife. 'I'll

say she is. Umpteen weddings; there's hardly a Saturday without one in the summer. As well as the usual babies and family groups and so on. And she's got a contract with some of the schools now, haven't you, love, taking pictures of all the kids? The parents love 'em, especially as we've started doing 'em in colour.'

'What d'you mean, "we"?' laughed Josie. 'How long have you been taking photographs?'

'Oh, come on, love; you know I help you with the sorting out and mounting. To be quite honest, she couldn't manage without me.' Jim winked at Frances and she thought again what a well-matched pair they were.

'Do you do all your own developing?' she asked.

'No, not now,' said Josie. 'I tried at first, but it became too much. No, Paul helps me out. You remember Paul Hepworth, of course. He does the bulk of it for me. In fact it's what he does most of now, developing and printing, more than the actual photography. He still has the shop on Caunce Street. He does a very good trade with holiday-makers' snaps.'

Frances did, indeed, remember Paul Hepworth. It was because of him that Josie had developed her interest in photography. She had been his assistant and had even been engaged to him for a while. Frances was glad, though, that her sister had married Jim Clegg, and she was sure that Josie was glad too. Paul, a widower, had been too old for her and too set in his ways. The woman he had married was much more suited to him, and it was obvious that Paul and Josie's former relationship didn't affect their present business association. Neither was Jim the least bit jealous; there was no need for him to be.

'Talking about Mum, though,' said Frances, when they had finished their coffee and biscuits and chatted a little more about Josie's flourishing career, 'I did notice a big change in her, even in the few weeks since I last saw her. I'm sorry if I seemed unsympathetic, but I have a full-time job as well, you know, like you – or I will have in a couple of weeks' time – and I won't be there to fetch and carry for her all the while. It's all right at the moment, during the school holidays, but when term starts . . .'

'Yes, I know what you mean,' said Josie, much more reasonable now. 'We're not there all the time, are we, Jim and me? I can see that if we were she'd have us run ragged as well. Yes . . . she's changed. It upsets me when I think about what an energetic person she used to be. Forever cleaning and polishing, cooking and baking – d'you remember the delicious cakes she used to make? – even before we moved to the boarding house. In Yorkshire, I mean, when she first married Dad. I bet she was the most house-proud woman in Haliford. Of course you wouldn't remember her then, not when we lived in Baldwin Lane.'

Frances had been a baby at the time, so she couldn't remember. But she had gathered from what she had heard over the years that she, Frances, had been Iris's undoubted favourite, the baby the woman had always wanted and never had. And so she had been fussed over, spoiled. Frances knew, to her later embarrassment, that it was so and that it had caused ructions between Iris and Josie. Josie had been only six years old when her new baby sister arrived, the baby that had caused her mother's death. It wasn't until much later, when Samuel Goodwin was killed in the war, that Josie and Iris had settled their differences. But now Iris's stepdaughters were united in their concern for the woman who couldn't have been a better mother had she given birth to them.

'She's still house-proud,' said Frances. 'I noticed that as soon as I arrived. The letter-box was gleaming and the step newly washed. But I hadn't realised it was somebody else doing all the work.'

'She may be in much more pain than we realise,' said Josie, 'though she doesn't complain all that much about it.'

'No, she just sits there,' added Jim. 'And that's something she never used to do. I remember your mam, always on the go, forever bustling around. I used to think she never sat down. Now, whenever we go, she's in the same chair.'

'Watching "the telly",' said Frances, smiling. 'That's what she insists on calling it, "the telly". I tell the kids in my class off for saying "telly" instead of "television", but I daren't say anything to Mum. She'd tell me I was getting too big for my boots. I wish I could have a decent conversation with her, though, about something other than television. Her life seems to begin and end with *Emergency Ward Ten*. Honestly, I think those doctors and nurses are more real to her than we are.'

'I don't think she's all that much different,' said Josie. 'Not in that respect. She's always liked escapism, and you can't blame her for that. Don't you remember how often she used to go to the pictures? You can't expect her suddenly to take an interest in Russia's sputniks or the CND. She's never taken much notice of world affairs – except during the war, when it affected us all – so I don't suppose she'll start now.'

'Or about the Common Market Treaty,' observed Jim. 'The only market Iris'd be interested in is the one in Abingdon Street. D'you think Britain'll ever be invited to join, Frances?'

'I shouldn't think so,' replied Frances. 'They don't seem to want us at the moment, France and Germany and all that lot. I think Harold Macmillan is quite keen on the idea, but I must admit I don't know a great deal about it so I can't blame Mum for not talking about that. But what does she talk about? Herself, mainly, and she never used to be like that. She used to take such an interest in us all. D'you know, she's hardly mentioned my new job at Wyre Bank? And that's after her pestering me to try and get back home.'

'Well, tell us about it then,' said Jim. 'We're all ears, aren't we, Josie?'

'I don't suppose I can tell you all that much, to be honest,' said Frances. 'I won't know much myself, not until I've met the staff and looked round the school. But I did meet the headmistress at the interview at the Town Hall. I told you about that, didn't I, Josie? But you weren't here, Jim. Let me tell you, she looks a real old battle-axe . . .'

'Try not to worry too much about your mother,' said Jim, driving Frances home about an hour later. 'Iris is only too happy to have a gofer at the moment.'

'A what?'

'You know, go for this and go for that, like you were saying.'

'Oh yes, I see,' Frances laughed.

'And as long as you're willing to do it she'll let you. But she'll have to manage on her own, at least part of the time, when you go back to school. So put your foot down, Fran. I should. Ask her what her last slave died of.'

'Oh Jim, I daren't. Honestly! You know my mother, I'm still frightened to death of answering her back.'

'Well . . . perhaps not. I know she's an old bossy-boots. Like your sister.' He gave her a nudge and she could see him grinning, though he kept his eyes firmly on the road. 'But don't let her get you down. You've got your whole career in front of you and goodness knows what else, a lovely young woman like you.'

'Thanks, Jim,' said Frances. She knew he wasn't flirting with her. He was far too happy with Josie. Frances and her brother-in-law had always been good mates. 'I feel so . . . so restricted, so hemmed in,' she said, 'especially after being at college, then living in Yorkshire. Auntie Alice was great. She fussed a lot, but I did feel I could come and go as I pleased. Mum treats me like a little girl, the way she always has done. She even made a fuss when I was coming out tonight, though she knew I was only coming to see you.'

'She'll get used to it,' Jim replied evenly. 'It's a novelty at the moment, having you at home. But you'll have to stick up for yourself. Iris was always a very self-willed woman . . . Now then, here we are.' He drew up at the gate of Iris's bungalow and switched off the engine. He looked at his watch. 'Quarter to eleven. I don't think she can complain at that, do you?'

'You never know,' said Frances darkly. 'Are you coming in, Jim?'

'Yes, just for a moment. I'll come in and say hello. Your mother doesn't go to bed early, does she?

'No, not until the little dot on the television fades away,' laughed Frances.

'Have you got your key?'

'Yes, at least I made sure I got my own . . .'

There was only one light burning in the living room, that of a standard lamp. It cast a dim glow on the black and white screen where some sort of magic programme was showing. But Frances took little heed of that for the light also revealed her mother, slumped sideways in her chair, her head lolling forward and the glasses she wore for viewing tumbled into her lap. She made no move or sound as they dashed across the room.

'Mum, Mum, whatever's the matter?' Frances kneeled at her side and seized hold of her wrist. 'Oh God, Jim, I can't feel a pulse. Mum, Mum . . . speak to me. Oh Jim, whatever shall we do? Supposing she's . . . she's dead? After all those awful things I've been saying. I feel dreadful. And I did love her, really I did . . .'

Frances's thoughts, at that moment, were not for herself but for her mother. She forgot about her new teaching job, her hopes for a bright future in her home town, praying that her mother would not die; that she might not, already, be dead.

Chapter 3

Iris was not dead. Neither was she completely unconscious, though, fortunately, she couldn't seem to hear what Frances was saying. She had, however, suffered a heart attack. The doctor was called, then an ambulance, and within an hour she was in the care of the doctors and nurses at Victoria Hospital.

'Oh dear, I feel so dreadful now,' said Frances as she and Josie and Jim sat drinking tea in the early hours of the morning. She had accompanied her mother to hospital, then Jim had picked her up in the van, after breaking the news of her mother's illness to Josie. They had persuaded her to stay the night at their home, which she was only too glad to do.

'I didn't realise how ill she was feeling. When she made a fuss about me going out I thought she was just being difficult. She said she had a pain – bad indigestion – so I gave her a couple of Rennies. Oh dear! It must have been the start of a heart attack and I never knew. Why didn't she say? She must have realised . . .'

'Probably not,' said Josie. 'Don't start blaming yourself, Fran, Mum's always taking Rennies. She eats too fast; she always has done, then she gets indigestion. She used to laugh about it; she said it was because they never knew where the next meal was coming from!' Josie gave a rueful smile. 'No, I don't think she would realise it was her heart, so don't go upsetting yourself.'

'But she must have been feeling quite poorly,' Frances persisted. 'More than any of us realised. Maybe that's why she had me dancing attendance on her. I feel so guilty: I can't help it.'

'Then stop it!' said Jim, a little sharply. 'We've all had a bit of a grouse about her, whether we should or not. She can be damned difficult at times and we're only human. Anyway, she's in the best place now, and if I know your mam she'll be sitting up and ordering 'em all about in a day or two.'

And that turned out to be the case. After a couple of days of special care Iris was admitted to the main ward where she was told she would have to stay for at least another week. She didn't seem to mind, although at one time she would have grumbled loud and long at being confined in a state of idleness.

'This is *Emergency Ward Ten* for real, isn't it, Mum?' Jim teased her, perching on the end of her bed. 'You've got your own real live doctors and nurses. How do this lot compare with the glamorous characters on TV?'

'Better! Tons better,' said Iris, beaming at a pretty dark-haired nurse who was passing. 'They can't do enough for you. Especially that one. She's a little love. And that friend of yours popped in to see me, Frances. Megan Ashcroft. Nurse Ashcroft, of course, we call her here.'

'Yes, I left a message to tell her you were here,' said Frances.

'Nice little thing. Could do with a bit more meat on her, though,' said Iris. 'She doesn't look strong enough to be a nurse. Wiry, though, I dare say. She's engaged to one o' t'doctors, she was telling me. She's done well for herself, I must say. I don't know him though. He's a – what d'you call it? – a gyna . . . something or other. Looking after women's insides.' Iris lowered her voice, exaggeratedly mouthing the words. 'Wombs an' all that.' She reminded Frances of Hylda Baker. 'That Dr Benson, though, the one that's looking after me. Eeh, he's a good doctor if ever there was one. "You've been very lucky, Mrs Goodwin," he says to me. "Very lucky indeed. You had us worried for a time, but you're going to be all right. And you've got a good family to take care of you when you go home, so you mustn't worry about a thing." '

Frances and Josie exchanged glances. It could prove to

be quite a problem when Iris came out of hospital for by that time Frances would be starting her new job. Infant school hours were, supposedly, nine till three thirty, but she knew that any teacher worth her salt put in considerably more time than that. Neither would she be able to get home at lunchtime. She and Josie had assured Dr Benson that their mother would be well looked after and they intended to keep their promise, but it would not be easy.

'I'll go round every morning, once I've got Valerie off to school,' said Josie, driving Frances home after one of their visits. 'Yes, I know I've said I'm too busy in the past, but she's our mother, isn't she? We've got to do all we can. And perhaps Mrs Kingsley, the woman who cleans for her, could be persuaded to come at least one more day. And I'm sure Eliza will . . . Yes, we'll cope, Frances, never fear.'

But Frances did fear that it would be others who would be coping with her mother's illness far more than she would be able to do in the near future. And she guessed that before very long her sister would be grumbling that she, Frances, was not pulling her weight. Once the new term started life promised to become very hectic. And tomorrow there was the staff meeting . . .

Frances's interview at the Town Hall had been back in June. It was the first time she had been inside the imposing Victorian building in Talbot Square and she felt the aura of solemnity and respect, reverence almost, the moment she entered. There in the marble-tiled entrance hall was a statue of Queen Victoria as an elderly monarch – the building had been completed fifty-eight years ago, in 1900 – surrounded by banks of plants and flowers on a green baize background. The wide staircase with an oak and wrought iron balustrade, and intricately carved heraldic beasts at each corner, led to the upstairs rooms, and was carpeted in a rich midblue. 'Tory blue', Frances surmised, as Blackpool since time immemorial had returned Conservative MPs.

Staff were being appointed for several local schools and so it had been an august body that Frances had faced that morning, consisting of headteachers of the respective schools, school governors, and a few members of the Education Committee. Because there were so many of them they were seated in the curved seats of the council chamber with the candidates, one at a time, seated in the chairman's stately oak chair, facing them across the huge leather-topped table. It was a daunting experience, especially after a long wait in an adjoining committee room, chatting with the other candidates about this and that, about anything, in fact, but the questions they had been asked. Some re-entered after their interviews confidently with satisfied smiles, others looked decidedly worried, but none divulged anything of the ordeal they had just been through.

Frances could remember very little about the interview or hardly any of the questions she had been asked; but she realised she could not have fared too badly because, at the end of the morning, she had been offered a post at Wyre Bank Infant School, commencing in September.

One person who had remained in her mind, however, was Miss Reynolds, the headmistress of that school. The woman had made a point of stating who she was before asking her question about the importance of reading in the school curriculum. She had a noticeable inland accent and Frances guessed she was from Wigan or somewhere near. Miss Reynolds had untidy mid-brown hair, and was wearing a nondescript fawn suit. On the whole she presented a homely picture, but all this was at variance with her forbidding stare through rimless glasses and her autocratic-looking hooked nose. She had seemed, on first acquaintance, to be aloof and unfriendly. Now, meeting her once more at the staff meeting at Wyre Bank Infant School, Frances wondered if the main problem was that the woman was short-sighted. From the way she peered at the sheaf of notes she held it would seem so.

At all events she had welcomed Frances and another new member of staff, if not effusively, then at least cordially. Frances knew she would not remember all the names of the various members of staff – nine, including the head-mistress – straight away. She had never been all that good at putting names to faces. In her previous school it had taken her a few days to remember the names of all the children in her class, although it helped in a Reception class when the children wore name tags. Seven-year-olds could not be subjected to such an indignity, Frances thought now, and she had just learned there would be thirty-six of them. Still, no doubt she would cope. Remembering their names could well be one of the lesser problems. It already seemed there would be a great deal else to contend with, including the introduction of a new reading scheme.

It was at this stage that Frances really began to notice Miss Cameron, the deputy head. The woman, neatly dressed in an elegant navy-blue suit, was turning the pages of the books that were being passed round the table, a look of contempt, bordering on disgust, on her face. She had a handsome, if disgruntled-looking, face with a well-sculptured nose and a determined mouth, painted in bright vermilion. Her sleek black hair was drawn back in a tidy bun. A more vivid contrast to the somewhat lumpy-featured Miss Reynolds would be hard to imagine. And Frances soon realised that it was not just their appearances that were out of harmony.

'I would like to give my opinion, if I may.' Miss Cameron looked coldly at the headmistress. 'It seems to me that by introducing rub—er . . . reading matter such as this we are doing nothing, nothing whatsoever, to educate the children. We should be trying to enrich their lives, surely, not pandering to their . . . their baser instincts.'

'Baser instincts?' said Miss Reynolds, not loudly, in fact quite reasonably, Frances thought. 'These are children we are talking about, Miss Cameron; five, six, seven years old.'

'Yes, yes, I know that. But I'm thinking of their parents as well,' Miss Cameron countered. 'In many cases they need educating, just as much as the children. And how is . . . stuff like this going to do it?' She picked up one of the offending books, holding it out to the group round the table. 'Just look at this. Father in his vest and braces and a two-day stubble on his chin! And the language!' She read out an example in her refined, rather high-pitched voice.

' "Flipping heck, Daisy, 'ow can I 'ear myself think with the row them kids are making? Tell 'em to put a sock in it." I ask you! And look at this.' She pointed to a picture of a grubby child sitting on a potty. 'And this . . .' Another one of a baby in a high chair about to place his bowl of cornflakes on his head. 'Not the sort of thing we should be encouraging our children to read, not in my opinion.'

'It's the sort of situation they can relate to,' said Miss Reynolds calmly, 'and surely they'll be more interested in reading about things that are relative to their own experience rather than children who live in country mansions and fathers who drive big cars. And that is the basis of many of the old reading schemes, you've got to admit. Anyroad . . . anyway,' she corrected herself, 'I would like to try it, for this term at least; then you will have the opportunity to tell me what you think. We won't know until we have tried, will we, any of us?' Frances had the distinct impression that what Miss Reynolds said she intended to be the last word on the subject.

Not quite though. There were still murmurings around the table, mainly from Miss Walsh now, the oldest member of staff. She appeared to be in her late fifties, tall and extremely thin with iron-grey hair drawn back in a bun, and dressed in a maroon frock with a lace collar that might have been fashionable during the war. 'I would like to make a point before this subject is closed.' Miss Walsh spoke very quietly, her head nodding gently in emphasis, although Frances made a guess that the timid appearance disguised a strong will. 'We mustn't forget that quite a number of our children come from *private houses*.' She stressed the last two words as though they were of the utmost significance. 'I know that the vast majority of them are from the estate – and they're no worse for that,' she added, although it was obvious from her condescending tone that it was definitely not a point in their favour. 'But we do have a responsibility to the others—'

'Thank you, Miss Walsh,' the headmistress cut in. 'We have a responsibility to all of them. And, as I've just said, we are going to try it for the next term. Are we all agreed?'

Her decisive voice conveyed that she would brook no further resistance, and though there were one or two resentful glances no one put forward any more arguments. 'That doesn't mean to say that we are going to forget all the well-loved favourites,' she went on, 'fairy stories and myths and legends and so on. They're all part of our heritage and we mustn't overlook them.'

There followed a discussion about the place of nursery tales in the education of children during which Miss Walsh and Miss Cameron were noticeably silent. Frances, who had hardly spoken so far, even braved a comment about how children loved repetition. She quoted 'The Three Billy Goats Gruff' and 'The Three Little Pigs', not exactly an earth-shattering observation, but it broke the ice for her – like an MP making his maiden speech – and she was rewarded by an appreciative nod and a favourable glance from Miss Reynolds. Frances was already beginning to change her mind about the headmistress, realising that the other two, Miss Cameron and Miss Walsh, both seemingly at loggerheads with the head, might be the ones to watch.

After the distribution of class lists, registers, attendance slips, new pencils, one for each child (and as precious as gold, Frances gathered) and classroom keys, the staff were then free to do as they chose. They could go home if they wished although Frances knew this would definitely be frowned on. There was so much work to be done in the classrooms – putting up pictures, arranging bookshelves, searching for equipment that had been hidden away in the stockroom – and all the teachers dispersed to get on with the jobs they had to do in preparation for the new school year.

'I'm sure you'd like to look round the school, wouldn't you, before you tackle your classroom?' said Mrs Aspinall to Frances. Miss Reynolds had asked this person to take Frances under her wing as they would be working in adjacent classrooms, both with groups of third-year children. Miss Jenkins, the other new teacher, whom Frances remembered from the interview, was being looked after by Miss Walsh. She decided she was lucky to be in the care of

Mrs Aspinall because she had liked the look of the woman straight away. Frances guessed she was in her late forties, round-faced and buxom, with untidy pepper-and-salt grey hair that rather resembled a bird's nest. She was wearing a limp cotton dress that had seen better days and her bare feet were shod in Scholl sandals.

'I'm Marjorie,' she said, as they clattered down the stone steps leading from the upstairs staffroom into the spacious entrance hall. 'And I'd be so pleased if you'd call me that. You're Frances, aren't you? I took a peek at a list the boss had, or else I'd never have known. They don't go in for Christian names much here. I expect you've noticed. Anybody'd think we were back in Victorian times. But I think it's because Miss Reynolds wants to make sure she maintains her position. I suspect she feels she'd lose some of her authority if she started being too pally with us all.'

Frances nodded. 'I think that's fairly common in a lot of schools. You're not on first-name terms until you've been there for years.'

'Yes, maybe you're right . . . Anyway, that's the hall.' Marjorie motioned towards the huge room behind glass doors which opened off the foyer. 'I expect you noticed it when you came in.' Frances had done so, comparing it in her mind with the cramped area that had passed for a hall in the village school near Haliford. 'That's where we have our morning assembly each day, and PE lessons of course.'

There was an iron climbing frame, often known as a Jungle Jim, at the back of the hall, and a stage, comprised of huge wooden blocks, at the other end.

'I see you have a stage,' said Frances. 'Well, a make-shift one, isn't it? Do you have concerts?'

'Hardly ever; just at Christmas,' said Marjorie. 'That's about all. Why, do you like concerts?'

'Mmm . . . yes, I suppose I do,' said Frances. 'We didn't have them at my last school because there wasn't much room for an audience. It's only a tiny village school. Yes, I think it would be a nice thing to do, especially with so many children, and there's loads of room.'

'Are you interested in drama then?' asked Marjorie. 'Or singing and dancing?'

'Yes, I used to have dancing lessons when I was a little girl, and I sing . . . a bit,' said Frances modestly.

'Do you play the piano?'

'No, I'm afraid not.'

'Pity,' said Marjorie. 'The reason I asked is because there are only two of us who play. Teachers who play the piano are getting to be as rare as hen's teeth. Miss Walsh and I take it in turns to play for assembly, God help us! I'm not very good; it's very much hit and miss with me, but Miss Walsh is even worse. She can't sight-read, that's her problem, though she won't admit it. She just goes blundering on—' Marjorie stopped abruptly. 'Sorry, I shouldn't have said that. It's very unprofessional, you see, dear, to criticise other teachers. My first headmistress drummed that into us. And I've never forgotten it.' She laughed. 'Well, I try to remember, though you can't help making comparisons sometimes between one teacher and another. The best thing is to keep your opinions to yourself. Miss Walsh is a good teacher, though, apart from her piano-playing. A bit old-fashioned, mind . . . There I go again!' Marjorie slapped her own hand in mock reproach.

Frances smiled. 'Never mind. We wouldn't be human, would we, if we didn't talk about people now and again? Do the children have their dinners in here as well?'

'In the hall? Goodness me, no,' replied Marjorie. 'All mod cons here, I can tell you. No, we have a separate dining room and our own kitchen as well. Meals cooked on the premises for us and the Juniors. No such thing here as green vans and dinners arriving in tins. We're very lucky.'

'And do the children all stay for their dinners?'

'The majority of them do. Some go home, because most of them live very near, but I think most of the mothers are agreed that they couldn't make a meal for the price they have to pay for school dinners. You can't blame them. They're very cheap, and good, too.'

'And what about the staff? Do they all stay as well?' asked Frances. 'No doubt we have to do dinner duty?'

' 'Fraid so,' said Marjorie, giving a wry smile. 'We have to take our turn. Nearly all the staff stay for dinner. Gertie tries to make school dinner something of an occasion.'

'Gertie?'

Marjorie smiled. 'Sorry – Miss Reynolds. Often referred to as Gertie – that's her name, Gertrude – though we don't let her hear us . . . These are our classrooms, by the way, yours and mine.' She pointed to two doors on her right, one painted red and one blue, leading off a long corridor. 'We'll come back in a few minutes. I'll just show you the dining hall.'

'What about the staff? Are they all . . . er . . . easy to get on with?' asked Frances, a trifle hesitantly, as they went on walking past more brightly coloured doors, a green, a yellow, then an orange one. 'I just wondered . . .'

'Ah, you've picked up a few vibrations, I dare say,' said Marjorie. 'It'd be surprising if you didn't. I don't think I'm being unprofessional in telling you that Miss Reynolds and Miss Cameron don't hit it off very well. You must have noticed it yourself, and if you hadn't then you soon would. Judith – that's Miss Cameron – is very resentful, you see. She thinks that the post of headmistress should have been given to her. She's always taught here in Blackpool. She'd been Head of Department in a mixed junior and infant school in South Shore. And so, of course, when this school was due to open nine years ago, she applied for the top job. And then what did they do but offer her the deputy's job and give the headship to an outsider, a woman from Wigan.'

'Miss Reynolds?'

'Exactly. It caused quite a lot of ill feeling, I can tell you. And not just with Miss Cameron. There were a lot of folk who were of the opinion that local jobs should go to local people.'

'Why do they do it then? Give the jobs to people from other towns, I mean?'

'I'm not sure. To bring in new ideas, to stop the system from becoming too insular . . . Maybe it was just a question of Miss Reynolds being the right person for the job. And I must admit she is. She's a jolly good head and she's got her

42

finger right on the pulse. She was brought up on a housing estate herself so she understands these kids, and their parents.'

'And Miss Cameron doesn't?' ventured Frances.

'She tries, I must give her her due. Different background, of course; her father was a doctor and she's never been short of the ready, you know.' Marjorie made a gesture with her fingers of counting pound notes. 'Still, I mustn't criticise her. They're different personalities, her and Gertie, and they both bring something of value to the school, each in her own way. It wouldn't do for us all to be alike, would it, dear?'

Frances was reminded of her Aunt Alice. That was a favourite expression of hers. 'I'm surprised Miss Cameron's stayed then,' she said. 'Why hasn't she tried to get another job?'

'Oh, she has, but it's easier said than done, Frances. Large infant schools like this are few and far between. She accepted this job because it was near her home. She looks after her old parents, you see, and she was travelling a long way before.'

'I wonder that she's not married. That seems a shame.'

'Why?' Marjorie gave her an odd look. 'You think it's the be all and end all, do you, marriage?'

Frances was aware of the asperity in her new friend's tone, although Marjorie was still smiling. She decided not to pursue the matter; she had only just met Marjorie Aspinall and she didn't want to appear nosy. She found she was already asking a lot of questions, some of them, probably, none of her business. But it was obvious that Marjorie loved to chatter, and Frances did want to find out about at least some of her new colleagues.

'No, not at all,' she replied. 'I was only thinking that Miss Cameron's a good-looking woman. I would have thought she might have been . . . married.'

'She should have been,' replied Marjorie. 'She was engaged to a fighter pilot. He was killed in the Battle of Britain. She never talks about it; the reason I know is because I've known Judith for a long time. I lived quite near her when I was a girl. I didn't know her well – I don't think anyone really knows her well – but I do understand something about her. All in all, I dare say Judith has quite a lot to be bitter about. Possibly no more, though, than some of the rest of us . . .' Marjorie stopped speaking and there was a few seconds' silence.

'Anyway, this is the dining hall.' She pushed open the swing doors at the end of the corridor. 'The kitchen is over there.'

The dining area was huge, a purely functional room with bare walls and a high ceiling. Formica-topped tables and wooden chairs were stacked at one end, and at the other end of the room was a metal partition which looked as though it could be drawn back when required.

'What's that?' asked Frances. 'Is there another room beyond there?'

'There is indeed,' said Marjorie, smiling. 'The Junior dining hall. This is where our territory ends, let me tell you. Go beyond here and you're setting foot in the enemy camp.'

'What? The Junior School? You're joking!'

'Only partly,' said Marjorie. 'Yes, maybe I'm exaggerating a little. But we call that the Iron Curtain.' She motioned towards the partition. 'It's very sad, but the Juniors and Infants don't get together as much as they should; hardly at all, in fact. Of course we have to go over with class lists when the children are moving up, and the heads meet if there's something of vital importance. But that's the crux of the matter really. Our Gertie and the boss over there, Jacob Entwistle, don't get on.'

'Oh dear,' said Frances. 'Why is that?'

'We're not sure. He's from the same neck of the woods as Gertie, funnily enough, and we think they knew one another, way back when. It's a bit of a mystery . . . So it's a question of never the twain shall meet.'

'So you don't know the Junior staff?'

'Some of them, just to exchange a few words now and again. We're often in the kitchen at the same time, getting our dinners. That's almost the only time we see them.'

44

Beyond the serving hatch there was a most impressive kitchen, empty, at the moment, of people. It was full of shining cookers and hot-plates, massive sinks and aluminium cupboards where the food was kept hot.

'And here endeth the guided tour,' said Marjorie. 'Come on, Frances. We'd best get back to our classrooms and get stuck in. Give me a shout if you want anything.'

'Thank you very much . . . Marjorie,' said Frances. 'You've been very kind. It all feels far less strange now, thanks to you.'

Wyre Bank School had been opened in 1950, to deal with some of the superabundance of babies, by then children of school age, born at the end of the war; and nothing had been spared in the way of amenities. The classrooms were big and airy with French windows opening on to a terrace that surrounded the playground. Each classroom had its own stockroom and cloakroom, and at the end of each corridor were rows of washbasins and toilets; even a drying room for the children's wet coats and mackintoshes.

As Frances stared in some wonder around her new place of work she recalled her previous school. It had been built in the middle years of Victoria's reign to accommodate the children of a small village on the outskirts of Haliford. Small wooden-partitioned classrooms, inadequate cloakroom facilities, smelly outdoor lavs, no dining room, not even a staffroom. But, for all that, it had been a happy place. It was the people who inhabited a building that made it what it was; in a school, the staff and children. Frances had met the staff, though she didn't yet know them all. From what she had observed, though, there were a few, it would seem, who were not conducive to a happy atmosphere. She had yet to meet the children.

Chapter 4

Frances stared at the sea of faces confronting her. Thirty-six of them. She had checked and double-checked as she copied their names from the class list she had been given, into the register, to ensure she had not missed any. A class register was sacrosanct, and woe betide any teacher who dared to defile its holy pages by rubbing out or making an alteration or – worst of all – getting the weekly or monthly totals wrong. Frances had made sure that the list of names, alphabetical, with six or so spaces left between the boys and girls in case there were any late admittances to the class – heaven preserve her, she hoped not! – was in her very best handwriting, or printing, to be more exact. She knew that first impressions counted for a lot and she was determined at least to start off in a tidy manner.

Thirty-six children, but it seemed more like a hundred as the faces, some eager, some artful, some rather apprehensive, stared back at her. However would she get to know them all, to remember all their names? They all looked alike . . . no, that was not true, Frances chided herself. Of course they didn't. There were fair heads, brown heads, a few ginger ones, and a variety of hairstyles and expressions on faces, but the school uniform did tend to produce an effect of similarity – of uniformity – as it was meant to do. The grey skirt or trousers, maroon jersey, white shirt, and maroon and pale blue striped tie were not obligatory, but Frances noticed that almost all the children were wearing them, save one or two who had a different coloured jumper or skirt.

On this vast housing estate, finance in some households was often a severe headache. In some families there were three, four or more children, and clothing was often handed down, becoming increasingly shabby. But, by and large, most mums and dads made their children's welfare a priority, and certainly, on this first day of term, the members of Class 3G (G for Goodwin, the name of the class teacher) looked clean, tidy and well dressed, a credit to their parents. Just how long they would stay so spruce, after a few playground fights, sorties into muddy puddles on the way home, to say nothing of spilled milk and dinner, remained to be seen.

'Now, children . . .' Frances's voice came out in a squeak, to her own ears at least, and she decided to try again. 'Now . . . Class 3G – that's what we're called, isn't it? – I think we'd better get to know one another, hadn't we? My name is Miss Goodwin—'

'We know, miss. We've seen it on t'door,' piped up a boy's voice from the back corner of the room. Frances wasn't quite quick enough to see who it was. A class comedian – or would-be comedian – she guessed, from the ripple of giggles that accompanied his remark.

'Oh, have you?' she replied, with her brightest smile. 'Well . . . that's very good then. You've only one new name to remember, and I've got thirty-six, so please try not to worry if I get you a bit muddled up at first. Just tell me if I get it wrong, and by the end of the week I shall know all of you, I promise.' So help me, God, she added silently.

'Right then, I'll call out your names, then you can answer "Yes, Miss Goodwin", if you're here—'

'Couldn't answer if we weren't here, could we, miss?' It was the same voice, from the same corner of the room, accompanied by the same outburst of laughter. Frances gritted her teeth, but this time she was quick enough to catch sight of the culprit, a dark-haired boy with rosy cheeks on a chubby face and a merry grin. A rogue, but a likeable one, she guessed.

'No, you're quite right.' She tried to smile at him, believing that it was wrong to quash children unless it was absolutely necessary – she had learned that at college – although at times you might feel like strangling the little

blighters. 'Of course you can't answer if you're not here.'
She was cursing herself for her pointless remark; children
could be so quick at noticing your mistakes, putting you at
a disadvantage, unless you were more than equal to them.
'I'm sorry, I don't know your name, dear.'

'Barry Cartwright, miss.'

'Very well then, Barry . . . Could you remember to call
me Miss Goodwin, please? Not just miss.'

'Orlright, miss . . . I mean Miss Goodwin.'

Frances let out a tremendous inward sigh as she opened
the blue-backed register. She discovered, to her horror,
that her hand was trembling slightly as she picked up her
fountain pen. It was an edict of Miss Reynolds – or could it
be the Education Authority? She wasn't sure – that registers
had to be written in ink and not in Biro. She grasped her
pen more tightly. What on earth was the matter with her?
Anyone would think she had never set eyes on a class of
children before.

'Right then, the register. Stephen Andrews . . .'

'Yes, Miss Goodwin . . .'

'Michael Baker . . .'

'Yes, Miss Goodwin . . .'

'Barry Cartwright . . .' She already knew him.

'Yes, miss . . . I mean, Miss Goodwin.'

One to watch unless she was very much mistaken, but
Frances held her tongue.

The names were mainly predictable: three Davids, two
Johns, two Michaels. The most unusual ones were Shaun,
Nigel and Donald, the latter name not being used very
much now. Frances wondered, fleetingly, if the appendage
of the famous cartoon character was added by merciless
children to this boy's name. It had been, she recalled, in
her previous school, with a timid little boy who had found
it hard to defend himself.

'Russell Dennis . . .' she called out, then wondered why
this name was greeted with hoots of unrestrained laughter.
She looked up enquiringly at the rows of boys and girls,
nearly all convulsed in giggles.

'Please, miss . . . Miss Goodwin . . .' It was the

irrepressible Barry again. 'You've got it the wrong way round. He's called Dennis Russell, not Russell Dennis.' The class, in unison, shrieked again. 'This is 'im, the one what's sitting next to me.'

Frances's eyes alighted on the auburn-haired boy sitting next to Barry. Hair of the bright orange hue that could saddle him with the nickname of Carrots or Gingernut, topped a thin, pale and freckled face that was wearing a surly scowl. She smiled apologetically at him, thinking that this was not her day at all.

'I do beg your pardon, Dennis. How silly of me.' She realised that her concentration must have lapsed for a moment, allowing her to make another blunder. She went on to explain that sometimes names could be used as either Christian or surnames. Dennis was one of them and so was Russell, hence the mistake. 'Can anybody think of any more?' she asked brightly.

'Yes, miss . . . Miss Goodwin. Please, miss, I can . . .' A shower of hands shot up.

'Stanley, miss . . .'

'Graham, Miss Goodwin . . .'

'James . . .' 'John . . .' 'William . . .'

An impromptu discussion followed as Frances explained that she didn't think the last two were used as surnames as such, but that often 'son' was added to a name, indicating that Johnson was the son of John and Williamson was the son of William. She got up from her seat behind the large desk to write examples on the blackboard – a spontaneous lesson, such as they told you at college to seize upon whenever you had the chance. Frances began to feel that the ice had been broken. The ginger-haired Dennis, however, who had been the cause of the diversion, sat sullenly, taking no part in it at all. Another one to watch, Frances decided, as she returned to the register and the list of girls' names.

Three Susans this time, three Lindas, Christine, Carol, Jennifer . . . They all answered dutifully. Girls, on the whole, were far more biddable than boys in a class; but it was the boys, Frances had to confess, that she found the most entertaining, and rewarding, once you got on the right side of them. This she was determined to do.

By the end of the day she felt she could put names to about ten faces – not bad going – Christian names, if not surnames as well. She had also managed to sort out the reading groups, with the aid of a list from their previous teacher, and she had given them a quick maths test (to the accompaniment of groans all round) to find out their competence, or otherwise, in this subject.

Dennis Russell – whom she still wanted to call Russell Dennis – she found was a fluent reader, one of her top group. And from the eagerness with which he had responded to the maths test she guessed that, when she marked the papers at home tonight, she would find that he excelled in this as well. Why, then, was he so sullen, she wondered. Neither she, nor the children, had managed to coax a smile out of him all day, in the classroom at any rate. She didn't yet know what his behaviour was like in the playground. She decided she would have to make some enquiries in the staffroom about this little boy, as to whether there was any reason – problems at home? – for his surliness.

Frances felt an empathy towards him, even though her first encounter with him had not been ideal. She had made him conspicuous, maybe to feel a fool, albeit unwittingly, and this was something that no child liked (and which no teacher was supposed to do). He reminded her of her brother-in-law, Jim Clegg, or at least what Jim must have looked like when he was a schoolboy; although she knew that Jim had always been a sunny-natured boy. Naughty, but appealing with it.

Dennis's desk-mate, the boisterous Barry, didn't appear, at a first showing, to have the academic ability of his pal. His was a superficial brightness, but Frances knew that if she managed to win him over he could be a sterling help to her in the classroom. As could one of the Susans, one of the Lindas, and little fair-haired Jennifer, a trio of fussy little misses, born monitors, who were continually pestering to help the teacher. They might well be regarded as fusspots or teacher's pets by some of the other children who were not that way inclined; but a boon, none the less, to a harassed teacher who often wished she had a dozen pair of hands.

It was well turned half-past four when Frances staggered on to the bus, bound for home, feeling as though she had been pulled through a mangle. Why had she imagined that teaching Third Year Infants would be easier than a Reception class? There were so many of them, all wanting their pencils sharpened, or their sums marked, or help with a word they couldn't spell, all at the same time, or so it seemed. Frances realised she was feeling the strain, not only because it was the first day, but because in Yorkshire she had had only twenty children in her class. And much more docile ones, too; at least, that was how she remembered them. (Were Yorkshire children more docile than their Lancashire counterparts, she wondered.) At all events, she told herself, it was only the first day. Things were bound to improve.

'You're late, aren't you?' Iris called out as Frances entered the house. Frances clenched her teeth and closed her eyes as she leaned back against the door. Lord, give me strength! she muttered silently, knowing that she must – must! – try to be patient with her mother.

'I thought you said you finished at half-past three,' Iris continued as Frances went into the hot, stuffy little sitting room. She was nodding pointedly at the wooden clock on the mantelpiece. 'It doesn't take an hour and a half to get home, does it?'

'No, Mum . . .' Frances collapsed into the chair opposite her mother, at the same time flinging her heavy bag of books on to the floor. 'It doesn't.' She tried to smile, but she knew it was only a faint movement of her lips to which her eyes would not respond. 'But I also told you, didn't I, that I would have quite a lot of work to do after school and that I might be rather late? And I'm afraid it'll be the same every day. There are all sorts of things to do – putting up pictures, making lists, sharpening the pencils ready for tomorrow. And on Thursday we have a staff meeting after school, so—'

'All right, all right, don't bother with the chorus.' Iris cut her off abruptly, apparently not interested in her daughter's first day in her new post. Frances felt hurt, although she might have guessed that this would be the case. Since she had come home from hospital last weekend Iris had been even more demanding. 'You're here now and that's all that matters. Better late than never, I suppose. But you might try and give a thought for me, stuck here on my own all day.'

'Why, Mum? Has Josie not been round? She said she would be coming.'

'Of course she's been. She says she'll come every morning. She's a good lass is Josie. I've got to admit our Josie does all she can to help her old mam.' The emphasis on the word Josie, then the tightening of Iris's lips, conveyed to Frances that her mother was criticising her, but she made no comment. 'And Eliza popped round this afternoon . . .'

'So you've not been on your own all day?'

'I never said I was, did I? I've been on my own since four o'clock, though, when Eliza decided she had to go. She brought some fishcakes, homemade ones. I remember she used to make 'em for high tea sometimes when she had the boarding house. D'you remember, Frances, when we stayed there during the war, before we had our own place? They were one of her specialities, them fishcakes. She made 'em with flaked haddock, and sometimes with a tin of salmon – red, when she could get it.'

'Yes, Mum . . . I remember.' Frances leaned back against the soft cushion of the armchair, closing her eyes. Fishcakes . . . it was obviously a more intriguing topic of conversation than her own first day in a new job.

'Anyroad, she's brought us half a dozen. Happen we could have 'em for tea, a couple each with a few chips. And the other two'll do for my dinner tomorrow. Mrs Kingsley could cook 'em for me. She'll be here in the morning to do a bit of cleaning. Will you see to 'em then, love, them fishcakes? Hey, come on, never mind going to sleep. You can't be all that tired, surely. You're only a young lass.'

Frances opened her eyes and looked steadily at her mother. 'No, Mum, I'm not really tired.' Just bloody exhausted, she added to herself. 'It's been a busy day, that's all. But I'll cook your fishcakes. Only one for me, though. I've had a big school dinner.' She rose, slipping off her jacket and picking up her bag of books. 'Just give me a few minutes to have a wash and sort myself out.'

'Hurry up, won't you, love? I'm starving. I've only had a bowl of tomato soup for my dinner. It's as much as I can do to open a tin of soup. How are you going to cook 'em, them fishcakes? Grilled, do you think, or fried?'

'Oh, grilled, I think, Mum. They're better for you done that way.'

'Mmm . . .' Iris pursed her lips. 'I think I'd prefer 'em fried. They'd be more tasty.'

'Very well, Mother,' Frances replied. If Iris didn't watch out she would have the blasted fishcakes served right on top of her head, complete with tomato sauce. 'Fried it is then. With chips and bread and butter. That do for you?' It had better do, Iris Goodwin, she thought. Oh yes, it had better do, or I might not be responsible for my actions.

By the end of her second week at Wyre Bank School Frances was finding, to her relief, that she was not nearly so tired at the end of each day. A little fatigued, but comfortably so, not dead on her feet as she had felt the first few days. She thought she had mastered the class and sorted out the troublemakers, showing them who was boss; now, maybe, it was time for her to relax a little more. She was beginning to realise, however, that she was not so much tired as bored. Not at school, of course; there was not a fraction of a second there that was not filled with some activity or other, even dinner times and playtimes often being spent in sorting out problems – missing coats, grazed knees, tête-à-têtes with Miss Reynolds, and so on and so on.

But Frances was finding she was increasingly restless at

home. Since term began all she had done of an evening was watch the television in the company of her mother, except for the couple of occasions when she had gone to visit Josie and Jim at Marton. She was not yet attached to a church or a society of any sort, nor had she any close friends with whom she could go out for an evening. Four years spent away from her home town, two at college and two teaching in Yorkshire, had left her very much out of touch with happenings in Blackpool. She wondered what had happened to Megan Ashcroft. She had seen her, briefly, when Iris had been in hospital, and the girl had promised, once again, to contact her when she had time, but so far she hadn't done so. A nurse's life could be even more chaotic than a teacher's, Frances supposed. Then there was the wonderful Bernard, of course, who appeared to take up so much of Megan's time.

Feeling very much out on a limb Frances thumbed through the pages of the local *Gazette*. It didn't mean very much to her; reports of the doings of this badminton group or the annual general meeting of that French circle or literary society or flower arrangers' group. And the people who were having babies, or getting married, or dying – hatches, matches and dispatches, Iris always called them – Frances had never heard of any of them either. She rustled the newspaper irritably as she tried to find the page where there was a crossword. Anything for a change. Iris, as usual, was engrossed with the doctors and nurses from *Emergency Ward Ten*, and though Frances quite liked that programme herself she felt like being awkward tonight; what her mother would call 'wrong-roaded'. She cast a baleful glance in Iris's direction although Iris, for once, had done nothing to deserve it (and, fortunately, did not notice).

Then as her eyes scanned over the columns of print she noticed something that made her look again, more carefully. This was just what she wanted, the very thing she had had in mind a while back, but with her mother being ill and then the hectic rush of the beginning of term it had gone right out of her mind. 'The Starlight Players,' she read. 'New members, both male and female, are required for this light operatic group. Rehearsals begin soon for our forthcoming production of *South Pacific*. Anyone interested should attend for an audition . . .'

Frances's feeling of restlessness had vanished in the time it took her to read the notice. The audition was next week and the venue was a church hall near the town centre, just a bus ride away. Frances decided she would be there, showing them how she could sing – and dance, too, if they required it – doing her utmost to become a member of these Starlight Players.

'Mum . . . I've been thinking . . .' she began, as the credits at the end of the programme appeared on the screen. Maybe now would be a good time to tell her mother, while she appeared to be in a reasonable sort of mood. Then she stopped, remembering that Iris had been dead against the idea of her joining an operatic group, 'jigging about on a stage', as she had put it. It might be better not to upset her just now; she could so quickly turn cantankerous again. Frances felt her courage wavering. Perhaps tomorrow . . .

'What, love?' asked Iris, smiling vaguely in her direction. 'Eeh, it's good, isn't it? I thought that young nurse'd fall for that good-looking doctor . . . Did you want to ask me summat, Frances?'

'No, it's nothing, Mum,' said Frances. 'I was just wondering . . . shall I make us a cup of tea?'

'Eeh, that'd be grand, love. And there's some shortbread biscuits in the tin. Eliza brought them today – they're homemade. I don't know what I'd do without Eliza, really I don't. Happen we could have a couple of those each . . . There was a time I used to make 'em meself. I thought nothing of knocking out a few dozen biscuits, and a couple of parkins and a fruit cake, and that was before I'd even thought about getting the dinner ready. Aye, those were the days, love. When you were only a tiny little lass, and Josie and Bertie were at school. And Samuel at work, of course . . .' Iris paused, shaking her head musingly. 'D'you know, I tend to forget about Samuel, he's been gone so long. Isn't that dreadful of me? It was because of you three,

56

you and Josie and Bertie, that I married him really. Well, that were one o' t'reasons.'

'Yes, it's a long time ago, Mum,' said Frances. 'It's not surprising that you forget. I can hardly remember my father at all.'

'No, love; you'd only have been what – six years old when he was killed.'

'Yes, I was six . . . and you hadn't been married to him all that long, had you?'

'No . . . six years, that's all. You were only a few months old when we got wed. Folks had a lot to say, I know that, but I knew he needed somebody, with three kiddies to bring up. Besides, I loved him. And now . . .' Iris looked down regretfully at her hands, the joints and knuckles swollen and misshapen, and she gave a heartfelt sigh. 'And now . . . deary me, I don't know, love; sometimes I feel I'm neither use nor ornament, and that's a fact.'

And Frances, remembering the times when her mother had been so good to them all, reproached herself for her impatience and, maybe, her lack of understanding and sympathy. She quickly moved across the room and kissed Iris's pendulous cheek. 'Come on, Mum, cheer up. You know that's not true. Don't start feeling sorry for yourself. We all love you.'

Iris nudged her daughter out of the way. 'Never mind all that soft soap,' she said, although Frances could see she was smiling. 'And I don't feel sorry for meself, not me. I never have and I never will. Go on, off you trot. Go and make us that cup of tea, there's a good lass.'

Iris's good humour lasted into the next day, so Frances plucked up courage to tell her about the Starlight Players. She had wondered whether she should make it a *fait accompli*, passing the audition first – as she was determined she would do – then telling her mother afterwards, but she decided that would not really be right. Iris would be sure to ask where she was going, and Frances hated telling lies, even white ones. Iris received the news placidly enough. Frances considered herself lucky to have got away with

merely a remark from her mother that she must be careful
not to neglect her job and a warning not to get too involved
with 'that fast crowd, drinking and carrying on till all hours'.
Iris had no idea, in point of fact, whether these Starlight
Players were 'fast' or otherwise, but the very fact that they
'careered about on a stage' intimated to her that they must
be so, all theatrical people, to Iris's mind, being tarred with
the same brush. Frances promised dutifully that she would
behave herself, and she set off in high spirits, the following
week, for her audition.

She was, if she were honest, experiencing a little
trepidation in going by herself, but she was not normally a
shy sort of girl and she felt she would soon be able to make
friends if – when – she became a member of the group.
There was nobody she could ask to go with her. She didn't
know any of the staff at school well enough yet to discuss
her interests with them, apart from Marjorie Aspinall, and
she seemed to be beset by problems at home, hinted at,
but never fully explained. Megan Ashcroft had finally
phoned Frances; they were to meet on Saturday afternoon
to have a mooch round the shops, then, perhaps, a cup of
tea together in the snack bar at RHO Hills. Frances knew
that amateur dramatics would not be Megan's scene at all,
at least from what she remembered of the girl. She recalled,
with some amusement, how Megan, when she had been
going through her 'holier than thou' phase, and her friend
Janet had reproached her for her somewhat provocative
style of dancing – to their way of thinking – when she had
appeared in the Children's Ballet in the Tower Ballroom.

Six people, including Frances, turned up for the audition
at a town centre church hall; four women and two men, all
roughly in the same age group, early to mid-twenties. All
that was required was a fairly strong and tuneful singing
voice, the man in charge of the proceedings informed them.
Not necessarily a trained voice, in fact that could be more
of a drawback in the chorus – which was what they were
aspiring to at the moment – as such voices tended to
dominate the others. And the dancing skills required were
minimal; anyone with a good sense of rhythm would be

able to master the steps required for the dances performed by the chorus of American marines and South Sea island girls.

Frances learned that the 'boss man', who would be producing the show, to be presented at Blackpool's Grand Theatre the following March, was Joe Markland, and the pianist, who very ably accompanied all the applicants, was his wife, Olive. The other three judges – although such a sober-sounding word was not really appropriate, the whole thing being very informal – were members of the committee, whom Frances was sure she would get to know in due course. In all probability they would be the singers who were to take the leading roles.

Frances felt that she acquitted herself very well. She chose to sing two contrasting songs from another well-known musical, *Oklahoma!*: 'I Can't Say No!', and 'Out of My Dreams'. Her voice had never been trained, but she had sung in church choirs and various amateur concerts. Neither had she ever learned to read music in the way that children do when they have piano lessons. Dancing lessons had been Frances's dream when she was a little girl, and Iris, who nearly always let her have her own way, had indulged her in her desire. But her knowledge of music, in theory as well as in practice, had grown along with her love of the art. Her very real enthusiasm showed, not only in the timbre of her voice, but in her mannerisms and expressions; and her little performance was followed by a ripple of applause from the other contenders and from the judges, whose smiling faces suggested to her that she had done well.

All six candidates, in fact, were told, to their delight, that they had been successful; and they were invited to attend at the same place, the same time, the following week when rehearsals would begin in earnest.

'That wasn't too bad, was it?' Frances remarked to the young woman sitting next to her, a bonny round-faced girl with dark curly hair, who had been eyeing Frances intently. 'I'm so glad we've all been accepted. It would have been awful if some had been refused. But I don't suppose you would come, would you, unless you felt you could sing?'

'No, I shouldn't think so,' replied the girl. 'Although I nearly got up and went home, I can tell you, when I'd heard you. No, I didn't really,' she went on, laughing, 'but I thought, Goodness! I'm not anything like as good as that. You were great, honestly.'

'Thank you,' said Frances, modestly, but feeling very pleased. 'I'm a bit out of practice though; I've not done much recently . . . I loved the numbers you sang. Gilbert and Sullivan songs are great favourites of mine.'

'Mine too,' said the girl. 'That's why I chose them . . . I remember you,' she went on, looking keenly at Frances. 'I kept trying to place you, then when that fellow – Mr Markland, isn't it? – called you Frances I knew who you were. You're Frances Goodwin, aren't you? You were in the Tower Ballet; I remember you were the girl in the swing.'

'Goodness me!' said Frances. 'Fancy you remembering that. Yes, you're right – I was – but it was ages ago. I was only thirteen; it's nine years ago.' She had been chosen that year for the special honour, the girl in the swing, swinging to and fro above the heads of the audience, waving to them and throwing flowers . . . and how she had loved it, fancying herself as quite the little princess.

'You've not changed, though,' said the girl. 'Hardly at all. I was in it as well, only that one year, but I was a couple of years younger, just one of the dancers, so you wouldn't remember me. I'm Julie, by the way, Julie Forrester.'

Frances smiled at her. 'Pleased to meet you, Julie. No, I'm sorry, I don't remember you. I'm amazed you remember me. Did you say you were in the ballet for only one year?'

'Yes. I changed schools the year after, and my mum said I had to concentrate on my studies, never mind "all that dancing lark".'

Frances grinned. 'That sounds just like my mother. Not that it stopped me. I was in the ballet for a few years, until I started studying for O levels.'

'Yes, I remember you a couple of years later,' Julie went on. 'I used to go and see it even though I didn't take part.

You were one of the principals then, weren't you? I remember you being dressed like Carmen Miranda, singing that "I-yi-yi" song. You were really good.'

'Don't remind me!' replied Frances. 'I was a precocious little madam, I know that much. I didn't half fancy myself, but I had a family that brought me down to size, thank goodness!' And friends, too, she was recalling. That was the rather suggestive song that Megan had objected to. Frances, also, had felt at variance with herself at that time, not able to equate her provocative performances on stage with her singing in the church choir. However, it had all been resolved, her mother's sudden illness having forced her, more than anything, to face reality. 'I'm glad I've grown up a bit since then,' she said, with a wry smile at her new friend.

Nobody seemed to be making any move yet to depart for home. Olive Markland, the pianist, went into the kitchen at the rear of the hall to make refreshments; and over a cup of tea Frances learned that Julie Forrester, who was twenty years old, worked in a local government office. Like Frances she lived in Layton, but at the other end, towards Bispham. They were pleased to discover that they could travel home on the same bus.

'See you next week,' Julie called out as Frances alighted at Layton Square.

'Yes, see you,' replied Frances, waving cheerily as she stepped off the bus. She had had a good time tonight. Life suddenly felt full of promise; a new job, new interests, new friends.

'Some enchanted evening . . .' she hummed to herself as she walked up the path. They would be singing that song soon. No, perhaps not that one; that was sung by the main characters, wasn't it? But there were lots of others: 'I'm in Love With a Wonderful Guy', and 'There is Nothin' Like a Dame', and 'Bali Ha'i'. Oh, it was all going to be so exciting.

'Frances?' called her mother as she entered the house. 'Is that you?'

Iris's voice was coming from the back of the bungalow. The front rooms, the living rooms, were in darkness. 'Yes, of course it's me, Mum. Where are you?'

'I've gone to bed. Where d'you think I am? I couldn't wait up any longer for you.'

'But I'm not late, Mum.' It was barely half-past ten. Usually Iris would still be up watching television at this time. Frances suspected her mother was being a wee bit difficult going to bed so early.

'Late enough . . . Anyroad, now I find I can't get to sleep. Make me a drink of Horlicks, would you, there's a good lass, and I'll take another of them tablets.'

'Righto, Mum, will do.'

'And fetch me library book an' all, would you? Seeing as I can't sleep I might as well have a read.'

'OK, Mum,' Frances answered cheerfully. She was determined that nothing, but nothing, was going to spoil the lovely evening she had just enjoyed.

Chapter 5

The following Saturday, as Frances approached the Winter Gardens entrance, where she had arranged to meet Megan, she was surprised, and a little miffed, if she were honest, to see that her friend was not alone. From the other side of Church Street Frances watched her, gazing up into the eyes of the tall dark man at her side, talking animatedly as she held on to his arm. This, then, must be the famous Bernard, but Frances hadn't bargained for him joining their girls' afternoon.

Megan caught sight of Frances and waved excitedly, like a little girl, pointing her out to her fiancé. 'This is Bernard, my boyfriend, that I was telling you about,' she said, as Frances drew near. 'Dr Bernard Conway, I should say, of course, Bernard, this is my friend, Frances. I've told you such a lot about her, haven't I, darling?'

'Indeed, you have,' replied Dr Bernard Conway gravely. 'I feel I know this young lady very well already.' Deep brown eyes, almost black, observed Frances keenly from beneath beetling eyebrows that nearly met in the centre of his forehead. A wide, autocratic forehead, from which the dark hair, greying at the temples, was already receding. This was a man not to be trifled with or taken lightly, Frances knew instinctively.

'How do you do, Frances?' He bowed his head as he took her hand; his voice was sonorous, like that of a priest intoning the responses in church.

'How do you do, Dr Conway?' replied Frances. Somehow she felt that she could not, yet, call him Bernard. Nor did he invite her to do so.

'I keep telling Megan, however, that I am not her

boyfriend, which is what she will insist on calling me.' He turned to Megan now, looking at her reprovingly. Fondly, though, Frances thought, but it was more the look of an indulgent uncle or father, rather than a fiancé. 'Such a childish word, Megan. I do wish you would remember that I am your fiancé.'

'Yes . . . yes, of course. Sorry, Bernard.' Megan's pale blue eyes blinked rapidly as she smiled up at him. 'Anyway, I said to Bernard – my fiancé,' she giggled, 'that he just had to meet you. But he's not staying with us, are you, darling?' Frances was relieved to hear that. 'He had an errand to do in town, and he's going back to the hospital now, aren't you, darling?'

'Yes, and I must hurry or I'll be late.' Bernard stooped and kissed Megan's cheek. 'I will see you tonight, my dear, as we arranged. Goodbye, Frances. I am pleased to have met you. I am quite sure we will meet again sometime.'

'Yes, I'm sure we will. Goodbye . . . Dr Conway.'

'Behave yourself now.' This remark was addressed to Megan. 'Don't go wasting your money on silly things you don't need. I know what you girls are like when you get together.'

'Oh, Bernard, as if I would!' Megan fluttered as the tall, slightly stooping figure, walked away. She turned eagerly to Frances, her blue eyes shining. 'Isn't he nice? I've been dying for you to meet him. I knew you'd like him.'

'Er . . . yes, he does seem . . . nice,' replied Frances. 'Very . . . er . . . dignified. You could tell he was a doctor, even if you didn't know.'

'Yes, couldn't you just?' said Megan happily.

Frances, quite frankly, felt that Dr Bernard Conway was a pompous, patronising sort of fellow, and their own family doctor, in spite of her remark, certainly did not have an overbearing manner like his. But she reminded herself that she mustn't judge too much on first appearances. She had only just met the man, and Megan seemed to be well satisfied with him. She must be, or she would hardly have made the decision to change her religion for him.

'He's rather older than us, isn't he?' asked Frances. 'Of

course, he must be, being a doctor. It's a long training, isn't it?'

'He's a specialist,' Megan reminded her, 'not just a doctor. He's a gynaecologist. Yes, Bernard's thirty-three, eleven years older than me, but it doesn't matter, does it? My father is twelve years older than my mother, and Mum and Dad think that an older man is much better for me. They like him very much, so I'm happy about that. In fact I'm very happy altogether.' She tucked her arm companionably into Frances's as they headed off down Church Street. 'Oh, it is good to see you again. I've really been looking forward to it. You must tell me all about your new job. Do you like it?'

'Yes, very much,' replied Frances. 'It's getting better all the time, now I've settled in. It's a big change from the school in Yorkshire, of course. I'll tell you more about it while we have our tea. Now . . . where are we going? Marks & Spencer, I suppose.' They were just approaching the Church Street store. 'Although the other branch, the one near Central Station, is better than this one, isn't it? They have a much better selection of clothes there.'

'I suppose so; I don't really know,' replied Megan. 'I don't buy many clothes at Marks. There's a little dress shop in South Shore, where Mum goes, and I usually get my things there. To be quite honest, I don't bother all that much about clothes. I'm in uniform most of the time.'

'It's nice to dress up, though, isn't it, when you're not at work?' said Frances, casting an appraising look in her friend's direction. Judging from Megan's tweed skirt, flat-heeled shoes and nondescript fawn jacket – not shabby, but several years out of date – it seemed as though fashion was not high on her list of priorities. All her garments looked as though they came from her mum's 'little dress shop'.

'Maybe,' replied Megan. 'But I haven't spent much on myself, not since I've been saving up to get married. I wondered if we could have a look round RHO Hills as well? I saw some lovely cups and saucers the last time I was in there, so I think I might go mad and buy them – for my bottom drawer, you know,' she added with a contented little smile. 'And they have all sorts of kitchen gadgets. Egg whisks and fish slices and spoons, and a really clever thing for cutting up onions – oh, all sorts of lovely things.'

Terrific! thought Frances. It seemed as though they were in for a scintillating afternoon. But she mustn't be uncharitable. She was really very glad to see Megan again.

'Yes, of course we will. Anything you like. And let's have a look in Sweeten's bookshop. That's near Hills, isn't it? I want to see if I can find some storybooks to read to my class. Something a bit different.'

They spent an enjoyable afternoon, each of them giving way to the other's preferences without irritation. Frances found a book of 'Stories for Seven Year Olds', which included modern material as well as the all-time favourites; and she treated herself in Marks & Spencer to a silky rayon waist-slip with a gathered tiered skirt, and a tan shoulder bag with a strap and buckle fastening, just the thing for school.

Megan, who could not be persuaded to buy clothes – apart from two pairs of nylon stockings, of a rather coarser denier than Frances wore – went into raptures over a tea set she had seen previously. It was what was known as a 'Harlequin' range, with cups, saucers and plates in six different colours; pink, blue, green, yellow, orange and mauve.

'You can use them with the pieces matching, or you can mix the colours up,' Megan explained delightedly to Frances while the assistant packed up the crockery carefully in a sturdy box, to be collected later.

She also bought the clever gadget she had mentioned for cutting onions, and a blue and white striped flour sifter to go with some other articles she had already acquired in this range.

'I can quite understand why you haven't much money to spend on clothes,' remarked Frances, indulgently, as they sat over their cups of tea and toasted teacakes in Hill's basement café. Megan had been like a child buying items for a doll's house, transparent in her joy over these treasures for her bottom drawer. 'If the wedding's to be next spring you'll have set a date by now.'

'No, we've decided to wait till the year after,' said Megan. 'I'd like a spring wedding, though, so it'll probably be the spring of 1960.' She sighed. 'It sounds a long time away, doesn't it? But Bernard says it'll be better if we wait a little while longer. He wants to make sure we get exactly the sort of house we want. On one of the Park Drives, I should think, so that we will be near the hospital. Of course, Bernard wants me to give up nursing when we get married and concentrate on being a housewife . . . and a mother, too, we hope,' she added coyly. 'We'd like a big family. Two boys and two girls at least. I never dreamed, Frances, that one day I would live in a house on North Park Drive. That's what Bernard's got in mind. It wouldn't matter to me where we lived, though, so long as we were together. I keep trying to tell him that.'

Frances nodded. There was really no answer to this eulogy. 'You're quite a long way from the hospital now, aren't you?' she remarked. 'Living in South Shore. How do you get to work? You ride a bike, don't you?'

'Yes, sometimes I go on my bike, sometimes on the bus,' replied Megan, 'depending on what shift I'm on. Bernard doesn't like me riding in the dark.'

'Have you never thought of living in?' asked Frances. 'Some nurses do.'

'No, I don't really fancy that,' said Megan. 'But I've got something in mind that I'd like to tell you about.' She leaned forward eagerly across the red checked tablecover. 'Actually, it was Bernard's idea . . . He thinks it might be a good idea if I moved into a flat near to the hospital. He thinks it would help to give me confidence and it would give me some idea of how to run a home . . . before we move into our own home, you see.' Dr Conway certainly seemed to have got it all mapped out.

'Anyway, Bernard has already found somewhere for me. It's on Newton Drive – that's quite near to the Vic, you know.' Victoria Hospital, she meant. 'It's part of a house, the downstairs part, quite a big one, so it would be better if

I could get somebody to share with me. That's what I wanted to ask you, Frances. Would you consider moving in with me? It's quite near to your school, isn't it? Well, not all that far away. Nearer than you are now, I should think.'

Frances was flabbergasted. She had had no inkling of what Megan was leading up to. 'Goodness . . . I don't know,' she stuttered. 'You've taken me quite by surprise!' She paused for a moment, then: 'I'm saying I don't know,' she went on, 'but actually I do know. I'm afraid I can't, Megan. I'm terribly sorry, but . . . I can't. There's Mum, you see. I've only just come back after being away for four years. She'd take a very dim view of it if I were to move away again so soon. Besides, she's been quite ill – you know that, of course – and she does rely on me quite a lot.'

'Yes, I know.' Megan nodded earnestly. 'It was just an idea. I suppose I didn't really expect you to say yes, but I'd much rather share with you than with one of the other nurses. But I should imagine I'll be able to find somebody quite easily. Bernard'll help me. I wanted to ask you first, though. We've been friends a long time, haven't we, Frances?'

Not always close friends, thought Frances, but she was touched by Megan's generosity, and she was growing very fond of the young woman now, gratified that Megan seemed to value her friendship so much. It was certainly an appealing proposition, the idea of sharing a flat. She felt claustrophobic at times in her mother's stuffy, overheated little bungalow. Her bedroom was tiny and there was very little room for her to spread out her possessions, or to find room to do her school work; the preparations of pictures and work cards and projects, all of which required a vast amount of space. However, it was an impossible dream at the moment, tempting though it might be.

'I'm sorry, Megan,' she said again. 'Truly I am. I would have loved it, and thank you so much for asking me, but I can't. I think it's a great idea, though, and I'm sure you'll soon find somebody to share with you. Now, I'll pay this bill, then we'd better be going, hadn't we? No, this is my treat this afternoon,' she said, as Megan started to get out her purse. 'I insist. It's payday next week; besides, it's so lovely we've met up again.'

Megan's pale blue eyes looked slightly moist as she smiled back at her friend. 'Yes, isn't it great? I'm so glad about it. We'll do this again sometime, shall we?'

'Yes,' Frances promised. 'Be sure to let me have your new address as soon as you move. I must admit I feel quite envious . . .'

'Please, Miss Goodwin . . .' It was one of the three Lindas who was standing at Frances's desk, her arm upraised and a somewhat smug expression on her face. She was a helpful child and Frances had found her and her two henchmen, Susan and Jennifer, a godsend with their desire to tackle all sorts of undesirable jobs – washing out paint pots, tidying cupboards, sorting out the jumble of books in a well-used book corner – but Linda, in particular, was also something of a telltale.

'Yes, Linda; what is it now?' Frances looked up from her task of marking the morning's spelling test. It was supposed to be a 'quiet time' in the classroom, the children engaged in silent reading after completing a work card in their jotters – a period of respite and calm for a harassed teacher – but it was the third time already that Linda had trotted out to the front with some minor anxiety.

'Please, Miss Goodwin, somebody's pinched my pencil sharpener.'

Frances sighed. That was the third item to go missing this week. Nigel had lost a rubber and Carol a packet of sweets – small things, admittedly, but nevertheless of great importance to a child. But so far Frances had done nothing other than to tell the children concerned to go and look again, very carefully. Their searches had proved fruitless. Frances desperately hoped there was not a light-fingered child in the class. That sort of thing was so difficult to pinpoint, and so distressing if it should prove to be the case. Frances always felt at a loss as to how to deal with it; which was probably why, she admitted to herself, she had done nothing about it . . . so far.

'You can't be sure somebody's taken it, dear,' she said now. 'Perhaps you dropped it on the floor, or it might be at the very back of your desk. Go and have another look.'

'I've already looked and looked, Miss Goodwin, and it's not there.' Linda's expression was indignant. 'I know somebody's pinched it, 'cause it was there just before playtime – I saw it – and now it's gone.'

'Please, Miss Goodwin . . .' Christine's hand shot up, another little miss who was inclined to tell tales. 'I know who it'll be what's pinching them things. He used to do it last year, in Miss Walsh's class. It's Dennis Russell.'

'Yes, it'll be him.' A few heads, to Frances's consternation, were nodding self-righteously, and there were muttered remarks. 'Yes, he did . . .' 'I remember, don't you . . .?' 'He pinched my new pencil . . .'

'Hey, shurrup, you lot!' Barry Cartwright's voice sounded above the whispering. 'You've got no right to say that about Dennis. You don't know, none of you. I sit next to 'im, an' I know 'im a lot better'n what you lot do, so you can just shut up!'

'Be quiet, all of you!' Frances silenced them. 'You as well, Barry, though it's very nice of you to stick up for your friend.' She had developed a liking for Barry, her sparring partner of the first day, finding in him, as she had thought she might, a great loyalty for his friends and an integrity beyond his years; this was despite his devil-may-care bravado and his lack of concentration with his work.

She was on the horns of a dilemma, though, now, and it would have to be sorted out, whether she liked the idea or not. 'Barry is quite right,' she said. 'You can't start accusing someone when you have no proof.' Why hadn't she heard about Dennis Russell's problem, she wondered, if what the children said was true? She felt, deep down, that there must be some truth in it; they were all so adamant. But none of the other staff had mentioned it to her.

'But we'll have to find out, won't we, one way or another? Listen, everybody, this is what I want you to do. Open your desks and take everything out – and I mean everything –

70

and put it on top. Then I shall come round and have a look.'

'And pockets as well, Miss Goodwin.' Linda's hand had shot up again. 'Dennis . . . I mean . . . some people used to hide things in their pockets.'

'Very well then, I suppose so.' Frances was hating this. 'If there's anything in your pockets, boys and girls, then take it out, please.'

Class 3G didn't seem perturbed by the chore. Anything for a bit of light relief, Frances supposed. They had been getting rather restless with their noses to the grindstone. The insides of the desks reflected the different personalities of the children, some in apple-pie order, others the most unbelievable mess, with sweet wrappers, stub ends of pencils, torn up paper, gloves and Balaclava helmets all jumbled together. Well, at least it was a good excuse for a tidy-up, but Frances was desperately hoping that she would fail to find the evidence she was looking for.

One look at Dennis Russell's face, however, was enough to tell her she had found the culprit. His eyes were downcast, his mouth set in a stubborn line and he was gripping tightly to both pockets of his trousers. Frances's heart sank.

'Come on, Dennis,' she said quietly. 'Empty your pockets, like all the others have done.'

'I have done, miss. It's all there, on top of the desk like you said.' He scowled at her from beneath his pale ginger eyebrows.

'I don't think so, Dennis.' Goodness, this was awful! She didn't want to force him or to look in his pockets herself. That, she knew, could be regarded as an infringement of his privacy. Even though he was only a child he did have his rights. 'Come along now, there's a good boy.' She was still speaking quietly. 'I don't want to involve Miss Reynolds . . . but I shall have to, I'm afraid, if you don't do as you are told.'

She didn't know why the mention of the headmistress should put the fear of God into the children, but it always seemed to do so. It wasn't as if Miss Reynolds was draconian in her dealings with them. For instance, she did not believe in corporal punishment. Canes and rulers, as implements of correction, were banned at Wyre Bank, and all teachers had to obey this dictum. But Miss Reynolds had the ability to make a child feel very, very small, very much aware of the gravity of his misdemeanours and the effect they were having on his teachers or his class-mates. Dennis was no exception. At the mention of Miss Reynolds's name he pulled out the contents of his pockets: a grubby handkerchief, two sweet papers, three pennies . . . and a rubber and a pencil sharpener.

'Oh, Dennis . . .' Frances shook her head. She felt saddened rather than angry at the sight of Dennis's face – his expression a mixture of belligerence and remorse – and guilty, too; although there was no reason, for heaven's sake, for her to feel guilty, was there? she asked herself. She was only doing what she had to do.

A deathly hush had fallen over the classroom and inquisitive heads were peering round, looking towards the back where Dennis's desk was situated.

'Right, everyone,' said Frances, in a decisive voice. 'Get on with sorting out your desks. Put everything back – tidily, mind – and the ones that finish first can clean the blackboards for me. Get on now; you heard what I said.' Then, in a quieter voice, 'Why, Dennis?' she asked. 'Why did you take these things?'

'Dunno, Miss Goodwin,' the boy mumbled. 'I didn't take them pennies, though. Me dad gave me them to buy some sweets. Them's the change.'

'And the missing sweets? On Monday, Carol's sweets?' Dennis hung his head. 'I've ate 'em, miss.'

'But you know it's wrong, don't you? A big sensible boy like you. And I know you can be very sensible when you try. You know it's wrong to take things that belong to other people, don't you?'

Dennis shrugged, still not looking at her. 'Dunno, miss . . . I mean, Miss Goodwin.'

'Please, Miss Goodwin, it's not really his fault,' said Barry. He grabbed hold of his friend's arm. 'I mean, he

72

can't help it, can you, Den?' Dennis didn't answer. 'He gets upset sometimes, don't you, Den? About his mum, y'see, and so he starts pinching.'

'About his . . . mother?' faltered Frances.

'Yes, she died, y'see, last year, didn't she, Dennis? When we was in Miss Walsh's class. An' he got upset and—'

'All right, Barry. Thank you very much for telling me.' Frances put an end to his chatter with a reproving little frown and shake of her head, which he seemed to understand. This was some other vital information that Miss Walsh had failed to pass on to her. 'I'm sorry, Dennis, to hear about . . . this. But it's still no excuse, you know, for . . . for what you've done.'

The bell, signalling the end of the morning session, sounded then, to Frances's relief. Several of the nearby children had been ear-wigging, and you could hardly blame them. 'Right, Class 3G, you may go. Line up at the door, quietly now. You stay behind, Dennis. I want a word with you when nobody's listening.'

She didn't make much headway with him, just a vague promise, indicated by a brief nod of his head, that he wouldn't do it again. She insisted that he must return the stolen articles to the children concerned with a suitable apology. It would be merely a mumbled 'Sorry', she guessed, but children, on the whole, were not ones to bear grudges and she felt sure that Nigel and Linda would be ready to forgive and forget. At least until the next opportunity for snitching came along. Children could be the most paradoxical creatures imaginable.

'What about poor Carol's sweets, though?' said Frances. 'You can't give those back, can you? Now, I think it would be a nice idea if you were to buy her some more. You've got three pennies there. You could get her some like the ones you . . . er . . . took, couldn't you?'

'It's me dad's change, miss . . . Miss Goodwin. But I don't suppose he'd know. I don't need to tell him, do I?'

'Er, no, not this time.' She didn't like encouraging him to be deceitful, but it was important to gain his confidence. 'Not if you promise not to do it again. And if he gave you

73

sixpence to spend – is that what he gave you?' Dennis nodded – 'then I don't suppose he'll mind if you spend it all. What sort of sweets were they?' she asked.

'Pear drops, miss.'

'Mmm . . . I like those, don't you?' she asked. Silly question, Frances, she told herself; he must have liked them or he wouldn't have pinched them. But the thought of those pink and yellow sweets had conjured up memories of Saturday spending money and visits to the sweet stall in Abingdon Street market.

'Yes, I like 'em,' Dennis replied seriously. 'But I like sherbet lemons better. Carol sometimes has them, so I think that's what I'll get her: sherbet lemons.'

Frances was touched by this small confidence. It was the first time the boy had opened up to her about anything at all. 'Very well, Dennis. Just see that you do.' She smiled understandingly at him. 'Run along and get your dinner, and we'll say no more about it, provided you remember what I've said.'

'OK, Miss Goodwin.'

'Right then. Off you pop, Dennis the Menace.'

He grinned at her small witticism and ran off, seemingly quite contented. Poor little lad . . . she had had no idea about his mother.

Frances felt quite drained by this occurrence, but she was determined to tackle Miss Walsh in the staffroom after she had had her dinner. No, tackle was not quite the right word. Frances reminded herself that she was still very much the new girl and that Miss Walsh was a teacher who required handling with kid gloves. Her first antipathy to the elderly teacher had not abated with further acquaintance; she felt, moreover, that the antipathy was mutual, that the woman was ill-disposed to her, too, though she did not know the reason, if, indeed, there was one. Maybe it was just a question of conflicting personalities.

'Miss Walsh.' Frances decided to approach her deferentially. 'I wonder if you could tell me something about Dennis Russell. I've been having – well, a bit of trouble with him.'

Miss Walsh didn't deign to answer at first. She dabbed

her lips with her crisp white napkin she had brought from home before placing it, with the greaseproof wrapping from her sandwiches, in the square plastic container. She was the only member of staff who brought sandwiches for lunch; she suffered, apparently, from digestive problems. Only then did she reply, although her steely grey eyes were looking, not at Frances, but down at the pile of papers in front of her, as though the young woman were wasting her time.

'What sort of trouble?' she asked coldly.

'Well . . .' Frances lowered her voice. 'I don't want to make an issue of it, but he's been stealing. Rubbers and sweets and . . . things like that,' she finished, her voice petering out as she seemed to be getting no response.

'Hmm,' Miss Walsh grunted eventually. 'Yes, I must admit there was a spell of that when he was in my class.' She spoke grudgingly. 'But I thought he had got over it. Of course, it's bound to have unsettled him, changing classes. I don't suppose he's used to you yet, Miss . . . er, Miss Goodwin. He was very attached to me, and we all have our different ways. Some children take a while to settle down, especially with a teacher they don't know.'

Frances bristled, but she made herself answer calmly. 'That's no excuse, is it, for stealing? But his friend, Barry – you know, Barry Cartwright . . .'

'Yes, I know him all right,' Miss Walsh answered darkly. 'Very impudent sort of boy. Slovenly mother, rough family . . .'

'Well, anyway,' Frances would not be sidetracked. It was not Barry, rough family or no, who was her concern at the moment. 'Barry told me that Dennis's mother died last year. I didn't know that, and . . . well, I feel that I ought to have known. It might have helped me to understand a bit more about him.'

Miss Walsh gave her a searching look, her eyebrows drawing together in a frown that implied, How dare you criticise me? 'Yes,' she answered frostily. 'Mrs Russell died last year, that's true. Just before Christmas, poor woman.' At least Frances was glad to see some expression of

75

sympathy. 'She had a brain tumour, I believe – quite sudden. And so, naturally, Mr Russell is finding it hard to cope on his own. Dennis is the only child, though, which is a blessing, I suppose.'

'They live on the estate, I dare say?' Frances ventured, relieved at even a slight thawing in the older teacher's attitude. 'Yes, I suppose it must be hard for Dennis if his father is out at work. Perhaps he has to let himself in the house – do you know if he does? I know some of the children do—'

'Good gracious me, no!' replied Miss Walsh. 'Dennis Russell is not one of the *estate* children.' Her emphasis on the word implied that such were the lowest of the low. 'Whatever gave you that idea?'

'Well, I don't know...' Frances floundered. 'I just assumed... I thought they might be short of money and—'

'If you had looked at the address in your register, girl –' Frances again felt herself bristling. How dare this woman call her 'girl'? – 'you would have realised where the Russells live. They are one of our private house families.' Frances noticed the accentuation of the two words, as she had done at the first staff meeting. Miss Walsh, undoubtedly, was a snob of the first degree. 'In fact they live in a very nice area, very near to Newton Drive.'

'The addresses mean very little to me, Miss Walsh,' Frances answered evenly. 'I've been away from Blackpool for four years and this is a district I don't know very well. All these avenues and groves and closes, they could be anywhere for all I know.'

'Then perhaps it's time you started to acquaint yourself with where the children live.' Miss Walsh peered coldly down her long nose at Frances. 'It does have some bearing on how they behave.'

'Not always,' Frances retorted, wondering at her bravery in answering back. 'Not if Dennis comes from what you call a "private house".'

Miss Walsh frowned with annoyance. She never liked to be put, even slightly, in the wrong. 'He was upset about his

76

mother,' she said, shaking her head irritably. 'Obviously he's still upset . . . about something. But of course he shouldn't steal. He will have to be broken of this . . . er . . . tendency before it gets a hold on him. You'd better tell Miss Reynolds about it.' She turned, pointedly, to the pile of papers in front of her and started shuffling them.

'I was hoping to keep Miss Reynolds out of it this time,' said Frances.

'Miss . . . er . . . Goodwin, Miss Reynolds is the head-mistress of this school, and she has to be informed of everything that goes on. Just see that you tell her. Now, if I can be permitted to get on with my work . . .'

'Cantankerous old bitch!' whispered Marjorie Aspinall, when Frances joined her, with their mugs of tea, at the other end of the staffroom. 'I couldn't help overhearing some of that. I'm sorry Dennis has started pinching again, but you can rest assured it's nothing to do with you. The cheek of it, suggesting that he hasn't got used to you! I think you've got a lovely way with the children, dear.'

'Thanks, Marjorie.' Frances felt grateful for the praise.

'It's possibly a bid for attention. Such behaviour usually is, and he's had a rough time, poor little boy. Jonathan Russell does his best, though. He's a very good dad.'

'You know them, do you?'

'Vaguely. I know Dennis, of course. I taught him two years ago – I had a Reception class then – and his mum often used to pop in to see me. She was a lovely young woman. And I know Jonathan just to say hello to. They live quite near us, you see. He has a garden centre – he's making quite a go of it – on the fringe of the estate, near Newton Drive.'

'The private house belt!' Frances grinned.

'Yes, that's right. Quite a large house, actually. Dennis is certainly not a latchkey child,' said Marjorie. 'Their house backs on to the garden site, so Jonathan is always there when Dennis gets home at tea time. He's not neglected in that way. It's difficult to know what the problem is . . . but I'm sure he'll grow out of it. I should mention it to Gertie, though. She does like to be kept informed.'

The headmistress was very concerned when Frances told her of Dennis's misdemeanour, but she decided not to intervene this time. Frances, indeed, had promised Dennis that she would not do so. They would give him another chance, but Miss Reynolds did want to be kept in the picture as to how he progressed. She agreed that he was a complex child, one who required careful handling, and a teacher who would be patient and sympathetic.

'As I know you are, dear,' Miss Reynolds said, to Frances's delight. Frances was recognising more and more the headteacher's ability to know the worth – or otherwise – of each child and each member of staff. There was not much that escaped the eagle eye of Gertrude Reynolds; and those who dismissed her as a somewhat untidy, fumbling individual – her short-sightedness could, at times, be a hindrance – with a pronounced inland town accent, were doing her a disservice.

Chapter 6

Frances attended her first rehearsal with the Starlight Players the following Wednesday. It was good to get away from her problems for a little while, to put all thoughts of Dennis Russell and the vindictive Miss Walsh right out of her mind and, she admitted to herself somewhat guiltily, to escape from her mother. Not that Iris had been too difficult recently. The doctor had prescribed some new tablets for her and these, she had told Frances, seemed to be giving her more relief from the pain of her arthritis. As a consequence she was more cheerful, much less querulous and demanding. But Frances still felt that Iris treated her very much as a little girl who had no separate life of her own beyond the boundaries of her home and family. Frances found she was missing more than ever the independence she had enjoyed in Yorkshire. The offer of sharing a flat with Megan had been tempting in the extreme, but she knew, alas, that she must put the idea right out of her mind.

But tonight's rehearsal was a welcome respite. It was good to see her friend from the previous week, Julie Forrester, again. Julie was already on the bus when Frances got on at Layton Square and they greeted one another excitedly.

'It's nice to have somebody to travel with, isn't it?' said Julie. 'And to walk through town with. Mum isn't too keen on me being out on my own in the dark, but I keep telling her the war was over ages ago. I think she still imagines us stumbling around in the blackout. I can't remember much about that, can you, Frances?'

'Not a lot,' replied Frances. 'I was nine when the war

ended, so I might remember a bit more than you. It sounds as though you have the same sort of mother as mine, eh? One who doesn't realise you've grown up?'

'You can say that again,' said Julie with feeling. 'If you ask me there's not much to choose between any of them. Here we are; this is our stop – the Winter Gardens.'

There was no need for their mothers to have worried, because Blackpool town centre was as busy at night as it was during the day, and almost as light, with the brightness of the shop windows and the glow shed by the streetlamps. Theatregoers were arriving in droves at the entrance to the Winter Gardens building for the season shows at the Pavilion and the Opera House. The Blackpool summer season would last for another month or so, right until the end of October, as the Illuminations, switched on at the beginning of September, attracted great crowds, both day-trippers and those who stayed for a weekend or longer. The twinkling coloured lights on the promenade were visible at the very end of Church Street and way above all loomed the Tower, its iron girders decorated with dancing lights that flashed on and off, and the 'crow's nest' at the top highlighted with neon striplights.

Blackpool was an exciting place in which to be out and about. Frances felt a thrill of delight at being part of the scene and a joyful anticipation at the rehearsal that lay ahead. She and Julie cast longing glances at the display of stylish – and expensive – shoes in the window of Vernon Humpage's as they hurried along Church Street to the nearby church hall. Such luxuries were way out of Frances's reach; Julie's too, she guessed, but there was no harm in looking. The window displays appeared even more appealing at night, like Aladdin's caves shining out in the darkness.

The rehearsal was enjoyable although all they were doing at the moment was learning the music and lyrics of the various songs. These were already quite well known, having been continually played on the radio and on records since the show opened on Broadway several years ago, and since then, of course, it had been performed in London and the provinces. Now a film of *South Pacific* had been released earlier that year. There was some talk at the rehearsal of organising a trip to Manchester in a few weeks' time to see the film and, maybe, to do some early Christmas shopping.

Tonight they went through the score of 'Bali Ha'i', 'I'm in Love With a Wonderful Guy' and 'Honey Bun', three of the numbers that the girls of the company would be performing, doubling as both island maidens and American nurses. There were not enough members for both, so there would have to be some rapid costume changes.

And while the girls enjoyed a cup of tea, the men went through their first rendering of 'There is Nothin' Like a Dame', the rousing number that Frances was sure would be a show stopper. She was thrilled with it all, every bit of it, and was already looking forward to next week when they would begin to learn some dance steps.

One thing Frances noticed was that the men and the girls didn't seem to mix very much, each of them chatting in their own little groups, apart from the ones that already knew one another. Maybe they would become more friendly and relaxed as time went on. Frances hoped so. It wasn't that she was dying for the company of men. She was enjoying the friendliness of the girls she had met tonight, but it would be nice for a change, she thought, to have a bit of male companionship, especially as she worked solely with women, each and every day.

It had been a good evening, however, and she went home, as she had done from the audition the previous week, feeling contented and as though everything was well with her world.

Frances stared in panic at the empty space in her desk drawer where she had placed the change from the dinner money. Most children had brought the correct amount of money, five shillings, either in two half-crowns or an assortment of florins, shillings and sixpences. But three of them had required change. Frances had wrapped up the appropriate money, to be collected at the end of the day, in separate bits of paper and labelled them; Mark, Geoffrey and Susan. Now, at the beginning of afternoon school, all the packets had disappeared.

Frances felt sick with apprehension as she scrabbled through the jumble in her drawer – she was not the tidiest of people – searching amongst the pencils, Biros, rubbers and blotting paper, attendance slips and confiscated toy pistols, transfers (to be stuck on hands) and marbles. No, it was not quite as bad as she thought. Susan's packet, containing a shilling piece, was still there, tucked underneath a tin box holding drawing pins, but the other two, one that held two half-crowns and the other a shilling, were well and truly missing. There was no doubt about it. Frances cursed herself. Why had she been such a fool as to leave the money in her desk, knowing . . . what she did know? But she had done it before – she suspected all the teachers did the same – with no awful consequences.

It might not be Dennis this time, she told herself, hoping and praying it would not be the little boy for whom, in spite of his awkwardness, she was developing quite an affection. But it must be somebody, and it was a very serious offence to take something from a teacher's desk, letting alone the fact that the teacher shouldn't have been such an idiot as to leave temptation there in the first place. Many of the families, Frances knew, were in dire straits financially. Almost half the children who stayed for dinner were on free meals, their names on a separate list at the bottom of the dinner register, though never referred to by the teacher or remarked on by their peers.

The children were coming in from the cloakroom now, a noisy cheerful bunch, shoving at one another, laughing and talking at the tops of their voices. The noise was Frances's fault. She should have been there to escort them in from the playground, but she had been otherwise occupied. She knew she had better shut them up now or she would be in trouble. It was a wonder Miss Walsh hadn't already been in to complain that Frances was neglecting her duties and that her unruly class was creating a disturbance.

She clapped her hands, something you were told at

college you should never do, but how else, she wondered, were you supposed to achieve a bit of law and order? 'Listen, boys and girls, I've something very serious to say. I was hoping I was wrong, but I've searched and searched and I'm sorry to have to tell you that there is some money missing from my desk.'

There were horrified gasps from several children, notably the girls, but, Frances was relieved to see, there were no accusing glances levelled at Dennis this time nor remarks made.

'You know what we will have to do,' she went on, feeling more and more sick. 'Empty your desks . . . and your pockets.' The search, however, proved fruitless.

'Miss Goodwin . . .' It was the ubiquitous Linda with her hand held high. 'Please, Miss Goodwin, he might've— I mean, whoever it is might've put it in his coat pocket. Or she might have, I mean, if it's a girl . . .'

'Yes, thank you, Linda. I know what you mean, and I've already thought of that.' Frances sighed. This was dreadful, even worse than before. 'Line up at the door, everyone, and we'll go and look in your coat pockets.' She had to go, like a policeman, to watch their every movement, though she was hating every minute of it. 'And there has to be no talking, none at all. We must not disturb the other classes.'

Frances's worst fears were realised, although she had guessed all along what would be the outcome, when the two packets of dinner money were discovered in Dennis's coat pocket. He had no defence; he merely scowled at Frances before lowering his head and muttering, 'Don't care . . .'

Barry put a friendly arm around his shoulders as he whispered, 'Den! Wotcher want to go and do that for, yer daft beggar?'

Dennis shrugged him away angrily. 'Gerroff,' he mumbled. 'It's got nowt to do with you, so you can just shurrup!'

'Leave him, Barry,' said Frances gently, trying to make as little of an issue of it as was possible. She wasn't sure how much the other children had noticed. The main thing was to get them back into the classroom and occupied, in the hope that they would forget about it. Dennis had done wrong, but she didn't think it would do any good to make an example of him in front of them all.

'We've sorted this little problem out now,' she told them, 'so go back to the classroom and get out your reading books. If you can be quiet for ten minutes, then we'll have the games and jigsaws out this afternoon, maybe even the paint and clay . . . Shhh!' she admonished, as there were a few shouts of 'Hurrah!' Miss Walsh would be out, breathing fire, as sure as eggs were eggs, if she heard this racket going on.

'I'll deal with you later, Dennis,' she told him in a lowered voice. 'I'm very disappointed, after all you promised.' But he refused even to look at her.

The problem was how to deal with him. It was too much for her to cope with alone this time; besides, she had been told in no uncertain terms that Miss Reynolds had to be informed about misdemeanours as serious as this one. The trouble was that the headmistress was away from school with the flu – she had telephoned in sick that morning – and she was not expected back for at least a week. Frances knew she would have to report the incident to Miss Cameron, the deputy head, who, she feared, would not show the same understanding as Gertie might have done.

She went in to see her at playtime. Judith Cameron, Frances could see at a glance, was revelling in her position as acting head in Miss Reynolds's absence. She was sitting at the head's desk, her cup of tea in front of her, tapping ash from her cigarette into her own personal ashtray, the one she normally used in the staffroom. Frances knew that Gertie disapproved of smoking, but there was little she could do about it in the staffroom where the teachers could do more or less as they liked. She would most certainly deplore it going on in her own private domain, but Frances supposed it was a question of the cat being away, and that Miss Cameron would have the good sense to get rid of the telltale odour before Gertie returned. She, Miss Cameron, had already told the staff that she intended getting a supply teacher the following day for her class, so that she could concentrate on her duties as head.

'Now, Miss Goodwin, how can I help you?' she asked, quite kindly, as Frances entered the room. Frances had not had a great deal to do with this teacher. So far, their paths had not had occasion to cross, but she did not feel that Miss Cameron was hostile towards her, as Miss Walsh so often seemed to be.

'It's Dennis Russell, Miss Cameron, a little boy in my class.'

'Yes, I know Dennis, although I've never taught him. What's he been up to? He's not – Miss Walsh was telling me about the incident last week – he's not been stealing again, has he?'

'Yes . . . yes, I'm afraid he has.' Frances felt annoyed that Miss Walsh had not kept the knowledge of Dennis's offence to herself, although she might have guessed that she would not do so. It was more than likely that she had also told Miss Cameron what a useless, ineffectual teacher Frances was. 'He took some dinner money change out of my desk. I know I shouldn't have left it there; it's partly my fault.'

'Yes, it was unwise, wasn't it, considering what you already know about Dennis?' Miss Cameron's bright red lips curved slightly in a sardonic smile; the sort of smile that often made the children she reprimanded feel about six inches high. Frances was determined, however, that she would not be intimidated.

'But you should be able to trust children, shouldn't you?' she said. 'And they should know that you trust them. You should be able to leave things in your desk and expect them to be still there when you come back.'

'In a perfect world, Miss Goodwin, maybe. But I am afraid that the children we are dealing with in this school are far from perfect. You have only to look at the homes that most of them come from. Estate families, five or six children, father out of work, or sometimes a guest of Her Majesty.' She gave a supercilious smile. 'Is it any wonder the children are tarred with the same brush?' She looked

85

away from Frances for a moment, idly surveying her long red-painted fingernails.

Frances felt her hackles rise. Here was another teacher with the selfsame attitude as Miss Walsh, one who regarded the estate families as being beyond all hope. Admittedly there were some, Frances felt sure, where the children were brought up in appalling conditions, but she was also sure that the majority were decent, hard-working people who did the very best they could for their kids – just as much, if not more so, than the private house families did. Besides, Dennis was from what Miss Cameron would consider to be a superior sort of home, wasn't he?

That is what Frances told her now, as matter-of-factly as she could. 'Dennis Russell is not from the . . . the estate, Miss Cameron. I believe his father runs a garden centre and they live in quite a big house. But his mother died last year, so maybe—'

'Yes, yes, I'm well aware of the boy's background,' Miss Cameron interrupted. 'It's just that I have a bee in my bonnet about some of these people. A feckless lot . . . The last school I taught at was very different . . .' She stared into space momentarily. 'But that's another story. Yes, Miss Goodwin, Dennis Russell will have to be dealt with, whatever the circumstances. He can't be allowed to get away with stealing, especially money. Don't worry; I will deal with him . . . and severely too.' Her tone was ominous, and Frances felt fearful for the child.

'What . . . what will you do?' she asked.

'If it were up to me I would see that he got a damned good hiding. The headmaster at my last school didn't disapprove of caning, and neither do I. I would cane him in front of the whole school if I had my way. But, as it is, Miss Reynolds does not approve of such a form of correction.' She pressed her red lips together in a tight line. 'And we have to do as she says, unfortunately. But I will think of a suitable punishment, Miss Goodwin, you can be sure. Just leave it to me.'

'Don't . . . please don't be too hard on him,' said Frances. She was feeling sorry, now, that she had reported the matter at all. She should have kept it to herself, dealt with it in her own way. But how?

'I said leave it to me.' Miss Cameron picked up her cigarette in a dismissive gesture. 'Thank you, Miss Goodwin. That will be all.'

Frances slept fitfully that night, so concerned was she about the little boy. She hadn't mentioned the incident to him again that afternoon, neither had she discussed it with her mother when she got home. Iris never wanted to listen to her school problems and she would probably have dismissed this as a childish prank. Maybe not, though. Something stirred in Frances's memory, something from the dim and distant past.

As she lay in bed she remembered, vaguely, that Josie had been involved in such an incident as this, pinching sweets from a local shop, during the war, when they lived in Haliford. And there had been no end of a row about it, Iris going on as though the little girl had stolen the crown jewels. Not that Josie had been the only offender. Frances had been only a tiny girl, but she seemed to remember hearing that another girl had egged them all on; and she wasn't sure, but she thought Jimmy Clegg might have been involved as well. Strange to think of that now, with Jim being a policeman. He had been a real tearaway as a lad, from all accounts, so maybe Dennis would turn out all right, given time.

She thumped the pillow and lay down again, trying to compose her mind for sleep. 'Please God, look after Dennis and help him to be good,' she whispered silently into the darkness, before she finally fell asleep; a childish prayer, but maybe He would hear.

Frances felt sick with dread all through the morning assembly, through the singing of 'Glad That I Live Am I', and the prayers led by Miss Cameron, wondering what that teacher had in mind as a punishment for Dennis. She was sure the woman would not have forgotten. Dennis looked a little paler than normal this morning, although he never had much colour, and he was more than usually subdued.

'Sit down, children,' Miss Cameron ordered, when they had muttered the 'Amen' at the end of the Lord's Prayer. 'I have something very, very serious to tell you all. We have a thief in this school. Isn't that dreadful? Come here . . . Dennis Russell.'

There were audible gasps of shock as Dennis shambled out to the front of the hall, his head down, shuffling his feet. Frances felt as though she was going to be physically sick, there and then, and she clasped her hands tightly in her lap, trying to hang on to her breakfast, and her emotions.

'Yes, this is the boy.' Miss Cameron pulled him roughly by his arm so that he was facing the assembled school, all two hundred and more of them. 'This is the boy who went into his teacher's desk . . . yes, you may well gasp.' She nodded towards the rows of children. '. . . and stole some money. Change from dinner money. His teacher had left it there because she felt she should be able to trust him, as we should be able to trust all of you.' Frances felt that she might have preferred it if she, too, were publicly castigated for her foolish action; but Miss Cameron was making out the crime to be entirely Dennis's.

'You are a thief, Dennis Russell. There is no other word for it – a THIEF!' Miss Cameron was not shouting. There was no need for her to do so, as a deathly hush had spread all through the hall. 'And so that everyone will know that you are, you are going to wear this . . . all day.' She reached to the table behind her and picked up an oblong card, some six by nine inches in size, on which were printed the words, in black Indian ink, 'I am a thief.' 'You will wear it all day in the classroom, and when you go out to play you will stand against the wall, still wearing it. And at dinner time—'

'Miss Cameron . . .' Frances jumped to her feet, her anger at this dreadful punishment making her braver than she would ever have dared to be in normal circumstances. 'Miss Cameron, Dennis can't possibly stand by the wall all

88

through dinner time.' The playtime, after the children had had their dinner, was at least half an hour long. 'No child can be expected to stand still for so long.'

Miss Cameron raised her pencilled eyebrows, surveying Frances coolly. 'Yes, Miss Goodwin, I fully realise that. There is no need to remind me. You didn't let me finish. At dinner time, Dennis Russell, you may join in and play with the other children, that is if any of them will want to play with you, which I very much doubt. Go along now.' She pushed him to one side. 'Go back to your class. I don't want to see you again. I am disgusted with you.

'Now, the rest of the school, please stand up. Turn, and walk out quietly.' While Miss Walsh, with a smug smile on her face thumped out 'Marche Militaire' on the piano the children of Wyre Bank Infant School filed out class by class, this morning, for once, very subdued.

As well they might be, thought Frances. It was a horrendous punishment, one chosen to humiliate and make an example of the culprit, the sort of thing that was very much frowned upon by liberal educationalists. Frances was reminded of *Jane Eyre*. Wasn't there some such punishment in that book? The ill-fated Helen Burns being forced to wear a placard with the word 'slattern', and all because her drawer was untidy? That, of course, was a far worse penance because that poor girl had been a virtual saint, guilty of no crime at all. Whereas Dennis . . . yes, he had done wrong, Frances was forced to concede, and how she would have chosen to deal with the offence she was not sure. But this way was too, too harsh.

She made no comment on it whatsoever throughout the day, either to Dennis or to the rest of the class. She couldn't say, 'It serves you right', or 'You've got what you deserve' because she didn't believe that. Neither could she be seen to take sides with him or offer him much comfort. It was an unwritten rule that teachers were supposed to support one another in their actions, certainly in their dealings with the children.

She was pleased to see that the class, too, passed no remarks. Barry had put a consoling arm through his friend's as they went through the classroom door, and this time Dennis did not shrug him away. Frances could have wept as she saw the look he gave Barry. His brown eyes – Frances had not noticed before what a deep, warm shade of brown they were – looked puzzled and tormented and so afraid.

'Never mind, Dennis,' she whispered. 'It will soon be over. It's only for today.' It would have been heartless not to say anything at all and these words, she felt, were a compromise between condemnation and compassion.

Dennis was silent all day, which was only what she expected, although, surprisingly, he worked as well as he always did, even taking his turn without demur at reading from the 'class reader', a simplified version of *Treasure Island*. Frances was hoping against hope for a wet playtime, then the poor little lad would escape much of his disgrace (although Miss Cameron was quite capable of extending the punishment to the next day, should this happen). The sky had been grey and overcast for much of the day, but her prayers were not answered until the afternoon when, to her relief, it bucketed down. On such occasions the teachers hurried to the staffroom to collect their mugs of tea, then hurried back before their charges got out of control.

'You've got your wish,' Marjorie Aspinall murmured as they poured out their tea. 'Poor little lad. I could have cried when I saw him standing there this morning.'

Miss Walsh had ears as keen as a wolfhound's. 'Poor little lad, indeed!' she snorted. 'Don't go wasting your sympathy on him, Mrs Aspinall. It's no more than he deserves, the little thief. Although I can't understand it.' She turned her steely glance on Frances. 'If it had been that ruffian he knocks around with, that Barry Cartwright, I could have understood it better. But not Dennis Russell. It certainly wouldn't have happened in my class, I can tell you that.'

'Vindictive old cow!' whispered Marjorie, as the older teacher swept out of the room. 'Take no notice of her.'

'The cheek of it!' spluttered Frances. 'Anybody would think I was teaching the kids to steal, like Fagin. I won't half be glad when today's over, Marjorie. And I'll be glad when Miss Reynolds gets back, too.'

'Won't we all?' said Marjorie. 'Good old Gertie. She's not so bad after all, is she?'

At the end of the afternoon Frances, without a word, took the offensive placard from Dennis's neck, tore it into pieces, and threw it in the waste-paper basket. If she was exceeding her authority by so doing, she did not know, neither did she care. That was the end of the wretched thing as far as she was concerned. 'Off you go, Dennis,' she said, quite impartially. 'We will say no more about it.'

If, however, she had expected a grateful smile or a word of thanks, she was to be disappointed. Dennis scowled at her, as he had done so many times. 'I'm gonner tell me dad of you,' he mumbled as he hurried out of the classroom.

Not of me, Dennis, surely not of me? thought Frances, feeling somewhat hurt. She had been in no way responsible for his awful disgrace. But children were such unpredictable, exasperating creatures. You never knew when you had them or how far you could trust them. The more she taught them and got to know them, the more she realised this.

She was not very surprised, therefore, when, at the end of the following afternoon, when all the children had been dismissed, an irate figure burst into her classroom. She had been half expecting him, although Dennis, today, had made no further comment about 'telling me dad of you'. One glance at the ginger hair, though a rather darker shade than his son's, and the thin, freckled face, told Frances that this, indeed, was Dennis's father. It was obvious that he had the temper to match his red hair.

'I've come about my son,' he began, 'Dennis Russell. You are Miss Goodwin, I take it?' Frances nodded; she felt as though she had lost her voice. 'Well, Miss Goodwin, I want to know what the hell you think you are doing, humiliating my son like you did? Good God, what age do you think we're living in? The Victorian age? Making the poor kid stand there with a bloody label round his neck. And just because—'

'Just wait a minute, Mr Russell.' Frances found she was able to speak, just. 'It wasn't my idea, you know, that Dennis should wear that . . . that thing. As a matter of fact I—'

'You're his teacher, aren't you? Don't try to tell me you've no say in what goes on because I don't believe you. If you're his teacher then I hold you responsible. You're trying to shift the blame, aren't you? Yes, I've heard about Miss Cameron – and I intend to see her as well – but why the hell did you go blabbing to her in the first place? Couldn't you have dealt with him yourself if he'd done something wrong? Though I can't see—'

'Mr Russell . . .' As she looked at him Frances had a feeling she had seen this man somewhere before, quite recently. He was the image of Dennis, that was true, but somewhere else, in some other context. She couldn't dwell on it now, however. 'Mr Russell,' she went on. 'It is a rule in this school that all bad behaviour, of whatever sort, large or small, has to be reported to the headmistress. And as Miss Reynolds is away at the moment I was forced to tell Miss Cameron. As a matter of fact, I agree with you – though of course I couldn't admit it to Dennis – that the punishment was far too severe.'

'I should damn well think it was. Making a public example of him when all he had done was to pinch a few sweets and a rubber. Good grief, find me a child that wouldn't do that, given the chance.'

'Is that what he told you?' said Frances. 'Is that what Dennis said? That he stole some sweets and a rubber? If that had been all he stole, then I can assure you—'

'What? Do you mean to say that there's more to it?' He was speaking a shade more quietly now, and more reasonably.

'Sit down, Mr Russell,' said Frances. She pulled forward one of the only two adult-size chairs in the room. Dennis's father flopped down on to it, his long legs stretched out in front of him, while she sat on her own teacher's chair behind the desk. 'Yes, I'm afraid there is more to it than just a few sweets. Dennis did steal some sweets last week, and a rubber and a pencil sharpener. But this time I'm sorry to tell you that he went into my desk drawer and took some money. Two half-crowns and a shilling – dinner money change.'

'He did what?' Mr Russell's brown eyes, the same deep warm brown as his son's, were alight with anger, but Frances felt that now it was levelled not solely at her, but at Dennis as well. 'The little liar! Wait till I get hold of him! Making out to me that he was so hard done by, that it was just a few sweets.' He paused, then: 'Are you sure it was Dennis?' he asked abruptly.

'Quite sure, Mr Russell. The money was in his coat pocket. I didn't like making a search, but I knew I had to do it. I looked in all their pockets, not just his. I was hoping that I wouldn't find it, I can tell you.'

The man let out a tremendous sigh. 'Good God, this is dreadful. Much, much worse than I thought.' He looked down, shaking his head sadly before looking across at her. 'I apologise, Miss Goodwin, for losing my temper. I shouldn't have gone for you the way I did.'

'It's quite all right,' said Frances. 'I understand how you feel. As I've already told you, I thought the punishment was too severe, even for the theft of money.'

'It may well do the trick, though.' Mr Russell nodded. 'The chances are he won't do it again. Tell me, what would you have done?'

'To be honest, I have no idea,' said Frances. 'Talked to him, I suppose. Tried to make him see how wrong it was. But of course I'd already done that when he took the sweets and the other things. I think that's what Miss Reynolds would have done if she had been here. The children take notice of her. She seems to be able to make them see the error of their ways. Although there would have to have been some form of punishment: missing games lessons, or playtimes, something of that nature. Miss Reynolds doesn't believe in smacking them. And neither do I.'

'Then we're agreed on something,' said Mr Russell with a wry grin. 'Although I must admit that sometimes I'm at my wits' end to know how to cope with Dennis. I'm going to be honest with you, Miss Goodwin, now I've found out what he's really been up to. He's stolen from me as well. Not much; just the odd shilling or half-crown. I've been trying to convince myself it was just an isolated instance, that he'd not do it again. But what you're telling me is dreadful. Why is he doing it, do you think?'

Frances felt at a loss. She knew herself to be an inexperienced teacher, not used to dealing with such problems, whereas this man was several years her senior – in his early thirties, she guessed – quite experienced, surely, as a father, in coping with a difficult child. Nevertheless she tried to answer confidently.

'It could be a bid for attention, Mr Russell.' Psychologists' jargon, she realised, but it was likely to be the explanation. 'I understand you suffered a . . . bereavement. I was so sorry to hear about your wife . . . Dennis's mother. When we consider that, maybe it is not too hard to understand. That is why I thought Miss Cameron was too severe.'

'Yes, thank you,' he muttered. 'Dennis took it badly, and so did I, of course. But I know I've got to get on with my life. What choice do I have?' He shrugged his shoulders, spreading his hands wide in an expressive gesture. Frances was more convinced than ever that she had seen him before. Then suddenly she remembered where it was . . . 'But Dennis,' he continued, 'he still misses her. I hear him crying at night sometimes, poor little chap. I've tried to make it up to him, to be both mum and dad, to show more affection, but . . .' He broke off, staring at her. 'D'you know, I've seen you somewhere before. I felt I had, as soon as I came in, but I can't quite remember.'

Frances smiled at him. 'Yes, I've been trying to place you, too. And now I have done. *South Pacific*, the Starlight Players?'

'Well, I'll be damned! Yes, of course. You're one of the new girls, aren't you? I saw you last week, but you were at the other end of the room. And you looked different, somehow.' He put his head to one side, surveying her thoughtfully. 'That's why I didn't recognise you.'

Frances laughed. 'It's probably my different clothes and my hairstyle. I don't wear it tied back when I'm out of school.'

'Yes, that must be it, your hair.' He nodded in a thoughtful way, all the while looking at her attentively. 'Enjoying it, are you, *South Pacific*?'

'Yes, very much,' replied Frances. 'Although we've only just started, haven't we? It was my first rehearsal. What about you? Have you been in these shows before?'

'Yes, it's my third year. But I've still only made the chorus. Mind you, that's all I want, all I'm capable of to be honest. But I enjoy singing.'

'So do I,' said Frances eagerly. 'Did your wife . . . was she a member?'

'No, Jean wasn't a member. She used to come in and help with the costumes and all that, but she wasn't a singer.' He smiled. 'She always said she was tone deaf. She used to go to her flower classes on a Wednesday night, while I was at rehearsals. We thought it was good to have separate interests, especially as we worked together during the day. She was learning how to make wedding bouquets and wreaths and all that sort of thing, to help with the business; to add a sideline. I run a garden centre, you know?'

'Yes, I've heard about that, Mr Russell,' Frances replied. 'I believe you're doing very well.'

'Can't complain. That side of the business, though, the bouquets and floral arrangements, I'm afraid it's come to an end since Jean . . . died. It was just starting up and I've never got anybody to replace her. Never felt I wanted to, to be honest.' He smiled at her, rather sadly. 'I'm Jonathan, by the way. You can't go on calling me Mr Russell if we meet at rehearsals, can you?'

'No, I suppose not. And I'm Frances.'

He grinned. 'Pleased to meet you, Frances. Although we didn't get off to a very good start, did we? I was as mad as hell yesterday when Dennis came home with that awful tale, but I've calmed down now, especially now I realise—'

'Where is Dennis?' asked Frances. 'He's not gone home on his own, has he?'

'He's waiting outside in the porch. It won't do him any harm. I didn't want him to listen to what I was saying.'

'Then you'd better not leave him too long, had you?'

'No, maybe not. Although it'll give him time to cool his heels, the little devil. He'll know I'm going to find out what he really did. But I don't think there's any more we can say at the moment, is there?'

'No, not really. Don't be too hard on him, will you? I think he's gone through quite enough already. Do you want to see Miss Cameron? Not today, but perhaps some other time?' Frances didn't see why the woman should escape scot-free.

'I might. Yes, I think I should, if only to try and save some other poor little blighter from the same harsh treatment. And I'm sorry I blamed you, Miss Goodwin. I can see now I've met you that you have Dennis's best interests at heart.'

'I try,' said Frances simply. 'And all you can do, really, is to go on showing Dennis that you love him and that you put him first, as I'm sure you do.' She stopped, a shade embarrassed. Who was she to be telling this parent what he should or should not do? 'And I'll do all I can to help him. Don't hesitate to come in and see me – or Miss Reynolds – if you have any problems.'

'Yes, we'll keep in touch regarding Dennis, though let's hope that's the end of it.' He rose to his feet, and so did Frances. He was tall, almost six foot, casually and neatly dressed in a sports coat and grey flannel trousers with an open-necked shirt. He must have come straight from work, but he had made the effort to change out of his working clothes. A nice man, she thought, but she still felt somewhat wary of him. That preliminary burst of temper had unnerved her.

'Goodbye then, Miss Goodwin.' He held out his hand. 'And thank you.'

'Goodbye, Mr Russell.' She felt her hand enclosed in a firm grasp. 'I'm glad we've managed to sort things out.'

He nodded briefly, then turned and strode out of the classroom. Frances collapsed on to her chair, feeling completely drained.

Chapter 7

Jonathan Russell was finding, to his surprise, and to his slight annoyance, that Dennis's teacher was intruding more and more upon his thoughts. He had not known, of course, when he saw her that first time at the rehearsal, that she was Dennis's teacher. He had just been aware of a new girl in the company – more than one, actually, but she had been the one he had noticed particularly – an attractive girl with longish blonde hair, bright blue eyes and a happy smile. She had not been smiling at him, however, but chatting easily with her new-found friends. She looked as though she was the sort of girl who didn't find it difficult to make friends.

After that first sight of her he had thought no more about her. Then, when he had encountered her at Wyre Bank School – when he had dashed in and accosted her like the proverbial bull in the china shop, he now recalled to his shame – he had failed, at first, to recognise her. She had looked so different, almost schoolmarmish, with her lovely hair drawn back too severely from her face, and in her workaday clothes, a dark skirt and a nondescript navy-blue jumper. *South Pacific* had been the last thing on his mind at that moment, so distressed had he been at what he had seen as the school's unreasonable treatment of Dennis. But she had won him over – Miss Goodwin . . . Frances, which was how he now thought of her.

Her voice had trembled more than a little as she had explained what had really happened, how Dennis had been guilty of much more than the theft of a few sweets. And Jonathan fully believed, after hearing this young woman speak so honestly and sincerely, that what had happened to

Dennis – his dire punishment – had not been her doing at all, that she had, in fact, disapproved most strongly of the form of correction, and he knew he could trust her now to help Dennis in any way she could to prevent any repetition of his wrongdoing.

Jonathan had been pleased to discover that his son had such a nice, understanding sort of young woman for his teacher, and so he had quickly changed his tactics and apologised to her. That poor girl; he suspected he had alarmed her much more than he had intended doing. Dennis had given him no inkling of what his new teacher looked like. The lad didn't often talk about what went on at school, and Jonathan didn't pester him to do so. He remembered how, as a boy, he had disliked having to give a blow-by-blow account of his day at school, which was what his own mother and father had insisted on. What the hell? he had used to think. I've done some sums, and reading and writing and spelling. What do you expect me to do at school?

His father, in particular, had been anxious that Jonathan should work hard and get what he called a white-collar job, not end up in a job such as he himself had, that of a gardener employed by Blackpool Corporation. Jonathan never understood his father's attitude. It was an honest enough living, surely, not badly paid, and Mr Russell senior, possessed of green fingers, had always appeared to enjoy his employment. He had been disappointed, though, when Jonathan, in spite of his reasonable School Certificate results – five credits and three passes – had gone into the self-same work with Blackpool Parks Department (inter-rupted by a two-year spell in the RAF at the end of the war). The affinity with the soil and growing things had been passed on from father to son, but Mr Russell had not seen this as a matter for rejoicing. Now that Jonathan had his own business and was doing quite well his father's attitude had mellowed a little, but the young man still felt that he was something of a disappointment. His father would have loved to boast that his son was, for instance, a chartered accountant, or a surveyor. And if the lad had gone on to university that would, indeed, have been a feather in his cap.

But Jonathan had left school at sixteen and had been glad to do so. Teachers, from what he remembered, had not, in his day, been personable young women such as Miss Frances Goodwin; attractive girls with blonde curly hair and big blue eyes. He remembered them, by and large, as crabby, spinsterish figures with spectacles and hair in a bun, or balding men in tweed suits – the young men, towards the end of his schooldays, had been serving in the forces – striding the school corridors, often with a cane in their hands. Or maybe he was doing them a disservice. Jonathan was only thirty-two, but already his schooldays seemed very far distant. He didn't often think of them, because he had not particularly enjoyed them or developed any fondness for any of his teachers.

It was not as a teacher, however, that he found himself thinking of Frances Goodwin. He had realised, to his surprise, that he was looking for her at the next rehearsal, which was the day after his encounter with her at the school. They had not spoken, though, other than to smile and nod a greeting when they caught sight of one another across the room, and to say 'hello' when they met in the queue for cups of tea. She appeared very much on her guard as she looked at him, glancing quickly away to resume her conversation with the bonny dark-haired girl with whom she seemed to be friendly.

He had been unable to stop himself from watching her, at the other end of the room, talking and laughing so easily with the other girls. Why they segregated themselves in such a way at rehearsals of the Starlight Players – one group of men and another group of girls, as though they were members of some obscure religious sect – he could never understand. But it was what they always did at first, becoming more matey and relaxed together as time went on.

As he watched he saw Frances throw back her head and laugh, in response to some remark made by the other girl; and at that moment, as sometimes happened, there was a silence in the room as everyone, simultaneously, stopped speaking. The sound of her laughter – happy, melodious, altogether bewitching – rang out across the room, and Frances, aware of the sudden quiet, put her hand to her mouth in embarrassment.

Jonathan was reminded of the song that featured so poignantly in the show they were rehearsing – 'Some Enchanted Evening' – that tender, so sentimental song about seeing a stranger across a crowded room, and about how that certain stranger's laughter would ring, evermore, in your dreams. Frances was not a stranger now, as she had been last week when he had seen her for the first time. But he still did not know her well, and he knew that that was what he wanted to do. He wanted to get to know Frances Goodwin not just as Dennis's teacher, but to be able to talk and laugh with her as easily as she was conversing now with her girlfriends. To invite her out, maybe, to share a meal with him or to go to the theatre. But she appeared unaware of his existence, except, perhaps, as the parent of one of her pupils. And, maybe, he tried to tell himself, he was looking too far ahead, too soon. After all, it was still not a full year since Jean had died.

Hard work, Jonathan had realised, had been the best cure – the only cure that he had found until now – for the overwhelming sadness and the inevitable bitterness that he had felt at Jean's premature death. Manual work that made him sweat and feel exhausted, heaving bricks and slabs of stone, digging in the hard earth, getting his hands dirty; this was something, even as a child, that he had always loved. Most small boys were not averse to it, but Jonathan had revelled in it. He liked the feel of the soil between his fingers, the heavy clay soil that was prevalent in the Fylde coast area, and the more crumbly loam, rich in humus, which was essential as a top soil for all kinds of growing things.

It was a fallacy amongst Blackpool folk that the heavy clay of the area was ideal for rose growing. He had often heard amateur gardeners say so, and, indeed, there was hardly a garden in the town that did not contain at least a few of the bushes; standard, hybrid tea or floribundas. The truth was that roses required, above all, a well-drained soil, and Jonathan, when asked, was only too delighted to offer advice about suitable soils, composts or fertilisers.

When he had first conceived the idea of having his own business, instead of working as an employee of Blackpool Corporation, he had thought, initially, of setting up as a market gardener. But then he had changed his mind, remembering the abundance of these businesses in the Marton Moss area; long-established family firms, many of them, growing the famous Blackpool tomatoes in their myriad greenhouses as well as every other kind of vegetable and salad requisite. These men – and women, too – were experts at their trade. Marton Moss, he had often heard, was like a little world apart from the rest of Blackpool and the Fylde. Jonathan did not think it would be a good idea to try to get a foothold there. Even in a market garden to the north of Blackpool, the part with which he was more familiar, he might face too much competition from the well-established firms.

And so he had hit upon the idea of encouraging people to work their land for pleasure rather than for profit; growing flowers, shrubs and trees, the things that would beautify a garden. More and more people were now taking an interest in their gardens. Jonathan remembered how, during the war, many folk had had allotments, as well as gardens, 'Digging for Victory' by growing their own vegetables to ease the food shortage. Now, these same folk were thinking of their gardens more as places of beauty than of usefulness. Garden centres, where they could come to buy seeds, bulbs, plants, shrubs, even half-grown trees, were springing up all over the country.

When Jonathan had found the house with the large plot of land to the north of Blackpool, on the fringe of the new Wyre Bank estate, he had known it was ideal for his purposes. The mortgage had, at the time, seemed astronomical, but between them he and Jean had managed to raise the necessary deposit and, with careful budgeting, to meet the repayments. Jean, by this time, had given up her well-paid office job to stay at home and look after little Dennis. But they had saved most of the money she had earned during the early years of their marriage, and a legacy from Jean's grandfather had come at just the right time.

Jean had worked just as hard as Jonathan in the setting up of the business; harder, in fact, he often thought, as she had the home and a small child to care for as well. She had never done much gardening in the past, but she had been a willing and enthusiastic pupil, working alongside him and continually encouraging him, to help get the business on its feet.

A gradually developing sideline had been the wedding bouquets, wreaths, floral arrangements and sprays that Jean was becoming so skilled at making, her own brain-child which, sadly, had been abandoned since her death. There was still the small shop where they sold house plants and cut flowers – chrysanthemums and dahlias at this time of the year, and the hot-house carnations that Jonathan grew year-round – and Heather, the young girl who had been Jean's assistant, now served there. But he hadn't had the heart to find anyone to take over the creative floral work that Jean had begun. Heather, though a good worker, was capable of making up only the simplest spray or arrangement.

Now, however, Jonathan was wondering if he might possibly try to find someone – a middle-aged woman, maybe, who liked working with flowers – to resume this part of the business. He had hated the idea of replacing Jean, which was why he had not done so much earlier. Nobody could ever replace her, not in any way, not in the business . . . nor in his heart.

That was what he had steadfastly believed in the early months of his bereavement; and it was what he still believed. But then why did the picture of Frances Goodwin, her blue eyes dancing with laughter, keep intruding on his thoughts? It was the first time since Jean's death that he had felt any desire for a member of the opposite sex. No – desire was too strong a word, surely, for what he felt for Frances. It was more of an affinity, a feeling that they would get on well together should the opportunity arise. But it was too soon, far too soon . . .

So Jonathan told himself as he stacked the blocks of crazy paving stone on to the lorry, ready for his next job. During the autumn and winter months, when there was not so much going on in the garden centre, he worked as a landscape gardener, building patios, rockeries, pools, walls or paths, sometimes redesigning whole garden areas. He had taken a part-time building course, fitting it in between his working hours in the garden, to learn the necessary skills. He experienced a very real sense of achievement when he viewed his finished creation, be it only a crazy-paved path or a low stone wall. And the physical exertion helped to clear his mind, for a time, of the problems that beset him.

Thoughts of Frances led him, inevitably, to Dennis. He was more worried than he could say – far more worried than he had admitted to Frances – about the boy's misdemeanour. How dreadful it would be if his son were to turn out to be a real bad lot, a hardened criminal, thieving or house-breaking. Jonathan knew, in his saner moments, that there was not much likelihood of this, that he was allowing his thoughts to run out of control, but Dennis definitely needed sorting out now, before this thing got any worse.

He loved his son so much. Dennis was a part of Jean, the only part that he had to hold on to now, except for his memories. The boy's moodiness, fits of temper, and now this lapse into real misconduct, had only started since Jean's death. Jonathan had tried, and was still trying, to make amends to the lad for his loss. He played games with him of an evening, took him to watch a football match occasionally on a Saturday afternoon, especially when Blackpool were playing at home at Bloomfield Road; and though he had never been much of a hand in the kitchen, he now tried to provide tasty and nourishing meals, such as Jean had cooked. The only time Jonathan went out was on Wednesday evenings, to rehearsals of the Starlight Players, and Dennis didn't seem to mind being looked after by their next-door neighbour on these occasions; Mrs Barker always said he was no trouble at all.

But it seemed as though all his love and care was not enough to compensate Dennis for the loss of his mother. It would take time, Jonathan supposed, for both of them to come to terms with it and to adjust.

Jonathan had known that Dennis had to be punished for his offence, though he had been loath to do it. He had spoken to him severely, deprived him of sweets and chocolate for a week and sent him to bed early every night. What else could he do? He didn't believe in smacking children. Dennis had seemed penitent enough, although he could not explain why he had stolen the money.

'I just did,' he said, though not as sullenly as he sometimes spoke. 'I don't know why, Dad. I'm sorry . . . I won't do it again.'

And Jonathan had made him promise that he would also tell Miss Goodwin that he was sorry. He had not enquired as to whether he had done so.

Dennis had hung back, looking rather embarrassed, when the rest of the class went out for morning playtime.

'Now, Dennis, what is it?' asked Frances, smiling kindly at the boy. 'Did you want to speak to me?'

'Yes, miss . . . Miss Goodwin.' He hung his head for a moment, staring at his feet; then looking her straight in the eye he blurted out, 'I'm sorry, Miss Goodwin. You know – for pinching all them things. My dad says I have to tell you I'm sorry.'

'Your dad says?' Frances raised her eyebrows enquiringly, but she was still smiling at him. 'And what do you say, Dennis? That is what is more important. Do you say you are sorry, really sorry?'

'Yes, Miss Goodwin. I am . . . honest. I didn't really mean to do it, see. It was just something that made me . . .' He shook his head confusedly. 'Something inside me.'

Frances took a deep breath. This could be a real breakthrough if she could get Dennis to talk about his feelings. He was usually so uncommunicative. 'What do you mean, Dennis?' she asked gently. 'Something inside you? Something that makes you want to behave badly, do you mean?'

'Yeah . . . something like that. I was thinking about me mum, y'see. An' I got all mad inside me. D'you know what I mean?'

'I think so,' said Frances gently.

'And . . . and I want to cry sometimes, miss . . . Miss Goodwin. But I can't cry; only babies cry.' Frances remembered, nevertheless, how Dennis's father had heard the boy crying at night. 'And I felt that I wanted to do something bad – real bad – so that's why I took them things, and the money.'

'I see. And did it make you feel better?'

'No, not really.' Dennis gave a weak smile. 'And it just got me into a load of trouble, didn't it?'

'I'm afraid so,' Frances grinned. 'It usually does when we do something wrong, and it's worse when it's something we know is naughty. We've all got that little voice inside us, you know, trying to make us do things that are wrong, and we have to refuse to listen to it. But there's another little voice inside us,' she went on, 'and it's this voice we must try to listen to, instead of the bad one. It's called a conscience.' The 'still small voice' was how Frances thought of it, but Dennis would not understand that. 'Have you ever heard that word, Dennis?'

'I think so.' The boy's forehead wrinkled in a frown. 'Once, when I was only a little kid – I was about five, I think – me mum took me to see a picture about a boy that was made out of wood.'

'Oh, you mean Pinocchio,' said Frances. 'Do you know, Dennis, my mother took me to see that picture, too, when I was a little girl.'

'Did she, miss?' Dennis looked more animated than Frances had ever seen him. 'Well, d'you remember, Miss Goodwin, there was that little thing – that Jiminy Whotsit fellow – and he was supposed to stop the wooden boy from getting into trouble. My mum told me he was his conscience, see. But he didn't always stop him, did he?'

107

'No, that's because Pinocchio didn't always listen to him. Jiminy Cricket, he was called, and he acted as his conscience because Pinocchio wasn't a real boy; he was only made out of wood. But you're not, are you? You're a real live boy, a sensible one, too, sometimes, who can think for himself. So just stop to think, will you, if you're tempted to do something naughty again? Just listen to that little voice, the good one – your own Jiminy Cricket, if you like – and then you'll be all right. OK, Dennis?'

'OK, Miss Goodwin.' Dennis beamed at her.

'Off you go then, or you're going to miss all your playtime.'

'So are you, miss. You haven't had your cup of tea.'

Frances laughed. 'No, I haven't, have I? And it's not worth going for it now. Off you pop; don't worry about me. Just remember what we've talked about, that's all.'

Playtimes missed in the sorting out of problems were par for the course, thought Frances, and this was just one more. It was all in a day's work.

An occasional visitor to Wyre Bank Infant School was the Reverend Adrian Glover, the minister of the local Methodist church. He came in to take an assembly every few weeks, and he had been invited to speak at the simple celebration that Miss Reynolds, now recovered from the flu, was arranging for the Harvest Festival. There was a newly built Church of England on the estate, and several of the staff were of the opinion that Miss Reynolds should invite the vicar of this church, rather than a Nonconformist, to take part in the school's acts of worship. But Gertie Reynolds stuck to her guns. She was a dyed-in-the-wool Methodist – her grandfather had been a Wesleyan minister – and as the school was a council one, not under the jurisdiction of the Church, as some were, then she would do as she liked. The fact that her deputy, Miss Cameron, and Miss Walsh, too, were members – though rather spasmodic ones – of the Church of England, made her more determined.

Frances had seen the minister a couple of times, but it was not until the afternoon of the Harvest Festival

108

celebration that she had a conversation with him. He had been invited into the staffroom to partake of a cup of tea and a chocolate biscuit – a rare treat, provided by the head herself, for a special occasion – with all the teachers (except the unlucky one who was on playground duty).

The Reverend Adrian Glover came to sit next to Frances. 'You're new here, aren't you?' he asked. 'I've seen you a few times, but I know you only started here this term. Your first teaching post, is it?'

'No, not at all,' replied Frances, feeling somewhat affronted that he should think she looked only twenty years of age and not almost twenty-three. She had not yet reached the age when she would deem it a compliment to be taken for younger than her years. 'I've been teaching in Yorkshire for two years, but this is my first post in Blackpool.'

'Yorkshire – that's my neck of the woods,' he replied. 'I'm a Yorkshireman and proud of it. I come from Leeds; Headingley, to be precise, not far from the cricket ground.'

'Yes, I guessed as much,' Frances smiled. 'Well, not the exact location, but I thought you were from Yorkshire. I recognise the accent. I was born there myself, you see, in Haliford.' The broad vowel sounds and the rather gravelly tone, as though he were speaking way back in his throat, were not hard to identify by someone who hailed from roughly the same area, although Adrian Glover's accent was by no means pronounced. 'That's why I went back there to do my training,' Frances continued, 'and why I took my first job there.'

'Yes, once a Yorkshireman, always a Yorkshireman – or in your case, a woman.' Adrian Glover smiled back at her. 'It's hard to break away, isn't it? I know I miss it a lot at times, especially the hills and dales; it's so flat round here. They call it God's own county, Yorkshire, don't they? And not without good reason. So – what are you doing here in Blackpool then? . . . Sorry, I'm afraid I don't know your name.'

'It's Frances, Frances Goodwin.'

'Pleased to meet you, Frances. You don't mind me calling you that, do you?'

Frances shook her head. 'No, not at all.' She found it a refreshing change after the stiff and starchy form of address that was common in the staffroom. She was still 'Miss Goodwin' to everyone except Marjorie and the other young woman, Greta Jenkins, who had started the same time as she had.

'And I'm Adrian,' he went on. 'I hope you'll call me that. It's what I am to most of my parishioners. I don't like to stand on ceremony, especially with me being so much younger than many of them. Funnily enough, though, it's the older ones who insist on calling me Mr Glover. They think it's undignified, I suppose, to use Christian names.'

Frances laughed. 'That's just what they're like here,' she said in a lowered voice. 'All terribly formal. You asked me what I was doing in Blackpool.' She spoke in normal tones again. 'I've come back because it's where my mother lives.'

She went on to explain about her mother's illness and how she was now needed at home. In return she learned that Wyre Bank Methodist Church was Adrian's second living. He had spent three years at a church in Bradford and had been in Blackpool for just over a year. So, in a quick calculation, assuming he had done two years' National Service, she guessed him to be twenty-eight or so, which was about the age he looked. He was not very tall, only an inch or two more than her own five foot four. His straight hair was a nondescript brown, neither dark nor light. In fact you might consider him to be a nondescript sort of person until he smiled. His smile was radiant and he had the most perfect set of teeth, white and evenly sized, that Frances had ever seen. Rather like an advert for Colgate, she couldn't help thinking.

By the time the bell rang signalling the end of playtime she felt as though she had known Adrian Glover for ages. He rose to his feet when she did and walked towards the door with her.

'Frances, just a minute before you go.' He put his hand lightly on her arm to detain her. 'I couldn't help noticing what a lovely singing voice you have. I could hear you right above all the others.'

'Oh dear!' Frances gave a little frown. 'I didn't realise I was so conspicuous.'

'Not at all; it was when you came forward with your class that I heard you. I was wondering if you might consider joining our church choir? It's mostly middle-aged people and we could do with some young blood . . . Not all middle-aged,' he added quickly, at Frances's look of misgiving. 'There are a few younger ones. Do you think you might consider it? Or perhaps you already belong to a church?'

'No, I don't; not at the moment. I'm C of E really, but I don't suppose that matters. Yes . . . yes, I think I might like to do that. Look – Adrian – I'll have to go now.' Miss Walsh, passing the two of them in the doorway, had given Frances a very disapproving glance. 'It's time I was getting back to my class.'

'Of course. I'm sorry I've held you up. Listen – I'll call and see you and give you more details. After school – then you can't be accused of neglecting your duties,' he added, with his dazzling white smile. 'Bye for now, Frances. It's been nice talking to you.'

'Yes . . . yes it has. Bye, Adrian.'

Frances felt a glow of pleasure and a feeling, too, of conviction that this was the right thing to do. Iris, once a regular worshipper, was no longer able to go to church; and of course Megan, the only friend with whom Frances might have gone along to a church service had, amazingly, become a Catholic. Frances had been brought up to attend Sunday school and church – and she felt glad that she was being pointed once more in the right direction. Besides, Adrian Glover was a very personable young man . . .

Chapter 8

'Our Frances's young man is coming for his Christmas dinner.' Frances, entering the living room on her return home from school, was just in time to hear the remark that Iris was making to her friend Eliza. 'You know, that young minister from the Methodist church. They've got ever so pally, the pair of them . . . Oh, hello, love. I hadn't heard you come in.'

'No, I didn't think you had.' Frances gave her mother a warning glance before sitting down opposite their visitor. 'Hello, Eliza. Good to see you again. He's not my young man, you know. Don't take any notice of Mum. I keep telling her not to call him that. We're just friends, that's all.' She turned to her mother. 'Don't you dare say anything like that in front of Adrian. I wouldn't know where to put myself, and neither would he. Now, think on!'

Frances raised her finger in mock reproof, but Iris, knowing she was only jesting, grinned back at her. 'As if I would! I'd be the last one to want to embarrass the lad. All the same—'

'Aye, it must be quite serious, all the same – eh, Frances – if the young fellow's coming for his Christmas dinner? Getting his feet under t'table.' There was a roguish gleam in Eliza's eyes that Frances couldn't help but respond to.

Eliza Pendleton must have been about the same age as Iris, but whereas Iris had aged quite noticeably, Eliza was pretty much the same as Frances remembered her from the time they had stayed in her Blackpool boarding house all those years ago. She was still blonde – though artificially so now, Frances guessed – buxom and constantly cheerful, a real tonic to have around, as she had been to countless holiday-makers; and Frances knew that it did her mother good to have her old friend visit her.

'Don't you start!' Frances said now, laughingly shaking her head at Eliza. 'Adrian's coming for his Christmas dinner because he can't get home to Yorkshire till the next day – with the morning service, you see. And he'd rather come here than go to some of the older ladies who have invited him. He's had quite a few invitations—'

'But he's accepted yours. Well, he won't be sorry.' Eliza nodded sagely. 'Your mam always puts on a good spread at Christmas, although she won't be able to run about like a scalded hen like she used to, will you, Iris?'

'No, more's the pity,' replied Iris, but not in the plaintive tone she sometimes used. 'But I shall be t'supervisor, you can be sure of that. Our Josie and Jim and young Valerie'll be coming, as usual, and Frances and her fellow – sorry, her friend. I dare say Josie'll do most o' t'cooking, but it's easier for them to come here than for us to go to their place. I have such a job getting in and out o' t'car these days. What about you, Eliza? Would you like to come and join us? You'd be very welcome.'

'No, thanks all the same. I'm going to our Arthur's. Me brother's, you know, in Blackburn. I usually go there for Christmas. Aye, it's a hectic time and it seems to get worse every year. I reckon you'll be glad when you break up, eh, Frances? I'm sure I don't know how you handle all them kids. Teachers deserve their money if anybody does, that's what I always say.'

'Thank you, Eliza.' Frances smiled. 'Not everybody would agree with you. We're usually told it's money for old rope – all those long holidays. We finish in a couple of weeks, but there's a lot to do before then. The Christmas play, and then the parties. It's hard work, but I'm enjoying it . . .'

Frances was relieved to get away from the subject of her 'young man', although it was true that she and Adrian Glover were becoming very friendly. Her mother, at first, had looked askance at the idea of Frances attending the Methodist church.

'Methodists?' she had said, with a loud and derogatory sniff. 'Them tub-thumpers? I don't know as how I hold wi' all that ranting and Bible-bashing. There's never been any Methodists in our family, nor in your father's neither. Church of England we were, born and bred. That's where yer dad and me first met, at St Luke's Church in Haliford. Anyroad, I dare say you'll please herself; you always do. Don't go taking too much on, though. You've already got your practices for this 'ere *South Pacific* carry-on, and now you tell me you'll be out at choir practice every Friday. And you'll have to go to Sunday services, morning and evening, if you're in t'choir. Seems to me you'll never be at home.'

Which was why Frances had turned down Adrian's idea that she should give him a hand with the newly formed youth club. Enough was enough, she decided. She was already feeling that her life was becoming very full, with the church and the Starlight Players in addition to her school work. And Iris, after all, did have first claim on her loyalties at the moment. Her mother would take only the very minimum of payment from her for her keep, considering, no doubt, that the way Frances looked after her – and she did try her best – was, in itself, ample payment. One of Iris's good points always had been, and still was, her generosity.

When she met the Reverend Adrian Glover all Iris's misgivings about the Methodist church and its 'Bible-bashing' preachers were laid aside. She took to the young man immediately. Frances had been impressed by his sermons – well planned, concise and easy to follow – and the common-sense teaching about life and its problems that they contained. Here was no high-falutin theologian with his head in the clouds, nor a ranting tub-thumper who made you squirm in your seat, but a young man who obviously had his finger on the pulse of life here in this vast housing estate and was anxious to share in all its problems, large and small. In very much the same way as

Gertie Reynolds did, thought Frances. Although the two of them were dissimilar in age and temperament they both showed such concern for the people in their care. Frances was no longer surprised that Miss Reynolds had chosen Adrian, rather than the local vicar, to share in the school's activities.

For her own part, Frances's admiration for him grew every time she saw him. She had invited him to tea about a month after they'd first met and was pleased that her mother had taken to him so readily. So long as Iris didn't frighten him away by making too many assumptions ahead of time. Frances was hoping that their friendship might develop into something more, but she was aware, also, that Adrian had to be very circumspect in his dealings, not only with her, but with other young women in the congregation. There were quite a few, she had noticed, who cast wistful eyes in his direction. He had invited her to his flat a few times after evening service but, as far as she knew, no one else was aware of their meetings and Adrian took good care not to pay her too much attention when they were in the company of other people.

In private he had made no move towards her, except in friendship. He had neither held her hand nor taken her arm, but she was aware of the warmth of his glance and the light of admiration in his clear grey eyes when he looked at her. They conversed so easily together, finding more and more interests in common: music, literature, love of the countryside and a fondness for the hills and dales of Yorkshire.

'It's the dog collar that attracts you, isn't it, Mum?' Frances said jokingly. 'It's a feather in your cap, isn't it, for your daughter to be friendly with a minister – even if he is "only a Methodist"?'

'Nowt o' t'sort,' replied Iris hotly. 'He's a lovely young man, with or without his dog collar. So polite and friendly – and so caring, Frances. I wouldn't mind if he were a dustman if he were t'right one for you – and I happen to think he is. Anyroad, time'll tell, I dare say.'

'Yes, I expect it will,' said Frances. 'But don't go reading too much into it, Mum, that's all. Adrian gets a bit lonely sometimes, and it's nice for him to have someone near to his own age to talk to. That's all it is.' But she couldn't help wishing there might be more.

Then as Christmas approached, just after she had quite categorically told her mother and Eliza that he was 'not my young man', Adrian was beginning to show signs that very soon he might well be. One Sunday evening, after he had driven her home in his shabby baby Austin – all a clergyman could afford, he assured her – he had stopped the car engine when they drew up outside the bungalow. There was an emotive silence, then, leaning across, he kissed her gently on the cheek, for the first time ever.

'Good night, Frances,' he said softly. 'I've enjoyed our time together.' He continued to look at her as though he was unwilling to let her go.

'Good night, Adrian,' she replied. 'So have I; I always do.' Then, as his eyes still held hers, 'Would you like to come in and say hello to Mum?' she asked.

'No . . . I don't think so. Your mother may well have gone to bed, and I don't want to keep you up with work tomorrow . . .' His voice petered away as he leaned towards her again. This time his arms encircled her and their lips met in a kiss that held more tenderness than passion. But Frances could see in the warmth of his grey eyes, shining in the light from a street-lamp, the promise that was there.

'Yes, but I'll see you again soon, Adrian,' she whispered as they drew apart.

There was no need for them to whisper. There was no one to hear, but the softly spoken words and the tender glances they exchanged were an intimation of the affection that was steadily growing between them.

A few weeks previous to this, at the end of October, preparations for the Christmas fair at the Methodist Church had been going on apace. Frances, week by week becoming more involved, had been called upon to help with the stall that the choir was arranging. It was to be the home produce stall, consisting of jams, marmalades, chutneys and pickles, all bottled by industrious housewives; home-made cakes and pies; and produce from gardens, such as cuttings from plants and early-flowering bulbs which would – with luck – bloom in time for Christmas, and dried floral arrangements with a Christmassy theme.

Frances felt very much aware of her shortcomings as the choir ladies, mostly many years older than herself, discussed what they would contribute, each one, she couldn't help thinking, trying to outdo the others.

'I'll make some buns. Er . . . fairy cakes, with jam and cream in them,' she offered. 'Will that be OK?'

They assured her that it would be most acceptable. Just how the buns would turn out Frances herself was not very sure. She was no great shakes at cake making, but her mother would be at hand to give advice even if she didn't actually do the baking.

'And what about the garden part of the stall?' asked one of the ladies, a Mrs Hatton, who, to Frances's amusement, was never seen without a hat, shaped like a plant pot, on her head. This helped Frances to remember her name, although many of these Methodist ladies, she had noticed, were reluctant to be parted from their headgear. 'Could you perhaps make us a floral arrangement, dear? Something with a few twigs and fir cones and a bit of glitter, perhaps. The simpler the better, I always think. Being a teacher you're sure to be bursting with good ideas, aren't you?'

They hadn't seen her efforts at making lanterns for the shepherds to carry in the nativity play, thought Frances. Washing-up liquid bottles covered with yellow crepe paper, crisscrossed with black tape, made very realistic lanterns. So it said in the October edition of *Child Education*, but Frances's creations looked for all the world like . . . washing-up liquid bottles covered with yellow paper. In the end Marjorie had come to her rescue and made some superb ones. Each to his own, Frances decided. One couldn't excel at everything.

'No, I don't think so,' she answered bravely now. 'I'm not very good at that sort of thing.' She was aware of self-satisfied smiles from the felt-hatted brigade. 'But I might be able to help you with some plants,' she added, with a burst of enthusiasm.

She had only just thought about it. She had visited Jonathan Russell's garden centre a few weeks ago to buy a chrysanthemum in a pot for Eliza's birthday and she had noticed that he had all kinds of house plants for sale. Perhaps he might be willing to let her have a few at cost price. It wasn't the same as rearing them herself, which was what the other women had done, but they should be able to make a little profit and it would add a touch of professionalism to the stall.

'I've got a friend,' she said. 'Well, he's not exactly a friend – he's the father of one of the little boys in my class – he has a garden centre and I wondered . . .'

A few of the women were dubious. The plants would not be 'home produced', which was what the stall was supposed to be; but after a lot of what Frances considered to be argy-bargy she was given the go-ahead. As the garden centre was on the edge of the housing estate, some of the choir members had had dealings with Jonathan Russell and felt he would give them a good deal.

'Frances, how nice to see you.' Jonathan greeted her in a friendly manner when she called at Russell's Garden Centre the following week. They used one another's Christian names with ease now, meeting, as they did, each week at rehearsals. But they still had not progressed much beyond the odd remark or two about how the show was going, or about Dennis's current behaviour. He was, Frances was happy to report, much improved. There had been no further incidents of things disappearing and he seemed much less moody and withdrawn.

Jonathan was very pleased to comply with Frances's request for plants. He led her to one of the greenhouses and helped her to choose a selection of pot plants that would be suitable for selling at the Christmas fair:

poinsettias, Christmas-flowering cacti, and the miniature orange trees that always looked so cheerful at this drab time of the year.

'I don't go there myself,' he said, as he picked up first one plant, then another, trying to select the most compact-looking specimens. 'To the Methodist church, I mean. To tell the truth I don't go anywhere. Never have time, nor inclination neither after what's happened,' he added in a quieter voice. 'But I'm glad to help. Only too glad, especially after what you've done for Dennis. He's a different boy; I would never have believed it. You've got a real way with those kids, Frances. Dennis thinks the world of you. It's Miss Goodwin this, and Miss Goodwin that.' He stopped abruptly, as though he feared he might say too much. 'Anyway, these plants: you can have them at cost and I'll give you one of each as my contribution. As I say, I don't go to church, but I don't argue with those who do. I'll see they're delivered on the Saturday morning. In fact I'll bring 'em myself. Come into the shop and Glenys can make you out a bill. You haven't met Glenys, have you? Glenys Mortimer. She only started here a couple of weeks ago. I told you, didn't I, that Jean – my wife – used to make wedding bouquets and all that sort of thing and I'd never found anybody to replace her? Well, I really think Glenys fits the bill. She's very competent.'

Frances followed him into the shop, which, she could tell at a glance, was already flourishing better than it had when she'd visited it a few weeks before. There was a display of Christmas floral decorations, skilfully created from dried flowers, twigs, fir cones and holly, with just the minimum of glitter or a red satin bow to add that seasonal touch, such as would make the Methodist ladies green with envy. Pot plants, like the ones Frances had already chosen, bloomed in profusion on the shelves, together with chrysanthemum plants in glowing shades of gold, russet and purple. On the floor was a selection of garden ornaments: gaudily painted gnomes with red hats and flowing beards – not to Frances's liking, nor, she made a guess, to Jonathan's either, but he would have to cater for

120

all tastes – as well as the less garish stone figures of tortoises, squirrels and hedgehogs. There was a good choice of weed killers, fertilisers, garden tools, watering cans and hoses, as well as a shelf full of colourful ceramic plant pots. The whole place was tidier and cleaner, showing all the signs of a thriving business. Frances guessed that this, in no small measure, might be due to the young woman who was, even now, busily engaged in making floral decorations.

'Glenys, I'd like you to meet Frances, or perhaps I ought to say Miss Goodwin – she's Dennis's teacher.' The young woman quickly put down her scissors and the roll of red satin ribbon and held out her hand in greeting as Jonathan introduced them. 'Frances, this is Glenys – Miss Mortimer, to be more formal – my new assistant.'

Glenys Mortimer was what might be called petite, an inch or two shorter than Frances, with dark hair cut in an urchin style, green eyes which added to her elfin appearance, and a very pleasant smile. Frances couldn't help but notice that she smiled just as charmingly at Jonathan as she did at Frances, and that the smile was readily returned.

'You can see the difference she's made to this place, can't you, Frances?' Jonathan continued. 'This is all Glenys's work.' He waved his hand expressively towards the shelf of floral displays. 'All ready for Christmas, as you see . . . Frances has chosen some plants for the church fair,' he said to Glenys. 'A dozen altogether, but just charge her for nine of them at cost. Could you work it out, please, and give her a receipt? Now, if you'll both excuse me, I've some loading to finish off outside. I'm starting a big job at Bispham tomorrow. Cheerio, Frances. Be seeing you.'

Glenys's eyes followed him as he went out through the door. 'He's such a nice man, isn't he?' she said. 'And so good to work for. I'm ever so glad I decided to come here, though I wasn't sure at first that I was doing the right thing. I worked at a florist's in Blackpool, you see, in the town centre. It was a nice steady job, but there wasn't much chance of promotion. My boss did all the floral arrangements – well, nearly all – and she seemed to think nobody else was capable. So when I saw Jonathan's advert

I decided to make a break. And I've not regretted it.'

'There's certainly a lot of scope for you here. You've made some lovely arrangements,' said Frances admiringly. 'Where's Heather, by the way?' She had just realised that the usual assistant was nowhere to be seen.

'Heather? Oh, it's her half-day. She's still here, but Jonathan wants her to do more work in the greenhouses now I'm in the shop. It's what she's best at: propagation, nurturing the young plants and all that. Apparently she has green fingers, but she's not all that good on the artistic side. Anyway, I'd better get on with this bill instead of nattering on. I like talking to customers, though. I think they prefer it when you're friendly towards them. Now, nine plants, Jonathan said, didn't he . . .?'

She uses his name a lot, thought Frances, as the young woman – rather younger than herself, she guessed – worked out the bill. It seemed as though she might be quite smitten with her new employer, and, unless Frances was very much mistaken, Jonathan, too, was not unaware of his new assistant's charms. Or did he just admire her competence? For reasons that she couldn't begin to explain Frances was experiencing a sense of unease. How would Dennis take it, she wondered, if his father were to have a new interest – a romantic interest – in his life? She didn't like to think of anything happening to upset Dennis. He seemed to be very much on an even keel at the moment.

'Have you known Jonathan long?' Glenys asked, when they had sorted out the payment. The question was casual, but there was an inquisitive, almost calculating, look in her green eyes. 'He said you were Dennis's teacher, didn't he?'

'Yes, so I am,' replied Frances. 'That's how I first met Mr Russell. No, I haven't known him very long. We're in the same operatic group – the Starlight Players – so there's that connection as well as the school one. But I don't know him very well at all.'

Frances might have only imagined that Glenys looked relieved. 'Oh, I see, Well, it's been nice meeting you . . . Frances. Maybe I'll see you again sometime.'

'Yes, I'm sure you will. Bye for now, Glenys.'

Frances was thoughtful as she rode home on the bus. She had called at the garden centre on leaving school and dusk was already closing in. She hoped her mother would not be panicking as she sometimes did when Frances was later than expected. But it was of Jonathan Russell, mainly, that Frances was thinking. She was trying to convince herself that it would be rather nice if he were to meet someone who could make him happy again. Not that he would want to forget his wife – he had obviously thought the world of her – but he deserved to be happy and he was plenty young enough to make a fresh start. Provided Dennis did not suffer by it . . .

It was the second time in the last week or two that Frances had entertained these thoughts about Jonathan Russell. The first time had been when a group of them from the Starlight Players had gone to see the film of *South Pacific* in Manchester. Frances was surprised to see that Jonathan's companion that day – at least, they had sat together on the coach – was Sylvia Bowland, the young woman who was playing the lead part, Nellie Forbush, the American nurse, in their production.

'I didn't realise those two knew one another all that well, did you?' Frances remarked to her friend, Julie Forrester. 'Jonathan Russell and Sylvia Bowland. They seem to be getting on very well together.' The pair were sitting a couple of seats in front of Frances and Julie on the coach, their heads close together, talking animatedly.

'I think they know one another from way back,' said Julie. 'I heard somebody say that Sylvia knew his wife quite well. Why, are you bothered?'

'No, why on earth should I be?' Frances looked at her sharply. 'But I did wonder who might be looking after Dennis today. Their neighbour, I suppose; I've heard Dennis mention her. And I find it rather odd that Jonathan can get away on a Saturday . . .'

'He's his own boss,' remarked Julie, 'so I suppose he can please himself; and he has a few people working for him, doesn't he?'

'And it's a slack time of year in the garden trade, I dare

say,' added Frances. 'Anyway, it's none of our business, is it?'

'You sound as though you'd like it to be, though.' Julie gave her a playful nudge. 'If you ask me, Jonathan would have come and sat next to you if you hadn't been with me. I saw him looking over here when he got on the coach. I wondered if I ought to move. In fact I've seen him looking at you – all moony like – at rehearsals sometimes. Don't tell me you've not noticed.'

'Of course I haven't noticed,' replied Frances indignantly. To her annoyance she could feel herself beginning to blush. 'What nonsense you talk, Julie. All moony indeed! And I couldn't care less who he sits with.'

'I think you'd make a far better Nellie Forbush than that Sylvia Bowland,' said Julie, lowering her voice confidingly. 'You're a much better singer than she is, but they say she always takes the lead. I believe she's thick as thieves with Olive Markland.'

'But they've all been in the company for ages,' added Frances. 'They're not likely to ask a newcomer like me to play a starring role, are they? It's nice of you to say so, Julie, but it's not really true. I think Sylvia's OK. She's probably one of those people who doesn't give her all until it gets to nearer the time. Anyway, I wouldn't have time to take a part like that. My mother's always telling me I mustn't neglect my school work. And then there's the church . . .' She lowered her voice. 'I'm getting quite friendly with Adrian.'

'Oh yes, your vicar friend.' Julie rolled her eyes eloquently.

'Minister, actually. They don't have vicars in the Methodist church. Anyway, he's asked me to go for supper again tomorrow night after the service.'

'You don't say! That should be a laugh a minute,' said Julie, pulling her mouth into a moue. 'You'll have to watch your Ps and Qs, won't you? I shouldn't imagine there'll be much chance of a bit of you know what with him, will there?'

'Oh, I don't know,' replied Frances with an arch little

smile. She wasn't going to admit that, so far, to her disappointment there had been no chance of it at all. 'He's only young, you know, and ever so attractive. Not handsome, but very . . . appealing. My mother thinks he's absolutely the bee's knees.'

'Well, that would put me off for a start, if my mother liked him,' joked Julie.

Frances laughed. 'Yes, I know what you mean. I told her it was just the dog collar that appealed to her. But I dare say he's just the same as other men, under the clerical collar.'

'And wouldn't you just love to know what's under that dog collar, eh?' Julie gave her another meaningful nudge. 'If anything . . .'

'Shut up, Julie! I've told you, he's just the same as anybody else. There's no reason why he shouldn't be, just because he's a man of the cloth.' She giggled. 'Daft expression, that, isn't it?'

'A man of the cloth,' repeated Julie lugubriously. 'Rather you than me, kid. Now, if he looked anything like Rossano Brazzi I might be interested. I'm really looking forward to seeing him in *South Pacific*, aren't you? I think he's gorgeous . . .'

They had booked for a matinée performance of the film, leaving time beforehand for a look round the shops and a snack lunch. They saw Jonathan and Sylvia again in the Kardomah café on Market Street. They were not alone, however, but with a group of four more of the Starlight Players, two men and two women. Frances and Julie didn't join them as there was no room at the table. Frances's eyes, as she ate her poached eggs on toast, kept straying, as of their own volition, to the table in the corner; but she looked away hastily when she saw Julie's knowing little grin. Jonathan did not appear to be taking too much notice of Sylvia now. He was deep in conversation with Joe Markland, the producer, but he noticed Frances and gave her a cheery wave and smile. She decided that she liked him very much, but Julie's idea that he was interested in her, Frances, was just ridiculous. And anyway, it was Adrian, with his thoughtfulness and his gentle unassuming manners, that she wished was with her that afternoon.

The film of *South Pacific* was a delight from beginning to end. The South Sea island settings; the imaginative use of light and shade – that yellow sky as the principals sang was really something; the singing and dancing, with the words, music and actions so perfectly synchronised; the superb acting and the poignancy of the tender love stories. Frances felt a lump in her throat and tears in her eyes more than once. She felt so much for the island girl at the death of her young lieutenant. John Kerr, who was playing the part, was so handsome in that lean rangy sort of way. He rather reminded Frances of Jonathan Russell, apart from the colour of his hair. The same tall, spare figure, his thin-featured face and the way the laughter lines wrinkled round his eyes when he smiled, just as Jonathan's did.

'Wasn't it wonderful?' Julie enthused on the way back in the coach. 'And Rossano Brazzi! Couldn't you just die for him?'

Frances, personally, did not care for him much, neither the actor nor the character he was playing, Emile de Becque, the French plantation owner. She found them both too sophisticated, with too much of the lady killer about them for her taste. 'Mmm, if you like that sort of thing,' she said now. 'But I must admit I prefer John Kerr. Now I think he's really dishy.' She did not say, however, that he reminded her of Jonathan Russell.

Both young women agreed that the two men in their own company who were playing the leading male roles were not a patch on the screen actors. One was an ageing, balding tenor who considered himself something of a Don Juan, and the other one they both thought was a weed. But it was, after all, only an amateur production, and what it lacked in professional expertise it would make up for in enthusiasm.

The sets, too, could not be compared with the real-life scenery of golden sand, azure blue sky and sea and waving palm trees which helped to make the film so memorable. But far from being disheartened each member of the company went home full of a renewed zest that this would be the best show they had ever put on. And for Frances and Julie, for whom it was their first show, the anticipatory thrill of playing their own small parts in front of an audience was rekindled.

Chapter 9

The performance of *South Pacific* was still a few months away, and before that Frances had her own production of the school nativity play to stage. In former years, so Marjorie Aspinall had told her, they had just had a tableau consisting of a dozen or so children who could be trusted to keep – comparatively – still and not fidget, to the accompaniment of Christmas carols played by Miss Walsh on the piano and sung by the whole school. And the louder the better, Marjorie had added, to drown out the inadequacies of Miss Walsh's piano playing.

'It seems a shame to me that so few children can take part,' said Frances. 'Why don't you do a proper nativity play to include all the children? Well, all the Third Year, at least. You know, with travellers to Bethlehem – that can involve lots of the kids who are not very good at learning lines – and animals in the stable, and innkeepers and their wives. And the "multitude of the heavenly host"; that takes care of at least ten angelic-looking little girls.'

'My goodness! You are ambitious, aren't you?' laughed Marjorie. 'I suppose we've never done it because nobody has ever suggested it; and, to be quite honest, I don't think anybody would have wanted to tackle it. There's a tendency here to say, "This is the way we've always done it . . .".'

'And this is the way it's going to stay,' added Frances with a rueful smile.

'Exactly; the stumbling blocks being Miss Cameron and Miss Walsh, of course. They don't like change, and sometimes Miss Reynolds feels she has no choice but to give in to them. Not always, though. When Gertie wants something badly enough she usually sees that she gets it. Look here,

Frances; if you feel you would like to tackle something on a bigger scale this Christmas then why don't you suggest it to the boss? Personally, I think it would be a great idea. The kids get so restless at this time of the year. So many wet playtimes, and they can't play out when they get home either, with the dark evenings. It'll help to channel their energy into something they'd enjoy. And you're so keen on amateur dramatics, aren't you, dear? I'm sure you'd make a really good job of it. Yes, you go ahead and ask Gertie. She can but say no.'

Miss Reynolds, however, did not say no. She seemed delighted at Frances's suggestion and gave the young woman her full support to go ahead and make arrangements in any way she liked, providing that, in the early stages, it did not interfere too much with ordinary lessons. Nearer the time, of course, it would not matter too much. Infant school children were generally too excited in the run-up to Christmas to settle down to work, and this would give them something to think about other than what Father Christmas was going to bring.

'It will give them more of an insight into the real meaning of Christmas,' said Miss Reynolds. 'Some of them, I fear, don't hear very much about that at home, and it's up to us to do what we can. Yes, Miss Goodwin, I think it's an excellent idea. I'm sure Mrs Aspinall will help you with costumes and props and all that sort of thing. She's very good on the creative side. And as the two of you have the older children it shouldn't disturb the rest of the school too much. Try not to let it, dear,' she added, with a meaningful nod. 'Not everybody will want to—' She hesitated, before concluding, 'Just keep it to the Year Three classes, if you can.'

Frances understood only too well what Miss Reynolds's eloquent glance implied, especially after her initial discussion with Marjorie.

Frances's misgivings were justified. Although neither of them had a 'top' class and, therefore, their children were not actively involved, Miss Cameron and Miss Walsh had a great deal to say on the subject of the nativity play.

'It's a ridiculous idea,' Miss Walsh was heard to comment in the staffroom, to whoever might be listening. She knew very well that Frances, for one, could not fail to hear. 'As if the children haven't enough to do with their lessons without expecting them to learn parts as well. They'll get too excited, far too worked up. And all the Third Year taking part! I've never heard the like. Personally, I like to keep a curb on all the excitement in the weeks before Christmas. I make sure my class are working right till the end.'

'Yes, I must admit I can't see any need for change,' added Miss Cameron, blowing a cloud of smoke in the direction of Miss Walsh, who wafted her hand vigorously. Smoking was one thing on which the two did not agree. 'A tableau has always been good enough till now, but it seems that what you and I say, Emily, doesn't count for much any more. And did you know . . .?'

It was the first time Frances had ever heard anyone use Miss Walsh's Christian name. Miss Cameron must be feeling very agitated to have done so in front of other members of staff. The two of them had their heads together now, talking quietly in what seemed to be aggrieved tones.

'How petty they are,' Frances remarked afterwards to Marjorie. 'Damn it all, it's only a school nativity play. It's not exactly a matter for the United Nations, is it?'

Marjorie laughed. 'You will find, my dear, that nowhere are women more small-minded than in an infant school staffroom. They seem to forget that there's a whole world spinning round outside, they are so concerned with their own piddling little affairs. I sometimes think it should be compulsory for teachers to do another job, in the big wide world, before they come into teaching. Not that I ever did, but I did get married, which gives you a very different perspective on things.' She gave a mirthless chuckle. 'And it also brings a whole new set of problems.' She stopped abruptly as she always did when she got on to the subject of her marriage. Frances sensed there was something badly wrong, but even after a term of friendship with Marjorie, she was still none the wiser.

'Take those two, for instance,' Marjorie went on. Frances

131

knew only too well to whom she was referring. 'Straight out of college and into an infant school, and they've been there ever since. What experience have they had of life, either of them? Judith was unfortunate, mind you, losing her fiancé – I told you about that, didn't I? That he was killed in the war? I guess that's what's made her so bitter and twisted. As for Miss Walsh, I didn't know her when she was younger, but I could guess she's always been pretty much the same.'

'Yes, she was probably born old,' remarked Frances. 'Some people are, aren't they? One of the Lindas in my class, she's a real old-fashioned little thing, not like a child at all. But I hope to goodness she doesn't turn out like Miss Walsh.'

'It's nowhere near as bad in a junior staffroom,' Marjorie continued. 'I did a short spell with juniors, on supply, and I noticed the difference. You usually get a good proportion of men teachers there and they do help to ease the tension, if you know what I mean. Men have a different attitude from women, on the whole, and they help to stop you from taking yourself too seriously. By the way, did you know what those two on our staff are belly-aching about now? It's about you giving the parts of the wise men to Dennis Russell and Barry Cartwright.'

'Oh crikey!' said Frances. 'I'm in the doghouse again, am I? And I will be even more when Miss Walsh finds out I want you to play for the carols instead of her.'

'Ridiculous giving a responsible part like that to a lad who is such a troublemaker.' It wasn't long before Frances heard the remark being cast about to be picked up by any listening ear. Not that there were many; most of the staff were giving her their full support. 'And as for that other lad who did all that thieving. Well, I ask you . . .'

Frances did not talk much at home about what went on at school. Her mother never appeared particularly interested, and if she were to tell Josie and Jim it would all sound so trivial. An infant school, with its blinkered view at its own microscopic part of life, would seem like the proverbial storm in a teacup to them. But for all that, she was enjoying her first post back in her home town, so long as she could come to terms with the back-biting and bickering.

Nor did she confide in Adrian. When she was with him all thoughts of school fled from her mind, even though it was through his contact with the school that they had first met. There was just one aspect of the school curriculum, however, that she was unable to forget, even when she was with Adrian, and that was the forthcoming nativity play. She was anxious for it to be a success because it had been entirely her own idea. As the day of the Christmas performance drew near she was very much aware of Adrian's support and encouragement. She wondered, in fact, how she could have managed to get through it all without the knowledge that he was there in the background, quietly urging her on and telling her to take no notice of criticism. And Adrian should know; in a vocation such as his he, too, would never be without his critics.

The nativity play, performed twice, once for the whole school and once for visiting parents and friends, was considered to be a great success by all who saw it. And the staff, with notable exceptions, were fulsome in their praise. Admittedly, there were minor catastrophes. One of the shepherds lost his tea-towel headdress at a crucial moment, dropping it in the manger, right on top of the Baby Jesus; King Herod's papier-mâché beard came unstuck; one of the angels, despite repeated instructions, had turned up in her navy-blue knickers, which were all too visible below her gauzy dress; and the third wise man dropped his gift of myrrh – which was, fortunately, retrieved by one of the oxen before it rolled off the stage. But all these little hitches, though they had Frances tearing her hair out, only added to the enjoyment of the performance, or so she was told by many delighted parents. Dennis and Barry had behaved themselves impeccably as the first two wise men.

'I was glad to see Dennis acquitted himself so well,' said Jonathan Russell with a grin, when she met him amidst the throng of parents, after the play. 'And it was a first-class performance, Frances. If Joe Markland discovers your talent he'll be roping you in as assistant producer for the Starlight.'

'Oh no, ta very much,' laughed Frances. 'I prefer to sing. This is as much as I can manage as far as productions go. It's all too nerve-racking. But I'm glad you enjoyed it, Jonathan. Parents are bound to be biased, though, aren't they, when their own children are taking part?'

'Maybe, but I can assure you it was a jolly good show.' Frances wondered, from his choice of phrase, whether Jonathan had been in the RAF. He was old enough, certainly, to have served in the war, rather than doing National Service. She realised there was a lot she didn't know about him, not that that was surprising. 'Here's your friend coming to talk to you,' Jonathan said now. 'See you, Frances.' He nodded at her, quite curtly, then walked quickly away.

Frances turned round to see Adrian approaching, a radiant smile lighting up his face. She smiled back at him as she dashed eagerly towards him. 'Adrian, what did you think of it? Was it OK?' At the back of her mind a little thought niggled. How did Jonathan know that the young clergyman was her friend? And had she only imagined that he looked rather piqued at Adrian's arrival on the scene? All thoughts of Jonathan Russell, however, quickly faded away as she saw the look of admiration in Adrian's eyes. Possibly more than admiration she thought – hoped – as she smiled at him. There was a look there that told of love, of passion, so far withheld.

Eagerly he seized hold of her hands, seemingly not caring about the throng of parents and children all around them. 'It was wonderful, Frances,' he said. 'I am so proud of you.' It was a few days after this that he kissed her for the first time.

'Take no notice of that daughter of mine,' said Iris to Eliza, soon after the New Year of 1959 had begun, 'if she tells you again that that young minister and her are just good friends. It's all my eye and Betty Martin. You should have seen 'em on Christmas Day. They couldn't leave one another alone. Well, not mauling one another, I don't mean that, at least

134

not in front of us. But he held her hand, all secret like, when we sat down to listen to the Queen's speech. Happen they thought we hadn't noticed, but I did.'

'Aye, you would, wouldn't you?' Eliza chuckled. 'I've never known you miss a trick, Iris Goodwin.'

'Yes, there's not so much escapes me. You should have seen the way they looked at each other. I've always thought that looks can speak volumes, and the way that young Adrian was looking at our Frances, well, I wouldn't be surprised if we were to hear wedding bells in the not-too-distant future.'

'Well, that's good news right enough,' said Eliza. 'Do you think so, Iris? How would you feel about your daughter marrying a clergyman? Of course I know he's not C of E, like you've always been. You set great store by that, don't you?'

'Oh, I've decided that it doesn't matter two hoots, so long as the lad'll make her happy. And that's all he seems to be, clergyman or no, just a lad who's in love with our Frances. And I can see he is. It just shines out of his eyes.'

'And hers as well?'

'Aye, I think so. I can tell you, Eliza, I'd die a happy woman if I knew she was settled with a nice young man like that. No, he's more than that. He's not just nice; he's a good man an' all, so kind and sincere.'

Eliza laughed. 'Well, you'd expect him to be good, wouldn't you, being a man of the cloth. Although I don't suppose they're all saints, not by a long chalk. There's good and bad in everything; that's what I've always found. But look here, Iris; what's all this about dying happy? You're not thinking of popping your clogs yet awhile, are you?'

'No, am I heck as like! Just a figure of speech, that's all. But we don't know, do we, none of us? We don't know the day nor the hour, as it says in the Good Book. And I'd like to think, when the Lord calls me, that I've left my family all nicely settled. Funny how I say "my family", isn't it? They're Samuel's family really, not my flesh and blood at all. I never see my own lot, my brothers and sisters. I don't even know how many of 'em are still living.'

'You've been better than flesh and blood to your Samuel's three,' replied Eliza. 'I know you don't see so much of Bertie now, but the two lasses have a lot to thank you for.'

'And I've a lot to thank them for, an' all,' said Iris. 'I know I grumble at them at times, and I shouldn't, because they're both as good as gold. Our Josie and me haven't always seen eye to eye, of course. Fur and feathers used to fly between us when she was younger.'

'Yes, for a lass who's not your own flesh and blood your Josie's an awful lot like you,' commented Eliza.

'Happen she is.' Iris nodded. 'Stubborn at times and wants her own way . . . like me. Aye, I know my faults. You're more aware of your own shortcomings, aren't you, as you get older? Yes, Josie's a good lass. She has a busy life, but she comes to see her old mam when she can.'

'Not so much of the old,' said Eliza. 'You're not much different in age to me, are you? And I don't consider myself old, I can assure you.'

'No, I've a few years to go before I reach my threescore and ten,' mused Iris. 'If I ever do. That's what I was trying to say, Eliza. None of us knows. And my old ticker's not in such good shape as yours, you know. I had that scare a few months ago, and it wasn't the first one.'

'But you've recovered from it wonderfully well,' said Eliza, in what Iris considered to be an overcheerful voice. 'You're looking tons better. And you've got your Frances back living here now. I know that must be a great relief to you. You never liked living on your own, did you?'

'I was all right till I started being ill. When you live alone you're your own boss, there's that to be said for it, and I've got to admit I'm not the easiest of persons to live with. Yes, I'm glad our Frances is back, though I don't know for how long, do I? If she gets wed I'll be on my own again.'

'Well, if she does, I don't suppose it'll be just yet,' said Eliza consolingly. 'Clergymen aren't all that well paid, are they? They'll have to save up. Cheer up, love. You're looking a bit down in the dumps and that'll never do.' She jumped smartly to her feet. 'I'll go and make us a nice cup of tea.

That'll cheer us up. And what about a piece of Christmas cake? I dare say there's a bit left, isn't there, of that one I made for you?'

'. . . Yes, you're very good to me, Eliza,' Iris went on, a few minutes later, as they sat with their cups and plates on their knees. The rose-patterned china had been a Christmas gift from Josie and Jim. The cup fitted into a ridge at the side of a fair-sized tea plate, big enough to hold a few sandwiches or, as now, a large wedge of Christmas cake. It was ideal for television viewing as it meant that you didn't have to do a balancing act with a cup and saucer and a plate as well. 'I don't know how I'd manage without you,' Iris went on. 'Our Frances can't always be here even when she's not at school. Would you believe she's gone in there today and the term hasn't even started yet? Says she has to put some pictures up and get things ready before the kiddies come back. She's keen, I'll say that for her. Always working, she is; marking books and making wall charts or whatever they call 'em . . .

'Aye, you're a good friend, Eliza. One o' t'best, and you mustn't think I don't appreciate it. You spend that much time here that I sometimes wonder why you don't move in wi' me.' Iris laughed, to show that she didn't really mean it, as her friend looked at her keenly.

'Well, that's as may be . . .' Eliza pressed her lips together tightly, before dabbing them with a holly-patterned serviette. She reached across for Iris's cup and plate. 'I'll just rinse these few bits under the tap for you – they're not really dirty – then I must be off. My neighbours are coming in tonight for a game of whist. Their sister's staying with them and she'll make up the four.' She glanced at the wooden clock. 'Time's getting on. You don't realise when you're chatting.'

Oh dear, I hope I haven't gone and put my foot in it, thought Iris, after her friend had departed, rather abruptly, she couldn't help noticing. She had only been joking when she had made that remark about Eliza moving in. Or had she? It was said that many a true word was spoken in jest, and maybe there had been a grain of wishful thinking in the words she had uttered so casually. Frances would not be here for ever. Even if she did not get married quite soon – and Iris hoped she would make a go of it with that nice Adrian Glover – the girl might well want to get a place of her own. Not that she had actually said so, but Iris knew that girls did that sort of thing these days, much more so than when she had been growing up. Girls were so much more independent now, and they often had a reasonable income, too, to make it possible for them to fly the nest.

When she was young, they had not had two ha'pennies to rub together, at least not the ones on her social level. Almost the lowest of the low they had been, she and her nine brothers and sisters, her frequently drunken father and her down-trodden mother, in their grimy hovel at the wrong end of Haliford. But she had bettered herself – quite considerably – by marrying first Alfred Collier, then, much later, Samuel Goodwin. That marriage, though, had been financially beneficial to them both, and Iris liked to think she had given as much as she had received, if not more, in that partnership.

She knew that she had done her best for the three children and they had turned out well, all of them. Samuel, had he lived, would have been proud of them, as she was. Josie was happily married and had a dear little girl of her own, and a good career as well. Bertie, too, was happily married – at least she assumed he was happy – to a girl from the Midlands area where he was teaching. They had a little boy and another baby was on the way, so they had informed her in their Christmas letter. Bertie was the one of the three children whom Iris had always felt she did not know quite so well. He had never been as outgoing as his two sisters, and he was the one who was not so closely in touch with her now. His living a good distance away was not the only reason. Now he was making a life of his own.

How did the old saying go? 'A son's a son till he takes him a wife, but a daughter's a daughter the rest of your life.' And so it was with her two stepdaughters, and for this Iris often gave thanks to the Lord. As she had mentioned to Eliza, Iris knew, only too well, her own faults. How the girls put up with her sometimes, God only knew, but thank goodness they did. Looking back on the antagonism that had existed, at one time, between her and Josie, it was a miracle the lass still bothered with her. But she did.

And as for Frances, well, Frances had always been her own special little girl, the one she had brought up from a tiny baby in arms, as though she were her own child. The girl probably had no idea how much she was still loved; Iris was not very good at showing her feelings. She sensed a certain restlessness in Frances of late, though she knew the lass tried not to show it too openly. Iris knew that her daughter was irked by her continual fussing and her insistence, still, that she should be home at a reasonable hour; even though Iris knew she could come to no harm with Adrian Glover.

There might well come a time before very long, even before her marriage, when Frances would want to break free. Iris wasn't quite sure why she should be anticipating this; after all the girl had come back from Yorkshire and had got a post in her home town so that she could help to look after her ailing mother. But Iris knew what was in Frances's mind, and she knew, also, that it was a thought that the girl did not dare to voice, not yet. As Eliza had said, there was not much that escaped Iris Goodwin. Iris knew, deep down, that this was the reason she had dropped that not-too-subtle hint to Eliza. And what would she, Iris, do if Frances expressed a wish to fly the nest?

Chapter 10

The Starlight Players' production of *South Pacific* took place at Blackpool's Grand Theatre towards the end of March. There were performances every evening from the Tuesday to the Saturday, and they played, especially towards the end of the week, to almost packed houses. Frances had booked seats for her family and friends for the Friday performance and they were there in full force: Josie, Jim and little Valerie, Iris and Eliza, and Adrian. Megan was on night duty that week and unable to come, but she and Frances met occasionally when her nursing duties – and Bernard – allowed.

Iris had argued at first that her theatregoing days were over. She wouldn't be able to manage the stairs, she said, and crowds made her all hot and bothered.

'I've booked seats in the stalls,' Frances told her. 'Right in the middle of the second row, and I won't take no for an answer. Oh, come on, Mum. You've got to be there. Adrian's going to take you and Eliza there and back in his car. I'd be so disappointed if you weren't there to see me. And you know how you used to love going to the theatre.'

'Aye, it were t'pictures I enjoyed, though, more than t'theatre,' said Iris. 'I always liked a good film. Clark Gable: he were my favourite. That was Hollywood, of course. Then when they started making decent pictures over here I liked John Mills, and James Mason. And I liked the variety shows when we came to live in Blackpool. Dave Morris at the North Pier; he were there year after year. And Frank Randle and Tessie O'Shea . . . Those were the days.'

Frances had learned to be patient while her mother reminisced, something she was doing more and more recently. 'No, I was never much for yer straight plays, and how folks understand a word of that Shakespeare stuff I shall never know. But *South Pacific* has some nice tunes in it. Aye, I like a good musical. Betty Grable used to star in some lovely ones . . . and Rita Hayworth, and Fred Astaire and Ginger Rogers.' We're off again, thought Frances. 'Aye, I'll come, love, if you're sure I'll be all right. I'm not so steady on my pins, but I must admit I wouldn't want to be stuck here on my own while everybody else is off enjoying theirselves.'

Iris vowed afterwards that it was the best show she had ever seen, and Frances considered that to be praise indeed. 'Aye, it were a grand little show,' she repeated, for the umpteenth time, as they all gathered in her living room at the end of the evening. Frances, on previous nights, had lingered to chat with her friends about how the performance had gone, but tonight, as Adrian was waiting for her, she had not hung around. She had taken off her costume – that of an American nurse for the final scene – but she was still wearing her stage make-up.

'All t'songs were lovely,' Iris enthused. 'I don't know which one I liked best. That one that the fellow sang – that French bloke; well, supposed to be French, but I didn't reckon much to his accent – I think I liked that one best. "Some enchanted evening . . ."' She broke into song, her tired-looking face, so aged of late, taking on a more joyful expression as though the years were, momentarily, dropping away. Frances was touched to see her mother looking so happy and engrossed in what she had seen. Oftentimes she took little interest in what was going on, apart from the 'telly', but tonight had been a special experience for her.

'No, that bloke that played the French chap, I thought he were the weak link,' she continued. It wouldn't be Iris if she couldn't find something to criticise. 'Fancies himself, doesn't he? He's got a nice singing voice, though. And that nurse, Nellie Whotsit; the lass that played her was lovely. Such a pretty girl.'

'Yes, Sylvia Bowland,' said Frances thoughtfully. 'She was good, wasn't she? We thought at first she was only

142

mediocre, but I must admit she's pulled all the stops out. They say she usually takes the lead.'

'Not that you wouldn't've done as well if they'd given it to you,' said Iris loyally. 'Our Frances was a grand little singer and dancer at one time, Adrian,' she went on, pointing towards the photograph on the sideboard of Frances in her ballet dress. 'Well, she still is, isn't she? That was her, in t'Tower Ballet. But I've shown it you before, haven't I?'

'Many times, Mum,' said Frances, embarrassed, trying not to sound too impatient. 'Adrian doesn't want to hear all that again. Anyway, they wouldn't give me a leading role. I've only just joined. You've got to be in a few years before they consider you for a big part.'

'Aye, and you've too much to do anyroad, with your school work,' said Iris, changing tack abruptly. 'You've spent enough time with 'em these last few months; happen you'll settle down again now. You did real well though, love. I was proud of you . . . I wish you'd go and take all that stuff off yer face, though. It makes you look like a tart.'

Frances sighed. 'Later, Mum. It's only stage make-up. We'd look like ghosts if we didn't have it on.'

'D'you think I could try some, Auntie Frances?' asked Valerie. 'Some of that make-up? Have you got a bit to spare? I think you look real lovely.' The little girl had seemed to be going to sleep, but had now perked up again.

'Indeed you can't!' said her grandmother. 'What an idea! That's just for grown-up ladies.'

'It wouldn't do any harm, Mum,' interposed Josie. 'She loves dressing up, and she is having dancing lessons . . .'

Frances was glad to have the attention diverted away from herself. Her mother made her feel such a fool sometimes, and in front of other people too. The discussion, led by Valerie, turned to the South Sea Island girls and how they had needed darker make-up. Frances still had traces of it on her arms and legs from an earlier scene. The little girl had been entranced by these scenes; the grass skirts and garlands of flowers, and the graceful dances of the island maidens.

Frances noticed her mother was nodding off to sleep now, but she came to with a start when Eliza said it was time for her to be going home. Frances went upstairs to fetch Eliza's coat, and then Adrian, who had promised to drive Eliza home, joined her in the hallway. They exchanged a loving – though not quite so lingering as usual – kiss whilst Eliza tactfully withdrew back into the living room to put on her coat.

'See you tomorrow, Frances,' whispered Adrian. 'May I meet you after the show? You won't be doing anything special, will you?'

'No . . . I don't think so,' replied Frances, though somewhat hesitantly. She knew that several of the cast would be going for a celebratory drink in one of the seafront hotels. She might have gone along with them . . . On the other hand, knowing of her mother's disapproval and the fact that they would probably be rather late, she might not have done. At all events, the problem was solved now. Adrian wanted to meet her, and she would much rather be with Adrian. 'No, of course not,' she repeated, more decisively. 'Where shall I see you then?'

'I'll wait just outside the theatre,' he replied. 'I'm not quite sure where I'll be able to park. I've . . . I've something rather important that I want to ask you.' He leaned forward and kissed her cheek again as Eliza emerged from the living room. 'Till tomorrow then, Frances . . .'

She felt a warm glow suffuse right through her. Unless she was very much mistaken, she thought she could guess what Adrian wanted to ask her.

'Aw . . . you old spoilsport,' Julie complained the next evening when Frances told her she would not be joining the revelry after the performance. 'There's ever so many of us going and it won't be the same without you.'

'Rubbish!' replied Frances. 'You know everybody now. It's not like it was at first with all of us huddled together in separate little cliques.' There had been a good deal more fraternising among the cast as time had gone on, early reticence and a certain awareness of the hierarchy between

144

the principal players and 'the rest' having been laid aside. 'Anyway, I can't say no when Adrian's offered to come and meet me.'

'I don't see why not,' said Julie. 'He doesn't own you, does he? And it's only for tonight. It's a special occasion.'

And it may well turn out to be a special occasion for me, too, thought Frances, hugging the thought delightedly to herself. 'Well, I'm not coming and that's that,' she said. 'But we're not going to fall out about it, are we, Julie? We'll keep in touch, won't we, after the show is over?'

'Course we will,' replied Julie. 'Nothing more sure than that. And we'll be doing another next year, won't we? Off you go then and have a jolly time with your old clergyman.' She grimaced and Frances laughed.

'Oh, I will. You'd be surprised!'

Adrian was waiting outside the theatre as he had promised. Frances hurried towards him and they kissed affectionately, but not too demonstratively. All the audience had gone, but several members of the Starlight Players were coming out, laughing and talking loudly. Several of them waved to Frances and called out to her.

'Cheerio, Fran. Sorry you're not coming with us . . .'

'Keep in touch now . . .'

'Be seeing you, luv . . .'

Jonathan Russell came out with Sylvia Bowland, his arm placed casually around her shoulders. They both smiled at her and nodded, but did not speak. Frances, for a brief moment, felt oddly deflated.

'Where's the car?' she asked, although she did not think they would be going straight home. She had removed all her stage make-up in case Adrian wanted to take her somewhere for a coffee. He did not drink. Being the leader of a flock of Methodists who, on the whole, abhorred intemperance – at least, they were supposed to – he knew he must set a good example, but there would be a few coffee bars open in the town centre.

'Birley Street,' he replied. 'I couldn't get any nearer. I didn't realise it would be so busy. It's Saturday night, of course; I was forgetting. I'm not used to being out and about in Blackpool on a Saturday night. Never mind the car.' He put his arm round her, something he had never done before in public, but nobody round here would know them and she noticed he was not wearing his dog collar. 'Let's have a walk on the prom. It's a lovely evening . . . and I whispered to your mother that you might be a wee bit late tonight. She won't mind.'

'Did you?' Frances looked at him keenly. 'When was that? I didn't see you.'

He grinned. 'When you went to get Eliza's coat.'

'Mum didn't say anything.'

'No, I guess Mum can keep mum when she wants to.' He drew her closer to him as they stopped for the traffic to pass on Bank Hey Street. Frances felt just a little peeved at the thought of her mother and Adrian plotting behind her back.

She forgave him though when he took her into his arms and kissed her, passionately, but so tenderly, as they stood by the sea railings, close to North Pier. The few passers-by, like themselves mainly courting couples, paid no heed to them. 'Frances . . . darling,' he whispered as they drew apart. 'You can guess what I want to ask you, can't you?'

'I . . . think so,' she faltered, taken aback for an instant, although this moment was not totally unexpected. 'But you'd better ask me all the same, hadn't you?'

'Frances . . . I love you so very much.' His grey eyes, luminous in the dark, were glowing with the love she knew he felt for her. 'Will you marry me?'

She did not even hesitate before answering. 'Yes . . . oh, Adrian, yes. Of course I will.' They kissed again, then, 'I haven't known you all that long,' he said. 'Six months . . . but they've been the happiest six months of my life, and I don't need any more time to know that I want to spend the rest of my life with you.'

He reached into his coat pocket and took out a small box. Frances hadn't anticipated that he would have already bought a ring. 'Here . . . if this doesn't fit we can have it altered. But I know you have slim fingers so I made a guess.'

He slipped the ring on to her finger, and it did fit perfectly. In the darkness she could see the glint of three small diamonds in a crossover setting. Not, perhaps, just what she would have chosen – a mite old-fashioned, but then Adrian was a rather old-fashioned sort of man. She guessed that, even though she was over the age of consent, he may well have asked her mother's permission first before popping the question. It would have been nice if they could have gone together to choose the ring, she mused, as she thought most engaged couples did today. He must have felt very sure about what her answer would be . . . But she was determined that nothing was going to spoil this wonderful moment which was, after all, the happiest in a girl's life.

'Oh, Adrian . . . it's perfect,' she breathed, moving her hand back and forth to see the diamonds glinting. 'I love it . . . and I love you too.' It was the first time she had told him this, but she knew it was true. He was just the right man for her. Everybody said so. Well, not Julie, admittedly, who, after all, had only met him once. But her mother, her sister and brother-in-law and Eliza and Megan; they all liked him very much.

'We're going to be so happy, darling,' said Adrian, 'although I can't imagine being any happier than I am at this moment.' They kissed once more before he said, 'Come along, love. We'd better go and break the news to your mother.'

Frances looked at him pointedly. 'I expect she will have guessed, won't she?'

'Maybe; your mother's pretty astute,' he replied in a guarded voice.

'She may have gone to bed,' said Frances. 'It's quite late.'

'Oh no.' Adrian gave a knowing smile. 'I think she will have waited up tonight.' Frances, more than ever, was convinced that her mother already knew. But supposing I had said no? she wondered. She guessed that if that had been the case her life would not have been worth living.

Iris looked up with an expression of delighted

147

expectancy as they entered the room. She didn't say, 'Well, have you asked her?' but the words were written all over her face.

'Mrs Goodwin,' said Adrian. 'We have something to tell you. Haven't we, my love?' He turned to Frances. 'Go on – you tell her.'

'Mum . . . Adrian has asked me to marry him . . . and I've said I will.' She held out her hand to display her ring. Her mother took hold of it and held it fondly to her cheek.

'Well, you'd be a very silly girl if you said no, wouldn't you?' She held her face up towards Frances. 'Come on, give yer mam a kiss. And you an' all, lad. I'm that pleased for you both. This 'un'll be a marriage made in heaven and no mistake.'

But marriage, though it was a natural progression from an engagement, was something that they did not discuss in any great detail. They decided that it would have to be a fairly long engagement, of eighteen months or two years at least. Adrian was in a flat at the moment, although the trustees of the church were looking for a suitable house to purchase, for use as a manse, on or near the estate. This would not be just for Adrian; for him at first, of course, but also for the incumbents who would come later. Methodist ministers did not stay in the same living for more than a few years, unlike Church of England vicars who often held the position for twenty, thirty years or more, if not for life. It was one of the drawbacks of the Methodist ministry, this constant moving about from parish to parish. Frances wondered whether her mother, steeped in the traditions of the C of E, had realised that when her daughter and Adrian finally got married the chances were that they might, before long, be living quite a distance away. It was something that Frances and Adrian had not yet talked about at length. He still had a year or two to do in Blackpool and, for the time being, he seemed very contented with the situation as it stood, glad to be able to tell the folk in his congregation about their engagement – there need be no more secrecy – and to involve Frances more and more in his parish work.

148

Megan was over the moon at her friend's news. Frances had not seen very much of her whilst she'd been rehearsing for *South Pacific*, but the week after the production they met in Jenkinson's café, on Saturday afternoon, for tea and cream cakes. This followed the inevitable scout around the shops, as Megan was still frenziedly shopping for her bottom drawer. This afternoon she had insisted on buying a plastic clothesline and coloured pegs from Hill's basement, although the wedding was still ages away.

'I'm so thrilled for you,' Megan enthused, licking the cream from her fingers with the relish of a little girl at a party. 'Mmm . . . that meringue was scrumptious! Thanks ever so much, Fran.' The cakes were Frances's treat, to celebrate her engagement. 'I really shouldn't have eaten two, but I couldn't resist them. Bernard says cream cakes are not very good for me, and he'll be cross with me if I put any weight on. It would be dreadful if I couldn't get into my wedding dress. I've already bought it, you know, from Diana Warren's. Yes, I'm absolutely thrilled to bits for you. It's lovely being engaged; to know that you belong to somebody.' She gazed dreamily into space.

'I wonder which of us'll be the first to get married, Fran, you or me. I want you to be a bridesmaid for me, but of course you could always be a matron of honour, couldn't you?'

'Well, you'll be married first, won't you?' replied Frances. 'Didn't you say it was next year, the spring of 1960? Adrian and I can't get married as soon as that. There are . . . well, all sorts of things to consider.'

'Yes, next spring. Just about a year from now,' said Megan happily. 'We haven't fixed the exact date, but we know where it's going to be. At the Sacred Heart Church.' This was the main Catholic church in Blackpool, near Talbot Square, right next door, in fact, to Jenkinson's café where they were now sitting. Fashionable Catholic weddings were often held there, just as Church of England ones were held at St John's.

'You've already bought your dress, you say, even

though it's a year till your wedding?'

'Oh, yes. I saw just the one I wanted in the window, you see. So I took Bernard along to show it to him, and he said it looked just perfect for me.'

'You showed it to Bernard? I thought a girl's wedding dress had to be a secret, from her future husband, at least. It's supposed to be unlucky, isn't it, letting your fiancé see it?'

'Oh, Bernard and I don't worry about silly superstitions like that. Anyway I tell him everything.' Megan's expression was a trifle smug. 'We have no secrets from one another. You can't have secrets when you're married, or even when you're engaged. You have to really trust one another. That's what Bernard says, and I agree with him.'

'Of course . . .' replied Frances. 'Have you found a house yet, or is it too soon?'

'Bernard's house-hunting, when he's not tied up at the hospital, but there's plenty of time. I'm sure he will find just the sort of house we want. He's very particular, of course. Everything has to be just perfect for Bernard.'

Frances decided not to comment on this remark. 'What about your flat?' she asked. 'You're still happy there, are you? Getting on well with your flatmate?'

'Oh, yes; Thelma and I get on quite well. When we see one another, that is, because we're often on different shifts. The trouble is she'll be leaving soon, so I'll be on my own again. Her family are going to live in Manchester and she's got a transfer to a hospital there. I don't suppose . . .' Megan hesitated. 'I asked you before; you were always my first choice, you know. You couldn't reconsider . . . about sharing with me? I'd rather have you than anybody; we get on so well . . . No, forget I asked. You told me before. It's your mother, isn't it? You can't leave her. No, it was silly of me.'

'Hold on a minute,' Frances laughed. 'Honestly, Megan, you rabbit on so much I can't get a word in. Yes, when you asked me before I did think it was out of the question. But now – well – I'm not too sure.'

'You mean you might?' Megan's face lit up with delight.

'Possibly,' Frances sighed. 'It's what I would like; make

no mistake about that. I came home mainly so that I could be with Mum, but I wouldn't say it's ideal, the two of us living together. There's hardly room to swing a cat round, you see, and I have so much school work to do. I can't do it in my bedroom, there isn't room. And when I spread the newspaper out on the table and get my paper and pens out I can hear Mum sighing and tutting. Then she starts coughing – putting it on half the time, I'm sure. She says the smell of the Indian ink gets on her chest and she can't concentrate on the "telly" with me messing about.'

'Don't you have two rooms?'

'Yes, but we don't make a coal fire in the other room, and Mum says the electric fire is too expensive to use for any length of time. Oh dear, I do seem to be grumbling about Mum, don't I, and I don't mean to. I know things are difficult for her, but I sometimes think she'd manage just as well without me. At least she wouldn't be aggravated any more by me leaving all my stuff lying about. She's always telling me I'm untidy.'

'Mmm . . . It sounds as though you're getting on one another's nerves more than a bit. Do you think she could manage, though, on her own? I would really love you to come and share with me, but . . .'

'Well, there's Eliza,' said Frances thoughtfully. 'She's always popping round. I've often wondered why they didn't make a home together, her and Mum.'

'Because your mum's none too easy, I dare say,' said Megan. 'It's different living with somebody than just seeing them every now and again. That's what Bernard always says. But I'm sure you and I would get on really well. Oh, Fran, I do wish you would think about it; seriously, I mean.'

'I already am,' said Frances. 'Leave it with me.'

'And how the heck d'you think I'm going to manage if you go swanning off to live with Megan? Leaving me here all on my own . . .'

Frances sighed inwardly, although she was trying hard not to let her exasperation show. She might have known what her mother's reaction would be; she would have been amazed if it had been any different, but she was determined to put her case clearly and logically and not to get annoyed.

'You're hardly ever completely on your own, Mum. You know that as well as I do if you're honest. Mrs Kingsley comes to do the cleaning, Josie calls every day, and Eliza's never off the doorstep from what I can see. And I'd come as often as I could manage. Adrian would bring me a few times a week. He's just as concerned about you as I am.'

'Huh! It sounds as though you're concerned, doesn't it? Making plans to abandon me. And you don't want to go worrying that young man of yours neither. He's got quite enough to do without ferrying you backwards and forwards. You're a very lucky girl to have a chap like that, I can tell you, and I hope you appreciate him.'

'We're getting away from the point, Mum. It isn't that I want to leave you, but in some ways I think you'd be better off without me.'

'How d'you make that out?'

'Well, I know I get on your nerves, being so untidy, and a lot of it I can't help. I've so much school stuff. And you get all fidgety when I start working in here. I've seen you. And there's not much room for me either.'

'I reckon you should be able to put up with it if I can. It isn't as if you paid me all that much. And it is your home.'

'I know, Mum. And you know very well I'd give you more money if you wanted it. It was your idea that I only pay a small amount.' Frances felt more than a little hurt at her mother's insinuations.

'It'll cost you a darned sight more in yer fancy flat.'

'I know, Mum.'

'It's the nights, Frances. That's what I'm worried about. I know I managed on my own before you came back, but I've got used to somebody being here now. I have to get up to t'toilet, and supposing I fell?'

'You never have, have you?'

'No, but there's always to be a first time.'

'Listen, Mum, what I've been wondering is this.' Frances leaned forward in her chair. She didn't go over to hold her mother's hands; that might have seemed too much like cajolery, but she did, briefly, touch Iris's hand as it lay on her lap. 'I've been thinking about Eliza.'

'Well, what about her?'

'Well, I was wondering if she might consider coming to live here with you.'

'And why should she? She's got her own little house, and a very comfortable one it is, too.'

'Yes, I know that. But she's always here, isn't she? And you seem to get on better with her than you do with anybody. I've heard her drop the odd hint, once or twice, that she doesn't really like living alone.'

Iris had gone quiet. Frances didn't know whether she was still disgruntled or was thinking the idea out.

Eventually Iris said, 'Aye, it's not a bad idea, I suppose. Happen I'll put it to her the next time she comes. I don't know what she'll say, mind. Don't go getting your hopes up. Although I reckon you'll get yer own way in the end. You usually do.'

That, coming from Iris, was rich, but Frances held her tongue.

That conversation took place on the Monday evening following Frances's meeting with Megan. On the Tuesday Frances decided she would go herself to see Eliza Pendleton, to broach the idea, tentatively at first, of her coming to live with Iris. She phoned to make sure it was not Eliza's day for a whist drive or her Townswoman's Guild meeting, and Eliza having assured her that she would be at home, Frances left school promptly, for once, and caught a bus to near the gates of Stanley Park, close to where Eliza lived.

Eliza greeted her warmly, but Frances felt somewhat ill at ease as she sat in the small sitting room – only a little larger than her mother's, but not so cluttered – whilst Eliza made a cup of tea. After all, what she was about to ask might be considered very presumptuous. She might very well be sent away with a flea in her ear.

Eliza smiled at her companionably when they were settled with their cups of tea. 'I think I can guess what you've come about, love, and I can't say I blame you. It's about what me and your mother were talking about last week, isn't it? I didn't realise she'd have let on to you so soon. Of course there's nowt settled yet, not properly. It'll need a lot of sorting out . . .'

'What? What do you mean?' Frances stared at her in surprise. 'I don't know—'

'You don't know what I'm talking about? Oh, deary me. I must've guessed wrong then, about what you've come for. Trust me to go and open my big mouth. But I'd best tell you now I've started. You see, love, yer mam and me, we've had an idea that it might not be a bad thing if we were to live together. Perhaps not yet, Frances. It's your home, love, when all's said and done, and I've no intention of pushing you out. But you're engaged now, aren't you, and you won't be there for ever.'

All Frances could do was to gape at her.

'It was yer mam's idea at first,' Eliza continued, 'and when she suggested it – oh, several weeks ago it must be – I thought: No, not on your life! But then, when I started to think about it, I realised it made sense. I know I've got a nice little home here and I'm very comfortable, but I get so lonely in the evenings. I still miss my Norman even though it's years since he went. Anyway, it was only a thought, for sometime in the future maybe. Don't go worrying your head about it. What was it you wanted to see me about, love?'

'But . . . that was it,' stuttered Frances. 'About you coming to live with Mum, that's if you wanted to. I – well – I sort of suggested it to Mum. But she never let on that you'd already talked about it. In fact she tried to make out that I was being selfish, wanting to go and leave her.'

'What! The crafty old . . .' Eliza shook her head be-musedly, but she was smiling, which was more than Frances was. Frances, at that moment, felt as though she could have throttled her mother. Putting her in the wrong, making her feel guilty . . . 'Yes, that's Iris all over,' said Eliza. 'She's got to get her two pennorth in. She's always got to have her little grumble. Now, what were you saying, love? That you'd suggested I might go and live there?'

Frances explained about Megan's flat and how she would very much like to go and share with her. There would be more room, she and her mother did tend to get on one another's nerves, but she wouldn't, of course, consider leaving Iris high and dry. 'And then I thought about you. But I realised it might be rather a cheek, so I came to talk it over.'

'Just wait till I see Iris! After the way her and me had talked about it—'

'Oh no, Eliza. Please don't tell her I've been. She said she'd ask you the next time you came round. It would be better if she thinks that – well – that she's doing me a favour. You know what she's like.'

'Don't I just! But I think I can handle Iris if anybody can.'

'She's not easy to live with, Eliza. And I know there's a lot for you to consider. This house, for a start. What would you do, that's if you do decide to move to our place? It would be a very big step for you to sell it. To move into somebody else's house, I mean. Oh dear, it's very complicated.'

'But it's not your problem, love. You're a kind girl and you're good to your mam, I know that, but you do have a life of your own. I'd rent this place out, I think, but we can sort all that out later. Then it would be there for me to come back to if . . . well, if ever I needed it.'

'You mean if Mum . . . if she wasn't there any longer?' Frances suddenly felt a chill of apprehension. 'You don't think she's likely to die, do you? Not yet?'

'We've all got to go sometime, love. No, I shouldn't think so, not yet. You mum's had two scares, but she's what they call a creaking gate. You've just got to be sensible when you get to our age and weigh up all the pros and cons. Yes, we'll come to some arrangement the next time I see her – tomorrow, more than likely. Then you can go ahead and make plans with Megan. She's that nice little nurse, isn't she? That one that looks as though a puff of

155

wind'd blow her over? And don't worry, love, I won't let on you've been.'

'I'm very grateful, Eliza. I know Mum can be difficult.'

'Never you mind. I'll give her a good hiding if she starts her monkey tricks with me! No – of course I won't; only joking! But I'll be able to deal with her, make no mistake about that. I'll just have to let her think she's being the boss.' Eliza chuckled. 'But you and I know different, don't we, lass?'

Chapter 11

'I might have known you wouldn't stay the course. What is it – six, seven months, and already you're off out of it.'

It was Josie who was objecting the most about Frances going to live with Megan. Iris now seemed very disposed to the idea. It had, of course, been her own idea in the first place, but she had not admitted this.

'It's nearly nine months, actually,' Frances replied, 'since I came home. Anyway, what's it to you? You know I wouldn't have dreamed of moving out unless Mum had somebody to look after her.'

'Yes, anybody except you. That's what it amounts to, doesn't it, Frances? You've been itching to be off ever since you came back. Mum would've been in a real mess if I hadn't called round every morning.'

'I don't see that that's any hardship to you. You're your own boss. You can do your work any time you like. Not like me. I have to leave the house before half-past eight every morning, and it's sometimes nearly five before I get home.'

'And don't we know it! You never shut up about it, do you? I'm sick of hearing how hard you teachers have to work.'

'Girls, girls, please!' Jim threw down his newspaper in exasperation. 'Give it a rest, can't you?' He turned to his wife. 'Josie, I hate to say this, but you're beginning to sound an awful lot like your mother.'

'How dare you?' Josie picked up the paperback book that was tucked down the side of her chair and flung it across the room at her husband. Not that she meant to hurt him, thought Frances, because she aimed it at his middle rather than his head. And if she had really intended to injure him she would have flung her cup or an ashtray or something hard. 'How dare you say I'm like my mother?'

Josie was grinning, though, and Jim was smiling back at her. This was just another of their frequent little spats, and Frances knew that it added a certain spice to their marriage. At the moment, though, she was caught in the middle of it, might be said to be the cause of it.

'Take no notice of her, Fran,' said her brother-in-law. 'She always has to have her little say – like your mother.' He glanced meaningfully again at his wife. 'As a matter of fact, we think you're doing the right thing – don't we, Josie?' He emphasised the last few words, and Josie, grudgingly, nodded.

'S'pose so . . . but I still say she hasn't given it long.'

'And I wonder how long you'd have stuck it, eh, if you'd had to live with your mam?' Jim went on. 'There'd have been all hell let loose with the pair of you together, and you know it.'

'I did live with her,' argued Josie. 'Before we were married I lived at home; when she had her first heart attack.'

'But you weren't on your own with her. Frances was there too. Besides, that's a long time ago. Your mother wasn't as difficult then, nothing like.'

'I know, I know,' sighed Josie. 'Sorry, Fran. I didn't mean to fly off the handle. But you know what I'm like.' Frances did; it would not be the last argument the sisters would have. Josie was a volatile creature and Frances, too, was not always placid and even-tempered. 'I suppose I'm rather worried about Mum, that's the top and bottom of it,' Josie continued. 'Worried that she'll be all right with Eliza. It hardly seems fair that we should expect somebody who's not one of the family to take responsibility for her whilst we carry on with our own affairs.'

'Eliza's just like family,' said Jim. 'Iris has known her for years, and I'd bet you a hundred pounds the pair of 'em'll be as right as rain together. Eliza'll not put up with any nonsense from her and that's for sure. Anyway, it's all settled, isn't it, and they both want to give it a try? Next week, eh, Frances, moving day?'

'Yes, at half-term. I move into Megan's place and Eliza comes to stay with Mum. She's got a young married couple renting her house for the time being. So it's all change.'

'And good luck to you, Frances, that's what I say,' said Jim. 'It'll give you a bit more freedom. Somewhere to entertain your young man, eh?' He winked at her. 'I know there's not much privacy at Iris's.'

'Adrian's got his own flat, you know,' replied Frances. 'So we're . . . well, we're OK.' She could feel herself blushing. She was discovering that what she had hinted to her friend, Julie, was very true; that Adrian, underneath his dog collar, was no different from other men. Not that they had gone 'the whole way', nor would they. She knew that Adrian would draw the line at that, and so would she. Frances knew that respectable girls, well-brought-up girls – like herself – walked up the aisle as virgins. Sometimes only just virgins, maybe, but, technically, virgins they were.

Frances had assured Megan that she would make herself scarce if, at any time, Megan wanted to be alone in the flat to entertain her fiancé. 'Oh no,' her friend had replied, obviously interpreting Frances's meaningful glance as implying something, to Megan's mind, that was quite shocking. 'Oh no, there's nothing like that at all with Bernard and me. He kisses me, of course,' she added coyly, 'but nothing else. I wouldn't, not until we're married. I know that Bernard wants me to keep myself pure, just for him. I would feel dreadfully guilty wearing a white dress if I'd done anything – you know – that was wrong.'

Frances guessed that she would have to watch her step, living with Megan. Adrian certainly wasn't as chaste as it seemed the saintly Bernard was, although Frances knew she could trust him completely not to let anything go wrong. But there would always be the times when Megan was on nights, and they would still spend some time at Adrian's flat. All told, Frances was happy that she was making the break from Iris. Megan might be somewhat prim and proper, but they seemed to complement one another very well and had never had any real disagreements.

'We can but give it a try,' she told Jim and Josie now.

'Eliza will still have her house to go back to if things don't work out. It's only a short let to the young couple, till they find their own place. And I'm not tied to Megan for ever, although I think we'll be OK together, funnily enough. She's so naïve and trusting, I always feel I want to take care of her.'

'I dare say she has a tough streak underneath,' said Jim. 'She must have, being a nurse. Anyroad, you take care of yourself, love; that's the main thing . . . Now, I'd best tell you my news. I've been made Road Safety Officer for the schools. What d'you think of that, eh? So you'll be seeing me at Wyre Bank in the near future, when I come to give the kids a pep talk. Happen you'd better not let on, though, that I'm your brother-in-law.'

'I don't see why not, Jim,' said Frances. 'It's a real feather in your cap, isn't it, being chosen to do a job like that?'

'I don't know so much about that,' said Jim. 'It's not exactly a promotion. I'm still a constable, you know, and it's not everybody that wants to have dealings with children. I wouldn't like to have to deal with so many of them all the time, like you do, but I've always liked kids. I think I get on well with them and I seem to be able to gain their confidence. It's important for them to think of the policeman as their friend, not somebody to fear.'

'And that's not all,' said Josie. 'You'll be seeing more of me as well. You know I have the contract for taking photographs at some of the schools? Well, I've just got a few more, and Wyre Bank is one of them.'

'That's great,' said Frances. 'Congratulations! Yes, we did have a photographer in last September, soon after I went there, but Miss Reynolds wasn't all that satisfied with the results. I didn't tell her about you though – I thought it might seem a bit pushy. But now she's got you anyway. She wouldn't realise that "Josephine Clegg, Photographic Studies" was my sister.'

'So you'll be able to tell her now, won't you?' said Josie. 'Tell her what a clever family you've got. The friendly school bobby is your brother-in-law and the photographer is your sister.'

'Yes . . .' replied Frances, but rather unsurely. Maybe it might be as well not to say anything at school about Josie, or Jim. Certain members of staff would be very quick to say that not only the new girl, but her family as well, were taking on too much at the school.

Frances moved into Megan's flat on the Friday of the Whit weekend, which was also the half-term holiday for the schools. The flat was more or less fully furnished with the essential items – table, dining chairs, a three-piece suite, beds, wardrobe and dressing table, all a trifle shabby, but sturdy and functional – but she took a few of her own bits and pieces, including a reading lamp, a record player and her collection of long-playing records (used very rarely, as it interfered with Iris's television viewing). Also, a new candlewick bedspread, two fleecy blankets, and some soft fluffy towels, all of which were a present from Iris. This gesture touched Frances deeply. She guessed it was her mother's way of saying she was sorry for having made such a fuss in the beginning. Iris, as usual, had not admitted that she might have been in the wrong, but this was a very practical way of making amends.

The two young women would be sharing the large bedroom, which held two single beds, but there was plenty of room for Frances to do her school work either in the bedroom or the spacious living room. There was a small bathroom and toilet combined, and an adequate-size kitchen with a Formica table, fairly limited cupboard space, a vitreous enamel sink, an electric cooker, and a small fridge. It was very luxurious compared to many flats, but there was no washing machine. Megan said she got round this problem by using a Hoovermatic rental service once a week. These little businesses were thriving at the moment. They were run by enterprising young men who rented out washing machines for around seven shillings and sixpence a time, to be brought to your home at, say, six o'clock in the evening and collected a few hours later.

They agreed they would take turns with the dusting and hoovering – there was a rather antiquated Hoover that

161

Megan's mother had bequeathed to them – and also with the cooking of the evening meal, depending on which shift Megan happened to be on at the hospital.

'It's all going to be wonderful!' Megan exclaimed, after Adrian had departed. He had made a few trips back and forth as his little car could not cope with all of Frances's belongings in one go. Megan was gazing round in delight at the living room. It had been brightened up considerably by her friend's additions of colourful cushions, in striking shades of red, yellow and blue, her shelf of books, her stack of records, and a few ornaments and vases which Iris had willingly parted with from her abundant store. 'Oh, I can't tell you how much I've been looking forward to having you here, and now you've come.' She clasped her hands together in delight.

'Sit down and have a little rest – you must be tired out with all that toing and froing – and I'll go and make us a cup of coffee. You like coffee, don't you? You can have tea if you prefer.' She didn't wait for an answer. 'I drink quite a lot of coffee now. It helps to keep me awake when I'm on nights. Bernard says too much of it isn't good for me, but he isn't here, is he? He won't know and we won't tell him, will we?' She grinned impishly as though she was behaving in a wildly wicked way.

'Yes, coffee's fine, thank you, Megan,' said Frances when she could get a word in. 'But let me come and help.'

'Oh, no. This is my little treat; I insist.' When Megan emerged from the kitchen a few minutes later, carrying a laden tray, she was wearing a frilly apron with a heart-shaped bodice, a smaller heart forming the pocket. She looked, Frances thought, for all the world like a little girl playing at 'house'.

Frances, with Megan's permission, entertained Adrian for dinner on Whit Sunday. It was a busy day for him as he was preaching both morning and evening and there was also a service of Holy Communion. Frances, who still sang in the choir, left the small joint of beef in the oven, hoping it would not be burned to a cinder when they returned; her cooking skills were minimal. It was somewhat well done, and she feared the potatoes, conversely, were too pale, but Adrian vowed it was the best meal he had tasted in ages.

Megan had dashed home after her attendance at Mass at the nearest Catholic church to make an apple crumble as her contribution to their first Sunday dinner together. She was disappointed that Bernard could not be there to make up the foursome, but he was on duty at the hospital until the evening. Frances, on the other hand, confessed – to herself – to being more than a little relieved at his absence. She had met him on several occasions, but had not warmed to him any more than she had done at their first meeting. Her first impression of him, that he was pompous, conceited and overbearing, had not changed. Megan, however, was rapturous in her praise of him and, Frances supposed, that was all that mattered. She was the one who was going to marry him, after all.

Adrian decided to take a complete day off on Whit Monday, and, after the evening service when he had taken her home he suggested to Frances that they should, for a change, behave as a couple of day-trippers, visiting some of the attractions of the seaside town that, so far, remained a mystery to him.

'The Pleasure Beach!' Frances exclaimed, delighted at the idea. 'I haven't been there since I was a little girl.'

'And I've always wanted to have a ride on one of your Blackpool trams, but I've never had the time,' said Adrian. 'So we'll go there on one, shall we? Then we can saunter back at our leisure. Stop for fish and chips if you like. I won't feel I really belong to Blackpool till I've had a meal of fish and chips.'

'You mean you never have?'

Adrian shook his head. 'No, not that sort. I sometimes grill a bit of fish at home, but that's not the same, is it?'

'Not at all. Your education's sadly lacking, lad. But we'll soon put it right.' She flung her arms round him and kissed him, more as a good friend than a lover, as they said good night at the door of her flat. 'I won't invite you in, if you don't mind. Megan's Bernard might be there by now.' She pulled a face. 'And I don't feel like listening to a theological discussion at this time of night.'

'And I don't feel like entering into one,' agreed Adrian, laughing. This was what had happened the one and only time that the two men had met, at Megan's flat, before Frances had moved in as an occupant. Catholicism and Methodism were, in many respects, poles apart, although there were points of agreement. Adrian, a believer in ecumenical relations between the churches, had tried to emphasise the similarities, whereas Bernard had been set on underlining the differences.

'No, I don't think I can stomach Dr Bernard Conway tonight. Enough's enough, and I've already preached two sermons. I'll see you tomorrow then, love. I'll pick you up bright and early. Can you be ready for ten o'clock?'

'Ten o'clock! That's not early.'

'It is on a Bank Holiday,' Adrian grinned. 'I think I've deserved a little lie-in. Till tomorrow then. Good night, darling.'

He kissed her again, and Frances felt a glow of happiness as she waved to him, striding briskly away down the road. The flat was in easy walking distance of both Wyre Bank School and the Methodist church, so Adrian had not used his car, although he had insisted on walking her home. Everything was working out so well for her: her flat, her job, her mother in safe hands, and, above all, the love of a good man. It was hard to imagine that things could be better.

Frances couldn't remember when she had had so much fun, and that was not a word that you would normally connect with a man who was an ordained minister. 'Clerk in Holy Orders'; that was the high-falutin title that was sometimes applied to them. But when Adrian dispensed with his clerical collar, as he had on this Whit Monday, he cast away much of the solemnity and piety that were associated with his profession. She had already discovered that he could chat, laugh and joke, even make love – within limits – at times, just as other, more worldly, men could;

but always retaining that certain air of restraint that made you unable to forget entirely that he was a clergyman.

Today, however, it seemed as though the final barriers might be down. Frances and Adrian were wholly at one with the happy laughing crowds of holiday-makers that thronged the Pleasure Beach. They sampled the daring delights of the bumper cars, the aeroplane ride and the ghost train. Then, as a brief respite from all this excitement, Frances opted for a sail through the River Caves, a remembered pleasure from her childhood days.

'All right,' said Adrian, with a twinkle in his eye, 'but only if you promise you'll go on the Big Dipper afterwards.'

Frances didn't like to say she was too scared, that until now her only experience of roller coasters had been the Little Dipper, designed purely for children. If Adrian was game, then so was she. So, with her heart in her mouth and butterflies dancing a wild fandango in her stomach, she promised she would. And with Adrian's arm tightly around her, holding her close at each mad, breathtaking descent, she found that the ride was far from being the frightening experience she had anticipated; thrilling, rather, and exhilarating.

'Well done,' he said, when they staggered out of the two-seater car. Frances, at any rate, was staggering. Even though she had enjoyed it her legs felt like jelly, although Adrian still seemed fit for anything. 'I'm proud of you, love. I know how scared you were.'

'Scared? What gave you that idea? Of course I wasn't scared. Well . . . perhaps a bit,' she admitted, 'until the first dip, then I was OK. Oh, Adrian, aren't we having a smashing time? I'm ever so glad you suggested the Pleasure Beach.'

'You suggested it; remember?'

'Oh yes; so I did. Well – whatever – it was a jolly good idea.'

'Some ice cream, I think, now. What do you say?'

'What? After a ride like that! We'll be sick.'

'Of course we won't. We might've been if we'd had it first. Come on; never say die. There are lots more things I want to do before the day's out.'

Not only did they have an ice-cream cornet, but, after that, a huge stick of candyfloss each. Soon their mouths and chins were coated with the vivid pink goo left behind by the spun sugar, and they laughingly took out their handkerchiefs, licked them, and wiped each other's face.

'My mum would never let me have this when I was a little girl,' said Frances. 'She used to say it was too messy.'

'And I think she was right, too,' replied Adrian. 'Look at the state of your hanky. She would be complaining if she was still doing your washing.'

'In fact it's the first time I've ever had candyfloss,' mused Frances.

'You're kidding!'

'No, honestly; it's the first time ever.'

'Mmm . . . Sounds like a day for firsts, doesn't it? The Big Dipper, and candyfloss. I wonder what else you're going to do for the first time, eh?' Had he not been a clergyman she might well have misinterpreted the roguish gleam in his eyes. But he couldn't mean that, surely? Not Adrian.

She laughed evasively. 'I don't suppose there'll be anything else. But there's a first for you, don't forget. Blackpool fish and chips!'

'Yes, all in good time. Now let's see if we can win a teddy bear.'

She watched whilst Adrian threw rings over skittles, finally winning, not a teddy bear, but a small Kewpie doll made of celluloid with a feather stuck in its head. She was glad it wasn't a teddy bear – she would have felt rather a fool carrying it home – but the doll fitted into her shoulder bag. Adrian wouldn't have a go at the rifle range, which did not surprise her. She knew he was a peace-loving man and he told her how he had abhorred the use of weapons, even in his National Service days, though certain usage of them had been unavoidable.

Neither did he wish to throw balls to make the man topple into the water. Frances had been fascinated by this sideshow as a child, and he was still there. Not the same man, of course, but some poor stooge sitting on a seat suspended over a tank of water, waiting for the ball to hit the lever that would catapult him into its depths. It wasn't deep and he was well protected in waterproof clothing, but what a way to earn a living, she thought. As her mother often said, it took all sorts!

On the way out they watched the Laughing Man in his glass case outside the Fun House. You could not help but join in the merriment yourself as the gigantic clown figure, with the smaller clown seated on his knee, rocked backwards and forwards, quite overcome with mirth, to the accompaniment of recorded laughter chortling away from somewhere deep inside him.

Frances was glad that Adrian did not suggest a visit to the Fun House itself, nor to Noah's Ark. The attractive frontage of the latter could be seen from the promenade, with its chunky, toylike animal figures parading, two by two, around the gaily painted boat. She remembered how Josie, seven years her senior, had persuaded her as a little girl into going into the ark, making out that it would be such a jolly place with funny animals like the ones outside. Instead, Frances had found it a terrifying place, not unlike the ghost train, full of dark, spooky corridors, sudden gusts of wind that blew your skirt over your head, and menacing figures at unexpected corners. Josie had been full of tricks like that when she was growing up, and it had been a long time before Frances, somewhat overprotected and pampered as a child, had forgiven her for that particular episode.

Having travelled to the Pleasure Beach by tram, one of the new streamlined cream and green ones, Frances and Adrian strolled back northwards along the promenade, hand in hand. It was a couple of miles or more to the town centre where they had parked the car, but Frances felt as though she could go on walking for ever.

'Fish and chips now; I'm feeling peckish,' said Adrian as they drew near to Central Beach.

This was a part of the town in which Frances had no desire to linger. It had long been the sleazy area of Blackpool, ever since the turn of the century, when the various pedlars, hawkers and sideshows had been turfed off the sands, only to end up across the road from the beach on what soon became known as the Golden Mile. At one time there had been freak sideshows there of a very sinister nature. Frances had heard her mother tell stories of giant rats; Fat Alice, the Fattest Woman in the World; plate-lipped and giraffe-necked women; even a vicar, the Rector of Stiffkey, starving himself to death – supposedly – in a glass case.

'You're joking!' said Adrian, when Frances told him this dubious story now. 'A vicar? Never!'

'A defrocked one,' she assured him, having heard the story, countless times, from Iris. 'He was kicked out of the Church for misbehaviour with young women whose souls he was supposed to be saving! Anyway, he ended up on the Golden Mile, starving himself in a glass case.'

'And what happened to him?' Adrian sounded as though he did not believe a word of it.

'Oh, he was mauled by a lion, and he died. Very tragic really. That was in Skegness, just before the last war. He was pretending to be Daniel in the lion's den.'

Adrian nudged her playfully. 'I'll believe you; thousands wouldn't!'

'It's true, honest . . . or so they say. Anyway, Adrian, I don't think you're going to get your fish and chips here. There are plenty of stalls, but I don't think I fancy stopping, somehow.'

As well as the fish and chip stalls there were tea stalls, amusement arcades, stalls selling seafood – cockles, mussels and shrimps – fortune-tellers' booths, rock sellers, purveyors of 'Kiss Me Quick' hats, mock auctions and sideshows. The latter might not be as dubious as those of the twenties and thirties, but it was still a far from salubrious area.

'No, I don't fancy it either,' agreed Adrian. 'Let's go into town and find a nice café.'

'There's Hesketh's,' said Frances. 'Near Central Station. They're supposed to be the best fish and chips in town. I remember going there when I was a little girl, but I've never been since. I can't think why.'

'Mmm, smells delicious,' said Adrian as they stood outside the café, savouring the aroma of freshly cooked cod – or haddock – and chips with the overlying fragrance of malt vinegar. 'It looks very crowded inside, though. Seems everybody has had the same idea as us. Look – there's a table over there in the corner. Hurry up, before somebody else grabs it.'

Frances narrowed her eyes as she smiled at him, making no move to dash inside the café. 'D'you know what we really ought to do, if you're bent on being a real Blackpool tripper? We should eat them out of the paper.'

'What, the fish as well?'

'Why not? That's what the hoi polloi do.'

'OK then; I'm game if you are,' Adrian grinned. 'This is certainly a first for me. Come on – let's get in the queue.'

'I hope we don't see any of your parishioners,' whispered Frances as they moved nearer to the gleaming chromium and tile counter. 'Whatever would they say?'

'Who cares?' laughed Adrian. 'Look, it's our turn. Go on – you ask. I don't know what to ask for.'

'Fish and chips twice, please,' recited Frances, as she had heard the people in front of her say. If she were honest, she, also, was not in the habit of frequenting fish and chip queues. At one time, when she was going through a rather snooty phase in her early teens, she would have protested that she wouldn't be seen dead in one. But she had matured a lot since that time, and today was a day for being reckless. 'Salt and vinegar, please,' she added.

'Cod or haddock, Miss?'

'Oh – er – haddock, I think. What about you, Adrian?'

'Yes, haddock for me, too.' Adrian's eyes were gleaming with delight.

'And a carton of mushy peas,' said Frances, as an afterthought.

'But how are we going to eat them?' whispered Adrian. 'We can't use our fingers for those.'

They were provided with a tiny plastic fork each, so that would have to suffice. Adrian watched Frances as she sprinkled first salt, from a giant metal shaker, then vinegar, in a red-topped bottle, on to the steaming fish and chips, then he did likewise. The assistant wrapped them, first in greaseproof paper, then in an outer covering of newspaper.

'We've nothing to drink,' Adrian pointed out; so they bought two bottles of fizzy cream soda, complete with straws, then Adrian pocketed the change from two half-crown pieces.

'What do we do now?' he laughed as they stood outside on the pavement, Frances holding the large newspaper parcel and Adrian a bottle of pop in each hand.

'We find somewhere to sit, that's what,' said Frances. 'On the prom, I think. I draw the line at eating them in the street. Besides we've got the pop to carry.'

But, as they walked seawards, dozens of holiday-makers all around them were enjoying fish and chips straight from the paper, many of them paying no heed to where they threw their rubbish. It was no wonder that Blackpool had a reputation for being an untidy town.

They found a vacant seat overlooking the sea, just across the road from Woolworth's. 'Just look at them all,' said Adrian, pointing towards the crowds of folk on the sands, packed so tightly together in places that it looked as though you couldn't put a pin between them. Men and women were sprawled on deckchairs, others, more frugally minded – deckchairs cost money! – were sitting on striped towels or raincoats, whilst children made sand pies and castles, or paddled in the rock pools or the shallows of the incoming tide. 'All herded together like sheep.' Adrian shook his head wonderingly. 'Why don't they spread out a bit? There are seven miles of sand to go at, after all.'

'They always do that,' answered Frances. 'The stretch between North Pier and Central Pier is always crowded. But they seem to like it that way. The herd instinct, I suppose. Perhaps they feel safer in a crowd, who knows? There'll be a great exodus in a little while though, when the tide catches up with them. Never mind, eh. They're happy, aren't they?'

'And so am I, Frances,' said Adrian, placing his hand over hers. 'Aren't you?'

'You bet I am,' she smiled back at him. 'And that must be one of the best meals I've ever had. Come on – didn't you say you wanted to go on North Pier?'

They deposited their rubbish in a nearby bin before sampling the pleasures of North Pier. It was the first time Adrian had been on the pier; and for Frances, too, it was as though she was experiencing it all for the first time. The bracing north-west breeze, increasing in intensity as they approached the jetty, the raucous cries of the swooping seagulls, the crash of the waves against the girders, the strains of a brass band playing in the pavilion, and, as they gazed back towards the town, the panoramic view of Blackpool – the hotels, boarding houses and seafront shops, stretching north and south in a long, long row; the cream and red Woolworth building; the cars and buses, and the trams sliding along the silver track; the milling crowds; and, dominating it all, the Tower, for more than sixty years the symbol of Blackpool.

'Magnificent, isn't it?' said Adrian. 'I would never have said it was a beautiful place, but it has a splendour all of its own, seen from here. I'm so glad I came to Blackpool.'

'And I'm glad you came, too,' said Frances, giving his arm a squeeze.

They returned to her flat, and as Megan was on duty at the hospital they had the place to themselves. They kissed and embraced on the settee, with ever-growing fervour, but Adrian made no suggestion that they should move into the bedroom. And, for that, Frances could not help but admire him. She could tell from the look of ardour in his eyes that his desire was every bit as strong as her own, but she knew that when she walked up the aisle as his bride – whenever that might be – it would be as a virgin. And that, she told herself, was the way it should be.

Chapter 12

'My parents would like to meet you,' said Adrian, one evening in June. 'I've told them so much about you, so – how about it? I could take a couple of weeks off in August and we could spend some time in Yorkshire. See your relations at the same time, if you like.'

Frances agreed that it was a great idea. It would be lovely to see Auntie Alice and Uncle Jack, as well as her cousin, Len, and his family.

Adrian decided, as they were travelling by car, that they would take a scenic route, stopping off at places of interest on the way. They lunched at Skipton, a busy market town of grey-stone buildings at the very edge of the moors. It was market day and they wandered amongst the stalls, which were strung out on the cobblestones on either side of the main street. There were stalls selling farm produce – chickens, eggs, butter and lemon curd; fruit and vegetables of every variety; pots and pans and crockery; towels, bedding, and materials in myriad colours and textures, seconds, many of them, from the nearby mills of both Lancashire and Yorkshire; and stalls with a mouth-watering selection of chocolates and homemade sweets.

'Yorkshire Mixture!' said Frances in delight, stopping by a sweet stall with its trays of treacle toffee, butterscotch, fudge and coconut ice prominently displayed. She pointed to a huge jar at the rear. 'You can't come to Yorkshire without buying a quarter of Yorkshire Mixture. Didn't you used to buy them when you were a little boy, Adrian?'

'Indeed I did,' he replied, 'and many times since. But a quarter won't go very far. We'd better have half a pound. And I never can resist those liquorice whirls. Now, those really take me back to my childhood. Let's have a couple of those as well.'

As the assistant tipped the jar over the scales, spilling out its contents of mixed boiled sweets – pear drops, butter drops, mint humbugs in black and brown stripes, multi-coloured fish, acid drops and aniseed – Frances thought that this was one of the things she loved about Adrian; his delight in the small, insignificant pleasures of life. What other man of her acquaintance would derive such enjoyment from the purchase of half a pound of sweets? And yet there was a much deeper, reflective side to him as well. She was lucky, so very lucky, to have met Adrian.

They had lunch at Whitaker's café, an old-fashioned establishment at the end of the main street, with a confectioner's shop downstairs and the café above, up a steep winding staircase. The gammon, egg and chips, and the curd tart to follow, were most appetising, so much so that Frances felt she could really do with a brisk walk instead of a ride in a car.

They did, however, make a stop at Bolton Abbey, a few miles east, to see the ruined priory. It stood near to the River Wharfe in a lovely setting of wooded hills and verdant meadows. Frances had visited the place before, but not for several years, and she was struck again by the quietude and air of serenity which seemed to emanate from the very stones of the ruins. This was the start of Wharfedale, a picturesque valley of limestone gorges, quaint hump-backed bridges and swirling stretches of river crossed by stepping stones. Frances would have liked to linger there, but Adrian insisted that the route would be out of their way and they must press on to reach Leeds before tea time.

'Another time, darling,' he promised her. 'We may even come back here later this week. But we've a whole lifetime ahead of us, haven't we?'

They headed now over Blubberhouses Moor – a wild stretch of bracken and heather-clad moorland where lone sheep grazed amidst the outcrops of limestone rock – before turning south towards the city of Leeds. The approach road was from the north, so they were able to avoid the city centre, arriving in Headingley in the late afternoon.

Adrian's mother seemed rather older than Frances had expected, although she might have guessed that the woman could be by no means young, having a married daughter a few years older than Adrian. There was only Mrs Glover to welcome them as Mr Glover was at work; he was employed as a local government officer in the city.

'Nobbut a tram ride away, down Woodhouse Lane,' Mrs Glover told Frances cheerfully, in her homely, quite pronounced Yorkshire accent, which took Frances back to her childhood days in Haliford. Iris, indeed, still retained more than a trace of the accent, although her tone was considerably more strident than that of Mrs Glover. 'He's bin looking forward to meeting you, has Bill. He has that! Na' then . . . a nice cup of tea for us, eh? Sit yerselves down an' I'll go and put t'kettle on.'

Adrian resembled his mother more so than his father, Frances realised when she met Bill Glover an hour or so later. Adrian was of the same build as his mother, not very tall and a little stocky, with the same candid grey eyes and winning – though rather hesitant at first – smile; whereas his father was tall and inclined to stoop, and, until you got to know him, appeared somewhat forbidding. He, too, seemed older than his years. Frances guessed that they must both be in their early sixties, roughly the same age as her own mother. Mr Glover could not be far from retirement.

It was obvious that they were very proud of their son. They were both life-long Methodists and they had been delighted, Mrs Glover explained, 'when our Adrian felt the "call".'

'Aye, he was allus a clever lad,' Mr Glover added. 'We thought he might end up as a teacher, like our Irene, but when the Lord calls I reckon you haven't much choice but to obey. Leastways, that's how me and Doris see it, don't we, luv?'

It was just as well that they did, thought Frances. Many parents, ambitious for their children, might have looked askance at a son deciding to go into the ministry of the church – especially the Methodist Church, which was not noted for awarding large stipends – rather than a more lucrative profession. But Mr and Mrs Glover took the view that their son was following a much higher calling. Frances could not help but be amused, though, at their quiet boasting, and at Adrian's embarrassment as he, alternately, cast his eyes heavenwards or looked down at his plate. She was reminded of the way Iris bragged about her – when she wasn't criticising her! – although Iris was much more vociferous than these two. Frances knew how disconcerting it could be and she was not surprised when Adrian tried to change the subject.

'Yes, my sister, Irene's, a teacher,' he said, although Frances already knew this. 'I told you, didn't I, Frances? At least she used to be. She doesn't teach now, of course.'

Frances wondered why he should say 'of course'. She knew that Irene's children were both at school so there would be nothing to prevent her going back to teaching, surely, if she wished to do so.

'Why doesn't she teach now?' Frances ventured. 'I mean . . .' she stumbled, as three pairs of eyes looked at her enquiringly. '. . . she could easily get a job, couldn't she? There's such a shortage of teachers.'

'Our Irene doesn't need to go out to work. Her husband has a good job,' said Mrs Glover, though not in a boastful sort of way. 'He's an accountant. He earns good money and I know he'd be most upset if he thought his wife had to go out to work.'

No, maybe she doesn't have to, thought Frances. But supposing she wants to? She kept quiet, however, whilst Mrs Glover continued.

'Besides, when you get married your place is in the home, isn't it, Frances?' Adrian's mother smiled at her so innocently that Frances knew there was no hint of censure in her words, nor could she possibly be aware of Frances's mildly rebellious thoughts. 'You have to be there to keep things nice for your husband and family. I'm sure I don't know how these wives manage who go out to work. Summat has to suffer, I'm sure o' that. No, our Irene's quite happy

176

in her home, just as I've always been. We could have done with the money, mind, when we were first wed. But Bill here said, "No wife of mine'll ever go out to work." And I never have done.'

Not even during the war? thought Frances. She knew that many women who had never worked before had taken employment in munitions factories. But her Aunt Alice had never done so, and she was one who quite easily could have worked. Aunt Alice was just such another as Mrs Glover, there to dance attendance on her husband, the 'bread winner'. Frances had always known that this was a trait of Yorkshire husbands, to keep the wife, the 'little woman', busy 'in t'kitchin'. Adrian was a Yorkshireman, too . . . Frances, for the first time since she had met him, was feeling a shade defiant. She stared fixedly at the plate of ham salad in front of her, not trusting herself to speak. But they were such nice people, Mr and Mrs Glover. Already she liked them very much, and she did love Adrian.

'So you're a teacher an' all, Frances?' She looked up to see Mr Glover smiling at her encouragingly. 'Adrian's told us you used to teach in Haliford?'

'Just outside, yes.'

'And now you're teaching in Blackpool, eh, near to our Adrian's chapel?' It always sounded strange, to Frances's ears, to hear the word chapel. It was a real old Methodist word, referring to their place of worship. The 'chapel' was the building, Adrian had explained to her, whereas the 'church' was the body of people who worshipped there, but more and more people of modern outlook nowadays called the building the church.

'For the moment, Dad,' said Adrian. 'I don't suppose I shall be in Blackpool for more than another year, then it'll be all change. And Frances'll have to get used to being a minister's wife, not a teacher.'

Frances gave him a questioning look, but Adrian smiled back ingenuously. He did not seem aware that he had said anything untoward.

'You've not fixed a wedding date yet, though, have you, lad?' asked his mother.

'No, not yet, Mum. You'll be the first to know.'

'Anyroad, Adrian tells us you're a Yorkshire lass,' said his father, 'and that's all to the good, isn't it, Doris? She's one of us.' He nodded at his wife before turning back to Frances. 'Born and bred in Haliford, weren't you, luv?'

Before she had a chance to answer Adrian spoke for her. 'Yes, "My girl's a Yorkshire girl, Yorkshire through and through . . ." ' He was quietly singing the words of the old music-hall song.

'Oh, I wouldn't say that,' retorted Frances. She was still smiling, but, deep down, she was feeling very contrary. 'Not through and through. I think of myself as a Blackpudlian now, more than a Yorkshire lass. I've lived there since I was seven, you know.' She had been tempted to say, 'tha knows', but stopped herself just in time. It would have seemed as though she was making fun of Mr and Mrs Glover and the way they talked.

'But you were at college near here, and you taught here for two years,' Adrian pointed out.

'Yes, I know, but Blackpool's my home now, isn't it?' Frances, to her dismay, realised that she sounded a trifle irritable. 'Well, we're not going to fall out about it, are we?' she said, trying to smile easily at them all. 'Lancashire, Yorkshire, what's the odds? It's only just across the Pennines, isn't it?'

'I've heard it said by folks from your neck of the woods,' said Mr Glover, with a gleam in his eye, 'that the only good thing to come out of Yorkshire is the road to Lancashire. That's your view, is it, Frances?' They all laughed and Frances felt a shade embarrassed.

'Of course not,' she answered. 'I've met Adrian, haven't I, and he's a very good thing that's come out of Yorkshire.'

'Well said, lass,' said Mr Glover, beaming at her. 'And d'you happen to know the next words of that song our Adrian was singing? "Eeh by gum, she's a champion!" And I reckon you are. Our Adrian's picked a grand 'un, and you're very welcome here. Isn't she, Doris?' Mrs Glover smiled and nodded her agreement. She seemed to agree with everything he said.

'You've scored a hit with my father,' said Adrian the next morning, as they drove along the road which led to Harrogate. They intended to spend most of the day in the spa town before visiting Adrian's sister and family at their home on its outskirts. 'He says you're a gradely lass.'

Frances laughed. 'I like him as well. In fact, I like both your parents. They've made me so welcome, Adrian.'

'And why shouldn't they? You're their future daughter-in-law, aren't you? The only one they're likely to have.' He took his hand from the steering wheel briefly to clasp her own.

'He's a real Yorkshireman, your dad, isn't he? The way he talks; he sounds just like my Uncle Jack – you'll be meeting him later this week – and I remember my own father spoke just the same. What I can remember of him, that is; he was killed when I was six.'

Adrian nodded. 'It's a pity about your dad. My father wasn't called up until nearly the end of the war – because of his age, you see – and he didn't go abroad. He puts a lot of it on, you know; his accent, I mean.' He laughed. 'I don't suppose for one moment he talks like that at work, not in the office. But Mum's never changed, nor would I want her to. She's always been the same, always there when I needed her. I remember when Dad was in the army, how reassuring it was to come home from school and find her there, in the kitchen, in her flowered pinny. Once – just once, mind – I got home and she wasn't there. The meeting at chapel had gone on longer than it should – Women's Bright Hour, they used to call it in those days – and I can see her now, bustling up the street in her tweed coat and brown felt hat. Nearly running, she was, because she knew I'd be standing on the doorstep. I wasn't any too happy, I can tell you. But looking back on it I realise it was a bit selfish of me.'

'More than a bit, I'd say, Adrian. And I dare say she made a big fuss, didn't she, putting herself in the wrong, getting you a nice hot cup of tea because you'd been left standing in the cold?'

'Yes . . . I suppose she did.' Adrian took his eyes from the road, momentarily, to glance keenly at her. 'What's got into you? You're suggesting I've been spoiled, are you, by a doting mother? Well, maybe I have, but I'm not the only one, am I? From what your mother has let slip, and your Josie, I gather there was a certain little lady who got far more of her own way than was good for her.'

Adrian's words were spoken lightheartedly and Frances was forced to smile. 'Touché, Adrian,' she said. 'Sorry, I asked for that. No, of course I wasn't suggesting you were spoiled, no more so than I was, at any rate. It's your mother's attitude I was questioning really rather than yours. She has no other life, has she, apart from you and your father, and your sister?'

'She has the church, or "chapel" as she still calls it.'

'Yes, I know.' Frances had to suppress a tut of exasperation. 'But what I mean is, her life is so . . . so narrow, isn't it?'

He looked at her sharply again, and this time his glance was cool. 'I don't understand what you mean. Go on . . . explain yourself.'

'I can't, Adrian. Not now. Just concentrate on your driving.' They were approaching the town and the traffic was a little heavier; she must not distract him. She was aware of an air of tension building between them, the like of which she had never known before. She could not allow this to happen, not with her and Adrian. She reached out and touched his arm. 'Sorry. . .' she said.

He smiled at her fleetingly and she was relieved to see that his eyes were warm again. 'It's OK, love. Tell me later, eh?'

And that was what she tried to do as they strolled through the Valley Gardens in Harrogate. 'I wasn't criticising your mum, Adrian, honestly I wasn't. If she's happy with her life the way it is then that's fine, but . . .'

'But what?'

'But . . .' Frances took a deep breath. 'But it wouldn't do for me. I would want more than that.'

Adrian pulled her closer to him, planting a kiss on her

180

cheek. 'What are you talking about, you silly girl? You've got more, haven't you? A lot more. You're a teacher. My mother never had the chance to go to college. She had to leave school when she was fourteen and work in the mill.'

'So did mine; so did a lot of them,' retorted Frances. 'That's not the point. What I'm trying to say is, how long am I going to be a teacher? You're talkng as though I'll be giving it all up when I— when we get married.'

'Well, you will, won't you, naturally?'

'What do you mean, naturally?'

'Well, for a start, we won't be in Blackpool, will we? When I get another living it will be somewhere else. We'll have to move and so – naturally – I thought you would give up teaching and help me with my parish work.'

'Be an unpaid curate, you mean?'

'We don't have curates in the Methodist Church.'

'Oh, don't be so difficult, Adrian! You know damn well – sorry – you know very well what I mean. Anyway, it's the Church of England I've had most dealings with till I met you. And I've seen them, any amount of them, vicars' wives – arranging the flowers, sick visiting, teaching in Sunday school, running the Mothers' Union, just as though they had no lives of their own.'

'But . . .' Adrian stood still, staring at her in amazement. 'Of course that's the way it is. Didn't you realise? If you marry a vicar – or a minister, whatever – then you marry his job as well.' His grey eyes were puzzled rather than angry. 'Come on, love, let's sit down. We must get this sorted out. I had no idea you felt like this. We must talk about it.' He led her to a vacant seat overlooking the rose garden.

'Perhaps that's something we've not done enough of,' said Frances quietly. 'Talking about it.'

'Yes, perhaps you're right.' Adrian nodded thoughtfully. 'But I took it for granted that you would want to . . . Maybe I shouldn't have done?'

'No, I don't think you should, Adrian. Nobody likes to be taken for granted.'

'But you help me already, don't you? You're in the choir,

181

and there's the Dramatic Society we were thinking of starting. You seem to be happy with it all, love. Naturally, I assumed that when we were married you would—'

'But I'm a *teacher*, Adrian,' Frances interrupted. 'I enjoy teaching. I want to go on doing it. I went to college and trained for two years because I wanted to teach. I don't want to . . . to give it all up. Maybe your sister is quite content to stay at home, but I don't think I would be.'

'My sister? Oh, so that's what has started all this, is it? Yes, I remember, at tea time . . . So that's why you went all peculiar.'

'It's partly that,' replied Frances. 'It started me thinking. You see, I like teaching.'

Adrian took hold of her hand. 'In spite of Miss Walsh?' he said with a gleam in his eye. 'I rather thought you'd be glad to get away from her.'

'I have got away from her, for six weeks. But I'll be ready for the fray again come September. I'm not saying I would want to go on teaching for ever and ever. I certainly wouldn't want to end up an embittered old spinster like . . . some of them. What I'm trying to say is that I've got a life of my own. I've got a career, and I want to carry on with it.'

'You're not keen on the idea of being a clergy wife then?' Adrian's eyes were unfathomable. She could not tell whether or not he was joking. She took hold of his hand, fondling each square-tipped finger as though she were counting on them.

'Yes, yes, of course I am. With this particular clergyman, not any old vicar.' She kissed him lightly on the lips. 'But I'm me as well, Frances Goodwin, and I want to go on being me, not just "the minister's wife".'

'You'll be Frances Glover by then,' he told her, pulling her head down on to his shoulder. 'Oh, darling, I'm sorry. I had no idea you felt like that. But we mustn't quarrel about it. We must try to reach a compromise. Surely we can do that. Perhaps you could get a part-time teaching post? Depending on where we are, of course. But I did hope, in a year or two, that we would start a family. You would have to be at home then, wouldn't you, darling, looking after the children?'

Children . . . They were not even married yet, had not even fixed the wedding date. Frances realised that they had never talked much about their plans for the future. Unusual, maybe, for an engaged couple, but Adrian had been more concerned with his immediate parochial affairs. Now they were looking a long way ahead, too far, it seemed, for Frances. Although she did love Adrian; she had no doubt about that.

'Let's just take things as they come, shall we?' she said. 'The main thing is that we should understand one another. I didn't mean to blurt all this out, not so suddenly, but it's as well that you should know how I feel. I do love you, Adrian. But it's just . . .' She shrugged.

'It's all right, darling. I understand,' he assured her.

But did he understand? Did she fully understand herself what was troubling her? Frances Glover, she repeated inside her head. It sounded rather strange, and yet it was not so much different from Frances Goodwin. The words of one of her mother's old sayings suddenly flashed into her mind. 'Change the name but not the letter, change for worse and not for better.' Now, why on earth should she be thinking that? She had not heard her mother quote it this time, not about her and Adrian. Most certainly not; her mother thought the sun shone out of Adrian.

His sister, Irene, resembled her father – tall, slimly built and dark-haired. Frances was made very welcome in their semidetached house, one almost identical in size and layout, and with a similar garden area, to the one where Mr and Mrs Glover lived. Irene's family typified the average, happy suburban family: dark-suited father coming in from a busy day at the office, two reasonably well-behaved children – a boy and a girl, Mark and Carol – and a mother busily engaged in the kitchen, often missing a good deal of the conversation that was going on, in her absence, in the living room.

Frances offered to help with the washing up, otherwise it was obvious that Irene would have tackled it all on her own; just as, the previous day, she had helped Mrs Glover. It was doubtful whether Bill Glover or Derek Patterson, Irene's husband, had ever washed or dried a pot in their lives, let alone buttered a slice of bread or boiled an egg or ironed a shirt. But Irene, as her mother had intimated, appeared very contented with her lot. She questioned Frances about her teaching post, as one teacher to another, and seemed very interested in the modern methods, only so she could compare them, however, with what was currently happening in Mark and Carol's school. She was very relieved, Irene said laughingly, not to be part of what she termed the 'rat race' any more. She was happy to serve on the PTFA committee, though, which was very concerned with the welfare of the children.

'But it will be Parish Committees for you, won't it, Frances, for now and evermore?' she said, laughing again. Irene seemed to laugh before and after every statement. 'Family Committee, Property and Finance Committee, Overseas Missions Committee – you name 'em, the Methodists have got 'em. I'm surprised they don't have a committee to decide how many committees they need. Still, you must have known all this before you decided to marry Adrian?'

Frances smiled and nodded. 'Er . . . yes. I was C of E, though. I don't remember quite so many committees, although I've not been actively involved for quite some time.'

'You'll be actively involved now, all right. You'll have your hands full with all those felt-hatted women.' Frances laughed at that. Irene was a lovely bubbly person. You couldn't help but like her. 'You won't have time for teaching, will you?' She didn't wait for an answer. 'When are you getting married? Adrian didn't say. I expect it will be next summer, won't it? That's what Mum thought. Ministers usually change over in August, don't they? We've just got a new minister. He seems very nice, quite young, like our Adrian. Well, he's not actually moved into the parish yet, but I've met him. I'm one of the church stewards, you see.'

'Oh yes, I see.' Irene, like all the family, was obviously very steeped in Methodism. 'I'm not quite sure when we'll be getting married. It could be next summer, I suppose. We haven't really talked about it very much.' Frances was aware that Irene was looking at her rather oddly. 'I mean, it all depends on Adrian, doesn't it, on where his next living will be?'

As soon as she had spoken the words she realised they sounded very feeble. Why should their getting married depend on Adrian's move? They could get married wherever they were, couldn't they? Before Irene could remind her of this she hurried on to say, 'Yes, I dare say it will be next summer. At all events we'll let you know in good time, then you can buy a new hat. Not a felt one, though!' She smiled warmly at Adrian's sister. She had taken an instant liking to her in spite of the young woman's tendency to stereotype her already as a clergy wife. And after all, why shouldn't she? That was what she was going to be . . . wasn't it?

Irene laughed. 'No, indeed! I've always fancied one as big as a cartwheel – like the nobs wear at Ascot – with masses of ribbons and flowers. And our Carol is dying to be a bridesmaid.'

And so, it appeared, were Len and Karen's two girls, Linda and Susan. Frances and Adrian visited the family later in the holiday, after they had left Leeds behind and were staying with Aunt Alice and Uncle Jack Rawlinson in Haliford. Len was cousin to Frances and Josie. Frances remembered, in the dim recesses of her mind, that her sister had at one time been quite keen on Len, then he had let her down badly by marrying a girl called Pamela who had been an evacuee friend of Josie. But that was all a long time ago, and Len was now very happily married to Karen, another young woman he had met through Josie. Linda, the daughter of his first wife, was twelve, and Susan was five.

All around her, it seemed to Frances, were happy

families, though this family was different from Irene's. Len was an electrician and when he came home from work he was dressed in overalls, not a grey business suit. But he sat down in an armchair, just as Derek had done, whilst his wife was busy in the kitchen preparing a superb steak and mushroom pie with heaps of fluffy mashed potatoes, tasty gravy and garden peas. Frances admired Karen's culinary skills and told her so as the two of them – inevitably – washed up afterwards.

'Oh, it's nothing,' said the young woman airily. 'I'm used to it now. I wasn't much good at first, mind, but I went to evening classes for cookery and now I can do it as easy as winking. You've got to be able to cook, haven't you? It's only fair to your husband. He wants a nice meal on the table when he comes home from work, doesn't he?'

'Er, yes . . . I suppose so,' said Frances uneasily. 'I'm not very good at cooking, I must admit. I can rustle up a meal of sorts, but nothing complicated. I don't really enjoy it, you see.'

'Oh, you will, you will. When you get married it'll make all the difference. You'll be doing it for the man you love.' Frances glanced across at Karen with a wry smile, which she quickly removed because she could see at once there was nothing ironic in the young woman's words. They were uttered in complete sincerity. 'You'll soon learn to cook. There's nothing to it, honestly. And your Adrian's such a love, isn't he? Fancy, a clergyman! I was a bit worried when Len first told me. I thought, oh crumbs! I'll have to mind my Ps and Qs. We don't go to church much now, you see. But he's quite normal, isn't he?'

Frances couldn't help but laugh. 'Yes, quite normal.'

'Oh, I think it's lovely, and now we've got a wedding to look forward to. Linda and Susan are dying to be brides-maids. Well, Susan is, at any rate. Linda's at the age where she's a bit embarrassed at dressing up. Not that we want to be pushy or anything, but – well – Len is your first cousin, isn't he?'

'We've not made any definite arrangements yet,' Frances said, concentrating hard on polishing the stainless-steel pan in her hands. Everything in Karen's kitchen gleamed. 'But I'll bear Susan in mind, I promise, and Linda too, if she likes.' She felt as though she was being swept along on a tide of enthusiasm which, as yet, she could not share. What's the matter with me? she thought for the umpteenth time that week. It wasn't as if she didn't love Adrian.

She watched as Karen stood on tiptoe, reaching up to place the pans on a shelf above the primrose-yellow breakfast counter. The kitchen was the height of modernity in springtime colours of yellow and green. Karen, too, resembled more a star from a Hollywood movie than a common or garden housewife. She reminded Frances of Doris Day and she almost expected her, at any moment, to burst into song. Her auburn hair was newly washed, curling prettily round her baby-doll face. Karen was only a couple of years younger than Josie – she must be about twenty seven or so now – but looked much younger. Her full skirt, held out stiffly with layers of petticoats, rustled as she moved, and the apron that covered it had deep frills and a heart-shaped top and pocket. Megan had an identical one, Frances recalled; and she was another one who couldn't wait to become a fully-fledged housewife instead of merely playing at it.

Women were constantly being exhorted, in the weekly magazines, to keep their husbands happy by looking as alluring as they could when he came home from work, and to be available in the bedroom as well as in the kitchen, it was intimated. This would ensure that he would not stray. Karen was obviously obeying this advice to the letter.

'I bet you can't wait, can you, to give up that boring old teaching job?' she said. 'I know I never want to see the inside of an office again as long as I live.' Frances kept her own counsel. She was getting very used to doing so this week.

She did, however, very daringly make a stand with her Aunt Alice later that week.

'Like I said to yer mam when she told me you were so set on going to college and being a teacher, "What's the

point?" I said. "What's the good of all that there education?" ' Aunt Alice was well into the age-old theme that
Frances had heard many times before, whilst Adrian was
off down the garden with Uncle Jack, admiring the vegetable patch and the rose bed. ' "She'll only go and get wed
in a year or two," I said, "and what's the good of it all
then?" '

'Education's never wasted, Auntie,' said Frances, but
Alice didn't appear to hear her.

'But yer mam wouldn't listen, not where you were
concerned. You were always the apple of her eye, but I'm
not condemning her for that, mind. "If our Frances wants
to be a teacher then that's what she's going to be," she said.
"I'm not going to deny her t'chances I never had." But I
was right, wasn't I? Three year you've been at it, that's all,
and now you're giving it up to get wed. Not that I'm
blaming you, luv. I think it's wonderful. And your Adrian's
a lovely lad. You're a very lucky young woman.'

'But I won't be giving it up, Auntie. I'm not giving up
teaching. Why should I?'

Alice Rawlinson gaped at her niece. 'Why should you?
Because you'll have a home to run, that's why, and children
in a year or two, God willing. And being married to a vicar
you'll have all sorts o' church things to see to. Our vicar's
wife's a real godsend to him. Some of us think she does a
darned sight more in t'parish than he does.'

'Adrian's a minister, Auntie Alice, not a vicar.'

'Same dog washed, I reckon.'

'And the parish is his responsibility, not mine.' Frances
was aware that she sounded more than a little peevish, but
she couldn't help it. She had heard so much this week of
what she must and must not do as a minister's wife.

'What on earth's got into you, girl?' Alice spoke crossly,
in a way Frances had never heard in all the time she had
known her. 'Don't you love this nice young man? Don't
you want to marry him? It seems to me that if you don't
want to help him with his work . . . well, you'd better think
about it, that's all.'

'I'm sorry, Auntie Alice.' Frances put down the pot towel

– goodness! the number of pots she had dried this week – and started to help her aunt to stack away the plates and dishes. Alice was banging them about, she noticed, with undue force. 'I didn't mean to answer you back like that. Of course I love Adrian. Of course I want to marry him. But times are changing, you know. Women have careers now.'

'Married ones don't, not in my book.'

'Yes, they do, Auntie. And teaching is a career that you can easily fit in round a family.'

'Huh! You have long enough holidays, I'll grant you that.'

Frances ignored this time-worn remark. 'And Adrian agrees with me that I should carry on teaching when we get married. For a while, anyway, possibly part time.' This was the compromise they had reached, although she knew that Adrian was not wholehearted about it.

'Oh, well then, it's none of my business, is it? Not if Adrian says it's all right. But I've never known a vicar's wife to be anything but a vicar's wife. Times are changing, though, as you say, lass.' Frances was glad to see that her little rosy-cheeked aunt was smiling again. 'Blessed if I can keep up with 'em sometimes.'

That was the trouble. Her aunt had never moved with the times. It was her view, in common with many of her generation – Mrs Glover was another example – that you could have a career, or marriage, but not both. But that seemed to be the view of Irene and Karen as well, both of them contemporaries of Frances. It wasn't that she was so dedicated to her teaching career that she intended to carry on with it for ever and ever. As she had said to Adrian, she dreaded the thought of ending up like some of the teachers she knew. But she valued her independence. She hated to think she might lose it and become just a boring old housewife.

These thoughts, and more, were flashing through Frances's mind as they drove home across the Yorkshire Moors at the end of their holiday. Josie had always been an independent girl. She had managed to combine a successful career with a happy marriage. Jim helped her, though, unlike the majority of husbands; they shared the housework as they shared everything. If she were to confide in Josie, however, her sister would be very quick to denounce her as self-centred, an accusation she had levelled at her many times before.

Her mother, too, was one of the most independent people Frances had ever known, until she became ill, that was. She had run her boarding house practically single-handed. Admittedly, she had been a widow and therefore had had no choice. But Frances guessed that if her father had lived the outcome would have been the same. She dare not voice her doubts to her mother, though. Adrian, to Iris, was beyond reproach.

And why was she having doubts at all? Frances didn't know. She only knew she was in a muddle and she would have to talk it over with somebody. She decided she would have a chat with Marjorie Aspinall. They would be back at school in a week or two, in fact they had a staff meeting next week; and she and Marjorie, despite the difference in their ages, had become good friends. Marjorie had carried on with her career throughout her marriage, although Frances continued to catch hints that the latter was none too happy. Yes, she would have a chat with Marjorie. Even if she couldn't help, it would be good to unburden herself.

But when she set eyes on Marjorie at the staff meeting the following week Frances realised it might well be her friend who was in need of succour. Marjorie's cheek was swollen and the flesh around one eye, though partially hidden behind dark glasses, was a purplish-yellow hue. Frances went cold with shock. She had had no idea that things were so bad.

Chapter 13

'I should watch where I'm walking, shouldn't I?' said Marjorie, before any of the staff had a chance to ask her how she had come by her injury. 'I fell off a step coming out of the butcher's – not round here; one in town. Tripped over my own big feet, I dare say, and before I could say "Jack Robinson", there I was, lying on the pavement outside.'

The members of staff were very concerned. Had she seen the doctor? Was anyone to blame? Should she really be here? She didn't look at all well . . .

'I'm as right as rain,' Marjorie assured them. 'It helps to take my mind off it, coming here. And the bruise will have gone by next week when term starts.' Frances noticed, however, that she was very quiet, not nearly so forthcoming with her sensible suggestions at the meeting as she usually was.

'You didn't swallow all that rubbish about falling off a step, did you?' Marjorie said, later that afternoon, as she and Frances walked towards their classrooms. 'I thought it might sound better, though, than the usual lame excuse of walking into a cupboard door.'

'You mean . . . you didn't fall off a step?' Frances had already reproached herself for jumping to a wrong conclusion. The reason Marjorie had given sounded plausible, although Frances had noticed one or two dubious looks from the staff, as well as the genuine sympathy. 'It wasn't . . . Surely it couldn't have been your . . .?'

'My husband? Yes – the very same.' Marjorie was blinking her eyes rapidly behind the dark glasses. Frances was horrified as well as being slightly embarrassed. It was the very first time her friend had shown much emotion at all.

'Come in here, would you, dear?' Marjorie opened her own classroom door. 'I'll have to talk to somebody. I don't usually, as you know. I've kept it all to myself, but I feel as though I'll go mad if I don't talk. D'you think they believed me?' she asked, leaning her elbows on her desk, looking across anxiously at Frances, who perched on the edge of one of the children's desks. 'Actually, I'm not all that bothered whether they believe me or not, not any more. Oh, to hell with it; I'll have to take these things off.' She snatched off the dark glasses, rubbing furiously at her eyes.

'Yes, I'm sure they believed you,' said Frances. 'Why shouldn't they? I did . . . But I'm so sorry, Marjorie. I had no idea things were so bad. I mean to say, your Kenneth – he looks so . . . so respectable. And he works at the Town Hall, doesn't he?'

Marjorie gave a hoot of laughter, though it was a mirthless one. 'Honestly, Frances; you're priceless. Do you really think because a fellow works in an office he doesn't know how to use his fists? Knocking the wife about isn't confined to your dustbin men or street sweepers or lorry drivers, you know. Although I've got to admit it's the first time he's done it.'

She stared into space, until Frances asked tentatively, 'What's the problem, Marjorie? I mean . . . I guessed you didn't get on very well. But I never thought for one moment that Kenneth was violent.'

Frances had never had much conversation with Kenneth Aspinall, but Marjorie had introduced them at one of the school functions, when he had come to collect his wife in the car. He was tall and distinguished-looking and smartly turned out – the antithesis of his wife, it might be said, who, even when she was supposed to be dressed up, always looked vaguely untidy; never dirty or slovenly, but just as though she had got ready in a hurry. Frances had thought her husband looked forbidding, and he definitely looked as though he could be moody.

'It's the first time he's ever hit me,' said Marjorie, 'although there have been times when we've nearly come to blows, I can tell you. Many's the time I've felt like landing out at him myself or throwing something at him, but I've managed to keep the lid on my temper. It's the moodiness I can't stand, you see, dear.' So I was right, thought Frances. 'The brooding silences he goes into, for no reason at all. And there's no getting through to him.'

'Didn't you know this when you married him?' asked Frances. Her friend was such a chatty person, and not moody at all. She couldn't imagine her wanting to marry someone who was the direct opposite.

'Yes, I suppose I did,' replied Marjorie. 'The strong, silent type, I thought. But I'd fallen in love with him, you see, and I thought it wouldn't matter.'

'Mmm. They do say opposites attract, don't they?'

'Yes, but it's as well to have a bit more in common than we've got. When I found that out it was too late.'

'But why did he hit you?'

'Something snapped, I suppose. There was a pile of ironing on the chair where he wanted to sit, and he'd already had to wait a few minutes for his tea. Oh, one thing led to another; you know how it does. He said I was a slut, the house was like a pigsty, and when I stood up to him, he landed me one.'

'But that's unforgivable, Marjorie, that he should hit you. Does he never think of helping you with the ironing and cooking and everything?'

'What? Huh, pigs might fly! Anyway, I'm on holiday at the moment, aren't I? I can't even make school an excuse. But that's not really the problem. We don't get on, that's the top and bottom of it; haven't done for years. Shall I tell you what it is that kills a marriage stone dead? It's lack of communication. It's not other women or poverty or sex – or the lack of it – or having an untidy home. It's not talking to one another; that's what drives the wedges in. And we stopped talking – really talking – years ago.'

'Oh dear.' Frances did not know what else to say. 'And what are you going to do about it?'

'What can I do, dear? I'm married to him, aren't I?'

'But . . . you don't need to be, not for ever, do you, if

you're so unhappy? I mean, couldn't you—'

'Get a divorce? No . . . no, of course not.'

'You're not a Catholic, are you?'

'No, you know I'm not. I'm not anything really. I'm not particularly religious at all. But I do believe that marriage is for life, and you can't start thinking about divorce when the going gets tough. And there are compensations.' Marjorie managed a weak smile and Frances guessed she was thinking about her little grandson, Robin, who was two years old. She had only the one child, her daughter Helen.

'What does Helen say?' asked Frances. 'Does she know you're so unhappy?'

'I think she might have guessed a little of it. But I don't talk to her about it. I can't. I saw her a few days ago – I couldn't stop her from coming round – and I told her the same tale about falling off a step. I think she believed me. It was Helen who made me go to the doctor's, and I do believe he swallowed it as well. It's strange, because I hate telling lies. But I couldn't admit to the truth.'

'But surely Kenneth must be sorry for what he's done?'

'Yes . . . yes, I think he is. He said he didn't mean it, and things are more or less on an even keel again now. But that doesn't alter the fact that, fundamentally, we're not right for one another. And I think we both know it.'

'Oh dear,' said Frances again. She felt so concerned for her friend that all her own worries, such as they were, had paled into insignificance.

'Cheer up,' said Marjorie. 'There's no point in both of us sitting around with long faces, is there? I don't intend to, I can tell you. I feel tons better already now I've talked to you; I do, really. Thanks for listening . . . And how about you, dear? You and Adrian had a good holiday in Yorkshire, did you? Thanks for the card. I'm glad you managed a day in Scarborough. It used to be one of our favourite places when Helen was small. It's not been all bad, you see. Anyway, that's quite enough about me. Have you fixed a date yet?'

'No . . . no, we haven't.'

'And what about Adrian? No sign of a move yet, to another parish? A living they call it, don't they?'

'No, I don't think he has anything in mind, not yet.'

Marjorie looked at her keenly. 'What's up? You've not fallen out, you two, have you?'

'Oh no, nothing like that,' Frances assured her. 'It's just that – well – I've been doing a lot of thinking during this holiday, and there are one or two things I'm not very sure about, not as sure as I should be, that is.'

'You mean . . . you're not sure you want to marry him?'

'Oh, yes – I want to marry him.'

'Well, what is it then?'

Frances sighed. 'It's hard to put into words. Anyway, I shouldn't be bothering you, Marjorie. You've enough to worry about.'

'Nonsense! You fire away, love. It'll give me something else to think about besides my own problems. Come on, spit it out. What's bothering you?'

Frances tried to explain, though it sounded very feeble; all about Karen and Irene, not to mention Adrian's mother, all so engrossed in the trappings of domesticity, and how she, Frances, didn't feel she would ever be able to have much enthusiasm for it all. Besides, there was her teaching career. 'I thought I'd talk to you about it, Marjorie,' she said, 'because it seemed to me that you had managed to cope with your career and your marriage as well. Now, after what you've told me, I'm not too sure.'

'Forget about me,' said Marjorie. 'What I do doesn't matter. I'm a fine example anyway, aren't I? It seems to me that you've some doubts as to whether you should marry Adrian at all. And if you are in any doubt, then I would say think again. Because marriage is for ever.'

'Oh, no. I love him. I want to marry him. But . . . I know it sounds silly, but . . . I haven't been swept off my feet by him.' She could see Marjorie's raised eyebrows and half-smile and she quickly went on to say, 'Yes, I knew it would sound daft, but I always thought that that was what would happen when I fell in love. I met Adrian, and I liked him, and he liked me. And – well – it just sort of grew from there. We were good friends first, but then our relationship changed and he asked me to marry him, and I suppose it was what I'd expected and so I said yes. And I knew my mother liked him.'

'You mustn't dream of marrying him just because your mother likes him.'

'Oh, no, no – I'm not. I love him . . . I'm sure I do.'

'The sort of love you've just described to me, the sort that grows from friendship, it seems to me that that might be the best sort. Tell me, Frances – can you talk to him? Really talk, about anything and everything? About worries you have?'

'Oh yes, of course I can. We talk about all sorts of things. And if I'm worried I tell him. I told him about wanting to go on teaching after we get married. He didn't agree with me entirely, but we were able to talk about it.'

'And you can have a good laugh with him, can't you?'

'Oh yes. We've had such a lot of fun this holiday.'

'And, pardon me mentioning it, but do you think you'll be happy with him in . . . other ways? I know you won't know yet, of course, what it's like . . . in bed. But it is important, Frances.'

Frances could feel herself blushing. 'No, I don't know about that, of course. We haven't . . . But I should think it will be all right. In fact, I know it will be all right.' She gave a satisfied little smile.

'Then, for the life of me, I can't see what you are worrying about. You're rather young, I suppose . . .'

'I'm twenty-three.'

'Still rather young to settle down, and I suppose that's what's worrying you, the settling down. But if you and Adrian are right for one another – and I happen to believe you are – then all that sort of thing will fall into place.'

'Don't tell me I'm a lucky girl, will you?' said Frances. 'You can't imagine the number of times I've been told that lately. Perhaps that's what's made me so stroppy.'

'All right, I won't. But I guess you already know it . . . Now, I think we've chattered for long enough, haven't we? There are pictures to put up and pencils to sharpen and goodness knows what else to do. Off you pop to your own classroom now, before Gertie comes along and catches us wasting time. See you later, dear, in the staffroom. I expect we'll all be having a cup of tea before we go home.'

Frances felt as though a great weight had been lifted from her mind. It had needed Marjorie's problems to put her own into perspective. Imagine being married to a man like Kenneth, someone with whom you had nothing in common. Poor Marjorie. I do love Adrian, she told herself, and we're going to have a perfect marriage. What Marjorie said was true. To be good friends, as they were, was far more important than any silly notions of romantic love.

It had been quite a straightforward staff meeting. There were no new teachers to be introduced this term, and Frances had felt much more confident than she had done at the same meeting exactly a year ago. They discussed the reading scheme which Miss Reynolds had introduced last year, and all the staff, with two exceptions, said how much the children had benefited from the more modern approach and the use of everyday, colloquial language. Miss Walsh and Miss Cameron kept quiet. They had had their say about it at various times throughout the year and obviously knew by now that this was a battle they were bound to lose. But then Miss Reynolds usually won, Frances was pleased to have noticed, with her own style of quiet persuasion rather than by loudly vociferous means.

One item at which all the staff had sat up and taken notice was Miss Reynolds's announcement that early in the new term they were to have a joint meeting with the staff of the Junior School. There were more than a few barely stifled gasps of astonishment. Such a thing had never been heard of before. It was well known that 'our Gertie' and Jacob Entwistle, the headmaster of the Junior School, did not get on, though nobody had discovered why. There were a few ribald remarks bandied around in the staffroom from time to time, that it might be an old love affair between the pair which had gone wrong. But, knowing Gertie, her staff didn't really think so.

Now, however, to their amazement, after her startling announcement Miss Reynolds gave an arch little smile and said, 'I know you are all aware that Mr Entwistle and I have not been exactly the best of friends. And I know you have gossiped about it . . . There is not much that escapes me.' A few heads were lowered as her shrewd, though quietly amused glance flickered round the room at the various members of staff. 'However, I have decided not to keep you in the dark any longer. Mr Entwistle was once engaged to my sister – not to me! – years ago, when we all lived in Wigan. He jilted her and married somebody else, and I happened to think he had let her down badly. She was very upset for a long time. But she's happily married now, and . . .' she gave another little smile . . . 'well, now I can't help thinking she had a lucky escape.'

There were a few polite ripples of surprised laughter. It was rare for Gertie to make even a faintly humorous remark. 'And that's enough said about that. It doesn't alter the fact that Mr Entwistle is a very good headmaster and he and I have decided to forget our old quarrel. What the meeting will be about is this.' She took a deep breath. 'As some of you may realise, next year – 1960 – will be the tenth anniversary of the opening of the Wyre Bank Infant and Junior Schools, and so Mr Entwistle and I thought it might be a good idea to have some sort of a joint celebration. More than one, maybe. Perhaps a party for the children, or a joint concert, with both schools taking part.'

Frances noticed, at that point, the disapproving glances that were exchanged by Miss Walsh and Miss Cameron, followed by Miss Walsh's pointed glance – not a pleasant one – across at Frances herself. She knew that they had still not forgiven her for what they considered to be the extravaganza of the nativity play, particularly as it had been followed, in July, by an end-of-term concert with every class taking part.

'And that is all I'm going to say about that particular matter at the moment,' said Miss Reynolds in a decisive voice. 'I don't want to hear your comments – not yet.' She raised her hand dismissively. 'Now, I want to have a word about discipline . . .'

Frances was enthusiastic about the forthcoming meeting. She had long thought that she would like to make the acquaintance of at least some of the members of the Junior staff, who, at the moment, were virtual strangers to her. She had met the First Year Junior teachers to whom they were passing on their 'top year' Infants, but with the rest she was only on nodding terms across the serving table in the kitchen.

'What did you make of that, then?' she had said to Marjorie. 'We're to be allowed beyond the Iron Curtain. That's where the meeting is to be held, isn't it, in their staffroom?'

'Wonders'll never cease,' said Marjorie. 'But it's about time, I must admit. What amazed me more than anything was Gertie divulging the family secrets. Just imagine – two women fighting over Jacob Entwistle!'

'She didn't exactly say that, not that they were fighting.'

'Well, you know what I mean. She said her sister was upset about it. I can't imagine anyone breaking her heart over him.'

'Nor me,' agreed Frances. 'He looks a dry old stick.' Jacob Entwistle was fiftyish, stocky and balding, with a silly little Hitler-type moustache. He bustled rather than walked and he was very rarely seen to smile. 'No, I can't imagine him ever . . . well, you know.'

Marjorie smiled. 'He has three children, I believe, so he must have had his moments. We've all had our moments, Frances.'

The bruising on Marjorie's face had gone by the time the new term had started and Frances was pleased to see that her friend was her old cheery self again. She decided not to refer to the matter of the rocky marriage unless Marjorie did so.

The joint meeting took place after school ended one afternoon during the second week of term. The Junior staffroom was much larger than its Infant counterpart but with the addition of the nine Infant staff it appeared very crowded. Frances glanced round at the noticeboard, already full even so early in the term, with pamphlets, notices of jobs, and missives from 'the office'; the table with its piles of newspapers and educational journals; the Formica counter holding rows of chunky beakers, kettle and aluminium teapot, and the – surprisingly – gleaming sink, and she thought how neat and clean it all was. Staffrooms, on the whole, were notoriously scruffy places; she guessed they had been having a tidy-up in honour of their visitors.

She knew most of the twelve teachers by sight, but several of them she had never spoken to. There were more women than men, as was usual in a Junior school, but here the ratio was not too unequal; seven women and five men, six if you counted Mr Entwistle. There was one man, however, whom Frances had not seen before. He was sitting almost directly opposite her across the table, on the second row of chairs. The staffs had grouped themselves, rather unsociably, in two distinct sets, one at each side of the large centre table. This man was noticeable because of his smart appearance. Men teachers were, on the whole, inclined to be less than spruce-looking, which was not always their fault; the chalk dust got everywhere. He was wearing a well-tailored sports jacket and his bright blue shirt matched exactly the colour of his eyes. Frances could see how blue they were because, at that moment, he looked at her and smiled. Covered with confusion – she realised she might have been staring – she gave a brief smile and hastily looked away. The next time she ventured a glance he was deep in conversation with his neighbour so she turned to Marjorie.

'Who's that? The fellow in the blue shirt on the second row?' she whispered.

Marjorie glanced across and gave a slight shrug. 'Search me. Never seen him before. I did hear they were having a new teacher, though.'

'Rather dishy, don't you think?'

Marjorie gave her a reproving nudge. 'Hey, watch it! You're an engaged woman. Don't you forget it.'

'I know, I know – I've not forgotten.' Frances grinned at her friend, who was smiling back; Frances knew she was only joking. 'But I can look, can't I?'

Marjorie winked. 'So long as that's all you do. I've got to admit he's an improvement on the rest of the men, whoever he is. Tall, dark and handsome, eh? That's a cliché if ever there was one . . . We'd better shut up,' she whispered as Miss Walsh, further along the row, was looking daggers at them. 'They're ready to start.'

Mr Entwistle, at the head of the table, was in charge, although he deferred frequently to Miss Reynolds who was sitting next to him. It was decided that there would be a joint party for all the children during the summer term to celebrate the schools' tenth anniversaries. They would open the partition between the two dining halls – the Iron Curtain, although Mr Entwistle did not refer to it as such – so that the children could dine together and, weather permitting, they would hold races and games on the grassed area which surrounded both schools.

But the most important item to be discussed, because it was to be held quite a while before the party, was the proposed concert. It was at that point that Mr Entwistle introduced the new member of staff. He turned to the man whom Frances and Marjorie had been discussing.

'This is Mr Avery. I know that several of you will not have seen him before. He has been teaching in Newcastle and has joined us this term. He is taking one of our Second Year classes, but not only that, he also holds the post of responsibility for Music. Mr Avery . . .' Mr Entwistle inclined his head stiffly, 'perhaps you might like to say a few words about some of the ideas you have?'

As soon as the man spoke it was obvious that he came from the Newcastle area. His accent, though not broad, had a definite north-country ring. Frances had met quite a few Geordies when she was at college and had come to love the sing-song way they talked. He explained that he intended to start a school choir, and a recorder group, and he hoped that all the classes, including the Infants, would be able to contribute in some way to the concert. That was what they were going to talk about now and all suggestions would be welcome.

'Why aye, man!' whispered Marjorie, when Mr Avery stopped talking. 'He's a canny lad!' Frances smiled.

These were various comments and suggestions from the other teachers. For her own part, Frances felt that she was still too much of a new girl, even after a year at the school, to put forward any ideas of her own. There was nothing definitely decided upon at this meeting – the ideas were many and varied – so the proposal that a committee should be formed, consisting of three teachers from each school, was agreed upon.

Frances had noticed that both Miss Walsh and Miss Cameron had kept very quiet throughout the proceedings, and when Miss Reynolds suggested that Miss Cameron, as deputy head, should serve on the committee, that lady answered frostily, 'I would rather not, if you don't mind. As deputy head I have quite enough to do in other directions.' And from the knowing glances that she exchanged with her henchwoman, Miss Walsh, it would seem to suggest that the pair of them had decided to boycott this concert.

'Fair enough,' said Miss Reynolds briskly. She turned to Frances. 'Miss Goodwin, you will be willing to serve on the committee, won't you?' Frances, to her dismay, felt her cheeks going red – she hated to be the centre of attention amongst so many people she didn't know – but she agreed that she would be pleased to do so. Mr Avery again met her eye and smiled, and Frances smiled back, though she was still feeling all of a fluster.

'Miss Goodwin has done some very good dramatic work since she joined our staff,' said Miss Reynolds, 'and I'm sure Mrs Aspinall, who is very artistic, would be only too pleased to assist as well.'

Marjorie, quite calmly, nodded her agreement. Then Mrs Clarkson, who was known to be talented at dress-making skills, was invited to be the third Infant representative.

Frances felt a glow of delighted anticipation. It should all be very interesting, to say the least.

Chapter 14

It was on the following Saturday that Frances bumped into Julie, her friend from the Starlight Players. They almost collided in the doorway of Marks & Spencer, then stood chatting by the stocking counter.

'Long time no see,' said Julie. 'It's been ages and ages, and you did promise to keep in touch.'

'Yes, I know I did,' said Frances. She felt rather guilty; she had promised, but then, so had Julie. 'You know how it is. There always seems to be so much to do and the weeks fly past so quickly.'

'Never mind; we'll be meeting soon, won't we?' Julie continued. 'Rehearsals start next week – for *Oklahoma!*'

'Oh, is that what they're doing this time? I hadn't heard.'

'You didn't know?' Julie stared at her in astonishment. 'You're coming, aren't you, to the first rehearsal?'

'Er . . . well . . . I'm not sure.' Frances, to her slight embarrassment, had not given the Starlight Players a thought for ages. Now, as she began to do so, the happy memories came flooding back. Should she go again this year? It would be lovely to take part in *Oklahoma!* – it was one of her favourite musicals – but, no, it would not be possible. 'I don't really think . . .' she faltered.

'Don't say you're not coming.' Julie looked very disappointed. 'I can't believe it. Not after *South Pacific*; we enjoyed it so much.'

'I'm so busy, Julie, honestly I am. I'm helping Adrian a lot at church, you know.' She was aware of her friend's slight moue of disapproval before she hurried on to say, 'I'm in the choir, and I've finally been persuaded to help with the youth club, and we're starting a dramatic society as well, for the youngsters. It's the first meeting tonight, actually; that's why I'm dashing around like a mad thing. I thought I'd make a few sandwiches – the kids are always hungry – so I've been to Burtons to get some bridge rolls, and I'm just on my way to Redmans to get some of their nice salmon paste—What's the matter?' she asked, aware of a broad grin – a somewhat sardonic one – spreading across Julie's face.

'He's getting you well trained, your Adrian, I must say. Salmon sandwiches and youth clubs and all that. You're beginning to sound like a vicar's wife already. When are you getting married?'

'Er . . . we don't know. Next year, probably. We haven't fixed a date yet.'

'Well then, if the wedding isn't just yet, surely you've time to be in *Oklahoma!* Oh, go on, Frances. I was looking forward so much to us being together again.'

'I can't,' Frances protested. 'It's not just church; it's school as well. We're planning a big concert for next year, with the Junior School, and I've been put on the committee. It may well turn out to be the same week as the Starlight Players' performance. Even if it isn't, I'll still have too much on.'

'Goodness, you are a busy bee, aren't you?' said Julie, sounding a little sarcastic. She moved, yet again, out of the way of a customer who was frantically waving a packet of nylon stockings at the assistant at the other end of the counter, at the same time giving a dirty look to the two young women who had nothing better to do than stand there chatting and getting in everybody's way. 'Come on, we'd better move or we'll be in bother. Let's go and have a cup of tea in the café upstairs. They have some lovely jam doughnuts.'

Frances started to protest once more that she hadn't time. 'Oh, I don't think—' she began, but at the look of exasperated disbelief on Julie's face she went on to say, 'Oh, all right then. Yes, that'll be very nice. But I mustn't be long, really I mustn't. I promised I'd call and see Mum on the way back from town.'

'How is your mother?' asked Julie, when they had carried their trays to a vacant table in the corner. 'She's managing OK without you, is she?'

'Yes, she's fine,' answered Frances. 'At least, she's as well as can be expected, considering her arthritis. That doesn't get any better; I don't suppose it ever will, but she hasn't had any more trouble with her heart, so we're all relieved about that. I wouldn't have left her, you know, if I hadn't known she'd be all right with Eliza.'

'No, I know you wouldn't,' said Julie, sincerely. 'You don't need to apologise to me. Why, what's the matter? Has somebody been saying —'

'No, not really,' said Frances. 'It's me. I sometimes feel guilty that I was only with her for such a short time – about nine months – before I got a place of my own. My sister had quite a lot to say about it at first, but then our Josie always does. But there's no need, really, for me to feel guilty about it because Mum's far better off living with Eliza than she was with me. Eliza understands her and they get on like a house on fire. They can talk about old times, you see, but Mum can't boss her about the way she tried to boss me. Yes, I've got on better with Mum since I left. I call to see her a few times a week. If Adrian can't take me I go on my own.'

'And it's working out all right with Megan, in the flat?'

'Yes, it's great. I don't see her all that much, especially when she's on nights, but we get on well together.'

'You've no idea how much I envy you,' said Julie. 'Here am I, still stuck at home with my mum and dad, still being treated like a kid. You are lucky, Fran.'

'Yes, I suppose I am,' said Frances. 'It's costing me more, though – a darned sight more than it did when I was living at Mum's. I don't know how I'll manage when Megan gets married next spring.'

'Next spring? You'll be wanting a flatmate then?' Julie was looking at her eagerly and Frances knew at once what was in her mind.

'Yes, I dare say I will . . . D'you think you could come and share with me, Julie? That would be wonderful. It would solve all the problems of trying to find sombody suitable.'

'If I can get away from Mum's clutches – yes, I'd love to. Let me know nearer the time, will you? I must try not to build my hopes up too much in case it doesn't work out. Now – are you sure I can't persuade you to be in *Oklahoma!*? It won't be the same without you, you know.'

'I'm tempted,' said Frances. She licked at the jam that was oozing out of her doughnut. 'Very tempted . . .' She wiped her sticky fingers on her serviette before saying, decidedly, 'No, I really can't manage it. But you'll be OK, Julie. It won't be like last year when we didn't know anybody. You know everybody now, don't you?'

'Yes, pretty well. Oh, by the way, I ran into Sylvia Bowland in town last week. You could have knocked me down with a feather when she stopped to speak to me. I always thought she was too grand to talk to mere members of the chorus. But I think she just wanted to show off her engagement ring. She's getting married; quite soon, she says, before the next show.'

'Is she? Good gracious! Fancy that.' Frances was silent for a moment as the thoughts flitted through her mind. Jonathan Russell; that would be whom she was marrying. She wondered why the thought should startle her so much. She should not have been surprised at the news. She had seen Sylvia and Jonathan together a few times and they had been very pally on that trip to Manchester.

'Hey, snap out of it!' Julie clicked her fingers in front of Frances's face. 'What's up with you? Oh, I get it. You thought she was going to marry Jonathan Russell, didn't you?'

'Why . . . isn't she?'

'No; it's somebody she works with, at the GPO. She's a telephonist there, you know, and she's known him for ages.' Julie grinned. 'You should have seen your face. I always knew you had a yen for Jonathan Russell.'

'Of course I haven't! What rubbish! I'm engaged, anyway —'

'What difference does that make? It doesn't mean you

stop fancying other fellows, does it?'

'It does to me,' replied Frances, with a show of indignation. 'Actually, I was thinking about Dennis – you know, Jonathan's son; he used to be in my class – and I was wondering how he would react if his dad got married again. He was a very troubled little boy at times.'

'Well, he won't be marrying Sylvia Bowland, that's for sure. But I did see him with a girl, arm in arm they were, coming along Church Street.'

'Oh? When was this?' Frances tried to sound unconcerned.

'A couple of weeks ago. They looked as though they might be heading for the Opera House. I was dashing to meet Mike outside the Regent, so I didn't notice where they went. Anyway, it's none of our business, is it?'

'No, none at all,' said Frances nonchalantly. 'What did she look like?'

'Small – very small, actually – and dark. Hair in an urchin cut.'

'Oh, yes.' Frances nodded. 'It sounds like Glenys Mortimer.'

'Who's she?'

'Jonathan's assistant at the garden centre. I've met her a couple of times. Yes, it must be her.' It had been obvious at their first meeting, Frances mused, that Glenys was setting her cap at her employer. Still, what did it matter? Even Dennis was no longer Frances's problem. 'Well, well, well . . .' She smiled brightly. 'You're as good as the Gaumont British News today, Julie. Any more titbits to tell me?' Aware of her friend's too knowing smile she decided to change the subject. 'Who's Mike?' she asked.

Oh, Mike was just a friend, Julie told her. They worked in the same office and had been out together a few times. It was nothing serious; Julie didn't want to get serious about anyone yet. She valued her independence too much and she certainly didn't want to get tied to somebody who would try to tell her what she must, or must not, do.

Frances, feeling that Julie might be having a dig at Adrian – she had never been all that smitten with him – was on the

207

point of protesting, but she decided against it. Julie wouldn't understand that when you fell in love and were planning to get married, then your own selfish wishes had to be put on one side. Or you had, at least, to reach some sort of a compromise, as she and Adrian had done about her teaching career. And she was not depriving herself of enjoyment by deciding not to join the Starlight Players again, as Julie seemed to be implying. She was only too happy to be helping Adrian, her future husband. Feeling more than a little smug in her self-denial, she said goodbye to Julie and dashed off to do the rest of her shopping.

The first meeting of the newly formed Methodist Church Dramatic Society went very well. The youngsters – some two dozen of them, aged from twelve to sixteen – were enthusiastic, and it was agreed that they should present a pantomime, *Cinderella*, the following January. Frances was to be the co-producer, along with Geoffrey Halstead, a keen, bespectacled young man of about twenty, who worked in the public library. He had aspirations to be a playwright and had already put together the first draft of a script for the pantomime.

It was the first mention Frances had heard of a pantomime. She had thought that the preliminary meeting was to decide on the type of production to be staged, but it now seemed that Adrian and Geoffrey, between them, had already made a decision. She felt a tiny prickle of resentment – he might have told her – but she decided to keep quiet as the script, at a first glance, appeared to be very good and quite professionally written.

It was decided that Geoffrey should be in charge of the acting, with help from Frances, whilst she also had responsibility for the musical numbers. She could not play the piano, something she often regretted, but there was a middle-aged lady in the congregation who was a talented pianist, so Adrian promised to try to enlist her services. She played for the women's meetings and the Sunday School, so Adrian was sure she would be only too willing to come along. He was a very persuasive young man, and few of the womenfolk, either young or old, were able to withstand his flattering cajolery.

Adrian had seemed a little preoccupied at times, throughout the meeting, and when he took her home later Frances found out why.

'Well, my love, we'll soon be able to fix a wedding date,' he began, when he was settled on the settee with a cup of coffee in his lap.

'Why? What do you mean?' Frances gave a slight frown. She could not help but be aware of the dictatorial tone to his voice, something she had noticed quite a lot recently.

'Because I think I've sorted out my next living,' he went on. 'At least, I hope to do so next week.'

'But . . . why didn't you tell me? It's the first I've heard of it. I didn't even know you were looking.'

'Of course you knew I was looking, Frances. Ministers have to start looking well in advance of a move. I thought you realised that. Anyway, I'm telling you now, aren't I? If I haven't mentioned it before it's because you always seem to have something else on your mind; school or concerts or something.'

'Go on,' she said evenly. 'Where is it?'

'Birmingham,' he replied. Frances's heart sank, though she was not sure why. 'I have a friend who is a minister in Birmingham – a fellow I was at college with – and he's leaving next summer to go to Africa.'

'Africa . . .?' she faltered.

'Yes, he's going on the Mission Field,' replied Adrian, with, Frances thought, a touch of impatience. 'And he thinks his church would be ideal for me. It's on a big housing estate, similar to Wyre Bank, I should imagine, just outside the city. Quite a lot of rehousing, I gather, from slum clearance areas. And quite a few social problems, too, of course. It should be a great challenge.' His grey eyes were alight with enthusiasm, but all Frances could do at the moment was stare at him. Why had he never hinted at what was in his mind?

As though unaware of her hesitancy he hurried on to say, 'Anyway, Arthur – that's my friend – has had a word with his church stewards, recommending me for the post, and I'm going down to meet them on Tuesday. And providing we take to one another – it has to be a mutual agreement, of course – then that will be that. If they offer me the living I shall take it . . . What's the matter, darling? You look a bit put out.'

Frances shook her head numbly. 'It's . . . it's rather a shock. Hearing that it's all more or less decided, and I didn't know a thing about it.' She was trying to speak calmly, to keep the lid on her temper which, she realised now, had been simmering all evening like a pan on a low light – his manner at the meeting had been very high-handed – and it was now ready to boil over. But she didn't want to cause a row, not about something as important as moving to another parish. She bit her lip. 'I would have been glad if you had told me sooner, that's all – asked my opinion. And I don't know anyone in Birmingham,' she added lamely.

'Of course you don't know anyone in Birmingham,' Adrian laughed. 'What a silly thing to say. Neither do I. You wouldn't know anyone wherever we moved to. But you soon will. You'll soon make friends. That's one of the duties of a minister's wife, making friends with the parishioners. You don't need to feel nervous about it. I'll be with you, darling. We'll be together, like we've planned, starting our married life.'

Yes, they would be together, but they had never done all that much planning, not about their marriage or where they would live or anything. Now it was Adrian who was making all the plans, and she was expected just to fall in with them. She wasn't sure what sort of a place she had envisaged for Adrian's next parish. Somewhere in Yorkshire, maybe, as the county was familiar to both of them. Perhaps a village similar to the one she had taught in near Haliford, or a seaside town something like Blackpool. But Birmingham! She knew very little about the place except that it was the second largest city in the country, a vast industrial place with factories and smoking chimneys and slum areas – Adrian had already mentioned that – and back-to-back houses and thousands and thousands of people. The very idea of the place was alien to her. She suddenly felt overwhelmed and insecure and . . . inadequate – yes, that was the word: unequal to the task that Adrian was thrusting upon her.

'But it's such a big place,' she said, in a halting voice. 'I'd . . . I'd feel lost in a place like Birmingham.'

'Don't be silly, darling,' said Adrian. She wished he would stop saying she was silly; that was the second time he had said it. 'We'll only be living in a little part of it. Near Edgbaston, it is, not right in the city centre. It won't be much different from Wyre Bank, you'll see.'

But Frances felt sure that it would be very different. She was realising, possibly for the first time, what a sheltered sort of life she had led. She had never lived in a big city. Haliford was only a small town, and Blackpool, though quite large, was friendly and familiar to her. The college she had attended in Yorkshire had been on the edge of a city, admittedly, but they had been secure in their own little academic world, only venturing into the town for occasional shopping trips.

'But you said it was a slum clearance area, didn't you?' she went on. 'Won't the people be . . . well . . .' She didn't quite know how to put it, '. . . er, different from us?'

'What do you mean, different?'

'Well . . . rough, sort of.' She hated it when Adrian looked at her in that way, his grey eyes resembling storm clouds rather than shining with love for her, as they often did. She guessed, before he spoke, what his next words would be.

'Well, that's a snobbish attitude to take, I must say, Frances.'

'I'm not a snob! I'm not!' she retorted. 'How dare you call me a snob?'

'I didn't say you were a snob. I said it was a snobbish thing to say.'

'Same thing.' Frances was angry, but her anger was tinged with more than a little guilt as she remembered what she had been like years ago. In her teens she may well have been a spoiled little madam with a snooty manner;

211

but she had grown out of all that ages ago. Miss Walsh, now; she really was a snob, with all her talk of 'private house families' and 'estate families'. But she, Frances Goodwin, was not like that. Was she . . .?

'We're only ordinary people, Frances, you and I,' Adrian was saying. 'Your family is working class, same as mine. We can't start looking down on people just because we happen to have had a rather better education. We've had more chances, that's what it amounts to.'

'I'm not; I don't look down on people,' she argued, although she didn't sound very convincing. Working class? she was thinking. Was that really what they were, both her and Adrian? Maybe they were, inasmuch as they had always had to work for a living. But her father had had a good job at the mill in Haliford – he had been an undermanager, not just a mill hand – and her mother had had her own private hotel. Frances had never thought of them, or herself, as working class.

'No, of course you don't, darling . . . I'm sorry.' Adrian placed his cup on the floor and put his arm round her. 'Certainly I've never known you to look down on anyone. Forget I said it. You get on well with all the parents at the school, don't you, and all the folks at church? And the children love you, I know that. I hear all sorts of nice things about Miss Goodwin when I come into school. Don't worry, love; you'll find the people in Birmingham are not all that much different. And I know you don't find it hard to make friends, do you?'

'No, not usually,' she admitted.

'Well then, there you are – try and look on the bright side. We've such a lot to look forward to. Now – we've a wedding date to fix, haven't we?'

They agreed upon the second Saturday in August 1960. The wedding would be at their own Methodist church, but as Adrian couldn't marry himself, he joked, he would invite one of his fellow ministers from a neighbouring parish to do the honours.

Frances began to feel more cheerful. All girls enjoyed planning their weddings and she was no exception. There

212

would be her dress to choose. She might ask Megan to go with her, although Megan's taste was rather frilly and fussy; probably Josie would be better. And bridesmaids to decide upon. Little Valerie, of course; and their relations in Yorkshire, both hers and Adrian's, had expressed a wish to be bridesmaids as well. And then there were Megan and Julie. Although by that time Megan would have to be called a matron of honour. Goodness; it seemed as though she might end up with quite a large retinue of attendants.

Thinking of Julie reminded her of their meeting earlier that day. 'I saw Julie this afternoon,' she told Adrian. 'You know, my friend from the Starlight Players. I hadn't seen her for ages. They're doing *Oklahoma!* next spring. She asked me if I was going to be in it.'

'And you told her no,' said Adrian. It wasn't even a question; just a bald statement – you told her no. Frances saw red.

'What makes you say that?' she answered back. 'Why should I say no? Just let me tell you, Adrian Glover, that if I wanted to be in it, then I jolly well would be.'

'Hey, steady on, darling. Keep your hair on.' The fact that he was smiling at her only made her more angry.

'You're not going to tell me what I've got to do and don't you dare forget it. As a matter of fact, I did say no, but only because it was what I'd already decided. What *I'd* decided, do you hear, not *you*. I'm too busy, and not just because of all I'm doing at the church. There's my mother to consider; I have to make sure she's all right even though I'm not living there. And then there's the big concert coming up at school. I told Julie I was far too busy, but I'd've been in it if I'd wanted to!' she said again.

'Yes, indeed, you are busy,' said Adrian, almost too calmly. 'I thought when you got yourself on to that committee at school that you already had quite enough to do.'

'I didn't get myself on to the committee! I had no choice. Miss Reynolds put me on, and I couldn't very well say no, could I? Anyway, it's all part of my career; I've got to do it.'

'Oh yes, of course, I was forgetting. It's your career.'

213

Frances looked at him sharply. If Adrian had been smiling she was sure she would have hit him. But he wasn't smiling. 'It won't make much difference now, though, will it, darling?' he said seriously. 'You'll have to give your notice in soon.'

Frances gave a start, a sharp intake of breath. Her notice; that made it all sound so final. 'Not just yet,' she replied. 'A term's notice, that's all they need. I don't need to hand it in till next spring.' That was a long time off.

'So long as you don't forget. I don't want to have to leave you behind in Blackpool.' Adrian smiled at her. 'Of course we're crossing our bridges, aren't we? They may decide they don't like me, those church stewards in Birmingham.'

Frances, in spite of herself – her misgivings, her self-doubt, her annoyance at him – found she was smiling back. 'That's not very likely, Adrian. They'll like you. I know they will.' Everyone – well, nearly everyone – liked Adrian.

The first meeting of the committee, set up to make arrangements for the Wyre Bank School Anniversary Concert, took place after school the following week. Mr Avery, the newly appointed music teacher, was in charge. Whether this was by accident or design Frances was not sure, but it was obvious from the start that he had a commanding personality. The others, not so used to organising such events as concerts – they had, so far, been only an occasional occurrence at either school – seemed happy enough to let him take the lead. He was well used to organising school productions, he told them; they had been a regular feature at his last school.

Frances, by the end of the meeting, had come to the conclusion that Marcus Avery was not only a born leader, but that he also liked the sound of his own voice. He had invited them to call him Marcus, a name which Frances thought suited him admirably: a trifle flamboyant and ostentatious. The three members of the Infant staff, however, did not take up his invitation, unlike his own colleagues who, whether they wholeheartedly approved of him or not – it was difficult to tell just what they thought of him – were all addressing him as Marcus as though they had known him all their lives. A much more free and easy staffroom, this, Frances decided, in spite of having a headmaster as formal as Jacob Entwistle.

The other two Junior representatives were Mrs Jeffrey, one of the Third Year teachers, and Mr Reed, who was the deputy head of the school. He had no doubt been invited along as another man so that Marcus would not be too outnumbered; not that that would have bothered the irrepressible Marcus Avery, Frances surmised.

He told them that he had already started a school choir, and very soon he would be forming a recorder group, both of which would be presenting items at the concert. Mr Reed, something of a Thespian, planned to put on an excerpt from *Toad of Toad Hall*, and also to dramatise several of the poems of A. A. Milne with his Fourth Year children; whilst Mrs Jeffrey, who was apparently a more than able pianist, would be producing 'Songs from around the World' in the appropriate national costumes.

The Infant teachers, Marjorie Aspinall, Wendy Clarkson and Frances, had looked uneasily at one another at all this abundance of ideas. They had not realised that so much planning would already have been done. They had all assumed that the first meeting was to decide, tentatively, who would do what and how many items would be required, not to come up with already fully fledged ideas.

'And what are our Infant colleagues going to offer?' asked Mr Avery. His raised eyebrows and patronising smile, to say nothing of his emphasis on the word 'Infant', seemed to suggest that mere Infant School children – and their teachers – were of little importance.

To make matters worse, both her companions, Marjorie and Wendy, looked straight at Frances, waiting for her to come up with an answer. She felt she could have brained them, but it was only to be expected, she supposed. She was the one who had been in charge of the previous dramatic productions, such as they were, so they were looking to her now to take the lead.

Think, think! she told herself in the few seconds before she opened her mouth; and, for heaven's sake, let it look as though you know what you are talking about. Don't start by saying 'er' or 'well'. She took a deep breath.

'Actually . . .' That was not a very good choice of word either, but it was too late now. '. . . We have quite a few ideas, but they are still in the early planning stages.' She spoke calmly and deliberately, meeting Marcus Avery's condescending half-smile with a level glance. 'Marjorie and I have the Third Year children, and we were thinking of songs about the sea, and holidays . . . and summertime.' She was making it up as she went along, from a vague idea that had been forming in her mind, but it sounded convincing enough. '. . . Seeing that we live by the seaside, and by that time we will all be thinking of summer holidays.'

'Mmm . . . very ambitious – for Infants. I'm impressed,' said Marcus Avery. 'And . . .? Any more ideas?'

'Yes.' It was Wendy Clarkson who spoke up now, to Frances's relief. 'I have one of the Reception classes, and I'm sure we could manage a percussion band. Yes, I realise it's rather noisy,' she added, with a touch of defiance, in answer to a grimace from Mr Avery, which he did not bother to disguise.

'That's putting it mildly,' he joked, grinning round for support – which he did not appear to be getting – from his colleagues. 'From what I've heard of Infants' percussion bands they're one hell of a din! Still, if we remember to bring our earplugs—'

'A percussion band,' Wendy interrupted. 'That will be the younger children's contribution. Just as tuneful, to my mind, as recorders played off-key, which is how they always sound to me.' Good for you, thought Frances, finding it hard to suppress a grin. 'And a medley of our favourite nursery rhymes. We can dress up for them,' Wendy added, improvising as Frances had done. 'I can only play the piano with one finger, but I expect Marjorie will play for us, won't you, Marjorie?'

Marcus Avery nodded. 'Playing the piano with one finger will not do, of course, for a concert performed in front of

216

an audience.' Arrogant devil, fumed Frances. Who the hell does he think he is? 'Although I dare say it might suffice in an Infant classroom. We have a few quite accomplished pianists on the Junior staff. Mrs Jeffrey here,' he nodded in her direction, 'and myself, of course.' Of course, seethed Frances, inwardly. Is there anything you can't do? 'We would be only too willing to offer our services, if you require them?'

'No thanks, Mr Avery,' said Marjorie. 'That won't be necessary. I play quite adequately . . . for Infants,' she added, with a meaningful glance at the Junior teachers.

'Good . . . good.' Marcus Avery made a steeple of his fingers. 'Let me see; we've got seaside songs, a percussion band and nursery rhymes. What about your Second Year children? What are they going to contribute?'

'That hasn't been decided yet,' said Frances firmly. That would, in truth, be something of a problem as Miss Cameron and Miss Walsh, both Second Year teachers, had so far refused even to discuss the concert; but there was no need to tell that to Mr Avery.

'Very well. Perhaps you will know by the time we have our next meeting? I would suggest we meet again in a month's time. Then we can have a progress report. Thank you, everybody.' Mr Avery smiled round at the other five in an authoritative manner. 'That will be all for today.'

'Well, of all the bumptious, arrogant so-and-sos I've ever met, he takes the biscuit,' stormed Wendy when they were safely back on their own side of the Iron Curtain. 'Did you ever hear the likes of that? Turning his nose up at my percussion band! How dare he?'

'I'm afraid he's typical of a lot of Junior teachers,' said Marjorie. 'Not all, by any means, but quite a lot. They seem to think that teaching Infants is a doddle – nothing more than baby-minding.'

'Huh! They want to try it, that's what I say,' said Wendy. 'I've also heard it said that if you can teach Infants then you can teach anything, and I think that's nearer the truth. Arrogant devil!' she said again.

'You don't fancy him then?' laughed Marjorie. 'I think Frances did when she saw him at the staff meeting. Changed your mind about him now, have you, Fran?'

'Not half!' replied Frances. 'Not that I ever did fancy him. I only said he was good-looking, and you've got to admit he is.'

'Handsome is as handsome does,' quoted Marjorie.

'And he can do nothing for me, thank you very much,' said Wendy. 'I'm perfectly satisfied with the one I've got.'

'And so you should be.' Marjorie gave her a nudge. 'There's something wrong if you're not, luv.' Wendy, in her late twenties, was newly married and had been somewhat starry-eyed since returning to school after her August honeymoon.

'Well, we don't have to meet up with him again for another month,' said Frances. 'And I'm not sorry about that.

'How are things?' she enquired of Marjorie, when they had said goodbye to Wendy. 'With you and Kenneth? If you don't mind me asking. You haven't said anything lately.'

'So-so,' replied Marjorie. 'No better, no worse. Well, certainly no worse. He hasn't hit me again, but like I said before, there's no communication between us. Ah well, that's life, I suppose. You have to take it as it comes. Count your blessings, Frances. You and Adrian are made for one another. I'm so pleased you've fixed a date, dear. That's something for me to look forward to. I will be invited, won't I?'

'Of course you will, Marjorie. We can't invite all the staff, but I hope you will be there . . . you and Kenneth. You're still a couple, aren't you? We'll have to invite him as well.'

'Yes, we're still a couple,' Marjorie sighed. 'For what it's worth . . .'

It was far less than a month before Frances saw Marcus Avery again. She looked up from her desk one afternoon the following week, after all the children had gone home, to see his tall figure standing there.

'Oh . . . hello,' she faltered, hastily putting down her red marking pen. 'Sorry, I hadn't seen you come in.' They always left their doors propped open, ready for the cleaners.

'Hello, Frances. It is Frances, isn't it?' She nodded, feeling rather bewildered. What on earth did he want? 'I've come to see how you're getting on with arrangements for the concert. At least, that's one of the things I've come about. It is you that's in charge, isn't it?'

'Well sort of. I've been here the shortest time – I only joined the staff last year – but, yes, it does seem to have fallen to me.'

'Any more bright ideas then?' He drew out the other adult chair and sat down on it, back to front, his arms resting on the support. 'Your Second Year colleagues? Mr Entwistle has hinted that we might be batting on a sticky wicket there.'

'Er, yes . . . possibly.' She wasn't going to give too much away, not to this supercilious fellow whom she hardly knew, although he didn't seem nearly so bad today. 'Miss Cameron – she's the deputy head – and Miss Walsh are not all that keen on the idea of a concert at all, but they've decided they are going to put on a display of gymnastics.'

'What! With six-year-olds?'

'Yes, why not? Just simple routines set to music, I gather. Marching tunes such as the children walk out to after morning assembly.' There was a selection of such pieces at the back of the Infant Hymnal by Carey Bonner, and Miss Walsh repeated these with monotonous regularity, but there was no need to tell him that. Nor that it was Miss Reynolds who had brought her influence to bear on the two rebel teachers, insisting that they must come up with something. Frances hadn't dared to approach them.

Marcus Avery grinned in quite a friendly manner. 'Just about Miss Walsh's level, I gather. Not much of a virtuoso, eh?'

'Maybe not, but then we can't all be accomplished pianists, can we? She does her best.'

He nodded. 'And another thing I came about . . . was to apologise.'

'Apologise? What for?'

'Oh . . .' He pursed his lips. 'I've a feeling I may have thrown my weight about rather too much at that meeting.'

'Did you? I hadn't noticed,' lied Frances.

'Oh, come on, you must have done.' He smiled at her and, somewhat unwillingly, she found herself smiling back. 'The truth is, Frances, I feel I have to justify my position – being given this special post, I mean – and the best way I can do it is by being assertive, more so than I would normally be.'

'I wouldn't have taken you for a timid sort of person,' Frances ventured. 'Although I think I know what you mean.' Indeed, she did. She had had to stick up for herself more than once since joining the Infant staff.

'No, I'm certainly not timid, but there are certain people who feel that the post should have gone to somebody already on the staff and not to an outsider like me. Especially to someone who was Emergency Trained, as I was.'

'Were you?' said Frances, in some surprise. 'I didn't realise that.' Emergency Training was a scheme brought in at the end of the war when there was a shortage of teachers, and many highly suitable people were taken into the profession after only a year's training, instead of the two years normally required.

'Yes, when I came out of the RAF I decided to do the year's training,' said Marcus Avery. 'And I've never re-gretted going into teaching. This is my first step up the ladder, though, in twelve years, and, as I say, some folks think I shouldn't have got it. But Mr Entwistle seemed to like what I could offer at the interview, so that was that.' He smiled at her again and, once more, Frances smiled back. She was deciding that she might have misjudged him.

'Why are you telling me all this?' she asked.

'Dunno really. So that we can understand one another, mebbe.' His Geordie accent was more pronounced when he was not putting on the style. 'We have to work together, after all, for this concert, haven't we, pet?' He glanced down at her hand. 'You're the young lady who's engaged to the minister, aren't you?'

'Yes . . . yes, I am. We're getting married next summer. Then we're moving to Birmingham.'

'You're moving? Oh dear, that's a pity. Still, that's a long time off, isn't it? There was one more thing I wanted to mention, Frances. I was wondering if we might persuade some of the staff to take part in the concert as well. To add a touch of – you know – class, professionalism.'

'To prevent it becoming too childish, you mean? Too *infantile*?' She emphasised the word.

He frowned, but at the same time he was grinning. 'I asked for that, didn't I? Yes . . . I'm sorry for my remark about the percussion band. It was uncalled for. Believe me, I couldn't teach Infants for all the tea in China.'

'It was a bit tactless, maybe. But what were you thinking the staff could do? I can't see any of ours—'

'Oh, you never know. A lot of people hide their light under a bushel. For instance, I believe you are a singer?'

'Me? Oh no, not really.'

'But you were in *South Pacific* earlier this year, I've been told?'

Who had told him, she wondered. 'Only in the chorus. I did used to sing solos when I was much younger, but I couldn't do it now.'

'Duets, maybe? I sing as well.' She might have guessed he would. His accomplishments seemed to be never-ending. 'After a fashion,' he added, although she felt the modesty was assumed. 'I was in an operatic society in Newcastle. Perhaps you and I could get together. I think we might do rather well.'

'To . . . sing duets, you mean?'

'Yes . . . that's what I had in mind.' Frances was aware of a humorous glint in his eye and, to her annoyance, she felt herself blushing.

'Oh, I don't know, Mr Avery . . .'

'Marcus, please.'

'All right then – Marcus – but I don't know. I'll have to think about it.'

'You do that then. And Mrs Jeffrey on our staff might be persuaded to do a piano solo. And I believe Mr Reed is a reciter of dramatic monologues. There's a wealth of undiscovered talent when you look around. Your fiancé wouldn't object, would he?'

'No, why should he? But I haven't said I'll do it yet.'

'Think about it, pet.' He unravelled his long legs from the chair and stood up. 'Must go, Frances. I've already taken up far too much of your valuable time.' He glanced down with a grin. 'I'd best let you get on with marking your sums. Bye for now then. It's been nice talking to you.'

'Goodbye . . . Marcus.' She stared after him as he strode out of the classroom, self-confidence positively radiating from him. She didn't believe for one moment his protestation that his assertive manner had only been put on. To be in control came naturally to him, although it was generous-spirited of him to try to explain. He didn't need to have done so. Nor had she taken any notice of his affectionate form of address. To say 'pet' – in the same way that Lancashire and Yorkshire people said 'luv' – came as naturally as breathing to Geordies. But Marcus Avery was an interesting character, to say the least.

Chapter 15

The nation had been thrilled to hear the news, in the February of 1960, of the engagement of Princess Margaret to an unknown young photographer, Antony Armstrong-Jones. A cause for rejoicing, indeed, especially as the announcement came only a few weeks after the birth of a second son, Andrew, to the Queen and Prince Philip. And now, only three months later, everyone was again in a frenzy of excitement about the wedding, which was to take place on 14 May at Westminster Abbey.

The event was not considered important enough for the children to be given a day off school as they had for the wedding of Princess Elizabeth, but Frances, with her mother and Eliza, watched the recorded highlights later that evening.

'Eeh, doesn't she look beautiful?' Iris enthused, gazing enthralled at the new bride, so dainty and petite, on the arm of her not much taller bridegroom. 'They make a lovely couple and I hope they'll be really happy, I do that. I thought it was a shame when they wouldn't let her marry that Group-Captain Townsend, but happen it's turned out for t'best in the long run.'

'Well, if they can't make a go of it then it's heaven help the thousands of other young couples who are getting wed,' said Eliza. 'They've got everything they could want, haven't they? Pots of money, nice clothes, big posh houses; they want for nothing, that lot. Not that I begrudge 'em any of it. I wouldn't want to be Queen, not for a gold clock, I wouldn't!'

'Aye, they'll have to make it work, that's for sure,' said Iris. 'Princess Margaret's a bit of a one, but she'll have to settle down now. It wouldn't do to have a divorce in t'Royal Family, would it? Goodness knows what it'd do to t'Queen if owt like that happened . . . not that it will.'

'But it did happen, Mum, didn't it?' said Frances. 'With Edward VIII – the Duke of Windsor. I don't remember it – I was only a baby – but I've heard enough about it.'

'Oh aye, him,' replied Iris. 'It was her that was divorced, though, not him. But they soon got shut of him; it wouldn't do, you see.'

'I thought you were all for him,' said Eliza. 'Haven't I heard you say that you thought they should've let him marry the woman he loved, no matter who she was?'

'I might've done at the time,' Iris admitted. 'Aye, I seem to remember having an argument with your Aunt Alice, Frances. But that was before I knew what a good king George VI would be. He turned out to be a grand 'un, he did that, and his daughter's not doing so bad, neither. She's a grand lass.'

Frances smiled to herself. She was sure Queen Elizabeth would be gratified to hear Iris Goodwin's words of praise.

Princess Margaret did, indeed, look beautiful in her very simple wedding dress, designed by Norman Hartnell. It had a tight-fitting bodice and a high V-neckline, and the material, it was reported in the newspapers, was white silk organza, some thirty yards of it. Her only ornament was a magnificent diamond tiara and her wedding ring, a plain gold band, was made from the same Welsh nugget that had produced the wedding rings for her mother and sister.

'Eeh, I wish t'telly was in colour,' Iris said later as they watched the Princess and her new husband board the Royal Yacht, *Britannia*, at Tower Pier, for their honeymoon in the Caribbean. 'Now, that's what I call a smart coat. Sunshine yellow, Dimbleby says it is. I wish we could see t'colour of it.' Princess Margaret's coat was very stylish, straight and loose-fitting with a small stand-away collar and three-quarter-length sleeves.

'And we've another wedding to look forward to on Saturday, our Frances and me,' Iris remarked to Eliza. 'Megan and that doctor.' She turned to her daughter. 'I bet

224

she's getting excited, isn't she? Has she got everything ready?'

'Oh yes; it's all been organised with military precision, Mum,' replied Frances. 'Bernard's seen to that. It'll all go like clockwork, you'll see.'

'You sound as though you're not right keen on Megan's chap, Frances,' remarked Eliza.

Frances smiled. 'He wouldn't be my choice, but it's Megan who's marrying him, isn't it, not me? And she seems very happy.'

'It was kind of the lass to invite me, I must say,' said Iris. 'Specially with me not being a Catholic. I don't want to feel the odd one out.'

'You won't, Mum,' Frances assured her. 'Megan's femily aren't Catholics. It's only Megan that's turning. And don't worry, Adrian'll look after you in church, and at the reception. You won't be on your own.'

Frances had been invited to be a bridesmaid for Megan. Not the chief one, her friend had explained apologetically. That would not be possible as she was not a Catholic. That honour was to go to Maria, Bernard's sister, and the two little bridesmaids, also, were nieces of Bernard. Megan was an only child and her parents seemed to lead isolated lives, very wrapped up in one another and in their beloved daughter, but with no close relatives living near. Frances knew that it would be a wrench to them to part with Megan, although they appeared delighted with her choice of husband, considering that she had done very well for herself. Neither did the fact that he was a Catholic seem to worry them. Whatever Megan did was pleasing to them; she was a much-loved, and loving, daughter.

'We are *Roman* Catholics, Megan. I wish you would remember that,' Frances had heard Bernard affirm, in his pedantic way, more than once to his fiancée; and to her, Frances, as well, when she had inadvertently got the title wrong. 'Catholic is a term which means world-wide, that is all. Even the Church of England refer in their creed to the Holy Catholic Church. But we are Roman Catholics because our faith was started in Rome, by St Peter himself, our first pope. The *true* faith,' he added.

Frances always saw red when he said that and she knew that Adrian did too. But he had advised her that it was better not to get into an argument with the fellow as he, against his better judgement, had done on a few occasions.

'The true faith, indeed!' she had stormed, one evening when she had had rather too much of Bernard Conway's deliberations. 'I don't know how you can sit there and let him say that, Adrian. Doesn't he realise there are different ways of approaching the same God? Our way isn't wrong, only different. The man's a fool.'

'Hardly that, love. Far from it. Bigoted, maybe, but then a lot of Catholics – sorry, *Roman* Catholics – are. But so are a lot of Methodists. It would be a question of the pot calling the kettle black, so I prefer not to argue.'

'You're a saint, Adrian.'

'No, I'm not. You should know that.' They exchanged knowing glances. They were both relieved that it was only a few months to their own marriage.

'But how Megan has let herself be brain-washed by that fellow is beyond me,' Frances went on. 'When she was at school, she was very anti anything that smacked of popery: priests dressing up and incense and ritual and all that. She even looked askance at me for singing in the church choir; we had a rather fancy uniform, you see. But I think, even then, she was led by the nose by her friend Janet, who was a much more forceful character. Megan always had to have somebody to look up to.'

'I think Megan looks up to you as well as to Bernard. She needs you, Frances. You'll keep up your friendship, won't you, after she gets married?'

'Of course we will. I'm very fond of her.'

'Good; I've a feeling she may be in need of friends.'

'Why? Don't you think she'll be happy with Bernard?'

'I hope so; I pray so. But we all need friends.'

Megan's wedding dress was a fussy creation of net and silk organdie, with a tiered skirt consisting of layered frills. Her veil was floor length, kept in place by a head-dress of artificial flowers. The bridesmaids' dresses were pink, a colour of which Frances was not particularly fond. With her blonde prettiness – Frances was not given to false modesty about her looks – she felt like the fairy on the Christmas tree, especially as all four bridesmaids' dresses, for the two older and the two younger attendants, were made in the same style. They had puffed sleeves, sweetheart necklines and gathered skirts, Megan's choice entirely; but this was Megan's day and no one wanted to deprive her of any of her rapturous delight in it all.

And Frances had to admit, when she saw her friend walking down the aisle on the arm of her father, that Megan looked every inch the fairy-tale bride. Her colouring – blonde hair, blue eyes and delicate complexion – was not unlike that of Frances, but Megan was much more ethereal. She was the picture of innocence as Frances knew, in truth, she was; a pink and white angel, as she smiled so adoringly at the tall, commanding figure, handsome in his morning suit, who stepped forward to meet her at the chancel steps. Frances found herself muttering a silent prayer before the service started. Please, God, let her be happy. You know – forgive me, God – that I don't care for him very much myself, but please let him be kind to Megan.

Despite her prejudices Frances was impressed by the service, which was a beautiful and a moving one. The hymns they sang were such as might have been sung at any church wedding. 'Praise, my soul, the King of Heaven' and 'O perfect Love'; the choice of countless brides down the years, although Frances guessed that Bernard would also have had his say. She did not care much for the use of incense – low church folk tended to have an antipathy to such practices – and the celebration of Nuptial Mass seemed, to her, to be a strange idea at a wedding; although Bernard had mentioned that it was usual at Roman Catholic marriage ceremonies. It was, however, only those who were of the 'true faith' who were allowed to partake of what Frances thought of as Holy Communion. The people at the left-hand side of the church – the bride's side – were conspicuous by their absence at the altar rail, whilst all the bridegroom's side followed the bride – a new convert – and groom in the partaking of 'the Host'. Adrian had told her that this was the word used by Roman Catholics to describe the bread consecrated in the Eucharist (the Lord's Supper, to Methodists).

'I don't see why the rest of us can't partake of it,' she had argued. 'All us Methodists and C of E folk. It isn't as if we don't believe. And I do want to join fully in Megan's wedding, to give her my support . . . even if I'm not all that keen on her future husband.'

'It's a difference in doctrine,' Adrian explained. 'We believe that the bread and wine are just a symbol. Catholics believe that the substances change into the actual body and blood of the Lord. Transubstantiation, they call it. They believe it undergoes a miraculous change at the elevation of the Host. You'll see the priest lift it up at Megan's wedding.'

'But that doesn't make sense,' Frances argued. 'How can they believe something that's so clearly impossible? I've told you, Megan's being brain-washed. She would never have gone along with something as preposterous as that in the old days.'

'Preposterous to us, maybe,' Adrian replied calmly, 'but not to them. Don't ask me to explain it, darling, because I can't. "There are more things in heaven and earth than are dreamed of in our philosophy." That's not the Bible; it's Shakespeare – *Hamlet*, I think – rather misquoted. What I mean is, we can't understand everything about one another's faith. Perhaps we're not meant to. The important thing, I believe, is that we shouldn't fall out about it. It's all caused such bloodshed in the past, but not any more, thank God.'

'You're a very tolerant man, Adrian.'

'I try . . . not that I always succeed.'

Frances was recognising more than ever, as their own wedding day drew nearer, the innate goodness of this man to whom she was engaged to be married. He was not without his faults, certainly, but then, who was? There were times when she disagreed with him, and many times when he annoyed her. But he possessed such integrity and human kindness, at the side of which she often felt aware of her own unworthiness. She sometimes felt that she was not good enough – in the true sense of the word – to be the wife of the Reverend Adrian Glover.

These thoughts were with her as she watched Megan, so radiantly happy, on the arm of her new bridegroom. Bernard's proprietary attitude towards her was nothing new. He had long behaved as though Megan were his property, but Frances feared that the young woman's subservience to him would now increase. There was nothing as yet, however, to cloud the happiness of this day. The wedding breakfast at the Imperial Hotel – one of Blackpool's leading venues for such events – was superb. Asparagus soup, poached halibut, roast duckling – most people had been expecting chicken, but Bernard was sure to have had his say and opted for something more unusual – and sherry trifle, followed by coffee and a slice of rich dark wedding cake. The toasts were in champagne; Megan's parents had not stinted on anything, and Bernard, to give him his due, thanked them effusively for all they had done and for the gift of his lovely bride. He promised to take the utmost care of his new wife and there were murmurs all around of 'Ah . . .' and 'Isn't that nice?' and 'Don't they look happy?'

They were to honeymoon in Paris for a few days, and then in Rome; and after Megan and Bernard had changed out of their wedding finery a Daimler car arrived to take them to the airport. Megan's going-away outfit was surprisingly chic. The light wool suit was deep pink, Megan's favourite colour, with a fashionable stand-up collar, nipped-in waist and straight skirt, and with it she wore a tiny matching pillbox hat. She threw her wedding bouquet of pink roses and carnations high in the air, with all the delight of a little girl tossing a ball in the playground, and there was a surge of eager hands to catch it. Not those of Frances, however. She stood back and the bouquet was caught by Maria, Bernard's sister, which was quite fitting as she was engaged and due to get married the following year.

'You didn't even try,' said Adrian, though not in any

reproachful way. 'What's the matter, darling? Are you too grown-up for such childish goings-on?'

'No, not at all,' she assured him. 'But there's no need for me to join in, is there? I know, don't I? I know that we're getting married in August.'

'Yes, it's our turn next, love.' He put his arm round her as they watched the wedding car drive away in a shower of confetti. 'Not long to wait now. Three months, that's all.'

Frances knew there was a lot to do in the next few months, most of it not connected in any way with her forthcoming marriage, but with the events at Wyre Bank School. The anniversary concert was to be held during the first week in June. There was to be a performance on the Wednesday afternoon for the children of both schools, so that they could all see what the others were presenting. This was by way of a dress rehearsal, and the performance proper, for the parents and friends, was to take place on the Thursday evening.

As the day approached Frances was finding herself, increasingly, in a highly nervous state. She had always suffered, to a slight degree, from stage fright. Most artistes did, whether they were leading players or just members of the chorus. If you did not experience the sensation of butterflies in the stomach then you were unlikely to give of your best. But this nervousness stemmed from something else. The duets she was singing with Marcus Avery: what would people think? No, not just people in general; Frances was not too concerned about them. But what would her mother think? And her sister, Josie? And what would Adrian think?

At first she had made up her mind that she would kindly, but firmly, say no to Marcus's suggestion. But then, on learning that quite a few of the staff, not just of the Junior School, but the Infant School as well, were willing to show their talents, she had said to herself, Why not? She couldn't be so churlish or immature as to refuse to take part in what was, after all, a very reasonable proposition. Marcus was not suggesting anything outrageous, merely that they should get together and sing duets. They were to practise after school once a week, and in case Frances was concerned about the impropriety of this, Mrs Jeffrey, who had agreed to be the accompanist, would be there as a chaperone. Not that this was stated in so many words, but Frances knew that Marcus was aware of the doubts that were in her mind, and why they were there. Because, right from the time he had sought her out in her classroom, way back in September, ostensibly to apologise for his arrogance, they had both known that a spark had been fused between them. A spark of awareness, of liking for one another, an affinity which, if it were allowed to do so, could grow and grow.

But this was a spark, at least to Frances's mind, which must not be kindled any further. And so she quelled the tiny flames of what she dared not think of as desire which arose every time she sang with him, telling herself that she was merely being moved by the words of the songs and the haunting melodies, not by the look of barely suppressed longing in Marcus's eyes. She was sometimes cool with him and abrupt, feigning an indifference she certainly did not feel, because she was a very happy engaged-to-be-married young woman, and he, she had learned, was a married man.

'Watch it now, with Casanova,' Marjorie had warned her when, before the concert committee's second meeting, Frances had admitted to her friend that she had agreed – though unwillingly, she assured her – to sing duets with Marcus Avery. 'I don't trust him. He has a look of Stewart Granger, and that's a fellow I never could abide.'

'Of course he hasn't,' Frances had laughed. 'He's nothing like him.' Although she had, if she were honest, noticed the slight resemblance to the said film star. 'Stewart Granger's real shifty-looking, and Marcus is a very nice person when you get to know him. He's not nearly so high and mighty as he seemed to be at that first meeting, you know.'

'OK, if you say so. Just watch your step, that's all. You don't want folks thinking that what you're singing about is true.' Frances, herself, had wondered about the wisdom of singing 'People Will Say We're in Love', from *Oklahoma!*, but it was a song that came over so well as a duet. 'He hasn't thrown any bouquets at you, has he? He didn't bring those, by any chance, did he?' Marjorie nodded towards the nature table where there was a jamjar filled with somewhat wilting Michaelmas daisies.

Frances burst out laughing when she saw where her friend was looking. 'Good grief! It's time I chucked those out, isn't it? The nature table is not exactly my forte, is it? No, he hasn't brought me any flowers . . . but, come to think of it, I do seem to have mislaid my gloves,' she added with a grin. 'Fear not, Marjorie, I know what I'm doing. I'm in no danger of losing my heart, I can assure you . . . or anything else. Anyway, I'm engaged to Adrian, aren't I? And Marcus is married.'

'Since when did that make any difference?'

'Well, it does to me,' Frances had replied primly. 'I think that girls who get involved with married men deserve all they get. He does say he's not too happy, though.'

'Oh, he does, does he? You've not gone and fallen for that old chestnut, have you? "My wife doesn't understand me", and all that garbage.'

'He hasn't said that. Only that his wife – Geraldine, she's called – is very much a career woman and that they seem to be going their separate ways.'

'What does she do?'

'She's in charge of personnel at Marks & Spencer. Quite a high-flier from all accounts. It really does seem as though she hasn't much time for Marcus at the moment.'

'Hmm . . . so he says. Have they any children?'

'No, they haven't got a family.'

'And how old is he? Do you know?'

'Mid-thirties, I suppose. He was in the RAF during the war, then he did his Emergency Training. Hey, what is this, Marjorie? Why are you quizzing me like this? I've told you, I couldn't care less about Marcus Avery. Just because I'm singing a few songs with him it's no big deal.'

Now, months later, the concert was almost upon them and Frances knew that all her worrying would not make a scrap of difference. It was too late to back out now so she might just as well make up her mind to give a good performance and, above all, to enjoy it.

She couldn't help but be relieved, however, when she learned on the eve of the concert that Iris did not feel well enough to attend. She was concerned, of course, for her mother's health, but when Eliza assured her that it was nothing to worry about, that Iris was just rather tired and her arthritis was more troublesome than usual, Frances decided that it was an 'ill wind'. But it was too much to hope for that Adrian might be suddenly called away . . . to arrange a wedding or funeral or something? And Josie, in her capacity as school photographer, was sure to be there.

The dress rehearsal was a disaster, but the teachers who had some experience of amateur dramatics, including Frances and Marcus, told one another that this boded well for the next day. A bad dress rehearsal meant a good first night, or, in this case, the only night; they would not have a second chance.

Several of the children forgot the words of the poems and songs and frequent loud promptings were heard; the cardboard model of Blackpool Tower fell down with a crash in the middle of a scene; Wendy's percussion band performance was marred by triangles clanging to the floor, cymbals coming in when it should have been the drums, and the whole ensemble finishing two bars ahead of the pianist; and Little Bo Peep, a charmingly dressed shepherdess, complete with woolly lamb, made a pool on the floor in full view of the audience.

The display of Music and Movement by the Second Year children was by no means synchronised, despite the frantic gesticulations of Miss Cameron and the shouts from a red-faced Miss Walsh, banging away on the piano. Frances had it in her heart actually to feel sorry for them. She knew that, despite their opposition to the whole idea, they had worked hard at this display and the ragged performance was the children's fault and not theirs.

Frances decided to have a word with Miss Cameron, the rather less antagonistic one of her two adversaries.

'Never mind, it'll be all right on the night,' she said. 'It's sure to be; you've put such a lot of work into it. Honestly, couldn't you brain them when they let you down like that?'

'Thank you,' Miss Cameron replied, with the merest hint of a frosty smile. 'Yes, we have worked hard.'

'Let us down? They haven't let us down at all!' Miss Walsh, who could hear a pin drop from fifty yards – Frances hadn't realised she was walking behind them – broke into the conversation. 'I think they did very well. All right on the night, indeed! If it was up to me there would be no night at all. It's ridiculous making children behave like performing monkeys. Teachers in my day were trained to teach reading and mathematics, not to be stage managers, or to pretend they're prima donnas.'

Frances had been feeling quite elated. In spite of the numerous blunders in the children's performances – there had been several, too, in the Junior School's items, though these were not so noticeable – she felt that she and Marcus had acquitted themselves very well. A lot of the children had clustered round, making a fuss of her.

'That was smashing, Miss Goodwin.'

'Don't you sing lovely?'

'I like yer dress, miss . . . You look just like a film star.' There had been favourable comments from several of the staff, too. Now she felt deflated. Marjorie had a dental appointment and had dashed off immediately after the rehearsal and now she had no one to talk to. Dispiritedly she crept into her stockroom and took off her dress. It was her pink bridesmaid's dress from Megan's wedding, subtly altered here and there to tone down the fussiness. She had felt she must give it another airing, and it had proved to be a great hit with the children. At least they liked my performance, she thought, but the niggling fears about tomorrow night were beginning to plague her again. She grabbed her shoulder bag and cardigan and dashed out of the classroom. She couldn't get away fast enough today from the unfamiliar silence of the echoing corridors and the feeling of deadness that had descended on the place now all the children had gone home. She was aware, too, of

an odd creeping sense of foreboding, a feeling that something – something not very pleasant – was about to happen.

She had the flat to herself as she usually did when she
arrived home. Julie, who had come to share with her soon
after Megan's departure, did not arrive back from work
until after half-past five. Julie had been only too keen to
become her flatmate despite Frances's warning that it
would be for only a few months; in August she would be
getting married and Julie would have to find someone else
to move in with her.

'Never mind, I'll worry about that when it happens,'
Julie had said. 'You don't know how glad I am to have a
place of my own. Mum's been driving me barmy lately
with her endless fussing. It's a miracle she's let me come at
all. It was Dad who persuaded her she had to let me stand
on my own feet. Actually, she thinks you're a good influence
on me, Fran,' Julie giggled. 'I think it's because you're
engaged to a vicar. She thinks you'll keep me on the straight
and narrow.'

Julie was a very amenable flatmate, easy-going but, at
the same time, dependable. In many ways she was easier to
get on with than Megan had been and not nearly so
exasperating.

Frances was glad to see her arrive home that evening
and her friend soon tried to set her fears at rest about the
concert. 'They're only a load of school kids,' she said. 'You
can't expect 'em to be perfect. And the parents'll think it's
marvellous whatever happens. I know it's important to
you, but it's not exactly Sadler's Wells, is it? They're only
kids off the Wyre Bank estate. You can't make 'em into
prima donnas.'

'That's what Miss Walsh said about me, that I was
pretending to be a prima donna. Honestly, Julie, I could
have wept. And I'm still worried sick about what people
are going to think. I wish I'd never said I'd do it. I could kill
Marcus Avery.'

Julie managed to calm her down. Why should anyone
think anything? They were acting, weren't they, that was
all, just like the Starlight Players? All sorts of couples sang

love songs together and sometimes they hated one another's guts. Look at Anne Zeigler and Webster Booth; everybody knew that they fought like cat and dog when they were off the stage. *Oklahoma!*, staged in March and a tremendous success, had contained 'lovers' who, in reality, never saw each other between rehearsals.

'I'm really looking forward to this concert,' Julie assured her. 'I wouldn't miss it for anything. Don't you worry about a thing, kid; you'll be fine. Anyway, it's only school, isn't it?'

Yes, it was only school, Frances told herself; and the thought was tinged with more than a little sadness because she had now handed in her notice and her post at Wyre Bank School was soon to be advertised. There could be no turning back. Not that she wanted to, but she had been happy during the short time she had been at the school.

The old adage about a poor dress rehearsal proved to be true because the concert was a triumph. The children's items all came up to scratch as did those of the teachers. There were not many who were brave enough to display their talents, but those who did gave very accomplished performances. Wendy Clarkson surprised everyone with her humorous monologues, 'Albert and the Lion' – always popular with Blackpool audiences – and 'Sam, pick up thi' Musket'; while Mr Reed recited dramatically two poems by Rudyard Kipling. Mrs Jeffrey turned out to be a brilliant pianist, there was a conjuror who, many said, could rival David Nixon, and Marcus and Frances brought the house down with their duets, 'People Will Say We're in Love' and 'Some Enchanted Evening'.

'Once you have found her never let her go . . .' They held hands and gazed at one another as they sang the final words of the song, and once again, more so than ever this time, her senses heightened by the intensity of the moment, Frances experienced the familiar flame of longing that she knew she had to extinguish.

As they turned to face the audience, acknowledging the applause with bows and smiles, Frances's eyes scanned the rows, searching for her friends and family. Julie was beaming all over her face and clapping like mad. So was

Valerie, bouncing up and down in her seat with excitement. Jim, at her side, was smiling fondly at her, but, as Frances watched, Josie put out a hand to restrain her daughter, and Josie's face as she glanced in the direction of the stage was as angry as a thundercloud. Frances met her sister's eye for only a brief second before she looked away, searching for Adrian. Adrian was not scowling, nor was he smiling or clapping; he was staring, into space, a thoughtful expression on his face. Frances did not know how to interpret that.

The final item was 'Jerusalem', sung by the Junior School choir and after that the cast, both pupils and teachers, were free to mingle with the audience. The children were the parents' responsibility now and after they had collected their belongings from the various classrooms, which had served as dressing rooms, they would get on their way home.

Frances pushed her way through the crowd, heading towards Adrian. He knew many of the people there, several of them being members of his own congregation. Frances could see him chatting to a group of them at the back of the hall. She was stopped by a hand on her arm.

'Frances . . . not so fast.' It was Marcus. 'I want you to meet my wife.'

She turned to find herself looking into the cool appraising eyes of a woman who was about her own height. A slim, dark-haired, sophisticated woman – she looked rather older than Marcus – whose glance did not falter for several seconds. It seemed an age to Frances before she spoke.

'How do you do?' Frances took the proffered hand, muttering some sort of response. 'I must congratulate you on your performance,' said Mrs Avery. 'Very professional, but then everything Marcus does is highly professional.' Was there a touch of sarcasm there? Frances was not sure; the woman's expression revealed very little. 'You sing very charmingly together.' She gave a polite little smile, but her eyes still held a frosty look.

'Er . . . thank you,' murmured Frances. 'Yes, we've . . . I've . . . enjoyed singing with Marcus. As you say, he's a real professional. It's nice to meet you, Mrs Avery, but will you excuse me, please? I've got to meet my fiancé.' She hardly glanced at Marcus as she hurried away.

Valerie stepped into her path. 'Auntie Frances, you were smashing! Your dress looks lovely; it's your bridesmaid's dress, isn't it, that you had for Megan's wedding?'

But Josie, hard on her heels, grabbed hold of her sister's arm, pulling her to one side, before she could answer. 'What the hell did you think you were playing at?' she hissed. 'You and that Avery fellow, gazing into one another's eyes in that ridiculous way! You made a real show of yourself.'

'Oh, come on, Josie, don't be silly. We were only acting. Surely you could see—'

'Acting my foot! All I could see was you making an exhibition of yourself. You've got a crush on the fellow. Anybody with half an eye could see that. I tell you what, it's a good job Mum wasn't here to see you behaving like that.'

'Behaving like what? I've told you, we were just acting a part—'

'And goodness knows what Adrian thought of it. You'll be jolly lucky if he doesn't give you a real good telling off. It's what you deserve, but he's too nice. Too nice for you, that's for sure.'

'Come on, Josie, that's enough.' Her husband was pulling at her arm. 'You've had your say, and I'm sure Frances didn't mean it to look that way. You've got to look the part when you're singing love songs. Even I know that.' He glanced helplessly at Frances. 'Come on, Josie; people are looking at us.' In point of fact, they weren't; everyone seemed to be minding their own business. 'Come along, love. We said we'd call and see your mother on the way home.'

Josie departed without another glance at her, and Frances, feeling sick with worry, hurried off to find Adrian. He was at the back of the hall, alone now, waiting for her.

'Whatever's the matter, darling?' He put his arm round her. 'You look worried to death. Or are you just tired? Yes, I'm sure you must be.'

She was amazed. He hadn't noticed anything then? It

was only Josie, who was always so critical of her, who had thought . . . what she had thought. But Marcus's wife had been decidedly cool too, she recalled. 'I'm all right,' Frances sighed. 'Come on; I've just to collect my things, then we'll go home.'

She paused briefly to say good-night to Jonathan Russell and Glenys Mortimer, who was clinging tightly to his arm. From the look of things she might soon be more than his assistant. 'Well done, Frances,' said Jonathan. 'I enjoyed the concert, all of it. Jolly good show.' Dennis, at the other side of him, glanced shiftily at Frances, in the way that children often did when they saw their teachers away from a classroom situation. She thought that the little boy looked rather less than happy.

'Good night, Dennis,' she said, giving him a special smile, which she was pleased to see he returned.

'G'night, Miss Goodwin.'

'No, I'm not all right, not really, Adrian,' she continued as they walked across the playground to where Adrian's car was parked. She didn't know why she was telling him, but she felt she must. 'It was our Josie. She's just had a go at me. She said I made a fool of myself singing those songs.' Frances was very near to tears.

'But why? Why should she say that?'

'Because they were love songs. And because . . . well . . . Marcus and I . . . we were looking at one another.'

Adrian smiled. 'But you were acting, darling, that's all. Didn't she realise that?' He opened the car door and Frances stepped inside. 'She surely wasn't suggesting you were . . . what – falling in love with Marcus Avery?' His tone suggested that the very idea was ridiculous.

'Something like that,' said Frances in a quiet voice.

'But that's ludicrous.' He seized hold of her hands. 'Besides, doesn't Josie realise that I trust you implicitly, darling?' That made Frances, for some reason, feel worse than ever. He kissed her briefly on the cheek before starting up the car. 'Don't let it spoil your evening, love. It was a great concert. I was very proud of you. Come on, let's go and see your mother.'

'It's late, Adrian. Anyway, Josie might be there.'

'All the better if she is. We can let her see that her ideas are nonsense. Your mother will be dying to hear all about the concert and you know she doesn't go to bed early. I bet she and Eliza sit up half the night chatting about the olden days.'

It was not Eliza, however, who opened the door of the bungalow to them, but Mrs Pearson, the woman who lived next door. Iris, she explained in hushed tones, had been taken ill earlier that evening. Mrs Pendleton – Eliza – had rung for an ambulance and had gone with her friend to Victoria Hospital. She had asked Mrs Pearson if she would stay at the bungalow to give the news to Iris's daughters who would, she guessed, be calling round after the concert at the school. Josie and Jim and Valerie were already on their way to the hospital, and now that Frances, also, had been given the news Mrs Pearson would get back to her own home.

'Thank you . . . thank you.' Frances could barely whisper the words. 'She will be . . . all right, won't she?'

'Let's hope so, dear.' Mrs Pearson's smile was sorrowful. 'But you'd best get up there as quick as you can.'

Chapter 16

'Frances . . . you won't go and leave me, will you?' It was the following afternoon and Iris was clinging tightly to her daughter's hand. Frances was surprised at the strength of her grip because her voice was very weak. She was in a very weak state altogether. The doctor had almost admitted, as much as a doctor ever would, that it had been touch and go last night. But she had pulled round and with the excellent care and attention she was receiving it was beginning to look as though she might make a good recovery. It was, however, her third heart attack, besides one or two minor scares, so it was inevitable, even if she recovered, that her heart would be weakened. Her mother was a fighter, though, Frances knew that; at least, she had always used to be.

'No, Mum, of course I won't leave you,' Frances replied. 'I'm staying right here with you unless the nurse comes and tells me to go. They don't like visitors staying too long, you know.' Not when the patient is as ill as you are, she thought, but did not say.

'No, no . . . I don't mean that.' Iris's head, on the pillow, shook a little and her voice was tinged with irritation. 'I mean . . . you won't go away and leave me. You won't go and live . . . in Birmingham, will you?'

Frances was speechless for a moment. What on earth could she say? The wedding was barely two months away. The reception was booked, the invitations sent out, the wedding dress and bridesmaids' dresses reserved at Diana Warren's. She couldn't cancel it all now. It was impossible. And yet . . . In that moment, as she looked down at her mother's face, still ashen with the vestiges of the pain she had suffered, and at the grey eyes – Iris still had such beautiful eyes – looking at her so lovingly, Frances recognised that this was the excuse for which, albeit unknowingly, she had been searching. Iris was handing her a lifeline, and she reached out to grab it.

'No, Mum,' she said, taking hold of both of Iris's hands. 'Of course I won't go and leave you. I shall stay here in Blackpool until you're quite, quite better. It'll be all right. I'll tell Adrian. He'll understand.'

Forgive me, God, she thought, because she knew, deep down, that her mother's illness was not the only reason – maybe not the reason at all – why she was making this momentous decision. Neither was it because she didn't love Adrian. He was such a good admirable man, worthy of any girl's love. She did love him . . . but she wasn't sure, perhaps she had never been sure, that she really wanted to marry him. All through their engagement she had made difficulties and excuses about their future together. Now was the moment to face the facts, to be completely honest with herself and with Adrian.

They had had only a brief glimpse of Iris last night as the doctors and nurses had fought to save her life. Frances and Josie, of necessity, had been obliged to speak to one another. The concert had not been mentioned – entirely forgotten in the trauma of the events that followed it – and now there was an uneasy truce between them. Josie and Jim had been to see Iris earlier in the afternoon. Now it was the turn of Frances and Eliza, and Eliza had withdrawn for a little while to let the mother and daughter have some time together.

'Eliza . . .' said Frances, as the two of them walked along the endless hospital corridors at the end of the visiting time. 'I've just said something terrible, and I don't know what on earth I'm going to do about it. I've gone and told Mum that I won't go to Birmingham, that I'll stay here. She looked so pathetic,' she went on, as Eliza, stopping in her tracks, turned to stare at her in open-mouthed surprise. 'I couldn't say no, could I?'

'You mean . . . you've said you're not going to get married?'

'I haven't actually said that, but I can't very well get married, can I, not if I've promised to stay in Blackpool? I can't live here and Adrian in Birmingham. Oh, Eliza, what the heck am I going to do?'

'Listen, love . . .' Eliza linked arms with her companionably as they continued walking. 'Your mother's a very demanding woman. She can be quite self-centred at times. I know that only too well. In normal circumstances I would have said don't give in to her. But now – well, I've got to admit it's rather different.'

'Her heart, you mean? I know it wouldn't do for her to get upset. That's why I said what I did. That's why I promised . . .' At least it's partly the truth, Frances assured her conscience, that 'still small voice' she could hear inside her head.

'Exactly. She's got you over a barrel, though she may not realise it. If you ask me she's been leading up to this for quite some time.'

'What do you mean, Eliza?'

'Well, it's difficult to put into words, dear. But ever since you told her the wedding date was fixed and that you would be going to live in Birmingham she has been . . . well, sort of quiet, preoccupied. You must have noticed, surely?'

'I know she hasn't made a big fuss about the wedding arrangements as I thought she might have done. Like she did when our Josie was getting married. But she was younger then and quite a lot fitter, even though she'd already had one heart attack.'

'And Josie was settling in Blackpool, remember.'

'Yes, of course. But I didn't think she was taking it so badly, about me going to live in Birmingham. It isn't as if it's the other end of the world. I know she's been rather quiet about it, but she hasn't said very much.'

'She has to me. She's kept saying how she'll miss you, and that once you're married she'll have lost you.'

'But she likes Adrian so much. She was over the moon when we got engaged. In fact I sometimes feel she almost pushed me into it. She must have realised we'd move away.

After all, he's a Methodist minister.'

'She's closed her eyes to it, love. That's what she's done, and now it's happened – or it's about to happen – well, she just can't face it.'

'You don't mean she's brought the heart attack on herself?'

'No, not exactly. . . No, of course not. Not even Iris could do that. But she's been worrying, and it hasn't helped.'

'And I've got to make sure she doesn't worry any more,' said Frances in a quiet voice.

'Well, that's up to you, dear. Perhaps you could just postpone the wedding, could you, for a few months, until you see how she goes on? Far be it from me to tell you what to do; it's none of my business really, is it? If she hadn't been ill I'd have said get on with your plans and never mind her; you can't let her rule your life. But now. . .'

'But now I can't. I mustn't upset her any further. Listen, Eliza, don't say anything to Adrian, will you?' Adrian would be waiting for them in the car park. The rules about visitors were very strict – only two people at the bed at one time.

'No, of course I won't say anything. As if I would.'

'No, what I mean is, I'll tell him in my own time. When we're alone. I'll have to choose the right moment.'

'Don't leave it too long, dear. There's a lot to be done – or undone – isn't there, if you've really made up your mind?'

'Yes, I have . . . I really have.'

Frances decided she wouldn't wait at all. If she put it off she knew she might lose her nerve. She broke the news to him as soon as they arrived back at her flat after taking Eliza home.

'Whatever are you saying, darling?' Adrian looked shocked beyond belief, as though his world was coming to an end, as she had feared he might. She knew he loved her very much. 'Are you saying that you don't want to marry me?'

'No, no . . . I didn't say that at all. Haven't you listened?

I just said not yet. We'll have to put the wedding off for a few months – longer, perhaps – until we see how Mum goes on. She's very poorly, Adrian. She nearly died, and she wants me here with her.'

'Yes . . . yes, I can see that. I realise it's been a near thing. But it seems so drastic. Everything is arranged – the reception, the invitations . . . the honeymoon. And that was to be my secret, darling. It was to be a lovely surprise.'

'Yes, I know. I'm sorry.' And, in that moment, Frances really was very, very sorry. 'But it'll only be for a little while, Adrian. We can't very well get married and live apart, can we? Me up here and you in Birmingham? You'll have to go there without me. We'll be able to meet.'

'I don't see how. Weekends are out, aren't they, with two services each Sunday?' Adrian sounded so glum. She would have thought, being a clergyman that he might have been more philosophical about it, seeing it as, not exactly the will of God, but as a trial that had been put in their way and which they must try to overcome. But he just sounded and looked miserable.

'What about your job?' he asked suddenly. 'You've given in your notice at Wyre Bank. It's been advertised, hasn't it?'

Her job! Until now Frances, unbelievably, had not given it a thought. She had not been in to school today because of her mother's illness. School seemed very far away at the moment, but she knew, if she were honest, that she had never faced up to the fact that she had actually handed in her notice. She had done it, but it did not seem real, perhaps because it had been done unwillingly.

'I don't think it's been advertised yet,' she said slowly. 'Maybe . . . it's not too late . . . to cancel it.'

The look Adrian gave her was unfathomable. If he was thinking that it was what she had wanted all along he did not say so.

He was thoughtful as he drove home leaving Frances in her flat. He knew that he should insist that they went ahead and got married as arranged, no matter what difficulties might be in the way; because he feared, deep down, that if he did not do so then he might well lose Frances altogether. He couldn't help feeling that she had latched on to the fact of her mother's illness as an undeniable excuse to postpone their wedding. To cancel it entirely, maybe, or was he being too suspicious? On the other hand, he could see the logic in what she was saying. They couldn't marry and then live apart.

Iris had a very strong hold over her younger daughter. He had seen this as soon as he had met the woman, although he had always liked Iris, admiring her guts, her down-to-earth attitude and the deep love she showed for her adopted family. Was it time now, though, to make a stand against her, to make her realise she could not hang on to her daughter forever in this selfish way?

Oh, what a confounded mess and muddle it all was, just when everything had been going along so smoothly. A new living, the promise of a nice flat for the two of them in Birmingham. Not that he had imagined it would always be easy, living with Frances. She had surprised him by taking that extraordinary stand about her teaching career last summer. He had realised, though it might well be against his better judgement, that he would have to go along with her decision to carry on teaching, if only on a part-time basis. He loved her so much he could not bear the thought of losing her.

But there was something else, just a small cloud of doubt, niggling away at the back of his mind. It was stupid, really, but he could not get that wretched fellow, Marcus Avery, out of his thoughts. He could not forget the way the two of them – that Marcus chap and his own lovely Frances – had looked at one another when they were singing that love song at the school concert. There could have been nothing in it though; he was just being ridiculous. Frances would never have mentioned it if there had been the least little bit of feeling between the two of them, and she had been so truthful and so upset about her sister having a go at her.

There was something about Marcus Avery, though, that Adrian did not like. Adrian tried, always, to see the best side of people, but this man managed, somehow, to rub

246

him up the wrong way. He did not know him well, only meeting him on the odd occasions he had called into the Junior School, so maybe he was being too condemnatory. But Mr Avery seemed so superior, so arrogant, the type of person who was always right, or thought he was. No, whatever was he thinking about? Frances would never allow herself to be taken in by such a fellow as that. She had too much common sense. And Frances loved him – of course she did – as much as he loved her. But Josie was no fool . . .

Adrian's thoughts were in a turmoil. He decided, as he always did to 'take it to the Lord in prayer'. It would help to clarify things in his mind. And he knew, come what may, that he had to trust Frances implicitly. A relationship without trust was no use at all.

The post had not been advertised. Miss Reynolds admitted that the office had been dragging their heels, fortunately, as it turned out, because she appeared delighted that Frances would not, after all, be leaving.

'I'm so sorry about your mother, dear,' she said, 'and about your wedding having to be postponed. But it's an ill wind, as they say. Of course you can have your job back, for as long as you want. I'll phone the office right away.'

Frances undertook the task of cancelling all the other arrangements: the reception, the flowers, the wedding invitations, the dresses. Luckily the manageress of the dress shop was very understanding and even gave her back the deposit she had paid as the dresses had not left the shop. There would be no difficulty in selling them to someone else and it would be far better, the manageress agreed, for Frances to choose again when the new wedding date was fixed; something entirely different might be chosen for a winter or a spring wedding.

The photographer had to be cancelled, too. That was to have been Josie, and here Frances, as she had anticipated, met with disapproval. The week after Iris's heart attack, Frances was on her own in her flat when Josie called, with the obvious intention of telling her what she thought of her. Not because of the cancelled photographic session –

that was neither here nor there because Frances wouldn't have been paying for the photos anyway, her sister pointed out, somewhat spitefully – but because of the impulsive way in which Frances had cancelled the wedding.

'But Mum's ill,' Frances argued. 'She's been terribly ill and she begged me not to go and leave her. What else could I have done?'

'You could still have married him.' Josie gave her a searching look. 'Don't think you can pull the wool over my eyes, Frances, even if you can fool Adrian. It was just an excuse. You could have got married if you really wanted to.'

'What? And live apart? What sort of a life would that be? Anyway, we will be getting married . . . eventually. We'll have to see how Mum goes on.'

'Don't pretend to be so self-sacrificing, Frances. I can see right through you. One minute you're gazing into some fellow's eyes – a married fellow, I might add – and the next minute you're cancelling your wedding. It looks very funny to me.'

'I couldn't help Mum having a heart attack, could I?'

'No, but it was very convenient, wasn't it?'

'How dare you? How dare you say that? I cancelled the wedding – postponed it, I mean – because Mum was ill and she wanted me to stay with her. But you can think what the hell you like, Josie. I don't care very much what you think.'

Without Jim there to pour oil on troubled waters, the bitterness between the sisters lingered. When Iris came out of hospital some ten days later, very much better, but still in need of care and attention – a district nurse was to call periodically, as well as the family doctor – they decided, independently, that they must try to patch up the quarrel.

'I'm sorry,' Josie mumbled. 'I may have spoken rather hastily. I was upset about Mum, that's why.' The apology was grudging, but at least it had been given.

'It's all right.' Frances, too, spoke in a mumble. 'We've both been upset, and you say things you don't mean when you're upset.'

Frances guessed, however, that Josie had meant every

word of what she had said, and her own guilty conscience – about letting Adrian down, about her real reason for cancelling the wedding . . . and about Marcus Avery – only served to make her feel worse than ever. For their mother's sake they had to behave as though there was nothing wrong, but Frances felt that relations between her and Josie had been so badly damaged that they might never be the same again.

Frances had seen Megan only briefly since her return from her honeymoon. With typical efficiency, Bernard had installed his new bride in a most desirable residence near to the hospital, and Frances imagined Megan was busy playing house in the real-life home of her dreams. But Megan had heard that Iris was in hospital and had taken time from her own nursing duties, which she had decided to continue for the time being, to pop into the ward now and again. One of her visits had coincided with visiting hours and that was when she had met Frances. She looked pale, Frances had thought, even paler than usual. Her few days in the Italian sun did not seem to have brought any colour to her skin, although, being delicate and fair-complexioned, it was possible that she had tried to keep out of it. There'd been a strange look in her eyes, though, a wariness, a distracted kind of look that Frances had not liked. Megan had not had the radiant appearance one might expect of a girl recently returned from honeymoon; like Wendy Clarkson, Frances's colleague had had, for instance, when she had come back to school after her wedding last August.

There had been no opportunity then to exchange more than a few words, and to Frances's question as to whether they had enjoyed their honeymoon Megan had replied with a polite, 'Yes, thank you – it was lovely.'

But Megan called at the flat the week after Iris had been discharged from hospital. It was half-past four and she had just finished her shift. Bernard, she explained, was on the evening shift and would not be home until nearly midnight, so she had decided to visit her friend. She knew they could have some time alone together because Julie did not get back till after half-past five. She spoke breathlessly and Frances guessed she had something on her mind. When Frances suggested that she might stop for tea Megan jumped at the idea; but first, she said, it would be nice to have a quiet chat, before Julie came home.

Frances went to put the kettle on and when she returned from the kitchen Megan was lying back in the armchair with her eyes closed. She looked exhausted, and when she opened her eyes Frances could see again the strain and anxiety there. Frances did not, at first, ask her what was wrong. Maybe there was nothing wrong; maybe she was just tired, and if there was something troubling her then she must be allowed to unburden herself in her own good time.

'Now then,' she said brightly, as she handed Megan a mug of tea. 'Tell me all about your honeymoon. Well, I don't mean absolutely all, do I?' She smiled knowingly at her friend, but the smile was not returned. You had to be careful what you said to Megan; she was so prim and proper, but Frances had thought, now she was a married woman . . . 'I mean . . . how did you like Paris? And Rome? Which did you like best?'

Frances was relieved to see a spark of enthusiasm return to Megan's eyes as she replied she had loved them both. They were both such wonderful cities.

'The Champs-Elysées was beautiful,' she enthused. 'All the blossom trees were in bloom, and the flowers in the Tuileries . . . And the Eiffel Tower. I couldn't believe I was actually looking at the Eiffel Tower. I'd always wanted to go to Paris, you know. Yes, I loved that part of it; Paris more than Rome, I think. Bernard preferred Rome, though.'

They had visited the Colosseum and the Catacombs, St Peter's and the Vatican City. Bernard must have been in his element, thought Frances, pontificating about it all to his new wife.

'And did you see the Pope?' she asked.

'Oh yes, we saw him all right, you might know.' Frances glanced at her, aware of the unfamiliar bitterness in her tone. 'I mean . . . yes, we saw the Pope. He came out on the balcony. It was Whit Sunday, you see, while we were there. Bernard was very thrilled.' Her voice sounded a little flat.

'You didn't have a private audience, then?'

'Oh no, nothing like that. Not for ordinary people like us.' Ordinary? thought Frances. When did Bernard Conway ever think of himself as ordinary? She thought that arranging an audience with the Pope would have been a piece of cake to such as him.

'Frances . . . Frances, can I talk to you?' Her somewhat uncharitable thoughts were stopped in mid-stream by the anxiety in Megan's voice.

'Of course you can. Megan, what's the matter? There's something wrong, isn't there?'

'Not really . . . wrong. I don't know. Perhaps it's me that's at fault. It might be. I know Bernard would say it was my fault if I told him . . . but I haven't.' She paused, biting her lip. 'You see . . . oh, Frances. I'm finding it so hard to say.'

'Go on, love,' prompted Frances. 'Never mind me. Pretend I'm not here, if you like. Just say it, whatever it is that's bothering you. Come on, Megan; we're old friends, you and me. It'll do you good to get it off your chest, whatever it is.'

'It's just . . . marriage. That side of it . . . you know what I mean.' Megan hung her head. 'You know . . . in bed. I never dreamed it would be like that. It's so . . . so awful.'

Frances could see she was near to tears. She had begun to guess it might be something of the sort that was troubling Megan, but exactly what it was she couldn't imagine. She did not like Bernard Conway, but she would never have suspected him of being odd; perverted, in some way, maybe?

'You mean . . . What do you mean, Megan?' she faltered.

'Oh, nothing peculiar,' replied Megan. 'I wouldn't want you to think Bernard was strange in any way. I do know about things like that.' She lowered her voice. 'Perverted people, sexual deviants and all that. I didn't used to know, but I've learned quite a lot since I started nursing. Things

251

I could never have imagined.' She was speaking quite freely now she was talking about other people and not herself.

'No, he's not peculiar, not really. At least – well – it's peculiar to me, I suppose. He's so . . . demanding, so insatiable.' She blushed and her voice dropped to a whisper. 'I did know that we would . . . make love. But not so often. Several times a night, sometimes, and in the morning as well. And I'm . . . I'm tired out. I'm exhausted. He can't seem to see how tired I am.' She stopped abruptly. 'I shouldn't be telling you this.'

'I don't see why not, Megan,' said Frances, quite matter-of-factedly. 'You've got to talk to somebody, haven't you? Haven't you tried telling him how tired you are? He's a doctor; surely he should understand. And you do look tired, love. You look worn out.'

'I am. And I'm worried because I never enjoy it. Sex, I mean.' She blushed again. 'I thought I would . . . but I don't. And I daren't tell him. So I just have to pretend that I think it's all right. Not that he bothers about what I'm thinking. I know that. Just so long as he's getting what he wants.' It was the first time Frances had ever heard Megan criticise Bernard, even slightly. To her confusion, she did not know how best to answer.

'Oh dear,' she murmured. 'I'm so sorry, Megan. Perhaps . . . perhaps it will get better. It's early days yet, isn't it? You've only been married – what? – just over a month. I dare say a lot of brides feel just like you do.'

Frances did not know; it was out of her realm of experience, but she guessed, also, that a lot of brides most certainly did not feel the way Megan did.

'I wouldn't want you to think I was criticising him in any way,' Megan went on. 'It's probably me, not him, that's at fault. I shouldn't have said anything, but I had to tell somebody how I felt. I couldn't tell anybody but you. Bernard's a wonderful husband in a lot of ways, and we're very happy . . . We are happy, really,' she repeated, almost defiantly.

'We've got a lovely house; everything I could possibly want. You should see the kitchen, Frances. There's an electric cooker, a fridge and a washing machine, and nice fitted cupboards, all in blue Formica. You must come round and see us, you and Adrian. I was sorry about the wedding being put off, but you're still engaged to him, aren't you?'

'Yes, of course.'

'Well, you'll have to come and see our house. That's one thing I'm looking forward to, having little dinner parties, and Bernard says my cooking's improving such a lot since we got married. He says I'm nearly as good as his mother now. And he's not mean with the housekeeping money. I only have to ask if I want a bit more. My wage goes straight into a joint account, you see, now we're married, and Bernard sorts it all out. So I've a lot to be thankful for, much more than a lot of girls have. A lovely house . . . and everything . . .' Her voice petered away.

Frances noticed she kept saying 'house' and not 'home' and wondered if there was any significance in that. It was, indeed, an imposing house, a detached one with four bedrooms, in a secluded part of Whinney Heys Road. Frances had seen it from the outside, but, so far, had not had a definite invitation to visit the newly married couple.

'And the important thing is to try to keep your husband happy, isn't it?' Megan was speaking breathlessly again. 'I mean . . . that's what you're supposed to do. To look after him . . . in every way.'

'It's important to be happy yourself as well, I would have thought,' replied Frances. 'He should be trying to make you happy. Marriage is a two-way thing, surely? And I don't see how you can be happy, Megan, if there's something as serious as this troubling you. It is quite important, you know, that side of marriage. At least, that's what I've heard people say.' She smiled. 'I wouldn't know, would I? Not from personal experience.'

'You'll be all right with Adrian,' said Megan in wistful tones. 'He's lovely, your Adrian. So nice and kind. Bernard's not a bit like him – I mean, Bernard's a different sort of person. He's rather . . . well, I've got to admit he can be terribly bossy at times,' she said in a confiding tone, as though Frances was not aware of the fact. 'It's with him being such an important doctor, you see. He can't help it. He's used to ordering people about. But I do wish he'd try to understand . . .'

'Make him understand. Tell him you're tired. Tell him you've got a headache,' Frances grinned. 'That's the usual excuse, isn't it?' But Megan did not respond. She just stared at her with worried, soulful eyes. 'Maybe you'd enjoy it more if you weren't so tired?'

'I might have an excuse soon,' said Megan. 'An excuse not to . . . you know . . .' How sad, thought Frances. So early in the marriage, to be looking for excuses. 'You see, I think I might be pregnant. I haven't said anything to Bernard yet, but I think I am.'

'Well, that's wonderful,' replied Frances, making the usual response to such news. 'That is, if you think so. Did you want a baby so soon?'

'Oh yes, yes. We both want children. Lots of them. Two boys and two girls at least, that's what we decided.' Frances nodded. Then Megan would have to get used to the means by which they were brought about, she was thinking. 'And it's not really surprising if I'm pregnant, is it? Bernard's a Catholic, you see – well, I suppose I am as well now, aren't I?' Megan added thoughtfully. 'So we can't take any precautions. It isn't allowed, so it's no wonder, really, that it's happened so soon. At least, I think it has. I've missed a period.'

'That's great news then, if it's what you both want,' said Frances brightly. 'What will you do about your job, if you are pregnant?'

'Oh, I shall give up nursing quite soon, I expect. Bernard really wanted me to give up as soon as we got married, but I managed to persuade him to let me stay on for a little while. He knows how much I love it.' She looked pensive for a moment. 'I've loved looking after the babies and children on the ward. But it's not to be compared with having a husband and children of your own, is it? That's what I've always wanted.'

'That's great then,' said Frances again, with a show of conviction she did not feel. She felt that Megan was trying to convince herself that she had achieved her aim in life – a happy marriage – but that she was, in reality, far more unhappy than she was letting on. 'And I'm sure you will be able to sort out . . . the other problem, when Bernard hears the news. You'll tell him soon, won't you?'

'Oh yes. Bernard's longing for a son, I know that. And we're so happy, Frances . . . really we are.' Her pale blue eyes seemed to be pleading with Frances to believe her. Poor Megan. She had imagined that marriage was going to be like a lovely story in *Woman's Own*, all china tea cups and lace doilys and cosy little breakfasts together: 'Would you pass the marmalade, please, darling . . .?' Frances recalled how Megan had loved playing at house in this very flat, and now the reality was turning out to be rather less than perfect, much more earthy and carnal than she had pictured.

'You won't say anything, will you, to Julie?' Megan gave a start at the sound of a door opening and closing; Julie, no doubt, coming in from work. 'Not about the baby, or about – you know – what I was telling you?'

'No, of course I won't. Not a word,' Frances whispered, then raised her voice as Julie came through the door. 'Hi, Julie. We've got a visitor. Megan's staying for tea. In fact, we've done so much chatting that I haven't even started to get it ready. Sorry.'

'Not to worry.' Nothing ever seemed to worry Julie. 'There's some chicken in the fridge, isn't there, left from Sunday, and we can soon knock up some chips.' She flopped down on the settee, tossing her cardigan and bag on to the floor. 'Hi, Megan. Nice to see you. How's married life?'

'Oh . . . it's lovely, thank you,' said Megan, like a polite little girl. 'I've just been telling Frances all about our honeymoon. I mean, all about Paris and Rome,' she amended hastily as she noticed Julie's grin and raised eyebrows.

Julie and Megan were not friends, only inasmuch as they were both friendly with Frances. They had met a few times at the flat and when they had all gone to choose

Frances's bridesmaids' dresses.

'So we're not going to be bridesmaids after all, you and me,' Julie remarked as they all started on their impromptu meal. 'So what d'you think of that, then? Missed our chance of a free nosh-up, eh?'

'It's only postponed, isn't it, Frances?' said Megan seriously. 'When is it going to be? Next spring, do you think?'

'Maybe,' said Frances evasively. 'It depends on quite a few things; on Mum, mainly.'

'And by that time I might be . . . well, I might not be able to be a bridesmaid,' said Megan, a little pensively. 'A matron of honour, I mean.'

'Why's that?' asked Julie, looking frankly at her.

'Oh, I don't know. No reason. But it's a long time off, isn't it? You never know what might've happened by then.' Megan looked down at her plate, concentrating hard on dissecting the leg of chicken.

'Is she pregnant?' asked Julie, an hour or so later, after their guest had departed.

'I don't know,' Frances replied airily. 'I suppose she could be. They're Catholics, you know. Why?'

'She seemed preoccupied, that's all. And with her saying she might not be able to be a bridesmaid . . . She looks tired, doesn't she?'

Frances nodded. 'Yes, I thought so, too.'

'A prolonged honeymoon, eh?' Julie grinned.

'Maybe . . .' Frances did not return the grin. 'I think she's just tired with nursing, and with looking after Bernard. I shouldn't imagine he helps her much.'

'D'you think they're happy?'

'I don't know,' said Frances again. 'I hope so. Yes, I think so. She'll be OK. Megan's tougher than she looks, you know. She has to be, being a nurse. Yes, she seems happy enough.' But Frances knew that her friend was far from happy.

Chapter 17

'Frances, could I have a word with you, please?' Frances glanced up from her desk one afternoon after school during the second week of the autumn term to see Marcus Avery coming towards her. It was infuriating, and ridiculous, the way her heart always gave a leap whenever she set eyes on him. Because there could never be anything between them. He had a wife, and even though Adrian had now moved to Birmingham he was still her fiancé.

'Whenever I come to see you you're always marking sums.' Marcus grinned as, without invitation, he sat down on the other adult chair.

'It's got to be done.' Frances put down her marking pen with a faint suggestion of a sigh at being disturbed. 'What can I do for you?' Her voice was polite, but cool.

'Oh, you could do quite a lot for me, pet.' She remained impassive, ignoring the sly smile and the innuendo in his remark. 'No, I've come to see you about something quite serious, actually.' He put on a more solemn face. 'You remember a little lad called Dennis Russell? Well, of course you must remember him; that's a silly thing to say. He's in my class this year and I'm afraid he's in a spot of bother – quite serious trouble, really.'

'Oh dear!' Frances, at once, was more than ready to listen. 'What has he been up to? Not what he was in trouble about in my class? I hope not.'

'Well, yes, it is, I'm sorry to say. I know about that little incident, of course.' Confidential reports on each child were sent from the Infant to the Junior School, stating any problems or serious misdemeanours. 'I gather he was all right all last year while he was in Mrs Jeffrey's class. But now, alas, he seems to be up to his old tricks again. And not just nicking from kids in the class. That would be bad enough, but it happens now and again and we can usually deal with it quite satisfactorily. No, he's been pinching sweets from the newsagent's – you know, the one on the estate, near the bus stop? Dennis and another couple of lads.'

Frances's heart sank. 'Not Barry Cartwright?'

'No, not Barry. He seems to be keeping his nose clean. A canny lad; I like him. He's a chatty, friendly little lad; most of 'em are. But I don't seem to be able to get close to Dennis, you know what I mean, pet? Somehow I can't manage to get his confidence.'

'Yes, I know. I found him difficult at first, hard to get close to. Go on – tell me – what happened? They were caught, I suppose?'

'Aye. Him and those other two. Third Year lads, they are, a year or so older than Dennis, but he seems to have met up with them in the playground or somewhere. Funny how they gravitate together, these delinquents. It takes one to know one, I suppose.'

'I wouldn't have thought of Dennis as a delinquent.' Frances sounded indignant, which was exactly how she felt. 'He's not a criminal, nor even a budding one, surely? It sounds to me as though he's been led astray.'

'Aye, well, it's easy to say that, isn't it? That's what they always say. "It was him what did it, sir, not me." Anyway, we are trying to nip it in the bud, make sure it doesn't happen again. Mr Williams – that's the newsagent – he came in and reported the incident to us rather than to their parents, seeing that they were all from this school. That's what's so awful, the school getting a bad name, but he seems to be a reasonable sort of fellow, thank goodness. He says he won't involve the police providing it doesn't happen again. It's up to us to see that it doesn't.'

'They've been punished, have they? Dennis and those other two?' Frances was remembering the awful humiliation Dennis had suffered at the hands of Miss Cameron. She had hoped it might have taught him never to do it again, but the incident was long enough ago for its impact to have lessened somewhat.

'Oh aye, they've had their playtimes stopped for a week, solitary confinement and all that. And the boss felt obliged to write to their parents. After all, it's their responsibility as much as ours. He doesn't believe in corporal punishment and neither do I. It would be all the same if I did, because it's a stipulation of old Jacob that there has to be no caning. It's a devil of a problem, though, knowing how to handle it.'

'You could always have a word with Jim Clegg, the Road Safety Officer. I told you he's my brother-in-law, didn't I? He could give them a pep talk about stealing and how it could get them into serious trouble. I thought of it when Dennis was in my class, but I didn't do anything about it. It wasn't so serious then.'

'Yes, it's an idea. A real live bobby might help to put the fear of God into them. But I was wondering if you could come and have a few words with Dennis, in private, like. The other two are not really my concern. More hard-bitten, they are, heading for real trouble if they don't watch out, but they're not in my class so I can't do anything. But Dennis is a different kettle of fish – at least I hope he is. I'll do my damnedest, if I can, to keep him out of trouble, but I don't seem to be getting very far with him. And I know he still thinks a lot about you. "I wish I was still in Miss Goodwin's class." That's what he said when I was trying to talk to him. "She was dead nice, Miss Goodwin." You've got quite a fan there, pet . . . and I can't say I blame him.' He grinned disarmingly at her. 'He's still rather a baby in some ways, compared with a lot of the lads. And so damned moody. I'm blessed if I can understand him.'

Frances was thoughtful for a moment, then: 'OK, I'll see what I can do,' she said, 'providing I'm not treading on anybody's toes. Mr Entwistle, for instance – he won't mind?'

'There's no reason why he should know, is there? It's just between you and me, surely?'

'Ye-es, maybe. But keep it quiet, won't you? I wouldn't want anybody to think I was pushing my nose into something that is none of my business. I do know Dennis's father, though – we were in the same operatic group – so perhaps we could look at it as more of a family matter. You say Mr Russell has been informed about this incident?'

'Yes; he wrote a very polite note expressing his concern. He said he'd dealt with Dennis – I don't know how – but the lad's still as moody as ever.'

'Goodness me, Jonathan must be worried sick about him. Dennis hasn't said there's anything wrong at home, has he? Anything worrying him?'

'No, I've told you, he says very little. I know there's only his father, of course; that his mother's dead. He's good to him, is he? He doesn't ill-treat him or anything?'

'Good gracious, no! Jonathan's a wonderful dad. But Dennis was missing his mum; perhaps he still is. That was the top and bottom of it when he was in my class.' And Frances had a good idea what might be troubling the little boy now. 'All right then; I'll see what I can do. When do you want me to come?'

'Tomorrow, after school? I'll keep Dennis back and get the other kids out of the way.'

'Very well, but don't expect any miracles.'

'Thanks, pet; you're a pal.' Marcus stood up, then he bent and gave her shoulder a squeeze. 'You'll do real well; I know you will. Cheerio then, Frances. See you . . .'

'Yes, see you, Marcus.' It had been a friendly gesture, that was all, but his slightest touch had been enough to set her pulse racing again. She had been determined, when she returned to school in September, not to get involved in any way with Marcus Avery, especially as Adrian was now down in Birmingham. Now she was being forced, against her better judgement, to make contact with him. But there could be no harm in it, she told herself, and she knew it was her duty to help Dennis.

Dennis looked up at her shiftily from beneath a scowling brow. Oh dear! She had hoped he might have been a tiny bit pleased to see her. Marcus had gone out of the room and left her alone with him, but she was at a loss, at first, to know how to start.

'Hello, Dennis,' she began.

''Lo, miss.' He continued to stare at her furtively for a few seconds before he spoke again. 'He's told you, hasn't he? He's told you . . . about what I've done. That's why you've come, i'n't it? I'm not a little kid, y'know. I don't need no Infant teachers comin' to tell me off. I'm in the Juniors now. And I can look after meself.'

'I've come because I'm a friend, Dennis,' said Frances. 'I'm a friend of your dad's, remember? Not just a teacher.' She smiled a little sadly. 'It seems to me you're not making a very good job of looking after yourself, are you? Or you wouldn't have got into all this bother, would you? Yes, I do know about it. Mr Avery told me.'

The boy nodded. 'Knew he had. He'd no business, telling you.'

'He told me because he knows that you and I are friends. Well, we always used to be, didn't we? Mr Avery wants to help you, Dennis. He wants to make sure you keep out of trouble. You like him, do you? You like being in his class?'

'He's orlright, I suppose. Yeah, he can be dead funny sometimes, cracking jokes an' all that. An' I'm in his recorder group an' all.'

'Yes, I heard you playing the recorder at the concert. You did very well, all of you. It was a good concert, wasn't it?'

'Yeah, it was orlright. I know you like him, miss – I mean, Miss Goodwin – 'cause you and 'im were singing all them soppy songs together, weren't you?' Dennis had been looking at the floor a lot while he was speaking, shuffling his feet. Now he looked straight at Frances. 'Is he your boyfriend, miss?'

Frances felt herself blushing, but at least she had managed to get Dennis's interest. She had got him talking, which was a very good start. She had thought, at first, he was going to clam up altogether. 'Of course he's not my boyfriend,' she said, laughing. 'Whatever gave you that idea?' Although she knew only too well what had given him the idea. 'Anyway, I'm engaged to Mr Glover – Adrian – you know, the minister from the church. You knew that, didn't you?'

'Yeah, I know. But he's not here no more, is he?'

'No . . . he's gone to live in Birmingham. But we're still engaged. I shall be getting married to him sometime soon.'

He looked at her impassively. Then, 'Why can't you marry my dad?' he blurted out.

Frances was so taken aback she could not find the words to answer. 'Your . . . dad?' she stuttered. 'But . . . why? What made you say that, Dennis? There's never been any thought of your dad and me . . . We've never . . .'

'But you know him, don't you?'

'Yes, of course I know him.'

'You and him, you were both in that thing, *South Pacific*. I came to see it. You were friends, weren't you, when I was in your class? He always used to be on about you.'

'What . . . what do you mean, Dennis?' she said faintly. 'On about me?'

'Well, telling me how nice you were an' all that. I know he liked you. He said I was lucky to be in your class . . . I know I was,' he added shyly. 'I was dead lucky. I thought he might've started going out with you. It would have been dead good, miss. I wouldn't have minded that. Then he started going out with Auntie Sylvia.'

'Sylvia Bowland?'

'Yeah, but that was because she used to be a friend of me mum's, see? And I didn't really mind that neither, but then she got engaged to that other feller. They've got married now.'

'Yes, so I've heard.'

'And now me dad's going out with that Glenys girl from the shop. She's always round at our house, Miss Goodwin, making our teas an' all that. They're not much cop, though. Not half as good as me mum used to make. And then they go out, her and me dad. They're always going out.'

'But they don't leave you on your own, do they?'

'No, course not. Mrs Barker, the lady next door, comes to look after me, else I go there. "Baby-sitting" she calls it, but that's daft 'cause I'm not a baby. Anyroad, I've heard Mrs Barker say to her husband that that Glenys has set her cap at me dad. I know what she means an' all. She wants to marry him.'

'And you don't want that to happen?'

'Do I heck as like! She's not like a mum, is she, miss? Mrs Barker says she's a silly little thing, just a bit of a kid. She didn't say it to me, but I heard her. She's daft, that Glenys, always giggling like soft girls do. She's not old enough to marry me dad, miss. You are, though . . .'

'I should imagine Glenys Mortimer and I might be about the same age,' said Frances thoughtfully.

'But she doesn't look as old as you, miss.'

Well, thank you very much! thought Frances, but she knew the remark had been meant as a compliment. They were getting into deep water here, though, and she had better put an end to any silly notions that Dennis might have.

'Listen, Dennis,' she said. 'I'm not going to marry your dad . . . you know that, don't you?' He nodded. 'And you'd better not go saying anything so silly to him, do you understand?' He nodded again. 'Is it because you don't like him seeing Glenys – is that why you've started getting into trouble again? That's what I've really come to talk about – you getting into trouble. Stealing, Dennis. That's what you've been doing, isn't it?'

He looked down at the floor again. 'I didn't mean to do it, Miss Goodwin. I knew it was wrong.'

'Then why did you do it? Was it to get back at your dad? Because of Glenys?' No, that was probably too deep for him; she was just thinking aloud. 'But you knew he'd be cross, didn't you?'

'I think I wanted him to be cross. Oh, I dunno.' Dennis shrugged impatiently. 'He never bothers with me. He's always with her.'

'Now, I'm sure that's not true. It may seem like it, but I'm sure he still spends a lot of time with you. Do you still go to the football match?'

'Yes, when Blackpool's at home.'

'And you still play games? Your dad was teaching you to play chess, wasn't he?'

'Yeah, we still play chess. She can't play,' he added defiantly.

'Well, there you are then. I know your dad cares a lot about you. Try not to be cross about Glenys. It'll only make you feel all horrid inside.'

'Her and me dad had a row,' he said, a trifle smugly. 'He's started going to the Starlight again – they're doing a new show – and she can't sing, so she can't go with him. And she was real mad. Are you in it, Miss Goodwin?'

'No, not this time,' smiled Frances. 'I've too much to do. I might be getting married before the next show. I've told you, no silly ideas!'

He was still looking at her plaintively.

'You won't ever do it again, will you, Dennis? Stealing from shops, or from anyone? That's why Mr Avery asked me to come, not to talk about your dad and his . . . friend. Do you remember, I told you once about that little voice inside you that tells you when you're doing something wrong?'

'Yes, Jiminy Cricket.'

'OK – Jiminy Cricket, if you like.' She smiled. 'I thought you might be too big to call him Jiminy Cricket now. But you haven't been listening to him, have you, Dennis? To the voice of your conscience; that's what it is, and we've all got one. We all want to do things that are wrong at times, but we have to listen to that little voice that tries to stop us. And if we stop listening – well, in the end that little voice stops trying to talk to us, and things get worse and worse.'

Dennis nodded. 'I know. I knew it was wrong, but I wanted to show 'em that I'm not just a soft baby. That's what they said.'

'Who, Dennis? The boys that were with you?'

'Yeah, them two lads, Bobby and Frankie. They said they'd done it before in Mr Williams's shop, millions of times, and he'd never caught 'em.'

Frances smiled. 'I dare say they might have done it once or twice, but you always get caught in the end. And you were with them that time, eh? How did you get mixed up with them?'

'They go home the same way as me. And they were laughing at me, 'cause I'd got my recorder with me. They snatched it off me and started chucking it about. They said it was only girls what played the recorder; they said it was a soppy thing to do. It isn't, is it, Miss Goodwin?'

'No, most certainly not. There are quite a few boys in Mr Avery's group, aren't there?'

'Yes, but it was me they was getting at; the others weren't there, were they? They said I had to go with 'em to Mr Williams's shop, else they wouldn't give me my recorder back. They remembered me from that other time, y'see, miss, when I was in your class. You know, when Miss Cameron made me wear that . . . that thing. They said I had to do it again, to prove I wasn't a big soft baby. I didn't dare say no, Miss Goodwin. I didn't know what they'd do to me. And I was feeling all mad about me dad as well, and I just didn't care any more . . . and that's what happened.'

'I see . . .' It sounded to Frances as though those two lads were bullies as well as thieves in the making, and that this could be a problem that needed expert handling. It was time now, though, that Dennis was on his way home. He was getting on for nine years old – as he said, no longer a baby – and there were no main roads to cross between the school and the garden centre, but she didn't want his father to worry about him being late, especially after the trouble he'd been in.

'Dennis . . .' She stood up, taking hold of his shoulders and looking him straight in the face. 'Promise me that you'll never, ever do that again. You won't steal, not from anyone, anywhere. Do you promise?'

'Yes, Miss Goodwin. I won't do it again. I promise.'

'I know now that it wasn't your fault. I don't think you were to blame at all. But you mustn't listen to boys who try to make you do wrong. I know it's not always easy. They've not bothered you since, have they, this . . . what did you call them? Bobby and . . .?'

'Frankie.'

'Bobby and Frankie; they're not still pestering you?'

'No, miss. Mr Entwistle told us he'd get the police if we were in trouble again. He was real mad, Mr Entwistle; I've never seen him so mad. I felt real scared of him and I think them other two did as well.'

'Good; it sounds as though that's what they need. Now, off you go home. And tell your dad you're sorry. You don't need to tell him you've been talking to me – perhaps it would be better not to mention it. Just tell him you won't do it again. And . . . try not to worry about Glenys. It'll all sort out, I'm sure. Your dad needs friends, you know – lady friends as well as men. Just try to be nice to him, not all – you know – moody and horrid. You'll feel better if you try to be nice.'

'All right; I'll try.' He gave a shy smile. 'Bye, Miss Goodwin.'

'Goodbye, Dennis.'

Frances breathed a heartfelt sigh as she watched him go. Poor kid. It really did seem, this time, as though he were more sinned against than sinning, as the saying went. She must tell Marcus to try to sort those bullies out. Bullying was a terrible thing when it got a hold in a school. You didn't see so much of it with Infants. Infant school children were renowned for tale-telling and bullying could, therefore, be dealt with quite speedily. But as they grew older there seemed to be a code of honour that they didn't snitch on their friends, or, indeed, their enemies. It was a wonder that Dennis had confided in her. Maybe it was because he saw her more as a family friend than a teacher.

Now, where was Marcus? She didn't want to go home without saying goodbye to him; besides, she had to tell him the outcome of her chat with Dennis. He was probably in the staffroom, but she didn't want to go looking for him. Frances was not sure why, but she felt it might not be a good idea for any of the rest of the Junior staff to see her on their premises with Marcus.

She glanced round at the classroom walls as she waited. It was a bright, interesting classroom with lots of different topics being pursued. Men teachers did not always bother about having a cheerful, stimulating classroom, but Marcus Avery appeared to be an exception. He was, of course, a very interesting person and one's environment, whether at work or at home, was often indicative of one's personality.

There was an unfinished frieze of *The Hobbit*, with Bilbo Baggins and several more of the plump little people in their green and yellow tunics. Frances would have thought that Tolkien was rather advanced for nine-year-olds, but experienced teachers were often able to pass on their enthusiasms to the children. There were also various brightly coloured posters from *Pictorial Education*, depicting the treasures of Ancient Egypt: the sphinx, the pyramids, the bright blue Nile with palm trees growing on the banks and some of the treasures of Tutankhamen's tomb. Teachers, in this free and easy, 'do as you like' approach to education which had been in vogue for several years now, were allowed to teach pretty much what they wished, provided they kept within certain guidelines and did not neglect the three Rs.

Marcus came in just as her eyes had wandered to another group of coloured pictures, of Hadrian's Wall and Roman centurions. Of course, Marcus hailed from that part of the country, near to Hadrian's Wall.

'Your interests seem to be many and varied, Marcus,' she observed as he sat down next to her.

'Oh aye, you could say that. I'm a man of many parts, pet. You don't know the half . . . Yes, we're doing ancient civilisations this year.'

'What, all of them?'

'Some of 'em; well, superficially, you know. Nothing too deep for nine-year-olds.'

'And you're a Tolkien fan?'

'Oh, yes. *The Lord of the Rings* is a great favourite of mine, so I thought I'd start the kids on *The Hobbit*. I suppose you might say I live in a dream world. Now, what's the news on young Dennis? You managed to get him talking, did you?'

Frances told him what had transpired, especially about the two lads she suspected might be incipient bullies.

'Ah-ha, he certainly didn't tell me all that. I rather thought they were mates of his, but I was wrong, wasn't I? I knew he'd respond to you. You're a sympathetic soul, aren't you, pet?'

'It might have helped because I know his father. I gather Dennis is feeling miffed because Jonathan has a girlfriend. He's not too keen on her, from what he said to me.'

'Oh well, that's none of our business, is it? We can't interfere in the fellow's love life.'

'No . . . and I'm pretty sure Jonathan wouldn't do anything to upset Dennis if he could help it. He's a very caring sort of father.'

'You seem to know him very well?'

'No, not all that well, not really.'

'You've not joined the – what are they called? – the Stardust Players, this time?'

'Starlight Players . . . no. I've only been in one pro-duction. My flatmate, Julie, is still with them. They're doing *The Dancing Years* this time. She keeps pestering me, but I'll probably be getting married next spring and that's when the show will be put on, so . . . I decided not to bother again this year.'

'But you're footloose and fancy-free at the moment, aren't you?'

'I wouldn't say that.'

'He's not here, though – your fiancé?'

'No, he's in Birmingham.'

'Well, there you are then . . .'

Frances stared down at her engagement ring, not meeting his glance, so she did not know what sort of look was in his eyes.

'Come on, Frances.' Marcus stood up abruptly. 'I'll run you home.'

'No . . . no, it's all right. It's not far. I always walk. But thanks all the same.'

'No, I insist. Anyway, it looks as though it might rain. Come on; you're ready, are you? Let's go then.'

Marcus's car was a green Hillman Minx, a couple of years old. There were still a few cars in the car park, but they did not encounter any of the other teachers. Frances was relieved, though she could not have explained why.

'Newton Drive, that's where you live, isn't it?' said Marcus as he quickly put the car into gear and spun it round.

'Yes. I hope it's not out of your way.'

'Wouldn't matter if it was. But, no, it isn't. I live in Layton – Grange Road – so I can easily go that way round.'

'Do you really? I never knew that. It's only a few minutes' walk from my mother's. She lives near the bowling green.'

At the speed Marcus drove it seemed only a few moments before they pulled up in front of the flat. 'Nice house,' observed Marcus. 'Very posh, in fact.'

'It's only a flat,' Frances explained. 'And it's not all that posh inside. Julie and I share the downstairs part. I used to share with Megan. She was a nurse, but she got married. She married one of the doctors . . .' She felt she was babbling stupidly. 'Anyway, I must get in now, Marcus. I usually start the tea. Thanks for bringing me home.'

'Hey, not so fast.' He put a hand on her arm to detain her. 'I was wondering . . . would you like to come and have a drink with me this evening? We could have a run out into the country.'

'No . . . no, thank you. I can't.'

'Why can't you? You've another engagement, have you?'

It would have been easy to say yes; to say it was choir practice, or she had arranged to see her mother, or she was going to the pictures with Julie. But none of those things was true and Frances was not in the habit of telling lies, even white ones.

'No, I'm not going anywhere. But . . . I can't, can I? What about your wife? What would she say? Anyway, there's Adrian.'

'Adrian isn't here, and Geraldine won't know unless I tell her, which I have no intention of doing. Anyway, she's going to night school. A friend picks her up at seven o'clock. Oh, come on, Frances. Don't be such a spoilsport. I'm not asking you to do anything wrong. Only to go for a drink. I want to say thank you for helping me with Dennis. And . . .'

I'd like to get to know you a bit better. We've never had the chance, have we? And where's the harm in that?'

'The harm is that you don't intend to tell your wife.'

'I shall tell her I'm going for a drink with somebody from school. That's not a lie, is it? And it's exactly what I have done, once or twice.'

'Oh, well . . . all right, then.' Frances felt it would be childish to refuse. It would make her appear so spineless and prissy. Besides, she didn't want to refuse. And, as Marcus said, where was the harm in it? 'What time? You'll call for me, will you?'

'I sure will, baby.' He put on a pseudo-American accent, then he grinned at her, reverting to his normal Geordie twang. 'I knew you would, pet. I knew you wouldn't go on saying no. Half-past seven? Is that OK?'

'OK, Marcus. I'll . . . I'll look forward to it.'

'So will I, pet . . . So will I.'

'Good for you,' said Julie when Frances told her about Marcus's invitation. 'It's about time you got out and had some fun. You've been too much of a stick-in-the-mud since Adrian went away. Not that you exactly hit the high spots when he was here, did you?'

'We enjoyed ourselves in a quiet way.'

'Well, off you go and enjoy yourself with Marcus. You never do anything now except go to choir practice or visit your mother. And I'm sick of asking you to come to Starlight with me.'

'But he's a married man.'

'So what? He's a colleague, isn't he, and he just wants you to have a drink with him, that's all.'

'But he's not going to tell his wife – not the whole truth, anyway.'

'He'd be a fool if he did, wouldn't he? Oh, don't be so blooming self-righteous, Fran. You've been so goody-goody it just isn't true since you've been engaged to that vicar. Forever worrying about what people'll say and all that. You nearly drove me potty when you were singing those songs with Marcus. As if it mattered, honestly!'

Frances knew she would have had a very different reaction if Megan had still been her flatmate. Megan would have been full of cautionary advice. Julie seemed to be the only person who was not impressed by Adrian's goodness and the true worth of his character. Frances knew, deep down, that of her two friends, Megan's judgement was more to be relied upon than that of Julie. (Except, perhaps, in the case of Bernard Conway. Megan had been quite blind to his faults before they were married, although she appeared much more aware now.) Julie, however, was much easier to live with. And Megan was not here to give advice . . . You could try listening to Jiminy Cricket, like you told Dennis, said a voice inside her head. But Frances chose to ignore it.

Chapter 18

Frances dressed with care, choosing to wear a lime-green dress she had bought from Marks & Spencer only a few weeks ago. She had worn it when she went out to dinner with Adrian, just before he moved to Birmingham, and he had said how much it suited her. It was a summer dress really, a linen and rayon mixture, perhaps not entirely suitable now the nights were drawing in and turning chilly as dusk descended; but it had elbow-length sleeves and she could carry a cardigan to slip on if necessary.

She took off the ribbon with which she tied her hair back when she was at school and brushed the pale golden locks loosely around her shoulders. Her hair was quite long at the moment. Adrian had admired her long hair and had persuaded her not to have it cut . . . She quickly stifled any thoughts of Adrian although she did keep her engagement ring on. To take it off would be very wrong.

Marcus's eyes widened appreciatively as she stepped into the car. Her dress had a fashionable shorter skirt and she had difficulty in keeping her knees covered. Marcus did not seem to be looking at them – he was looking through the rear-view mirror – but she carefully covered them with her cardigan.

'You don't drive, Frances?' asked Marcus as they zoomed off along Newton Drive.

'No, there's never been any need for me to drive,' she answered. 'I can walk to school and to church, and when Adrian was here he used to run me about. I must admit, though, I'm missing the car. I have to get the bus to my mother's, and to my sister's, and that's quite a way; she lives at Marton.' Her visits to Josie's, however, were now infrequent. Relations between the two of them were still somewhat strained.

'You should get yourself one of those new Mini-Minors. It's a canny little car, nippy in traffic, good on petrol; sixty miles to the gallon on a run, I've heard. I'm very tempted myself, except that there's not much room for my long legs.'

'I still wouldn't be able to drive, though, would I?'

'You'd soon learn, clever girl like you. Driving's a piece of cake. Take some lessons . . . I'd teach you to drive.' He turned to grin at her.

She smiled back unsurely, but did not answer. He didn't mean it anyway; how could he? The idea of owning a car was very tempting, provided she could afford it. There was always hire purchase, but her mother had always been dead against getting anything on the 'never-never'. 'It would certainly make life easier if I had a car,' she replied. 'I've never really thought about it till now. I could drive down to Birmingham, couldn't I, instead of going by train? If I manage to learn to drive, that is . . .' On the other hand, the idea of owning a car was perhaps not very practical. She would need it for only a few months if they went ahead with their plans for a wedding next spring or summer . . . Once again she pushed the intrusive thoughts to the back of her mind.

'To see your fiancé, you mean?' Marcus's voice held a touch of wry amusement, or was she imagining it? 'Yes . . . maybe you could, pet. Tell me, what are you doing with yourself while he's living it up in the big city? I'll bet he's having a rare old time.' She didn't comment as she knew his words were ironic. 'What about you, eh? Are you staying at home sewing? Preparing your bottom drawer?'

'No, I'm not much of a sewer,' she answered flatly. She was not sure that she liked his sarcastic tone. 'I go to see my mother – I told you, didn't I, that she'd been quite poorly? That's why the wedding was postponed – and my sister. And Megan, my friend who's a nurse. Well, she was, but she's given it up now; she's expecting a baby. I still sing in the church choir, and I help with the youth club now and again. Not as much as I did when Adrian was here, though. And I go to the pictures now and again with Julie. And I've quite a lot of school work to do, of course.'

'Of course.'

'There's always a lot of preparation to do when you're a teacher, isn't there?'

'It all depends.'

'On what?'

'On whether you want to be a slave to it; I certainly don't. You're not exactly hitting the high spots, are you, pet?' Julie's words exactly, she recalled. 'And now you're going out with me.' He turned to smile at her, not at all sardonically now, just a warm friendly sort of smile, and she felt her heart miss a beat.

'Just for tonight, Marcus, that's all,' she said quietly, but he did not reply. 'And . . . what about you? What do you do with your time, when you're not at school?'

'Oh, this and that. Quite a lot, in fact. Like I said, I don't intend to be a slave to my job. I work hard while I'm there, and I care about the kids – you know that, don't you, pet? – but "all work and no play" . . . you know what they say.' And Marcus was certainly not a 'dull boy', Frances mused.

'I play darts once a week – mebbe twice sometimes if there's a match – at the pub in Layton, the one at the top of the hill.' That was a surprise. She would have thought he was too sophisticated, too suave, for such a mundane pursuit. A working man's hobby, wasn't it, playing darts at the pub? But then he hailed from the very north of England, where men were men and the women stayed at home. Women in the area known as Tyneside were not encouraged to frequent public houses, or so she had heard. And hadn't she also heard Marcus say that he was a man of many parts?

'And I'm going to night school,' he continued. 'I've enrolled for two classes.'

It sounded as though he were never at home. 'What are you studying?' she asked. 'It seems as though you're going to be very busy.'

'Car maintenance. It'd be handy to know what to do if

this little lady ever broke down. Not that she ever has, touch wood.' He tapped the wooden dashboard in front of him. 'And French – conversational French.'

'Can't you speak French? I thought everybody learned French at school. I know I did.'

'Ah, but can you speak it? I'll bet you can't. Textbook French, that's all we learned at school. *Je suis, tu es, il est . . .* and so on. What good is that in the real world?'

'It's good groundwork. I used to enjoy French lessons.'

'Well, this is conversational French, learning to speak it like the natives do. The teacher's a Frenchwoman who married an English soldier. She was involved in the Resistance movement, from what I've heard, and she helped him to escape from occupied territory. Real storybook stuff. Anyway, she's a damned good teacher.'

'Mmm . . . it sounds very interesting. I was thinking of going to night school myself – to give me something to do now Adrian's not here – but, somehow, I never got round to it.'

'Come to the French classes with me.'

'What?' She stared at him in disbelief. Surely he didn't think she'd been hinting? 'Oh no, I couldn't.'

'Why couldn't you? You've just said you used to enjoy French lessons at school. And you're at a loose end.'

'I haven't said that. I'm quite busy, actually.'

'Visiting friends and relations, that's all. Make some time for yourself, Frances. Pursue your own interests, why don't you? You'd enjoy it; you know you would.'

'But . . . I couldn't go with you.'

'Why not?'

'Well, it wouldn't be right, would it? What would your wife say?'

'For God's sake, Frances, will you shut up about what Geraldine would say? You were on about it this afternoon. She won't say anything, will she, because she won't know? And if she did, what would it matter? We'd just be colleagues, one from the Juniors and another from the Infants, who happen to be attending the same night-school class. Where's the harm in that?' That's what he had said before, she recalled. Where was the harm?

'Besides, I told you, didn't I? Geraldine and I . . . we go our separate ways. We have done for ages now. She's at night school herself tonight, doing creative writing. And if she's not there, then she's at her writers' circle, or poetry reading with some of her cronies. She fancies herself as a novelist, my wife.' Frances was aware of his slightly disdainful tone.

'Oh, that sounds interesting,' she replied. 'Has she had anything published?'

'No, of course she hasn't!'

'Don't be so disparaging, Marcus. You should try to encourage her. It all sounds very clever to me. I'm sure I could never do anything like that.'

'I do try – or at least I used to do. But, I told you, we've drifted apart.'

'I'm surprised she has time to do all that as well as her job. She has quite a responsible job, you said?'

'Oh yes, Geraldine's quite a busy little bee, I've got to give her that. She's never still, always dashing off doing something or other.'

'But not with you? You don't do things together?'

'We used to at one time. But we're different people, two entirely different people, and we've become more different as time has gone on.'

'But surely your interests coincide? You said you were interested in Tolkien, and I know you read widely. And it sounds as though she's a literary person.'

'What are you trying to do? Start a Geraldine Avery fan club?' Marcus sounded angry and Frances glanced apprehensively at the oncoming traffic – too close for comfort at times – as he pressed his foot even harder on the accelerator. 'I've told you, we don't get on and that's that. Just shut up about it, can't you?'

Neither of them spoke for several moments as the car sped along the Garstang Road. Frances was beginning to wish she hadn't come. It had been a mistake. She shouldn't have listened to Julie. It was hardly fair to blame Julie, though. She had already made the decision to go before

277

she even spoke to her friend.

'We'll stop here,' said Marcus as they turned the bend in the road approaching St Michael's on the Wyre. 'There's a nice little pub.

'I'm so sorry, Frances,' he said when he had parked the car at the rear of the low whitewashed building. He turned and took hold of her hands. 'Please forgive me. I didn't mean to shout at you. It's hardly your fault, is it, that Geraldine and I don't get on?'

'It's all right, Marcus,' she mumbled. 'I shouldn't have said anything. It's none of my business.'

'I know you were only trying to help. You're such a kindly soul, aren't you, pet? I don't really like talking about it – about Geraldine and me – because there's nothing I can do about it any more. It's just the way it is. Let's forget about it, eh?' He rubbed at her hands. 'You're cold, aren't you? Come on, put your cardie on – it's a bit nippy out there – and we'll go and get something to warm you up.'

The pub was a mixture of old and new. There was a log fire blazing in the fireplace, one which, in the olden days, was big enough to encompass in its warmth a settle or two chairs; oak beams ran along the ceiling from which were suspended hanging baskets of dried flower arrangements; and a delft rack held blue and white plates of various designs, and an assortment of Toby jugs. The wooden benches were comfortable enough with padded seats and backs of floral chintz and the oak tables, though highly polished, looked as though they were from the same era as the inn. Early nineteenth century, Frances guessed. There was a very modern jukebox in the corner, however, and through a doorway at the far end they could see a small bowling alley and a game in progress.

'What are you having, pet?' Marcus asked as they found an empty table near the fire.

Frances realised she was quite cold; not just her hands, she felt chilled all through. It might have been a mistake to wear her summery dress. 'Oh . . . a rum and Coke, please, Marcus. It'll help to warm me up.'

'Bacardi and Coke?'

'Yes, that's right.' She knew this was the 'in' drink, what you had when you holidayed in Spain or Majorca.

'I really meant it, about night school,' he said when he had returned with their drinks, a brimming tankard of ale for himself and her Bacardi and Coke. 'You would enjoy it. I know you would. We have a great time at the classes. Everyone's so friendly.'

'But the classes have started, haven't they? It's too late to join.'

'Not at all. We've only had two lessons so far and people are still joining.' He put his hand over hers. 'Please say you'll come, Frances.'

'Where is it held?'

'At the new Secondary Modern School at Bispham. I could pick you up in the car.'

'It's out of your way.'

'Not all that much. Anyway, what does it matter when you're in a car? It would only take me a few minutes to nip along for you.'

At the speed you drive that's very true, thought Frances. 'I might,' she said. 'I'll think about it and let you know.'

'Good girl.' He squeezed her hand then let it go. 'They're talking about having a trip to France next summer if enough people are interested. A couple of days in Paris and then on to another part, possibly the Loire Valley.'

That idea, to Frances, sounded wonderful . . . but impossible, of course. By next summer . . . goodness know what might have happened by next summer. She was beginning to realise, though, how very limited her boundaries, so far, had been. She had never been abroad. She had been to London only once, and that had been just a brief visit, with her brother and sister and Iris, soon after the end of the war, staying for two nights at a cheap little hotel near Euston station. The furthest she had ever been was Torquay, and Iris had soon decided, on their one and only visit there, that the place was too posh, not a patch on Scarborough or Whitby or – of course – Blackpool.

'That trip sounds lovely,' she said now. 'I know I wouldn't

be able to go, but it sounds very nice. I've never been abroad.'

'You haven't?' Marcus sounded surprised. 'Well, well, well; your education's sadly lacking, isn't it, pet? In quite a few ways, I dare say. I'll have to take you in hand, I can see.'

She concentrated hard on the glass in her hand, not looking at him. The Bacardi and Coke was certainly warming her up inside and making her feel a little light-headed as well, happy and carefree, as though nothing mattered very much. She leaned back against the padded cushion, smiling as she listened to the song the jukebox was playing. 'Que será, será . . . Whatever will be, will be . . .' sang Alma Cogan. That song came to an end, then the strains of another, very familiar, tune drifted across to them.

'Listen,' said Marcus, reaching for her hand again. 'Listen, pet; they're playing "our song".'

'Some enchanted evening . . .' It was Rossano Brazzi from the film track of the show, singing the song she and Marcus had sung at school; the night she had had the row with Josie, the night her mother had been taken ill, the night Adrian had told her he trusted her . . .

'. . . The sound of her laughter will ring in your dreams.'

With a determined effort she pulled herself back to the present day, to the situation she was in at this moment; sitting in a pub, miles away from home, with a man who was not her fiancé; a married man . . . Firmly she extricated her hand from Marcus's grip. 'So I hear,' she said in a casual voice. 'We went to Manchester to see the film, when the Starlight Players were doing the show. It was an excellent film. Have you seen it, Marcus?'

'Of course.' He nodded his head, smiling bemusedly at her.

'I would have thought,' she continued, speaking very matter-of-factly, 'that you might have joined an operatic group instead of going to night school. Like the Starlight Players, for instance. You told me you used to be in one in Newcastle, didn't you?'

'Oh, yes, I was. But of course I used to take the lead

there. And if I joined one here I'd just be in the chorus, wouldn't I?'

'That's where everybody has to start, Marcus.' But that would not suit Marcus Avery at all. Frances guessed he was not accustomed to taking a back seat.

She was fully in control of her faculties when they drove back home. The next drink she had was a grapefruit juice, and she was pleased to see that Marcus, too, did not drink any more ale, just a bitter lemon. His driving was not dangerous or erratic, just speedy, but she was glad he was not taking any chances.

'Thank you for a lovely evening,' she said as he drew up, for the second time that day, outside the flat. 'I've enjoyed it.' She really had. Marcus was good company, and apart from holding her hand once or twice and making the occasional two-edged remark he had not overstepped the bounds of what she considered to be correct behaviour. She was beginning to convince herself that it would be perfectly in order for her to go to those French classes, provided she kept things, as she had done tonight, on a safe, purely friendly, footing. She decided she would not invite him into the flat; anyway, Julie would probably be in soon if she was not there already.

'I've enjoyed it too, pet,' he replied. 'We must do it again?' She did not answer the query in his voice, but reached for the door handle. Marcus leaned across and kissed her gently on the cheek. 'Good night, Frances. See you soon. Let me know about night school.'

'Yes, I will. I'll think about it. Good night, Marcus.'

It had been just a gentle friendly sort of kiss, she told herself, but it remained in her memory long after he had driven away.

After a good deal of heart-searching, Frances agreed to join the French classes. She had told her mother and anyone else who asked that she was going with a friend from school who picked her up and brought her back in the car every Tuesday evening. It was not a lie, she told herself, only a slight deviation from the truth. Iris, very much wrapped up in her own concerns, was not bothered anyway, not so long as Frances made time to visit her, as she still did, a few times a week. To her colleagues on the staff, Marjorie in particular, she said she was attending night school with a girl friend who was fortunate enough to have a car. Now that was a lie, rather more than a white one, but there was no way she could admit the truth to Marjorie. The only person who knew the truth of the situation was Julie, and she was adopting, very much, a live-and-let-live attitude.

Not that there was anything worth telling lies about, not at first. Marcus called for her at ten past seven on a Tuesday evening, drove her to the French class at Bispham, and drove her home again afterwards. They were not even in the same group when the class divided up to practise their conversation, and at the tea break they both mingled with their own class members and those of other classes: keep fit, flower arranging, china painting, cookery and all the other folk. Frances had feared she might see somebody she knew – not that it would have mattered; she wasn't doing anything wrong – but, so far, all the people she met had been strangers.

'Let's go for a drink,' said Marcus, one evening in October. 'You're not in any hurry to get home, are you?'

'No . . . but do you think we should?'

'Why ever not?'

'Well, we might see somebody who knows us.'

'For heaven's sake, you're not starting all that again, are you? I thought I'd got you out of that silly way of thinking. What does it matter if we do? We're just two colleagues who happen to go to the same French class. Come on, I want a drink, anyway . . . and unless you want to walk home you'll have to come with me.' She glanced unsurely at him, but, as usual, he was grinning cheerfully.

'Oh, all right then, just one.'

The Red Lion was a large public house on the main road with lots of rooms; a public bar, a snug, a snooker room, a restaurant. Frances glanced uneasily into each of them as they passed, but she saw no familiar faces.

'Give over,' said Marcus. 'You're forever looking over your shoulder like Lot's wife. Relax and enjoy yourself. We won't be meeting next week. It's half term. Let's make the most of it. Cheers, pet.' He raised his tankard of beer and she responded with her own Martini and lemonade. 'Cheers, Marcus.'

They chatted easily, as they always did, mainly about the French lesson and the people they had met there. 'You're glad you decided to come, are you?' asked Marcus.

'Very glad. I realise now I needed another interest in my life apart from school and family . . . and church.' Although she didn't go there so regularly since Adrian had left. She did not always manage to get to the Friday choir practice, or to both Sunday services, making the excuse of pressure of work and family commitments. The truth was that the tone of the place had changed dramatically since Adrian's departure. She had heard it said, oftentimes, that you should go to church to worship God, not the minister, but Frances realised now that her main reason for attending Wyre Bank Methodist Church had been Adrian. Now he was no longer there several others, besides herself, were far less regular in their attendance. Frances, however, would soon be seeing him again, a meeting she was anticipating with mixed feelings. She hadn't yet decided what she was going to tell him about the French classes.

'I'm sorry we're not meeting next week,' she said. 'Although I wouldn't have been able to come. I'm going down to Birmingham to see Adrian.'

'Are you indeed?' Marcus countered her remark, as he always did any mention of her fiancé, with a raised eyebrow and a half-smile. 'That will be nice for you. I'm sure you're looking forward to seeing him again, aren't you?' Again there was that touch of irony in his voice that made her feel . . . oh, so very guilty.

'Yes, of course I am,' she retorted. 'I haven't seen him since August.'

'Tch, tch, tch . . . that's dreadful. Are you going by train?'

'Yes, it's quicker than the coach, although these new motorways they're building should help to shorten the

283

journey. I prefer the train, though.'

'If you'd had your own car, like I suggested, it would be even better. You've not thought any more about it?'

'No, not seriously. It wouldn't be worth it.'

'Why not?'

'Well . . . with me getting married. Adrian has a car. We wouldn't need two.'

'Oh yes, of course, you're getting married, aren't you?' Marcus nodded soberly. 'I keep forgetting . . . You'll be glad to hear your little pal Dennis is managing to keep on the straight and narrow,' he said, in an abrupt change of the subject, something he was very good at. 'Almost a model pupil, I'm pleased to say. He's palled up with young Barry again. A bit of a ruffian, that one, but there's no malice in him. He's a good influence on Dennis.'

'Yes, I always thought so.'

It was inevitable when two teachers got together that for part of the time they would talk shop. Marcus told her that her brother-in-law, Jim Clegg, who had come in to talk about road safety, had been asked, later, to have a chat with the miscreants about stealing; how it could lead to the Juvenile Court and prison, eventually, if they didn't mend their ways. Frances hadn't known about this. She still saw Josie and Jim only infrequently.

'Oh dear, Dennis would be very chastened,' she said, 'at the sight of a policeman.'

'Yes, he was, but it wouldn't have been fair to lecture the other two culprits and not him. It was all done very tactfully, though. None of the other kids knew about it. Anyway, enough of school, eh? Another drink, pet? Another Martini?'

'No . . . no, thank you. I'll just have a grapefruit juice.'

Marcus grinned. 'Cautious little lady, aren't you? You know where to draw the line, is that it?'

'I hope so, Marcus.'

That was the first night he kissed her, not just on the cheek as he had done previously, but a long lingering kiss that left her breathless . . . and longing for more. As he kissed her again he slipped his hand inside her coat, gently fondling her breast. She did not resist, neither did she object when he lifted her jumper and cupped her breast in his hand. She leaned against him, moaning softly, scarcely aware of what she was doing. It was not the drink that had intoxicated her – she was always careful not to drink enough to do that – but the very presence of Marcus. He had long had that effect on her and she knew she would not be able to resist him much longer, should he suggest . . .

He did not suggest anything further, not that night. He drew away from her, straightening her clothes, then stroking her hair. 'Good night, Frances,' he said softly. 'Take care of yourself in Birmingham. I'll be thinking about you, pet. See you after half term, hmm?'

'Yes . . . I'll see you, Marcus.'

She tried to tell herself that this would not do. It was wrong; she was behaving shamefully and it was up to her to put a stop to it. She would go to no more French classes. She would tell Marcus so after the half term holiday. She argued with herself in the train all the way to Birmingham. It was easier to convince herself of her perfidy when Marcus was not there.

The weekend was not a success although Adrian was delighted to see her and she had to admit that it was pleasant to see him again, too. She felt the fondness she had for him returning. But she did not feel that she had his wholehearted attention. She was not his only, nor his primary, consideration. She was sharing him with his church, his parish, his flock; the many and varied miscellany of people who were now his spiritual responsibility. More than that in some cases, for she could see that many of them depended on him for advice on marriage guidance, family problems, money worries. His preaching, too, had become more dynamic, more down-to-earth, more suited to an inner-city, very working-class area.

In turn, she was guarded with him, having decided to make no mention of the French conversation classes in case she accidentally spoke Marcus's name. But the classes were now an important part of her life, and suddenly she found she had very little to say to Adrian.

She did not stay with him in his flat. That would not have been appropriate. She stayed, instead, with an elderly couple with whom he had become friendly. They were pleasant enough people and they thought the world of Adrian, but Frances was glad when it was time for her to go home. They had made no wedding plans. Frances thought then that maybe she should break off the engagement. No, she told herself. You do that and you are playing right into Marcus's hands. And there can be no future with Marcus, you silly little fool. Marcus is a married man . . . She would tell him she was not going to see him again, and when she got home she would write to Adrian and apologise for being so offhand with him. She would tell him how much she loved him.

But back home in Blackpool she realised the fact that Marcus was married made no difference whatsoever. The next time she set eyes on him she knew, beyond any doubt, that she had fallen helplessly in love with him and there could be no turning back. And she suspected that he felt the same way about her.

The knowledge was there between them at the next French class. They drove straight home and Marcus showed no surprise when Frances invited him into the flat 'for coffee'. Julie was visiting her parents and she had promised faithfully she would not be back until after half-past eleven when her father brought her home in his car. Julie had not asked Frances why she needed an empty flat; she knew, only too well.

'Frances . . .' said Marcus, when she had made the pretence of getting out the cups and saucers and filling the kettle. 'You don't really want coffee, do you?' He had followed her into the kitchen and he took the sugar basin out of her hands, setting it on the table behind them. He put his arms round her and kissed her. 'Come on, pet. You know what we both want. It's been there, between us, ever since we set eyes on one another . . . hasn't it?' She nodded. 'You know we can't hide from it any longer.'

'Yes, Marcus. I know.'

'Where . . .?'

She led him into the bedroom. She felt no embarrassment as he undressed her, then himself, and laid her gently
on the bed. There was never any embarrassment between
them, either that first time or afterwards – many times
afterwards. What they were experiencing seemed so right,
so inevitable, so completely wonderful that it could not be
denied. It was only later, when she was alone in her single
bed, that the feelings of remorse engulfed her. This
oppressive guilt would not go away.

'Miss Goodwin, would you come to my office after school
finishes this afternoon, please?' said Miss Reynolds, one
day in January, soon after the start of the new term. 'There
is something I would like to discuss with you.'
     Frances wondered why Miss Reynolds should want to
see her. She didn't think she was 'on the carpet'. The smile
on the headteacher's face had belied that. Besides, she
knew she was on good terms with the woman she thought
of as her boss; far too good, she knew some members of
staff thought. They usually referred to Miss Reynolds as
'the boss' – or Gertie – although, strictly speaking, all the
staff were employed by the local Education Authority. They
were the ones who had the power to hire and fire, although
it was very rarely a teacher was sacked. Frances had never
known it to happen. Sometimes, however, certain matters,
particularly those within a school, could be left to the
jurisdiction of the headteacher, usually with consultation
with the board of governors. It turned out that it was one
of these issues that Miss Reynolds wanted to discuss with
Frances.
     'Sit down, Miss Goodwin.' The woman smiled in a
welcoming manner. 'I wanted to have a word with you
before I speak to the rest of the staff, although Miss
Cameron, of course, as my deputy, does know about this
matter. The point is this. Our school has been granted two
Special Responsibility posts which are to be awarded, at
my discretion – and with the agreement of the governors –
to the teachers whom I consider to be the most deserving.
Now, I would like to know, if it would be possible for me to

consider you; or will you be leaving us in the near future? I know your wedding was postponed; I wondered if it was likely to take place soon?'

To say that Frances was surprised was putting it mildly. She was dumbfounded, quite speechless for a moment. She had been at the school for a little more than two years, and already, here was Miss Reynolds considering her for a post of responsibility; what was generally known as an SR post. She did not answer the question about her wedding plans. Instead, 'Why me?' she gasped. 'I haven't been here very long. Some of the teachers have been here ever since the school opened. Might it not cause trouble, Miss Reynolds? I mean some of them might well be resentful if the post was given to a newcomer like me.'

Miss Reynolds nodded understandingly. 'You may well be right, Miss Goodwin. I know only too well what you mean – and don't think I haven't weighed up the situation – but you would have to leave it to my judgement. And, believe me, I know what I am doing. I'll speak plainly, my dear, but I'm not going to mention any names. To do so would be extremely unprofessional. You understand that, don't you?' She made a steeple of her fingers, pausing, as though weighing her words carefully before she spoke again.

'There are some teachers, I have to say, both in this school and in others – very good teachers, in their own way – but who, nevertheless, are not prepared to go the extra mile. They come in at ten minutes to nine, they leave as soon as they can after a quarter to four, do all that is required of them and no more. They are diligent – to a point – and some of them care about the children in their charge, although there are others, unfortunately, who do not. I must hasten to add that I don't think there are any of that sort on this staff. I like to think that all my teachers are caring people.

'But, with some of them, there is not that extra something, that extra sparkle, that makes an excellent teacher, and that is what I have seen in you. I noticed it straight away at your interview, and when you joined my staff I

288

knew that my assessment of you had been correct. You have done some very good work since you came here – in drama and music especially – and I know that the children respond well to you.'

'Thank you, Miss Reynolds,' said Frances, humbly. She was not used to hearing such a eulogy of praise from anyone, especially Miss Reynolds, who was often quite stinting with her compliments. 'I've tried to do my best. I've enjoyed being here.'

'Which reminds me,' said Miss Reynolds, 'you have not answered my question, have you? Will you be getting married soon, you and Mr Glover, because, if you are then all this will be purely hypothetical, won't it?'

Frances shook her head and there was a silence for a few seconds before she spoke. 'No, Miss Reynolds. I'm afraid that Adrian and I . . . will not be getting married . . . not at all.' Only at that very moment had she made the decision which, for ages now, she had known she really ought to make.

'Oh dear. I'm sorry to hear that. You mean your engagement is broken off? You've decided . . .?' Miss Reynolds's short-sighted eyes, behind the rimless spectacles, were peering at her, perplexed.

'Yes, I'm afraid so,' said Frances, glad that she was not wearing her engagement ring. She did not always wear it at school as it was apt to get clogged with paste or paint, but the decision not to do so recently had not been entirely for that reason. 'We've decided that we're . . . we're not really suited to one another . . .' Her voice faded away because she knew that what she was saying was not strictly true. They had not decided; it was she who had made the decision, but Adrian would know about it very soon, just as soon as she could pluck up courage to write to him.

It was Miss Reynolds's surprising announcement that had brought things to a head in Frances's mind. She knew now how much she wanted to stay here. The thought of getting promotion so early in her teaching career was a real incentive for staying, but that was not the only reason. If she were honest, Frances knew this was not the reason at all.

'Oh dear, that's such a pity,' said Miss Reynolds. 'Mr Glover – Adrian – is such a pleasant young man, isn't he? And a very good minister; I was very impressed with him. I would have thought that the two of you were very well suited. But it's not for me, or anyone else, to say, is it, dear? It's your own affair. I'm sorry, though . . . except that it means, of course, that you will be staying here. You will, won't you? You'll apply for one of the posts I mentioned?'

'Ye-es,' said Frances, a little unsurely. 'They're going to be advertised, are they? I thought you said—'

'That it was up to my discretion who I awarded them to? Well – yes – it is; I will have the final say, but it will have to be with the agreement of the board of governors. And I will have to advertise the posts within the school, to any of the staff who wish to apply. That is the ruling. If there had been a vacancy – if you had been leaving, for instance – one of them would have been advertised further afield, but as it stands it's just open to the teachers who are already here.'

'There may be fierce competition.'

'There may well be . . . or there may not. Some people, I know, do not want extra responsibility. And some already have enough responsibilities at home; a husband and children to consider. The monetary award will not be great, as I'm sure you realise. But it's the next step up the ladder, so to speak, if you should wish, at any time, to apply for a deputy headship. There are some teachers – I can think of one or two here, without mentioning any names – who regard SR posts as merely rewards for long service. I know there will be a certain faction here who will think it should be given to the oldest member of staff. But that is not my view. I believe in rewarding those who have shown they are willing, as I said before to go the extra mile.

'Anyway, dear, I'll leave you to think about it. I'm so sorry about your broken engagement, but I suppose if it hasn't to be then it's better to find out now rather than later. I'm sure Mr Right will come along for you one day,

Miss Goodwin,' she added with an attempt at a coy little smile. 'In the meantime you've got your family, haven't you, and a job you enjoy doing. It's obvious how much you enjoy it. Speaking personally, I know how much my teaching career has always meant to me. It's been a very great blessing, a compensation, you might say . . .

'Thank you, Miss Goodwin. Off you go now, dear. I'll be speaking to the rest of the staff shortly. It might be as well, though, if you keep our little chat to yourself, you understand?'

Back in her own classroom Frances sat at her desk, bemusedly staring into space, trying to collect her muddled thoughts before she went home. A compensation, Miss Reynolds had said. Her teaching career, as well as being a blessing, had been a compensation. For not having a man – a husband and children – Frances supposed she meant. It wasn't likely that Gertie would ever have a husband now; she wasn't the marrying kind, anyway. She was married to her job. She, Frances, enjoyed her job – and now she was being encouraged to take the first step up the promotion ladder – but she wasn't married to it. She had been engaged to be married. Everyone, including Adrian, thought she still was. But now she had burned her bridges. She had told Miss Reynolds that the engagement was off. Now she had to find the courage to tell other people the same news, in particular, Adrian.

She sealed the envelope and addressed it to Adrian. Now, she told herself, this burdensome guilt would diminish at last. She did not need to feel guilty about Marcus's wife. Geraldine no longer cared about her husband, or he about her. But the feelings of shame, of self-reproach, of . . . sinfulness were still there. She never seemed to be free of them. Only in Marcus's arms did she get any respite, and his tender rapturous lovemaking had the power to make her forget everything except the here and now.

Chapter 19

Adrian was saddened, but not altogether surprised, to receive the letter from Frances telling him she thought it would be better if they ended their engagement. The fact that she had returned the ring in a registered envelope made it all the more final. He wished she could have had the courage to tell him to his face when they'd been together just after Christmas instead of this, to his mind, somewhat cowardly 'Dear John' approach. He had known then – before then, if he were honest – that their relationship had deteriorated. They had seemed ill at ease with one another in the short time they had spent together. It had not been ideal, Adrian staying with friends from his former church and Frances in her flat. He had travelled to Blackpool on Boxing Day and had to be back in Birmingham two days later because of parish commitments. He had felt that Frances was relieved to see him depart.

He could, of course, have ended the engagement himself knowing the way things were heading. But the truth was he still loved Frances. He guessed he had always loved her more than she had loved him, although she may not have known it. He could not, however, sacrifice everything for her and her desires; this move to Birmingham, for instance, to which, he knew, she had always been opposed. His was a vocation to which he believed he had been called, and he felt it was the Lord, again, Who had called him to work in this inner-city area. Maybe he had known all along in his heart of hearts that Frances was not cut out to be the wife of a minister, but he had loved her – he loved her still – and had hoped that she might come round to his point of view. Which was that husband and wife should work together in a vocation such as this, equal partners, more or less, sharing the same ideas and ideals.

He loved her for her enthusiasm, her gaiety, her friendliness, her concern for the children she taught. That was what had first brought her to his attention: the way she cared for the children, evoking a natural friendly response from them. Apart from her beauty, of course; her lovely face and golden hair and her trim, shapely figure. Once you looked at Frances you were compelled to look again; you would not be a real man if you failed to do so. Not that she flaunted her beauty in any way. She was well aware that she was pretty – he had seen her smiling in a satisfied manner at her reflection on occasions – but she possibly did not know the effect that her loveliness might have on the opposite sex.

He wondered, fleetingly, if there might be someone else in her life. Thoughts of Marcus Avery once more drifted into his mind. But she had not said so and as he had always found her to be completely honest he dismissed the idea. They had drifted apart, that was what she had said; she felt she could not share wholeheartedly in his work in the way he wanted her to, and now Miss Reynolds was offering her the chance of promotion she felt that that was really where her ambitions lay, in furthering her career. And there was, also, her mother who was still in far from perfect health.

If he had any criticism of Frances it was that she was possibly the tiniest bit selfish, although that was not her fault. Iris had spoiled her as a little girl. From what he could deduce she had been petted and indulged, even though she had been brought up in the days of wartime austerity. She had never really wanted for anything or had her desires seriously thwarted in any real way. This, no doubt, was at the root of the antagonism – most of the time well concealed, but at other times quite obvious – between her and her elder sister. Frances had never had to face up to any severe troubles or disasters in her life, apart from her mother's heart attacks. She had lost her father during the war, but Adrian guessed that he had never been all that close to his children. It was Iris, the stepmother, who seemed to be the mainstay of that family.

Adrian wondered how Frances would cope if troubles should come upon her. He wasn't sure why he was thinking this way, but he felt a strange sort of premonition about her. He guessed, though, that beneath that light-hearted, sometimes seemingly heedless, exterior there was a strength of character, a tenacity, ready and waiting to be drawn upon. There was no one, or very few, who got through life without their share of misfortunes. If she needed him, though, he would still be there for her. Was he being too optimistic in hoping that, one day, she might change her mind and turn back to him? At the moment, yes, he probably was; but who could tell what the future might hold.

'Never in all my life have I felt so humiliated,' said Miss Walsh to Miss Cameron, a couple of hours after the interviews for the Special Responsibility posts had taken place. The two of them were alone in the staffroom, the rest of the teachers either having gone home or working in their own classrooms. 'Marjorie Aspinall getting one of the posts was bad enough, although she has been on the staff for a reasonable length of time. But she's so . . . so slovenly. So untidy, such a fat, blowsy sort of woman.'

'I don't think her figure has anything to do with her suitability for the job,' said Miss Cameron, with a wry smile. 'The woman can't help being fat.' She blew a ring of smoke expertly across the room, taking care to avoid Miss Walsh's face, but Emily Walsh, at this moment, was far too agitated to bother about cigarette smoke.

'Of course she can help it! She's no discipline. You don't need to get fat. I never have, and neither have you, Judith. She's an untidy sloppy mess, and so is her classroom. I reckon nothing to all these so-called models made out of cornflakes packets and toilet rolls and cotton reels and goodness knows what. Creative modelling, Miss Reynolds calls it. Says it develops the children's inventive powers, helps them to create their "own little imaginative world". Creative rubbish! And she can't even write tidily on the blackboard. I tell you, Mrs Aspinall is a disgrace to the profession. How she managed to impress the board of governors I'll never know.'

'Hmm . . . She has other qualities, though, Emily. You and I may not agree with all she does, but I can't help thinking she's a good teacher. She's reliable, and always very helpful to the younger members of staff.'

'Huh! You can say that again! One in particular.'

'And I've hardly ever known Marjorie Aspinall to have a day off work in spite of – well – I think we all know she has personal problems to contend with. She gives a good impression, you see, Emily. She has a bright colourful classroom, lots of activities going on . . .'

'Too many if you ask me.'

'. . . and that's what they seem to go for these days. It's not Marjorie you're really concerned about, though, is it? That's only one of the posts, the one for Arts and Crafts. It's Frances Goodwin, isn't it? That's what has really got your goat, especially her being awarded the one for Music and Drama.'

'Well, of course it is. I tell you, Judith, I was never so humiliated in all my life as when Miss Reynolds came out and said that the post was being given to her. That young chit of a girl! And she can't even play the piano! Only been here five minutes and she's got them all eating out of her hand, silly fools that they are.'

'I did try to warn you, you know. I told you it was no use you applying for that post. I could see the way Miss Reynolds's mind was working. She more or less told me—'

'And how could I have lived with myself if I hadn't applied, if I hadn't spoken up about it? I told them straight – Miss Reynolds and all the rest of them – that I'd been teaching for forty years and that posts like that were introduced as a little reward for long service, for such as me. I don't think they all realised that. And I'm sure that's what the powers that be had in mind when they brought them in, not to be handed out like dolly mixtures to young kids who have no experience.

'Of course they were all so smarmy and oh-so-polite to me, told me that as I'd done forty years I should be thinking about retirement and taking it easy, not taking on extra work. And one of them, that rather common woman who manages the greengrocer's shop – what she knows about education I can't imagine! – she said they were trying to encourage the teachers who had that little bit extra to offer, not those who had had their day. Those weren't her exact words, but I knew what she meant. Oh yes, I knew all right.'

'So it could have been no surprise to you really, when you heard the result?'

'Of course it was a surprise. I thought some of them might have had a modicum of sense, but it seems not.'

'We always knew Miss Reynolds would have the last word. I did try to tell you, Emily.'

'Whose side are you on anyway?' snapped Miss Walsh 'I always thought you would stick up for me, Judith. It's common knowledge that you and the boss don't see eye to eye. That headship should have been yours; I'm not the only one who thinks that. But now it seems to me as though you're siding with her.'

'Not at all.' Judith Cameron sighed. 'But I suppose, particularly over this last year or so, I've stopped minding about it quite so much. I got tired of forever arguing with her, always putting forward a contrary point of view. I'd made up my mind in the beginning that I'd be as damned difficult as possible, give her a jolly good run for her money. But not any more. I suddenly thought, what the hell? What would I want with a headship anyway? Too much damned responsibility. No, I'm all right as I am, in a nice little deputy's job. She makes sure she doesn't give me too many extra duties; she likes to do it all herself. So, in many ways, it's quite a cushy little number. And the money's not too bad. If you'll take my advice, Emily, you'll try and forget all about this and just enjoy your last few years, like I'm doing.'

'But I feel such a fool. Besides, I can't stand the girl.'

'No, I realise that. You've never really liked her, ever since she joined the staff, have you?'

'I can't abide her! Those baby-blue eyes and that simpering smile. She's got Miss Reynolds wrapped round her little finger, and that takes some doing. She has had right from the start. And the way she carried on with that chap from the Junior staff last summer, that was downright disgraceful! All dressed up like a film star, singing those silly love songs! It should never have been allowed, not in a school concert, not in front of all those children.'

'I don't think they thought anything about it. Children don't; they just take things as they come. I must admit she's a pretty girl. You can't condemn her for that, Emily.'

'Pretty? Huh! Can't say I've noticed, but she's too much influence here, I'll tell you that. She's got all her family in on the act as well. Her sister always in and out taking photographs, and that Road Safety fellow, her brother-in-law.'

'That's hardly her fault. Just a coincidence.'

'A very funny one, if you ask me. She should never have been given that post. What has she done to deserve it? It's . . . it's outrageous. I can't believe it.' Miss Walsh was going red in the face, the veins standing out on her sinewy neck and Miss Cameron looked at her in some alarm. 'Tell me, Judith,' she went on, her voice getting louder and shriller, 'you've got to tell me, you've got to be honest with me – would you have given it to her? Why has she got it and not me? It should have been mine, you know it should.'

'No, I wouldn't have chosen her,' replied Miss Cameron carefully. 'But she's been chosen because of the work she's done, in music and drama. That's what Miss Reynolds said.'

'Music! What music? She can't even play the piano. It's me that plays the piano, day in and day out. And what thanks do I get? A slap in the face.'

'And because she has the makings of a very good teacher, a lot of potential, that's what the boss said.'

'A good teacher? Her writing's atrocious! You should see the state of her Record Book. I sneaked a look at it one day. Sprawly, messy writing – she's just as bad as her blowsy friend. They're a good pair, those two.'

Judith sighed again. 'I don't suppose, in the long run, it's the tidiness of the writing that counts. It's the ideas behind it. Look, Emily, you really will have to try and come to terms with it or you're going to make yourself ill.'

'I feel like going and having it out with Gertie Reynolds, telling her just what I think of her – and her board of governors.'

'You'll be making a big mistake if you do. Her decision is final. You'll only make yourself look foolish.'

'And her. That . . . Frances Goodwin!' It was an effort for Miss Walsh even to utter the girl's name. 'I can't begin to tell you what I'd like to say to that one!'

'Emily . . . don't.'

'She's not engaged to that young minister any more; did you know that? He's obviously seen through her, the little minx! He's well rid of that one and no mistake.'

'Emily, you mustn't let your personal dislike of her get the better of you. She's got the job, whether we like it or not – and if I'm honest, I don't – but there's nothing we can do about it. Just try to accept it. You're going to have to, you know.'

'Accept it? I shall never accept it. I shall be watching her.' Emily Walsh's eyes were narrowed with hatred and her mouth, before she spoke again, was set in a grim line. 'I shall be watching her every move. One false step and that little madam will get what's coming to her.'

Frances was surprised to receive a phone call one day in February, during the school lunch break, from Mrs Ashcroft, Megan's mother.

'Hello, Frances, my dear.' The woman sounded vaguely troubled. 'Megan asked me to give you a ring.'

'Hello, Mrs Ashcroft. There's nothing wrong, is there?'

'Well . . . we hope not, dear. Not very wrong . . . but our Megan has been admitted into hospital. Her blood pressure's very high and she's developed something they call toxaemia. I don't understand all that much about it, though Megan does, of course. Anyway, Frances, she's feeling a bit low, in need of somebody to cheer her up, and she wondered if you could find time to go and see her.'

'Of course I will, Mrs Ashcroft. It's Saturday tomorrow; I'll go tomorrow afternoon. Is she likely to be in long, do you know?'

'Oh yes, didn't I say? They're keeping her in until the baby's born. That's why she's feeling a bit fed up, you see. It's another two or three weeks yet, but they say she has to have complete rest. They're trying to bring her blood pressure down. It's important to do that, apparently, before the baby's born. Oh dear, we do hope everything is going to be all right. Her daddy and me, we can't help worrying.'

'I'm sure it will be,' Frances replied. 'She's in the right place, isn't she? They'll take good care of her at the Vic, and . . . er, Bernard will be there, won't he, to keep an eye on her?'

'Oh yes, that's one blessing. Bernard's one of the main men, isn't he? He'll make sure nothing goes wrong. Anyway, that's all I wanted to tell you, dear. You're keeping well, are you, Frances?'

'Yes, fine, thank you.'

'Megan was telling me about your engagement . . . I was so sorry, dear. Or perhaps I shouldn't have mentioned it? I didn't mean to upset you.'

'No, it's all right, Mrs Ashcroft. I'm not upset . . . not now. We decided it was for the best.'

'I see . . . yes. And how's your mother? She's keeping quite well, is she? No more – you know – upsets with her heart?'

'No, thank goodness. She's as well as can be expected. She's relieved I'm staying in Blackpool, I think.'

'Good . . . well, I'll say bye-bye then, dear. Thank you for saying you'll go to see Megan. Her daddy and I will be going again tonight.'

'OK, Mrs Ashcroft. Bye for now.'

Frances had been rather concerned about Megan for some time now. Her pregnancy, as the months advanced, had not sat well on her. She had put on a tremendous amount of weight, which Megan assured her, in her confident nurse's manner, was only fluid and was nothing to worry about. Her face had become red and puffy, her ankles were swollen and the huge bulge she carried in front of her seemed to be not a part at all of what had once been her delicate, slender frame.

Megan's face lit up with delight as she saw her friend approaching her bed the next afternoon and she clasped her hands together excitedly, like a small girl at a birthday party. Frances was glad to see, as she kissed her cheek, that her face was rather less puffy now and her eyes were bright, always a sign, or so she had been told, of good health.

'Hello, love,' said Frances. 'How are you doing? I've brought you some choccies, see. I don't know whether you're allowed to have them, but I don't see why not.'

'Ooh, lovely! Thanks ever so much, Fran. Dairy Box, my favourites! I'm sure one or two at a time will do me no harm. Best not to let Bernard see them, though. He'll be sure to think of a reason why I shouldn't have them.'

Frances made no comment. She hoped she would not encounter Dr Conway this afternoon. She guessed that, as he could visit his wife any time, he would avoid the regulation visiting hours. Megan soon told her that this was, indeed, the case.

'Bernard pops in every day before he starts his rounds, and when he's finished, if he has time. He's at home at the moment – he's on late today – so I'm sorry, but you won't be seeing him.'

'Oh, what a pity.' Frances tried to look regretful. 'You must feel quite at home here, Megan, amongst friends. The nurses remember you, do they?'

'Oh yes, some of them, but it's a huge place, you know. You can't know everybody. But, luckily, Shirley is on this ward now. You remember, the girl I was quite friendly with on the Children's Ward? She's doing a spell in Maternity now, so I'm glad about that. But the hours drag at times, Fran. They wake us up so early – before six – so it's such a long day. You don't realise when you're nursing, you're so busy, but I'm seeing it from a patient's point of view now. And sometimes, when I've nothing to occupy my mind, I start thinking.' Her pale blue eyes, for a moment, looked very frightened. 'Oh dear, I wish it was all over. I wish I knew that it was all going to be all right.'

'Of course it'll be all right. Why shouldn't it be? They're excellent here, aren't they? You know you've always said so yourself; you've said what a very good hospital it is. They're satisfied with your progess, aren't they?'

'Oh yes, I've been better since I came in here. They've managed to get my blood pressure down. I can't help worrying, though, sometimes.'

'Only natural. I'm sure I'd worry as well. But you must try not to. Have you thought of any names yet, for the baby?'

'Oh, yes.' Megan smiled and her eyes no longer looked quite so fearful. 'Michael Joseph or Stephen Joseph. We both like Joseph, you see, and it's Bernard's father's name as well. We can't quite decide about the other. I'd like to include Bernard, too. Michael Joseph Bernard . . . or do you think that's too much?'

'It's your baby.' Frances smiled. 'You can call it whatever you like. And if it's a girl?'

'Oh, I don't know. We haven't thought of any girls' names. Bernard wants a boy, you see.'

He would, thought Frances. 'And . . . what about you?' she asked.

'Oh, I'm not bothered what it is, so long as it's all right. But I know Bernard badly wants a son. Men always do, don't they?'

'They seem to . . . yes,' Frances replied. 'Some of them.'

'It will serve him jolly well right if it's a girl,' Frances remarked later to Julie. 'Bombastic devil! On the other hand, I wouldn't like to be in Megan's shoes if she fails to produce his son and heir.'

'Surely it wouldn't matter, even to Bernard, so long as the baby was all right . . . and Megan, of course,' said Julie. 'It's more important for her to be OK, isn't it?'

'I don't know . . . I hope so,' said Frances uncertainly. 'I can't help feeling rather worried, Julie. They're Catholics, as you know, although it's hard for me to think of Megan as a Catholic, remembering what she was like before. What I mean is this; I have an idea – I'm sure I've heard it said – that if there's a choice to be made about whether to save the mother or the baby – you know, if things should go wrong – then Catholics always insist on saving the baby.'

'Surely not now, Frances. We're in the 1960s. Surely the same dogmas don't hold good now, even if they used to.'

'I don't know. It's only what I've been led to believe.'

'But Bernard's a doctor, a gynaecologist. I know you don't like him, but he'll be on hand at the birth. He'll make sure his wife is all right, won't he?'

'I hope so, Julie. I hope to God he will. Megan has not been too happy with him since they got married. I didn't tell you before, because I understand things improved after she became pregnant. But she does deserve some happiness, and she was so looking forward to this baby coming . . . until she got frightened. She seemed terribly scared this afternoon. Oh, I do hope nothing goes wrong for her.'

It was Mrs Ashcroft, again, who phoned to tell Frances the news about Megan's baby. She had given birth on the last day of February to a baby girl who weighed 7lb 8oz, a very large weight for a young woman with such a small frame as Megan had.

'And she's all right, is she? And the baby as well?' asked Frances anxiously, the fact that Bernard had not got his longed for son not at first registering with her, so concerned was she to know her friend was in no danger.

'Yes . . .' Frances could hear Megan's mother breathing a heartfelt sigh. 'Yes, we think she's going to be all right now, thank God, although it was touch and go, Frances. She had a very bad time. She was in labour for almost twenty-four hours, poor lamb.' Mrs Ashcroft's voice broke a little. 'And in the end they had to put her out. It was a forceps delivery, she was losing a lot of blood. Oh dear, I don't know very much about these things. I've only had the one child myself and I had a rough time too, like Megan. But I know they can cope much better today; they know so much more about it all. Yes, she'll be all right, I'm sure. She's in good hands, and Bernard's there, of course.'

'May I go and see her,' asked Frances, 'or is it only close relations?'

'Just wait a day or two, dear. They're a bit fussy about visitors in the Maternity Ward, but towards the weekend she should be feeling strong enough.'

Frances was so relieved she felt as though a burden had been lifted from her shoulders. She was not quite sure what she had feared, or maybe she had refused to let those fears formulate fully in her mind. When she saw Megan the following Saturday any remaining anxiety about her friend vanished, for Megan appeared to be in reasonable health – pale, but bright-eyed and obviously delighted with her baby girl.

'Look at her, Frances,' she said, nodding towards the cot at the foot of the bed. 'Don't you think she's beautiful? I suppose I shouldn't say so myself, but I can't help it. I think she's just perfect.'

She was certainly a lovely baby, with rounded cheeks and a faintly mottled skin, such as all healthy babies had. Her hair was just a wisp of pale golden fluff covering the top of her head, and from what Frances could see there was nothing of the dark swarthiness of Bernard about her. She was all Megan.

'Yes, she really is beautiful,' she said. 'You're a clever girl, Megan.' She kissed her friend's cheek before sitting down on the bedside chair. 'What are you going to call her?' She remembered how Megan had said they had not thought of any girls' names.

'Maria Veronica,' replied Megan. 'Maria is after Bernard's mother – and his sister – and we both like Veronica. It's a saint's name as well, of course.'

'And Bernard . . . he wasn't too disappointed that he hadn't got a son? I'm sure he was only too relieved you were both OK, wasn't he?'

'Oh, no . . . I mean, yes, I think he was glad it was all over and that I was all right. It was quite bad, Frances. They had to put me to sleep in the end, because I couldn't . . .' She shook her head confusedly. 'I don't really want to think about it. Anyway, it doesn't matter now, does it, now I've got Maria? But I think Bernard was disappointed. I caught a glimpse of his face when I was coming round and he looked – I don't know – so disillusioned. He's tried to hide it. We talked about names and all that and he was ever so nice to me, but I know he's not all that pleased.'

She took hold of Frances's hand. 'Shall I tell you a secret? Don't let on to Bernard . . .' As if I would, thought Frances. '. . . but I wanted a little girl. I didn't dare tell him, but I really, really did.' She smiled shyly. 'And she is lovely, isn't she, Frances? I'm a very lucky girl, I know I am.'

Frances felt a lump come into her throat. She did so hope her friend would know some real happiness and that she would enjoy looking after her baby without the threat of ill health, or any other problems.

'And there's always another time, isn't there?' Megan said brightly. 'Perhaps the next one will be a boy, then Bernard will be pleased as well. They've told me I'll have to be careful, though, with me having such a bad time. But it's true what they say about labour pains, that you forget about them when the baby's born. At least I nearly have.' Her face darkened for a moment. 'I'm sure I will . . . soon.' She tried to smile. 'I shouldn't be talking like this to you, should I, an unmarried lady? I'll be putting you off.'

'Oh, don't worry about me,' said Frances. 'I've heard it all before. I'm not completely naive, you know. I expect your mum is thrilled to bits, isn't she? And your dad. How do they like being grandparents . . .?'

Frances stopped on the way out of the ward to speak to Shirley, Megan's friend, who had once worked with her on the Children's Ward. 'I'm glad they're both well, Megan and the baby,' she said. 'She is OK, isn't she?'

'Oh, yes, she'll be fine now,' replied Shirley. 'It was touch and go, mind you. She had us worried for a time. Dr Templeton's a brilliant doctor, though. If anybody could pull them both through it's him.'

'Oh, I see. Bernard – Dr Conway – he didn't deliver the baby then?'

'Oh no, Dr Templeton's Megan's doctor. It was considered to be the best policy, and it was what Megan wanted. She's grown quite attached to him. He insisted on being there, of course . . . her husband.'

From her tone of voice Frances guessed that Shirley was not enamoured of Dr Conway. She did not comment, however, except to say, 'I gather he wanted a boy, but Megan is over the moon with her little girl. I'm so pleased for her.'

'He'll have to be satisfied then, won't he?' said Shirley. 'Because she can't have any more.'

'What? She can't . . .? Does she know?' asked Frances, feeling perplexed. 'But she was talking about—'

'Oh, yes, she knows,' said Shirley. 'Well, it isn't so much that she can't have any more, but she shouldn't. I'd put it stronger than that; I'd say she mustn't. If she did, then there might be a very grave danger. I shouldn't really be saying this, but I know you're her best friend, aren't you?'

'Yes . . . I suppose I am,' said Frances.

'I know she always speaks so highly of you, and I'm not saying anything Megan doesn't already know.'

'She knows there's a risk?'

'Oh, yes; she's been told.'

'And Dr Conway; he knows as well?'

'Well, of course he does. He would, wouldn't he?'

'Yes, that was a silly thing for me to say,' replied Frances. 'But . . .' she hesitated, not knowing just what to do. She didn't want Megan to think they had been talking about her; on the other hand her friend's life might be in danger. 'But she's talking about . . . the next time,' she said in a whisper.

'Is she indeed?' said Shirley. 'Thanks for telling me. I'll have a word on the QT. I won't let on you've told me, but I'll try to impress upon her about the dangers. Now, if you'll excuse me, Frances, I must get on. Nice to see you again.'

'I shouldn't worry, if I were you,' said Julie, later that day. 'Dr Conway's a sensible fellow, surely? He'll be aware of the dangers if anybody will. Damn it all, it's his wife,

Frances. He's not going to put her to any risk, is he?'

'No, I suppose not,' replied Frances. She felt it would be wrong to discuss in any great detail her friend's marital problems. But how could they ensure, Bernard following the tenets of his faith to the letter, as he did, that Megan did not become pregnant again?

Marjorie Aspinall was waiting for Frances when she arrived at school on Monday morning. She popped her head out of the classroom door when she heard Frances's footsteps coming along the corridor and beckoned to her to come in.

'I've something to tell you. Bad news, I'm afraid.' Marjorie hesitated for a moment. Then, 'Kenneth's left me,' she said. 'He's packed his bags and gone. This weekend.'

'But . . . why?' Frances perched on the edge of a desk, looking concernedly at her friend. Marjorie looked stunned, her eyes puzzled and faintly disbelieving, but not, Frances was relieved to see, as though she was ready to burst into tears. 'Have you had a row? I thought – well – I rather imagined things were better. You hadn't said anything lately.'

'No, no row,' said Marjorie flatly. 'Nothing like that. He just told me he was leaving me. Should have told me ages ago, he said.' She paused. 'He's got another woman.'

'Another woman? But . . . didn't you know? You'd never suspected?'

'Not in the slightest. Never once did it enter my head. Bloody fool I've been, haven't I?' She gave a bitter laugh. 'They say the wife is always the last to know. Well, it's true because I hadn't a clue, not a bloody clue.' Frances had never heard Marjorie swear before and this disturbed her somewhat. Her friend must be very angry, and humilated, and hurt. And Frances, also, was feeling a slight stirring of guilt, though not about this.

'Who . . . who is it?' she asked faintly. 'Do you know?'

'Oh, yes, I know now. Quite brazen about it, he is. Some girl he works with in the office – her name's not important. She has a flat near the park and he's gone to live with her.

She's twenty-four, about the same age as you, Frances. Would you believe it? Twenty-four years old! Younger than our own daughter. Well, they say there's no fool like an old fool, don't they? And that's what Kenneth is – a silly old fool. He'll realise it though, before long. He'll be crawling back, I'll be bound, with his tail between his legs.'

'But Kenneth, of all people! He seems so unlikely. You said how moody he was, didn't you? How he never talked to you?'

'Well, he's obviously found somebody he can talk to now, hasn't he? Or perhaps they don't talk. Maybe actions speak louder than words – I don't know. I only know he'll live to regret it.'

'You mean he'll want to come back?'

'I'd bet you any money he will.'

'And . . . you mean to say you'd have him back?'

Marjorie didn't asnswer straight away. Then: 'He's my husband, Frances,' she said.

'But if you're not happy together, and you've told me often enough that you're not, wouldn't you be better off without him? You could make a new life for yourself. You've got your home and your job . . . and this new responsibility post now. Anyway, I thought you were fed up with him.'

'So I was, at times. But I'm married to him, aren't I? He's my husband. And if he thinks I'm going to stand by and watch some little trollop walk off with him, then he's another think coming. Do you know, he had the nerve to tell me he wanted a divorce?'

'And you wouldn't consider it?'

'Not on your life, I wouldn't! I shall never divorce him. Not that I'll need to. You mark my words, he'll be back. Maybe not yet, but he'll get fed up . . . or she will. And you can bet it's her that's done most of the running. Some girls are not content with single fellows. Oh no, they have to get their claws into the married ones. And some fellows have no more sense than to be led along by the nose, or by something else, more likely, if you ask me. That'll be the top and bottom of it: sex. That's what it always is.'

'But I remember you telling me once that it was important.'

'So I did. So it is. But other things have to be right as well. You can't just have sex on its own. But I was talking about marriage then, wasn't I, if you remember? Not just . . . a bit on the side.'

Frances, by now, was feeling dreadfully ill at ease. She had told Marjorie nothing at all about her relationship with Marcus. Her affair, she thought, with a stab of guilt, for she had to admit, if only to herself, that that was what it was. She had not dared to tell her older friend that she was seeing him outside of school hours. She had guessed what Marjorie's reaction might be, and this outburst now proved it. Could it be, she wondered, that Marjorie had guessed and was having a dig at her, for her involvement with a married man? She was being very vehement in her condemnation of such young women. No, that was not possible. Marjorie didn't know. Nobody knew.

'I'm really sorry, Marjorie,' Frances said now. 'And I hope it all works out in the way you want it to. I mean . . . if you want him back, then I hope he comes to his senses.' It was difficult to know what to say, and she knew she was being hypocritical, too. She hoped he came to his senses . . . How could she, in any honesty, have said that? However would she feel if Marcus came to his senses? But it was different with her and Marcus.

'Thanks, Frances,' said Marjorie. 'Don't say anything to the others. They'll find out, of course, soon enough, but I don't want to be the talk of the staffroom. Not today, not till I've had a chance to get over it a bit. Look, it's ten to nine. You'd better go and get yourself sorted out before the kids come in. Sorry I kept you. Ah well, another day, another dollar, I suppose. Maybe it'll help to take my mind off things . . .'

Chapter 20

It was not like that with her and Marcus, Frances tried to tell herself. Geraldine, Marcus's wife, had very little time at all for him now and if he were to leave her it would not worry her in the slightest; not when she had got used to the idea because she was, Frances gathered, rather neurotic. Marcus had hinted several times that he might leave her. He had not made a definite promise, but Frances knew that was not possible. Not yet. He had to choose the right moment to tell her. That was why there still had to be all this secrecy. Marcus did not want Geraldine to find out from someone else. Neither did Frances want her mother – or anyone else for that matter – to know about Marcus. Not that there was any chance of Iris finding out. She very rarely left the house these days and, besides, she did not know the same people that Marcus knew.

This was the one thing that Frances hated about her friendship with Marcus – the secrecy, the furtiveness of it all. They still met each Tuesday evening at night school, behaving there, in front of the other students, as though they were colleagues who happened to travel there together. No one suspected that they were anything more than good friends. Sometimes, on these Tuesday evenings, they drove out to a pub on the outskirts of the town, not too far away, to Hardhorn, maybe, or Staining; somewhere where they were not likely to see anyone who might recognise them. They would have only one drink, then they would find a secluded lane nearby and there, on the back seat of the car, Marcus would make love to her.

Frances preferred the times when Julie, by prior arrangement, had gone to visit her family or had gone out with

Mike, the boyfriend she saw spasmodically. She never came home until well after half-past eleven, which gave Frances and Marcus almost two hours of uninterrupted bliss. Far too short, but Frances knew, for the moment, that she would have to content herself with these occasional, clandestine meetings; until such time as they were able to make their feelings for one another known to everyone. Frances looked forward so much to that time. It was not in her nature to be devious.

What Marcus told his wife about the evenings when he returned home late, she had no idea. He did not talk about her much, and Frances did not ask, remembering well the time she had almost had her head bitten off for her pains. It was sufficient for her to know she was doing the woman no harm. She would never have entered into this relationship if she had felt she was causing any hurt to Marcus's wife. Girls who get involved with married men deserve all they get. She recalled making that remark to Marjorie, soon after she had got to know Marcus Avery. And so they did, so they did . . . It may well have been a priggish, self-satisfied sort of thing to say, but Frances did believe that nice, well-brought-up girls, such as herself, did not get themselves involved with men who were married. But, of course, with Marcus it was so very different. Marcus and Geraldine no longer loved one another. It was Marcus and Frances now. She loved him so much, and she knew that he loved her, too.

When she was with him she was in no doubt. Every smile, every gesture, every fond embrace, every act of love – each time better than the last – proved that he did. But when she was away from him, it was then that the niggling little fears– not exactly doubts, for how could she doubt him? – began to trouble her. For she could not remember him ever saying the words, 'I love you'. He had told her she was beautiful; he had said how well they got on together (in every way they seemed to be compatible); he had said how much his life had changed since they had met. But he had never actually spoken out loud the words that she so wanted to hear, 'I love you, Frances.'

She had told him, many times, that she loved him. She had even asked, 'Do you love me?' And his reply had always been, 'Of course I do; you know I do, pet.' So that was as good as saying it, she supposed.

He was very sensible, very careful and solicitous on her behalf that nothing should go wrong, and for this she had every reason to be grateful to him. She had hesitated, just for a moment, that very first time. 'Marcus . . . we can't, we mustn't. Supposing . . . ' But he had calmed her fears. 'Don't worry, darling,' he had said. 'I'll take care of everything.' And so he had, that first time and every time afterwards. Some men, she knew, would have been careless about such matters, not paying any heed to what the outcome might be. But not Marcus. He wanted to protect her, until such time as they could admit their love for one another.

He had been surprised, too, that first time, and Frances had been grateful for the way he had shown such gentleness and understanding. He was not always gentle now in the way he made love to her. The heights of rapture he was able to make her reach had amazed her. But that first time: 'I'm sorry, darling,' he had said. 'I had no idea . . . I had assumed . . . Please forgive me; I'm sorry if I hurt you, but I really did think . . .'

'Because I'm engaged?' At that time, last November, she had still been engaged to Adrian.

'Yes, I suppose so,' Marcus answered, a little testily. 'Naturally, I thought you and he . . .'

'He's a clergyman, Marcus,' Frances answered in a small voice. 'He . . . well, he wouldn't . . .'

'Never mind about him, not now, darling.' He had kissed her, smothering all her words of protest about Adrian. They had never talked about her fiancé, just as they never talked about his wife. At that time, at the start of their relationship, she had suffered dreadful pangs of remorse when she thought about Adrian down in Birmingham. Once she had made the decision to break off her engagement and written to Adrian, the guilt had lessened somewhat. She had told Marcus, of course, of what she had done.

'That's good, pet,' he had said with a cheerful grin. 'I knew you would, sooner or later. It's only fair to the chap. And after all, you and him – well – it was never really right, was it?'

Oh yes, it was, her conscience had protested, that 'still, small voice' inside her that begged her, so often, to stop and listen to it, and to which she was finding it increasingly easy to shut her ears. If you stopped listening to that little voice, in the end it stopped trying to talk to you. That was what she had told Dennis, and how very true it was. Oh yes, at one time I loved Adrian, she had wanted to cry out; maybe not enough . . . but I did love him. And there were so many people who had believed it was right, that they were made for one another. But, of course, she had said nothing.

'I'm pleased about your responsibility post,' Marcus had said, this being the catalyst that had sparked off her decision to end her engagement. 'Just think – it took me twelve years, and you've managed it in less than three. It must've been one in the eye for Miss Walsh right enough. I'd watch her if I were you, pet. Don't leave her alone with your beaker. She'll be slipping arsenic into your tea.'

Frances wondered if she might have detected a touch of envy in his remarks, but she had dismissed it, being more concerned about the way he had, once again, adeptly changed the subject. She had hoped, forlornly, it now seemed, that at the news of her broken engagement Marcus might have come to a decision of his own to tell his wife that he had met someone else, that he wanted a divorce. Was that, in fact, what Marcus wanted? Sometimes, when she was away from him, Frances felt she had no idea what Marcus wanted, where they were heading, or what would be the outcome of it all. But when they were together he was able to make her forget everything but the here and now.

'There's someone over there that I know,' said Marcus in an edgy sort of voice. It was an evening in early April and they had driven out, after their French class, to a pub they

314

had not visited before, in the Cleveleys area. 'Over there, near the door, the woman in the red jacket. No, don't stare, you idiot!' he hissed as Frances leaned forward to get a better look. 'Don't make it obvious, for God's sake! I'm going to pretend I haven't seen her. If we keep still and quiet she may not notice us.'

'Who is it anyway?' asked Frances, peeved at being called an idiot. Even as she spoke she was aware that the woman had turned her head slightly and was now looking in their direction.

'One of Geraldine's cronies. She's in the same writers' circle, or poetry group, one or the other. I can't remember which. I've met her a few times. They came to our place for supper once, soon after we moved here. Geraldine invited them, her and her husband.'

'The fellow that's with her?'

'Yes, I suppose it will be.' Marcus ventured another quick glance. 'Yes, that's him. Can't remember his name. Archie or Andy . . . Archie, I think. He didn't make much of an impression on me. He's one of those poetry chaps, like his wife. She's Daphne; I do remember that.'

The woman, Daphne, was not looking at them now. She and her husband were holding an animated conversation, their heads close together. She'll be telling him she's seen Geraldine's husband over there with another girl, thought Frances. Well, what the heck did it matter? It was about time it was all out in the open. She was sick and tired of all the secrecy. Maybe this would make Marcus realise he had to tell his wife.

'I'd forgotten they lived at Cleveleys,' he was mumbling, staring moodily into the depths of his glass. 'How could I have been such a bloody fool? Yes, it's their local, come to think of it. I remember now; they live just round the corner. Oh Lor . . . let's hope they don't see us.'

'What does it matter?' said Frances irritably, remembering he had once said the exact same thing to her. Maybe the difference now was that they had something to hide. 'We can't hide away in corners for ever.'

'Of course it matters! She might tell Geraldine.'

'So what? You've been saying for ages you'd tell Geraldine yourself.'

'Shut up, Frances, can't you! I can't tell her at the moment. She's not been well. I've told you time and time again I'll decide when it's the right moment to tell her. Oh no, oh, my God! She's seen us. Bloody hell! I might've known this would happen. For God's sake, Frances, act naturally. Don't say anything unless you have to.' He was speaking hurriedly, hysterically almost, in a frenzied whisper. 'Just leave it to me. I'll do all the talking . . .

'Hello there, Daphne.' His voice changed to one of forced bonhomie. 'I thought it was you, and your husband. Archie, isn't it? I was just saying to Frances, I'm sure that's Geraldine's friend over there. But you look different somehow.' He put his head on one side, frowning as he looked at her closely. 'Yes, it's your hair, isn't it? You've had it cut.'

'Yes . . . yes, I have indeed, Marcus.' The woman, a very attractive woman with short dark hair, was looking at him keenly, a humorous, but very shrewd, glance in her blue eyes. She knows, thought Frances. There is no use trying to pull the wool over this one's eyes. The woman now shifted her appraising glance to Frances who smiled back quite ingenuously. Marcus had told her to behave naturally, although there had been nothing natural about the way he had been panicking. Anyway, wasn't it time they stopped behaving like a couple of criminals? Marcus and Geraldine's marriage was virtually over.

'This is your local, isn't it? I thought I might see you here,' lied Marcus. 'Oh, I'm sorry – I haven't introduced you. This is Frances . . . Frances Goodwin, a colleague of mine from school. Actually, she's on the Infant staff and I'm on the Junior, but, for our sins, we've ended up on the same committee.'

For our sins? thought Frances, cringing inwardly. What a thing to say! A Freudian slip, perhaps, but Marcus was chattering away inanely, obviously not aware of all he was saying.

' . . organising a joint concert for our schools. That's

where we've been tonight, to a committee meeting. One of our staff lives in Cleveleys and we've been to her house. So we thought we'd just have one for the road, didn't we, Frances?' She smiled and nodded her agreement. 'This is Daphne, by the way. Daphne . . . I'm sorry, I forget your surname.'

'Thomson,' the woman replied coolly, shaking hands with Frances, at the same time giving her a curt, unsmiling nod. 'I thought Geraldine said you went to night school on a Tuesday, Marcus? A French class, isn't it?'

'Yes . . . so I do, usually. But this was considered more important tonight. Overtime, actually, but teachers have to attend all kinds of extracurricular meetings. No one realises—'

'No, I'm sure they don't,' Daphne broke in. 'And I'm sure you and . . . er . . . Miss Goodwin will be wanting to get home, so I won't keep you. Another hard day at school tomorrow, eh?' She raised a questioning eyebrow. 'What I came across to say, Marcus, was that we were so pleased to hear Geraldine's good news. She's waited a long time and I know how thrilled she must be. Do give her my love, and tell her I hope she'll soon be feeling better. I gather she's not too well at the moment. She missed the last meeting.'

'No . . . she's not too well. Just a stomach upset, you know. Nothing to worry about. I'll tell her I've seen you, and that you send your congratulations. Come on, Frances. Drink up . . . Oh, I see you have done. I promised Geraldine I wouldn't be late, but she knows what teachers are like when they get talking.' He gave a forced laugh as he rose to his feet, almost pushing Frances towards the door. 'Cheerio, Daphne; be seeing you.'

Daphne walked with them to the table near the door where she rejoined her husband. 'Hi there, Archie,' Marcus called, briefly raising his hand, but he did not stop. His agitation was all too obvious now, to Frances, at least, if not to these friends of his wife.

'Phew!' he gasped as they stood on the pavement outside. 'That was a close shave. We pulled it off though. Thanks, pet.' He squeezed her arm. 'She won't suspect anything, not Daphne. Come on, I really did say I wouldn't be late. We won't have time for . . . anything else tonight.'

'What was all that about?' asked Frances, still feeling very piqued, as they walked towards the car. 'Congratulations? Good news? What's she done then?'

'Oh, that!' Marcus gave a casual laugh. 'Something and nothing really. Geraldine has had a short story accepted by a magazine called *People's Friend*. Anybody'd think she'd written *War and Peace* the way all her cronies are going on about it.'

'But that's very good,' said Frances. 'You didn't tell me.'

'Why should I? It's Geraldine's hobby, not mine. But obviously she's pleased about it. Like Daphne said, she's waited a long time. Some of these would-be writers wait for ever to be published. I should imagine it's quite a feather in the cap for her writers' group; reflected glory and all that. Come to think of it, I rather think Daphne Thomson's a member of both those groups Geraldine goes to. Anyway, never mind, eh, pet?' He opened the car door and ushered her inside.

'We'd best play it cool for a week or two, though, mebbe?' he said, not looking at her, as they drove away.

'What do you mean, play it cool?'

'Well, not meet . . . You know what I mean; I don't have to spell it out, surely? There'll be no night school anyway, over the Easter period, nor over the summer term.'

'Yes, but some of us were going to meet unofficially, weren't we? Mrs Beecham said we could meet at her house.'

Mrs Beecham was the French teacher, and she had agreed to entertain a dozen or so of the keener members of the class at her home, during the summer, when there was no tuition, to practise their conversational French. It was mainly for the ones who were going on the holiday to France. Marcus and Frances were not among that number, but they had expressed an interest in going along to the meetings, knowing it would give them an excuse to be together.

'We'll go, pet. Don't worry . . . we'll go.' Marcus reached

across and patted her knee. 'We'd better just watch our step. You know what I mean.'

No, I don't know, Marcus, she wanted to argue. It's time you told her. I'm sick of all the subterfuge, all this shillyshallying around. For goodness, sake, behave like a proper man and face up to the facts . . . But, of course, she said nothing.

They hardly met at all for a few weeks. One evening during the Easter break from school, however, Marcus arrived at her flat unexpectedly, desperate, he said, for her company. He had missed her so much. They drove out to the inn at St Michael's where they had had their first drink together so many months ago. Seven months, to be exact. Frances had felt sure that by this time they would have come to some arrangement about their future together; but still Marcus seemed content to carry on as they were, furtively, much more infrequently now, and with no talk of the time that lay ahead. And because she loved him so much she made no protest.

Their lovemaking that night, in a secluded lane in the deep still darkness of the countryside, was more frenzied than ever, and yet, more tender. And, at last, Marcus did utter the words that Frances had been longing to hear. 'I love you, Frances,' he breathed, kissing the long hair behind her ear. 'You know I love you, don't you? Whatever happens . . .'

'What d'you mean, Marcus?' She felt a sense of misgiving, though she was thrilled to hear his declaration of love. ' "Whatever happens"?'

'Nothing . . . nothing at all, darling. I didn't mean anything. I just want you to know I love you, that's all.'

'And I love you too, Marcus,' she sighed. 'I'll always love you.'

The next time they met was at Mrs Beecham's house in Layton, not too far from where Marcus, and Frances's mother, too, lived. Rather close for comfort, Frances pondered, especially on a light May evening, but the avenue was deserted and no one saw them arrive together at the house. When they left, after an enjoyable couple of hours spent drinking coffee and chattering away in French, it was dark. Frances found herself, to her annoyance, glancing furtively around as they came out of the gate. Again, there was no one in sight, only a couple of cars parked nearby, and their own friends who were leaving at the same time. What on earth am I worrying about? she asked herself, but the feeling of foreboding that had been with her for a few weeks now, ever since they had met Geraldine's friends in Cleveleys, would not go away.

They drove straight home and Marcus kissed her as they sat in the car outside the flat, but he refused her invitation to come in for yet another cup of coffee, even though Julie was out for the evening.

'No, best not to, pet. You know how it is,' he said, squeezing her hand. 'See you soon . . . ' He leaned across her to open the car door.

No, I don't know how it is, Marcus, she thought as the car zoomed away. I don't know how anything is . . . I don't even know you any more.

They went again, the following week, to the home of Mrs Beecham, leaving early this time to drive to a secluded lane that Marcus had discovered near the village of Staining. Neither of them noticed the small black car that had been parked opposite the house, following them. In fact it had followed them unobtrusively for several weeks now.

Frances could hardly wait for the next week to come, anticipating, with an eagerness she could hardly contain, a repetition of the rapturous lovemaking they had enjoyed in the lane near Staining. But Marcus decided he must go straight home. Geraldine, it seemed, was not well again, although he did not elaborate on this. The mere fact, however, was enough to plunge Frances once more into the depths of depair. Not only that; she was becoming more and more aware that what she was doing was wrong . . . sinful; the word she had heard so often in her youth when she and Megan had belonged to that religious sect came back to haunt her now. She was behaving in a wicked and sinful way. She knew it now without any shadow of doubt.

She also knew it was time to make a break from Marcus. Things were going wrong. Just how wrong she was not sure, but it was no longer the same. He was . . . different. She still loved him. Sometimes she felt she loved him more than ever, but she knew they were getting near the end of the road. And she would have to tell him . . . soon. Not tonight, though. Her mind was in too much of a muddle to tell him now. She did not linger, waiting as she sometimes did, for more than one kiss. Instead she pulled away from him.

'Good night, Marcus. I mustn't keep you. I know you're anxious to get home.' She pulled open the car door and hurried up the path, feeling more wretched than she could ever remember feeling in her life. But her troubles were only just beginning.

She sometimes saw him at dinner-time when the Junior and Infant teachers collected their meals in the kitchen. They would exchange a few friendly words over the hotplate, no more, no less, for fear of inquisitive ears and prying eyes, of the children as much as the teachers. But the following day there was no sign of Marcus, either in the kitchen or the Junior canteen. Frances glanced warily towards the staff table, but he was not there. She wondered if he was taking a day off school. Maybe he was not well, but she did not dare to make any enquiries. It was while she was eating her cottage pie, in the company of the rest of the staff – apart from Miss Walsh, who still brought sandwiches – that she heard the news. It was Miss Cameron who told all of them together.

'I've just been talking to Mrs Jeffrey,' said Miss Cameron, in quite resounding tones. You had to speak loudly to make yourself heard over the din made by more than a hundred children. 'It seems they've rather a crisis over there at the moment. Mr Avery's wife has been rushed to hospital. Last night it was. She'd taken an overdose, a load of aspirins or something and she's—'

'She's not dead, is she?' someone asked.

'No, she's not dead, but she—'

Frances felt the bile rush to her throat and her hands, holding the knife and fork, begin to tremble. Scarcely knowing what she was doing she pushed her plate to one side and stood up. She had to get away. She couldn't listen to any more. Fortunately she was on dinner duty, which involved parading up and down between the children's tables, making sure there was no undue noise or commotion, so she did have some excuse for leaving the staff table so abruptly. She was in no state, anyway, to worry about what the rest of the staff might be thinking. She was aware of Marjorie Aspinall looking at her anxiously, but the rest of them did not appear to have noticed anything untoward.

She did not know how she managed to get through the rest of that dinner hour, endeavouring to quell the noise, persuading the slow eaters to try just a little more of the cottage pie. There was not much trouble with the chocolate pudding which followed. Dishes were very quickly scraped clean of the stodgy mixture smothered in pale brown chocolatey sauce. It had never been a particular favourite of hers, but today Frances did not even attempt a mouthful. It would have choked her; besides, she did not dare to go back to the staff table while the teachers were still sitting there. She could not bear to hear them talking about Geraldine Avery; about what she had done, why she had done it.

Why *had* she done it? Frances grew cold at the thought. She could feel the trickles of perspiration running down her face and neck, even though she was icy cold, and her hands were trembling again. She grasped hold of the back of a chair to steady herself. It could not be because of her, Frances, surely? No, of course it couldn't. Geraldine didn't care about Marcus any more. Marcus had told her so. There must be some other explanation. Geraldine hadn't been well. Perhaps she had reason to be worried about her health . . .

Not until the last child had finished his pudding was Frances able to leave the dining hall. She went to her own classroom instead of going to the staffroom, as she usually did, and it was there that Marjorie came to find her.

'I thought I'd find you here.' Her friend placed a mug of strong tea in front of her. 'Here, drink this. I've put plenty of sugar in it; you look as though you need it.' Marjorie perched herself on the edge of a desk and when Frances dared to look at her she found that her friend's eyes were full of concern. Shrewd and perceptive, but understanding, too. She knows, thought Frances. Perhaps she's always known.

'You've had a shock, haven't you?' Marjorie said gently. 'I could tell. You and Marcus Avery – you've been seeing one another, haven't you?'

'Yes, we've been friendly... for a long time now,' said Frances quietly. 'How did you know? Have you ... have you always known?'

'No. I wondered, I must admit, but I didn't know. To be quite honest, Frances, I thought you'd have had more sense.' Marjorie's voice, for a moment, was quite sharp, but almost immediately it softened again. 'But it's no time now to be going on at you. I can see how upset you are. Here, love, drink your tea before it goes cold. I only guessed just now, when you jumped up from the table. White as a sheet you were, love.'

'The others ... did they say anything?'

'No, I don't think they noticed. You were on duty anyway, weren't you, and they were all too busy listening to the gory details.'

'Gory details?' Frances breathed, hardly able to utter the words. 'But she's not ... dead, is she?'

'No, she'll be all right, but it was touch and go, apparently. You see – I don't know how I'm going to be able to tell you this, dear, but I'm afraid I'll have to. You see ... I'm sorry, love, but Geraldine Avery is expecting a baby. She's about four months pregnant and—'

'She's ... pregnant? But ... but she can't be! That's not possible.' Frances could hear her own voice, shouting hysterically, not sounding like herself at all. 'Marcus and me, we've been friendly since last September. November, it was, actually, when we started... That means that he and Geraldine ... No, it couldn't be. You must've got it wrong, Marjorie.'

'No, I'm sorry, love. It's perfectly true. She was pregnant – still is, I think. That's what he – Marcus – was so worried about, that she might lose the baby.'

'But he said he loved me. He said he was going to leave his wife.' Frances was trying to push away the thought that he had not said it recently, not, in fact, for ages. 'He said that he and Geraldine . . . that they didn't care any more, they went their separate ways.'

Marjorie gave a sad smile. 'I know, love, I know,' she said kindly. 'You've been duped. Taken for a ride, deceived, whatever you want to call it, it all amounts to the same thing. You're not the first girl to fall for a pack of lies, and you certainly won't be the last. I've been through it, remember, and I should know,' she added with a touch of bitterness. 'Oh no, I know it's not just the same. I was the wife, and you're the . . . girlfriend. But we've both been taken in, haven't we?'

'Marjorie . . .' Frances looked pleadingly at her friend.

'Yes, love? What is it?'

'When you found out about your Kenneth, you spoke so disparagingly about . . . about girls who went after married men. And I felt so guilty when you said it. Did you . . . were you getting at me?'

'No, of course I wasn't. I didn't know, did I, about you and Marcus? I was just bitter – still am, I suppose – and I had to let fly. But you're my friend, love. I care about you. Oh, Frances, you must try and see that he's not worth it. He's been conning you all the way along. He's no good, love. He's a rotter, a thoroughly bad lot. He must be, to treat his wife like that, and to let you think—'

'He loved me, Marjorie,' said Frances quietly. 'I know he did. It was so good. It was magic, what we had. I just can't believe that he would . . . Why did he do it?'

'I don't know, love. I honestly don't know. Yes, I dare say he did love you, in his own way. I could tell the two of you got on very well, and you're such a pretty, lovely girl, he'd find it hard to resist. But he had a wife, dear. And in the end, it's the wife who holds the trump card. You might have known he'd go back to her in the end.'

'You mean you still think Kenneth will come back to you?'

'Of course. But it's not Kenneth and me that we're concerned about just now, is it? It's you. You've had a shock, dear. I know it must have been dreadful for you, hearing it like that at the dinner table, and what I've just told you, well, that's even worse. But you'll get over it, Frances. You must. I know it will be hard at first, but you must try to put it all behind you and—'

Frances did not appear to be listening. 'Why did she do it, Marjorie?' she asked. 'Did they say? Had she found out about . . . about Marcus and me? Everybody's talking about us, aren't they?' Her voice was getting louder. 'I know they are.'

'Hush, dear.' Marjorie looked somewhat anxiously towards the door. 'No, of course they're not talking about you. Nobody knows anything about you and . . . Marcus. Anyway, do you really think he would be such a fool as to tell them, even if that was the reason? Not that I think it is, not for one moment,' she added staunchly. 'No, the general opinion seems to be that Geraldine Avery is rather neurotic and being pregnant won't have helped. They think she's got herself into a state about . . . everything. But you will have to try and behave quite normally, dear, or people might begin to get suspicious.'

'At least Miss Walsh wasn't there,' said Frances, with an attempt at a smile. 'The eyes and ears of the world.'

'Yes, that's one mercy. She'll have heard all about it by now, though, you can be sure. So don't you give them any fuel for their fire, Frances. Just behave as though nothing has happened. And if anybody mentions it, just say how sorry you are, how dreadful, something like that. You can do it, dear. I know you can.' Marjorie smiled encouragingly at her. 'You're a strong girl, aren't you? Just prove how brave you can be.'

'But what about Marcus? What am I going to say to him? When he comes back to school—'

'That's his problem, isn't it? He's the one who has the explaining to do. Just take it a day at a time, Frances, and don't look too far ahead. Try to put it all behind you, although I know that's easier said than done. Come on now, love. Best foot forward. The kids'll be in soon so I'd best be off and let you get yourself sorted out. Chin up, love. "There's worse troubles at sea," as my mam always used to say.'

Frances struggled through the afternoon somehow. She even went to the staffroom at playtime and bravely answered a few of the teachers' comments about Geraldine Avery. Yes, it must have been a dreadful shock for Marcus. Yes, she had heard his wife was rather nervy, but she hadn't known she was expecting a baby. No, she, Frances, did not know Marcus all that well; they'd sung those duets together, but that was a long time ago. Yes, she agreed, he did give the impression of being rather supercilious. She could feel Miss Walsh's gimlet eyes upon her, but she steadfastly refused to look in her direction.

Putting Marcus out of her mind, though; that was impossible. She knew, deep down, that what Marjorie said was true. He had deceived her. All his tales about he and his wife not getting on had been a tissue of lies. Snatches of conversation came back to her. '. . . Geraldine's good news . . . She must be thrilled . . . She's waited a long time.' It must have been the baby they were talking about. No wonder Marcus had hurried her out of that pub with some tale about Geraldine having a story published. Maybe she had – Frances would probably never find out now – but she was pretty sure it had not been a story that Daphne person had been talking about. A wild idea came into her mind that maybe the baby was not Marcus's, but vanished as soon as it appeared. Frances could face up to facts when she had to, although it had taken her a long time to do so, and it had been an awful way to find out. She had been on the verge of telling him it was over, she reminded herself. Now there was no need for her to do so.

She had to speak to him, though. She knew she was being foolish. She was not sure why she was doing it; maybe she was rubbing salt into the wound to punish herself for her wickedness; or maybe she still loved him and was unable to believe, even now, that it was all over. Whatever the reason, as soon as school was ended she hurried to the nearest phone box and dialled Marcus's number.

He answered quickly, giving his number and name. The tension was apparent in his voice and she very nearly replaced the receiver, but she hung on.

'Hello? Hello? Who is it?'

'Marcus, it's me, Frances.'

'Frances, what the hell do you want?' She couldn't believe the harshness in his voice.

'I just wanted to say...' What was it she wanted to say, for goodness sake? She didn't know. 'I wanted to say... I'm sorry about Geraldine. If there's anything I can do...' What on earth am I babbling on about? she thought. She was talking nonsense and she knew it. But she wanted to give him a chance to speak to her, lovingly, intimately, like he used to do.

'No, there's nothing you can do, Frances.' His voice was cold and hard. 'You've already done quite enough. Please don't ring again.'

She heard the receiver go down and she stared unbelievingly at the phone in her hand through a cloud of tears.

Chapter 21

'And about time too.' This was the greeting Frances received when she stepped over the threshold of her mother's home a few days later. 'We've not seen hide nor hair of you for nearly a week now, have we, Eliza? I might've popped me clogs for all you knew.'

'Oh, come on, Mum; that's not fair,' said Frances, slipping off her cardigan. As usual, the fire was banked high, in spite of the warmth of the late spring day. 'I did ring to tell you I'd got a cold. It wouldn't have been fair of me to come and breathe my germs all over you, now would it?'

A white lie – no, more than that; an outright lie, she supposed – but she had felt unable to face her mother until she had recovered somewhat from the shock of what had happened. Only now, with the weekend behind her, a weekend which she had spent trying to take stock of, and make sense of, the situation, did she feel calm enough to sit and chat with Iris about the inconsequential things they always talked about. Iris, thank God, had never known about Marcus; now there was no need for her ever to know.

'Tek no notice of her,' said Eliza, grinning. 'I think she got out of bed the wrong side this morning. Sit yerself down, Frances, and I'll go and make us a cup of tea. Are you going to stop and have your tea with us? I got a nice piece of hake from the fishmonger's this morning. There's plenty for three. I thought you might call round today.'

'Oh, I don't think so, Eliza, thanks all the same. I didn't tell Julie I'd be stopping.'

'There you are, you see.' Iris gave a discontented sniff.

'The minute she arrives she wants to be dashing off again. You'd think she might—'

'All right, all right, Mum,' Frances broke in. 'I'll stay. Thank you, Eliza. That would be lovely.'

'We're pleased to see you, love,' said Eliza with a meaningful glance, eyes raised heavenwards, as she went out of the door. 'It's nice to have a bit of fresh company.' Frances guessed that her mother was being more than usually truculent.

'Don't put yerself out on my account,' said Iris huffily, 'if you've summat better to do.'

'I haven't, Mum; really I haven't.'

'Huh! I must say you look well enough. A bit peaky perhaps, but there doesn't seem to be any sign of that cold you were on about.'

'No, I'm feeling much better now. I've managed to throw it off.'

She listened dutifully to Iris's news. She'd had a letter from Bertie – and about time, too! – saying that they might be coming to Blackpool for a holiday in the summer. Wonders would never cease! She thought he and his fancy wife had forgotten all about her. And Josie had popped in this morning but, as usual, had had to dash off after five minutes to take some more of her blessed photographs . . . Frances was glad when Eliza rejoined them. Her mother certainly did seem to be more contentious than ever today.

Her next remark almost made Frances spill her cup of tea all over the carpet. As it was, the liquid splashed over into the saucer and she could feel her hands begin to tremble. 'You'll have heard about that Avery fellow, won't you?' Iris nodded eloquently. 'About his wife trying to commit suicide? As soon as Eliza told me I said, "Avery – that rings a bell. I'm sure that was the young chap our Frances was singing them duets with." And Eliza says, "Aye, it's him all right. He's a teacher at Wyre Bank. In t'Juniors, though." Anyroad, his wife—'

'Yes, yes, I do know about it, Mum,' said Frances, speaking as quietly as she could so that her voice did not run out of control. How on earth did her mother and Eliza know, she wondered. But of course, come to think of it, Marcus lived only a few streets away, and Layton, like many other communities, was sure to have its fair share of gossips. 'We were all very sorry to hear about it. But Mrs Avery's all right.'

'It's no thanks to him, from all accounts, that Marcus Avery,' said Iris. 'It was him you did that singing with, wasn't it?' Frances nodded weakly. 'Aye, I recognised t'fancy name. Anyroad, they say he's been carrying on for ages with another woman, and his wife found out, and she tried to do herself in, poor lass. And to make matters worse, she were expecting a baby.'

'How... how do you know all this?' asked Frances in a faint voice. She felt, in fact, that she might be about to faint at any moment. Holding the cup as steadily as she could on the saucer, she placed them on the floor, then she gripped hold tightly of the chair arms. 'Who... who's told you?'

'How do I know? I should think all Layton knows by now. Eliza knows their next-door neighbour, don't you, Eliza? She belongs to the same whist club. They meet in one another's houses each week. I don't go, though. I've never cared much for whist; besides, I can't get about now. Anyroad... you tell her, Eliza.'

'Aye, well, I only know what Mrs Rigby was telling me. She's their next-door neighbour.' Eliza was not such an avid gossip as Iris; nevertheless she plunged eagerly into the scandalous tale. 'They've been trying for a baby for ages, apparently. That's what Geraldine – that's Mrs Avery – was telling Mrs Rigby. Ever since they were married, that were five years ago. Newcastle way, they come from, then they both got good jobs here. Of course you'll know that, won't you?'

She paused to take breath. 'Ever such a nice couple they were, Mrs Rigby says. Well, her more than him – she never reckoned much to him; a stuck-up sort o'chap he is; he thinks he's "it" – but they were right fond of one another. And her, Geraldine, she'd never hear a wrong word about him. They weren't all that young, mind. Mid-thirties or thereabouts, a bit old to be starting with a first baby. Anyroad, when they found out she was pregnant, after all this time, they were over the moon.'

'But I thought— I mean, I'd heard that Mrs Avery was a career woman,' said Frances. 'That she . . . that they . . . didn't get on very well.'

'Nowt o' t'sort,' replied Eliza. 'I don't know who's told you that. They were as happy as Larry. Aye, she might've been keen on her job when she thought there was nowt else. But when she knew about the baby she was tickled pink. That's what Mrs Rigby says. And she thought the world of him, that Marcus fellow. That's what made it all the worse when she found out—'

'Yes, would you believe it, all t'time he'd been carrying on behind her back,' Iris chimed in.

'Aye, she got suspicious, like. Found out he was telling lies.' Eliza took up the tale again. 'So she had him followed. One of them private detective blokes. It seems he said he'd been going to night school. Oh yes, he'd been going to night school all right, but he'd been taking a young woman along wi' him. And afterwards – well – they were getting up to all sorts of hanky-panky.'

Frances could bear it no longer. These gossiping old women, prattling away about something that was none of their business. And it hadn't been like that at all.

'But it wasn't like that!' she blurted out, unable to stop herself. 'Geraldine and Marcus, they were always having rows. It isn't true to say they got on well. They didn't! Not . . . not . . . all the time . . .' Her voice petered away as the two women stared at her in astonishment.

'And how would you know?' said her mother, with a searching look that seemed to pierce right through to the heart of her.

'I know . . . because . . . because . . .' Frances knew that the time for deception and lies had come to an end. She had never been a deceitful girl and it would be such a relief, now, to be able to admit the truth, awful though it was. She looked pleadingly at her mother. 'Mum, it wasn't like that, like everybody's saying. It wasn't just another woman. I know it wasn't . . . because . . .'

'Because it was you.' Iris finished the sentence for her. 'It was you, wasn't it? That's what you're trying to tell me.'

Frances looked desperately at her mother, longing for some glimmer of understanding, of compassion in her grey eyes, but she looked in vain. Iris's eyes were as cold and as hard as steel.

'It was you. You were carrying on with that fellow, behind his poor wife's back. And she was expecting a bairn, an' all. Well, I've heard some things in my time, but I never thought I'd hear the likes of that. From my own daughter's lips, telling me she's been carrying on with a married man. No . . .' Iris paused, giving her a strange look, as though she no longer recognised her. 'No . . . you're not my daughter, are you? I've never had a daughter of my own – the Lord's never seen fit to give me one – but I've treated you as though you were my own flesh and blood, God help me. From a tiny baby I've took care of you. I've loved you as though you were my very own. And now . . . now you've the nerve to tell me—'

'Mum . . . Mum, I'm sorry,' Frances gasped. 'I didn't mean to—'

'Oh, you're sorry, are you? It's a bit late to be sorry now, isn't it? I wonder if you're going to say you're sorry to that poor lass who's nearly lost her baby, the one whose husband you took.' Iris's face was getting more and more flushed and Eliza was eyeing her anxiously.

'Come on now, Iris. Calm down. You mustn't get yourself worked up like this. You know Frances is a good girl. I'm sure she didn't mean—'

'Good girl? Huh! No girl as carries on with a married chap is good in my book. I want nowt to do wi' her any more. She's no daughter of mine, I tell you. I won't have her . . . Oh, oh, my God . . . Oh . . .' Iris's hands were clutching at her own throat; she was trying desperately to get her breath. 'Oh, Eliza, for God's sake . . . help me. Oh . . . Frances . . .' These were the last words she uttered before she collapsed sideways in the chair.

Frances and Eliza were at her side at once, Frances with

her arms round her mother, while Eliza was feeling her wrist, frantically seeking for a pulse.

'Oh, Eliza, what have I done?' gasped Frances. 'I'm so sorry, so dreadfully sorry. Do you think she's . . .?'

'No, she's not dead,' said Eliza grimly. 'But there's no time for self-reproach at the moment, love.' She smiled at Frances sadly. 'Go and ring for an ambulance, there's a good lass.'

Iris didn't regain consciousness and she died early the next morning. Frances could not forgive herself, nor did she feel that she wanted to. She would have to live with this burden of guilt for some considerable time, and she knew that it served her right. What she had done was unforgivable. She had caused her mother to have the final heart attack that had killed her. Surprisingly, Eliza did not seem to condemn her. Rather the opposite; Frances found the older woman's sympathy and quiet understanding a great solace.

'But it was my fault, Eliza. I caused it. That's why she had the heart attack, because of what she found out about me,' Frances cried, time and time again, in different words, but always with the same feeling of culpability. They were sitting together in the living room of her mother's bungalow, the place Frances still thought of as 'home', even though she had her own flat.

'No, not entirely, lass,' Eliza tried to console her. 'I'm not saying it had nowt to do with it, but it would have happened anyway, sooner or later. Quite soon, is my guess. She's been living on borrowed time, you know, ever since she had the last one. She was lucky to pull round from that and I've seen her getting steadily worse this last month or so. And she'd been feeling poorly all day. I know she had; that's why she was so bad-tempered when you came. She couldn't always help it, love.'

'But I made it worse, didn't I? If it wasn't for me she'd still be alive. Oh, Eliza, whatever must you think about me? About me and . . . Marcus Avery? I'd no idea you knew him. I loved him, you know, I really did. And I thought he loved me. But it doesn't seem to matter any more, not now.'

'I didn't know him, love. I've never set eyes on him as far as I know, nor his wife, neither. I only know what Mrs Rigby's told me; you know what women are like for scandalmongering when they get together. And I can be as bad as the rest, God forgive me. But I don't think his wife ever found out who it was he was, er, friendly with, and you can rest assured that none of 'em will find out anything from me.'

'Thanks, Eliza. Sometimes I feel as though I wish everybody knew. I've been so wicked, I'd deserve it, everything they're saying about me. I know that's what you must be thinking.'

'No, not me, lass. You've not been wicked, and you're one of the most straightforward people I know . . . normally. No, you've been a bit foolish – more than a bit, happen. You're not the first and you certainly won't be the last girl to lose her head over a fellow. And I'll bet he led you on, didn't he? Telling you he loved you and his wife didn't understand him and all that malarkey?' Frances nodded. 'Well then, stop trying to punish yourself. Folks'll forget about it. It'll be a nine-days' wonder, you'll see.'

'But I keep thinking about Mum. She was so angry with me. All those awful things she was saying, before she . . . collapsed. She'd turned right against me. She looked at me as though she hated me. I can't get it out of my mind, Eliza.'

'She'd had a shock, love. And you know what Iris was like. She was never one to mince her words. Listen here, Frances; there was nobody in this world she loved more than she loved you, and she didn't mean what she said. She would have forgiven you.'

'But she died, Eliza, before she could tell me – if she ever would have done. I'll never know, will I?'

'That's often the way of it, lass. Death can come so suddenly with all sorts of things left unsaid, and words spoken that perhaps shouldn't have been. But your name was the last word she spoke, love. You mustn't forget that.'

And that was the only consolation that Frances could draw from this awful calamity.

But if Eliza was able to forgive and to minimise the part that Frances's revelation had played in her mother's death, it was certainly not so with her sister. Josie, of course, could not know exactly what had happened before Iris had suffered the fatal heart attack. She had not been there and no one was going to tell her; but that young woman was very good at putting two and two together.

They all met at Iris's bungalow after the formalities at the hospital had been completed, and one look at her sister's face was enough to tell Frances that Josie had some inkling – though goodness knows how she knew – of what had been happening.

'It was you, wasn't it?' Josie rounded on her sister. 'That was what made Mum have a heart attack, because she had found out about you. It was all your fault.'

'About me? I – I don't know what you mean.' Frances knew only too well. She also knew that her bold assertion that she wanted to come clean, that she would deserve it if everybody knew, was now going by the board. Pushed into a corner her automatic reaction was to defend herself. 'No, of course it wasn't my fault. I don't know what you're talking about.'

'Don't try to come the innocent with me! Of course you know. Everybody knows. Everybody's talking about you and that – that Avery fellow. You've been carrying on with him ever since that concert.'

'I haven't. That's not true!'

'Of course it's true! That's why you threw over that nice young minister, because of—'

'It wasn't, Josie. Really it wasn't.'

'Josie . . . Josie, that will do!' Jim got hold of her arm. 'Leave it, love. You promised you wouldn't—'

Josie shrugged him away. 'Never mind what I promised. And I can't leave it. Why should I? She caused my mother's death, Goody Two-Shoes there! Butter-wouldn't-melt-in-her-mouth Frances! Mum found out, didn't she, about you and that Marcus fellow? And it made her ill, so ill that she died. And it's all your fault.'

Frances knew that she could prevaricate no longer. 'Yes,' she replied, in a voice that was almost a whisper. 'She found out, but that wasn't what—. She'd been feeling ill for a while, Eliza said . . .'

Eliza spoke up now. 'Your mother had been feeling poorly all day, Josie. In fact she'd not been feeling well for some time. You noticed, surely, when you popped in yesterday? Although I know you didn't stay very long. Don't start blaming Frances, dear. It won't do any good. Your mum's gone and we've all got to stick together now. Iris wouldn't want you falling out, would she? It wasn't Frances's fault, you take it from me. I always had the feeling Iris wouldn't be with us for very long. That's why I never sold my house.'

'Don't make excuses for her, Eliza,' said Josie, more calmly now, but still with that coldness in her voice and in her eyes that Frances couldn't bear to meet. 'I knew Mum was ill; of course I did, but I didn't think she was going to die, not yet. She had a hand in it.' She pointed her finger viciously at her sister. 'And you won't convince me otherwise.' She turned to Frances, her eyes blazing with an anger that amounted almost to hatred. 'I'll never forgive you for this, Frances, not as long as I live. Oh yes, you were always Mummy's little favourite, weren't you? Well, I'm glad about one thing, and that's that she found out at last what you're really like.'

'Josie, for God's sake, give over!' Jim took hold of his wife's arms and pushed her bodily into the nearest chair. 'Don't you think Frances has already suffered enough? Just leave it, love.'

'Frances, Frances, it's always Frances, isn't it? Well, dear little Frances will have to take what's coming to her.' There was a malicious glint in Josie's eyes as she looked at her sister. 'You might like to know that you're the talk of the Wyre Bank estate. I wouldn't like to be in your shoes when you go back to school. Not that it doesn't serve you right. It does!'

'Josie!' her husband bellowed at her. 'You've said quite enough. For God's sake, shut up! If you say one more word about it—'

'Oh, leave me alone, can't you?' Josie jumped up from her chair. 'She was my mother as well, you know.' She ran out of the room, but Jim did not follow her. Instead he looked helplessly at Frances. 'I'm sorry, love,' he said.

'Is it true, Jim?' asked Frances, in a small voice. 'That everybody's talking?'

'I wouldn't say everybody. Some of them, maybe.'

'But how do they know?'

'Use your loaf, Fran,' said Jim, but not unkindly. 'How do you think they know? You live on the edge of the estate, don't you? Somebody's sure to have seen you and . . . Marcus. You have been seeing him, haven't you?'

'Yes, but it wasn't like they're saying.'

'You don't know what they're saying, Frances. And I don't intend to go into the rights and wrongs of it now. But if you thought you could keep it a secret, well . . .' Jim shrugged his shoulders in a movement that said, quite clearly, You must have been naive.

'But you and Josie – how did you know?'

'We're both connected with the school, aren't we? Josie taking photographs and me doing the road safety talks. Neither of us will listen to tittle-tattle, I can assure you. Yes, I know Josie's upset – don't worry, she'll calm down – but you know your sister won't indulge in idle gossip. Yet we both realised there must be some truth in it. There is, isn't there?' His smile was very sympathetic.

'Yes, but it's all over now. And I'll have to face the music when I go back to school. What am I going to do, Jim?'

'You'll have to be brave, love. And I know you can be. You've not committed a crime, Fran. You've fallen in love – is that what you thought it was? –' she nodded, 'rather unwisely, but it's hardly a hanging matter. Anyway, I'd better go and see how Josie is, then we'll have to get down to some details. The funeral's on Friday, we said, didn't we?'

It was quite a small group of mourners who gathered at

338

the church in Layton Cemetery for the simple service, followed by the burial: Frances and Eliza, Josie and Jim, Bertie and his wife, Alice and Jack Rawlinson, Len and Karen, and Iris's neighbour, Mrs Pearson.

To Frances, it all seemed very unreal. She knew she would have to face reality with a vengeance when she returned to school on Monday, but, for the moment, there was this other very sad occasion to be lived through. The feeling of numbness that seemed to have half paralysed her thinking helped her to a degree. She had looked at the pale waxen figure of her mother lying in the coffin – the first time Frances had ever seen a dead person – but that, too, had seemed unreal. She had heard people say that dead people looked as though they were sleeping, but Frances could not agree. Her immediate reaction was that this was not her mother. Iris was not there. The face, the features, the whole form was like an empty shell, a house that was lived in no longer. The spirit had departed, and it was the spirit, Frances understood even now, in her quiet grief, that gave life. Iris had been such a spirited, lively woman, so active and energetic at one time, until illness had overtaken her, making her querulous and dissatisfied, a shadow of her former self.

It was the old Iris that Frances found herself remembering now, the loving mother of her childhood and teenage years. Eliza had tried to convince her that her mother had loved her till the end, just as much as ever. The memory of Iris's last bitter words would not go away, but she tried to persuade herself that her mother was now out of her suffering – a well-worn truism, but one she must cling to – and with the Lord Whom she had always tried, to the best of her ability, to love and serve.

Frances and Josie had not spoken since the day after Iris's death. It was impossible that relations and friends should not have noticed, but they made no comment. They all met at Iris's bungalow, which was still Eliza's home, after the funeral. It had seemed fitting, almost as though Iris was still there with them; and at the end of the afternoon, when the two sisters found themselves alone in the kitchen, Josie did, finally, break the silence between them.

'I'm sorry,' she began, though her face was still unsmiling and her eyes void of any emotion. 'I said some things that – that maybe I shouldn't have said. Mum was ill . . . She would have died. I realise that now.'

'Thank you,' Frances muttered. 'I've reproached myself for what happened, time and time again, I can assure you. But I have to try and believe that it was inevitable, or I'll go mad with it all. But . . . Marcus and me . . . I want you to know that—'

'I don't want to know anything, Frances.' Her sister gave her a hard look; there was still no spark of warmth in her eyes. 'That's your affair. You have to live with what happened, and you'll have to face the consequences. But as far as Mum's concerned, she wouldn't want us falling out. That's all.' She turned her back on Frances and started putting the pots away in the cupboard.

Frances was almost sick with apprehension when she walked into Wyre Bank School the following Monday. She hurried straight to her classroom, seeing only Marjorie, who called in to offer her condolences about Iris's death.

'Thank you,' said Frances. 'It's been a terrible shock. Coming back to school would have helped, in normal circumstances, helped to occupy my mind, but as it is . . . Oh, Marjorie, I feel so scared at the thought of meeting them all. Have they said anything, about . . . you know?'

'They wouldn't say much to me, would they?' replied Marjorie, guardedly. 'They know I'm friendly with you. Yes, I've got to be honest, there are a few tales going round. Just hold your head up high, love. I doubt if anybody'll say anything to you. Besides, they know you've just lost your mother, don't they?'

Frances nodded. 'Is Marcus Avery back?'

'Yes, I believe so.'

'I . . . I can't face him, Marjorie.'

'Then don't. I've told you, he's the one with the explaining to do. Come on, Frances; be brave. The first day will be the worst. If you can get through that you'll be all right. And you've got my support, you can be sure of that.'

It was not so bad as Frances had feared. She was aware of a few sheepish glances in her direction and one or two silences when she approached, but that could have been because of her bereavement. Death did tend to be an embarrassment to some people. Several of the staff said how sorry they were about her mother. Miss Reynolds, of course, was genuinely sympathetic; Miss Cameron, too, to Frances's surprise, had offered her condolences very graciously.

Miss Walsh was the exception, but this was no surprise. The woman did not even glance in her direction, but Frances knew that the thoughts she was harbouring were far from pleasant, and the feeling of dislike and hostility emanating from her was palpable.

Marcus Avery was not in the canteen, to Frances's relief, when she went to collect her dinner. If he had been she knew she would have hung back until he had gone. She did not even look to see if he was in the Junior dining hall, but Marjorie, obviously knowing what was in her mind, whispered that she thought he had been going home at lunchtimes. There was no need to explain why. Frances knew, with the sick, shameful feeling that the thought always evoked, that it would be to keep an eye on his wife.

But he was waiting for her when she arrived home that afternoon, sitting in his car outside the flat. He opened the car door as she approached.

'Frances, I had to see you. I didn't want to come to your classroom – you know how it is – but I wanted to say how sorry I am . . .'

She stared at him, speechless for a moment. The words would not come.

'. . . about your mother. It must have been dreadful for you.'

'Yes . . . yes, it was,' she mumbled. 'It was . . . very sudden. It was a shock.'

'And I'm sorry for the way I spoke to you on the phone.

341

I didn't mean it. I didn't know what I was saying. I was upset and—'

'Of course. You would be.' She looked at him impassively, amazed at how little she now felt for him.

'Get in the car, Frances. I must— I've got to try and explain.'

'No, Marcus. There's no point.' She started to walk away, but he leaned out and grabbed her arm. 'Then let me come in, just for a minute. I can't leave it like this.'

'No! I've told you. There's no point. There's nothing more to say.' Even so, she lingered, taken aback by the look of abject misery in his eyes.

'Frances, I didn't mean to hurt you. Please believe me, I didn't. You're such a lovely girl . . . and you know how it was, between you and me. There was always . . . something. I didn't mean it to go so far, but then . . . I fell in love with you.'

She stared blankly at him. 'You told me lies. About your wife. You said—'

'I know! I know damn well what I said. It all got out of control. I didn't mean to hurt either of you.'

'That's what I can't forget . . . or forgive, Marcus.' Still refusing to get into the car, she looked down at him, noticing for the first time the innate shallowness that there was behind the undoubtedly handsome looks; the weak mouth and the shifty glance in his blue eyes. 'I can't forget that, between us, we made your wife so unhappy. I'm partly to blame, I know, and I can't forgive myself, but it was because of what you said, what you made me believe.'

'I know. But she's going to be all right.'

'And . . . the baby?'

He had the good grace to flush slightly, the first time she had seen him do so, and hang his head. 'Yes . . . it's OK, we think.'

'Then you'd better go home to her, Marcus. Don't try to see me again. It's better if you keep away.'

She turned her back on him and walked up the path. When she entered the flat he was still sitting there. Only after several moments did she hear the car zoom away. She

342

felt cold and empty inside, drained of all emotion, but she knew that the love she had been so sure she felt for him had died.

Chapter 22

'She will have to go, Miss Reynolds. There is no question about that. I, for one, refuse to teach on the same staff as her for much longer, and Miss Cameron here agrees with me.'

Gertrude Reynolds looked at the two teachers who faced her across the desk, Miss Walsh angrily vociferous, Miss Cameron rather less so. Miss Reynolds had the impression that Judith Cameron might well have been coerced into this, possibly against her better judgement. Her deputy had not been quite so antagonistic of late, and for that Gertrude was grateful. But Emily Walsh – she was a vindictive woman if ever there was one, and Gertrude knew that this present dilemma was going to need very careful handling. It was one of the most difficult and delicate cases she had ever come across in all her years of teaching.

'I . . . er . . . think I can understand how you feel,' she began. 'There has been a lot of talk and I know you feel that it won't do the school any good. But we must try to get things into proportion and not let our personal dislikes influence us.' She looked meaningfully at Emily Walsh. That teacher had had her knife into young Frances Goodwin – she had never understood why – ever since the girl joined the staff.

'Things will settle down. People will gossip less as time goes on. And it isn't as if Miss Goodwin has committed a crime, an offence of any kind. If she had been found guilty of stealing or dishonesty, then there might be a good reason for—'

'No offence? Of course it's an offence and what she's

345

done is extremely dishonest. Stealing another woman's husband? Driving the poor woman to suicide . . .'

'We must be thankful it didn't come to that,' Miss Reynolds interposed carefully. 'And we don't know for sure that it was because of Miss Goodwin and her . . . relationship with—'

'Of course it was because of her! And it's a crime as far as I'm concerned. She's broken one of the Ten Commandments. She's committed adultery.' Miss Walsh was going red in the face, her normally quiet and refined voice getting shriller and shriller.

'All right, Miss Walsh,' Gertrude Reynolds sighed. 'I understand how you feel – at least, I'm trying to. But, surely, we must try to show a little compassion. The poor girl has just lost her mother. She must be going through a great deal of personal agony.'

'And serve her right, too,' muttered Miss Walsh. 'Not that I don't feel sorry about her mother . . . I do.'

Then it's a pity you didn't tell her so, thought Judith Cameron. She felt a certain empathy towards the poor girl who was at the centre of this scandal that had overwhelmed the school. She knew that some sort of action would have to be taken, but just what, she was not sure. That was why she had come along with Emily Walsh to see Gertie, to make sure that Emily's spiteful streak did not get the upper hand.

She glanced at the two of them now; Emily, almost purple-faced in her self-righteous sanctimonious indignation, and Gertie, obviously dithering, for once unable to come to a decision. What did either of them know about love . . . or lust, whichever it had been? Nothing, she guessed, whereas she, Judith, had her memories. Life had not been altogether kind to her. She had lost the only man she had ever wanted to marry. There had been a few before Neville, but he was the only one she had really loved. And there had been others since, just casual affairs, but one had been with a married man. So Judith understood how easily things could get out of control.

Miss Reynolds turned to her now. 'What is your opinion

about all this, Miss Cameron? Miss Walsh has implied that you, er, agree with her.'

'It's a tricky situation, Miss Reynolds,' Judith replied carefully. 'And I have to agree that it is the school that is important. We can't let anything interfere with the smooth running of the school and the children's welfare. On the other hand—'

'Quite,' interrupted Miss Walsh, not giving Judith a chance to state a contrary point of view. 'The school is suffering and the girl will have to go. If it was up to me I'd see that she was sacked, given her cards. She's a disgrace to the profession! And him, of course, that Avery fellow. The pair of them are as bad as one another. I knew as soon as he came that there would be trouble. Him and his fancy concerts . . .'

'That will do, Miss Walsh,' said Miss Reynolds, firmly. 'We're getting away from the point. And as far as Mr Avery is concerned I understand from Mr Entwistle that he is already looking for another post. They will be going back to Newcastle as soon as he finds one. That is what his wife wants to do.'

'And good riddance too.'

'But one can't go about high-handedly sacking teachers,' the headmistress continued, ignoring Miss Walsh's interruption. 'I haven't the authority to do it, nor would I want to. Miss Goodwin is a very good teacher and she has more than proved her worth since she has been here.'

'The Office should be informed about what she's done.' Miss Walsh would not be dissuaded. 'And I'm warning you, Miss Reynolds, if you don't tell them what has happened then I most certainly will. And what I said before still goes. I refuse to go on teaching with that – that girl!'

Miss Reynolds closed her eyes. Dear God, give me strength, she prayed. It was not just a figure of speech; she really meant it. 'I dare say they already know at the Office,' she said quietly after a moment or two. 'There is not much that they don't find out about. But you will find, Miss Walsh, that even the Chief Education Officer himself would be unwilling to give a teacher the sack, certainly not in this case. In fact, I've never known of an instance where a teacher was dismissed. It is very difficult to give teachers their notice, except for the most heinous crimes.'

There was one teacher, however, whom Gertrude would be only too pleased to get rid of at that moment. But she knew she could not, in all fairness, suggest to Miss Walsh that she should be the one to go; to retire or to find another post.

'Might it be possible for Miss Goodwin to be transferred?' asked Judith Cameron now. 'It might be a solution, if it could be done without, well, too much fuss.'

Gertrude sighed again. 'That had occurred to me,' she said. 'For Miss Goodwin's sake, it might be as well if she were to take a post elsewhere, to get away from all the gossip.'

'I don't see that she deserves any sympathy,' said Miss Walsh. 'Why should we care how she feels? She's a bad influence and she's not a fit person to have charge of young children. That's what the rest of us feel.'

'It's what some of you may feel,' replied Miss Reynolds. 'Not all of us. I don't mind admitting to you that I do not want to lose Miss Goodwin.' She was aware of Miss Walsh's baleful stare. 'She's been a foolish girl, I agree, but I can't believe there is any malice or real badness in the young woman. She has made a mistake, an error of judgement, but may I remind you that the person who never made a mistake never made anything?' She thought Miss Walsh would explode at any minute. 'But, for the sake of the school,' she continued calmly, 'I am prepared to see if I can arrange a transfer for her.'

'As far away as possible!'

Miss Reynolds ignored Miss Walsh's remark, turning instead to Miss Cameron. 'You have said very little.' She looked questioningly at the woman who was her deputy, aware of much more empathy than usual emanating from her. 'I take it you agree with me, Miss Cameron, that I should contact the Office and see if there is a suitable post elsewhere for Miss Goodwin?'

'Yes . . .' Judith Cameron gave a quiet sigh. 'I don't see

348

what else you can do. I suppose I feel rather sorry for the girl. Oh yes, I know I've not always agreed with her; there have been times when I've actively opposed her,' she added, in reply to a furious stare from Miss Walsh, 'but that doesn't alter the fact that she was – is – a good teacher. And, like you say, we can all make a mistake, can't we?'

She was rewarded by a smile of quiet understanding from the headmistress, a very rare occurrence between the two of them. But, for once, they seemed to be in agreement and for this Gertrude Reynolds was grateful.

'Leave it with me,' she said. 'I'll see what I can do.'

That poor girl, thought Gertrude, when the other two teachers had left. She had lost her mother and her love affair had come to an end – if that is what it was – and now she was about to lose her job. No doubt another one could be found for her, but she was sure to feel that her removal from Wyre Bank was some sort of punishment. Gertrude remembered then how the young woman had been engaged to that nice young minister, but she had lost him as well. If she had married him then none of this would have happened. Life was a funny old thing, Gertrude decided. You never knew what was round the next corner. As far as affairs of the heart were concerned she had no experience whatsoever, but that didn't mean that she could not try to understand or show compassion. She would do her utmost to see that the Office dealt leniently with the girl.

There had been instances of this sort of thing before, in other schools; relationships developing between teachers who worked in close contact with one another, one, or both, of them, married. The matter was always dealt with discreetly, one of the parties being offered another position away from the source of the problem. Gertrude hoped that this dilemma could be solved satisfactorily.

Frances could not help but be aware of a subtle change in the atmosphere of the school, at least as far as her dealings with the staff were concerned. No one was openly hostile towards her, nor did they shun her – apart from Miss Walsh, which was only to be expected – but there was a certain wariness in the way they spoke to her. And it was not only the teaching staff; she had noticed that some of the parents and the dinner ladies were eyeing her somewhat guardedly. She guessed they were embarrassed. Not all of them, of course. Marjorie was as cheerful and uninhibited as ever and so was Wendy Clarkson, who she had come to know quite well since the time of the concert.

It was towards the end of her first week back at school, following the death of her mother, that Miss Reynolds asked to see her.

She smiled kindly at her when Frances entered the room at the close of afternoon school. 'Do sit down, Miss Goodwin. There is something of importance I want to discuss with you.'

Frances had expected that, sooner or later, she would be hauled over the coals for her misdemeanour. It was too much to hope for that she would get away scot-free, nor did she really want to. She was still suffering from a guilty conscience and felt that it would be a relief to tell Miss Reynolds that she was truly sorry for what had happened, that she hadn't intended it to turn out like this, that she had believed that Marcus Avery had really loved her. But would Miss Reynolds be interested in listening to the ins and outs of it all? Probably not; it was doubtful that she had ever been in love. At all events she did not appear angry now. Her short-sighted eyes were full of sympathy.

'I won't beat about the bush,' she began. 'I dare say you might have some idea why I wanted to see you.'

'Er . . . yes, I think so,' said Frances. 'And I want to say I'm sorry, Miss Reynolds. I didn't mean to—'

'All right, Miss Goodwin,' the headmistress interrupted. 'I think the least said about this matter the better, don't you? I know you well enough by now to realise that you will be feeling very contrite. However, we can't ignore the fact that not everyone is prepared to be as tolerant as I am, and as most of the staff are. So, mainly for your own sake, my dear, it has been decided that it might be as well if you were to leave Wyre Bank and take up a position elsewhere.'

'What?' This was something Frances had not expected

at all. 'You mean you want me to leave?'

'It isn't so much what I want, Miss Goodwin, or what you want. But the general consensus of opinion – and I must admit I agree – is that it would be better, especially for you, if you did leave. Certain teachers on the staff are very antagonistic towards you . . . I don't need to say any more, surely? You must be aware of it.'

Frances nodded. 'I've always been aware of it, ever since I came here. But it's not just because of this. I can't seem to do right for . . . some people.'

'I know, I know. But this time the teachers concerned do have a point. They feel that what has happened is upsetting the school. If you stayed you might find that things could be very difficult for you. You could be made to feel uncomfortable, very unhappy.'

'You say teachers,' said Frances, 'but it's only one teacher, isn't it?'

'Yes, it is.' Miss Reynolds gave a sigh. 'I'll be honest with you. This teacher – she has refused to work with you any longer. It would make matters easier – for me as well – if she were to retire, but she will not do so and she would never get another post at her age. Nor could I expect her to.' Miss Reynolds leaned forward, her arms resting on the desk. 'Frances . . .' It was the first time she had ever used the young woman's name, 'I am trusting you not to repeat what I have just said . . . not to anyone. I am really being most unprofessional. But I don't want you to think I am unsympathetic, my dear.

'However, to get down to brass tacks.' She straightened the pile of papers in front of her in a matter-of-fact way. 'I have been in contact with the Office and a position has been found for you at Park Gates Junior School. You will be starting there in September and you will be taking a First Year Junior class.'

'A Junior school? But I'm Infant trained, Miss Reynolds.'

'It makes very little difference.' Miss Reynolds shook her head. 'They always say if you can teach Infants successfully then you can teach anything. And you have been very competent with the classes you have taught.

These will be seven- and eight-year-olds, only a year older than the ones you have been teaching. I'm afraid beggars can't be choosers, Miss Goodwin.' Her tone was much more down-to-earth now, almost as though she regretted her earlier show of compassion.

'There was no post available in an Infant school. They had all been advertised and filled. But this post at Park Gates has just become vacant. The teacher has suddenly decided that she wants to retire and the head, Mr Knighton, feels he would like someone younger on his staff. I gather most of them are middle-aged.'

'Park Gates . . .' Frances was still trying to recover from the shock of being told she was being summarily dismissed, because that was what it amounted to. 'That's near the town centre, isn't it?'

'Yes, a much older building than this, of course. Built towards the end of the Victorian era, I believe. But I dare say you'll find the children are pretty much the same. A mixture of backgrounds, such as we have here. A lot of children from the boarding houses and shops, too, I should imagine.'

Then I should feel quite at home, thought Frances – she, too, had been a boarding house child – although the idea of the move, and the reason for it, filled her with trepidation. Would they all know, she wondered, the teachers at this Park Gates School, what she had done, why she was suddenly appearing on their staff without an interview?

That was what she asked now. 'I don't have to have an interview then, to see if I am . . . er . . . suitable?'

'No, Mr Knighton will take my word as to your suitability, although he will want to meet you, of course, before the new term starts. There is just one thing, however, Miss Goodwin. I'm afraid you will have to lose your responsibility post. This is just an ordinary position, although there is no reason why, if you prove your worth, you may not get it back . . . eventually.'

'Yes . . . I understand,' said Frances. She understood only too well. An enforced removal and a demotion to boot, but she supposed it could have been worse. She could have been given the sack, told she was no longer a fit person to have charge of impressionable young minds. She guessed, if Miss Walsh had had her way, that was precisely what would have happened. Instead she supposed she must be thankful for small mercies.

'Thank you, Miss Reynolds,' she said. 'You've been very kind. Thank you for being so . . . tolerant with me. I know I don't really deserve it. I shall miss Wyre Bank. I've enjoyed being here.' She could feel the tears pricking her eyelids and she blinked rapidly. 'Anyway . . . thank you.'

'All right, Frances.' Miss Reynolds smiled at her again. 'Let's leave it at that, shall we? You're having a fresh start; that's the important thing. And I wish you all the luck in the world, my dear.'

'Never mind,' said Julie, very calmly, when Frances told her the news. 'You've still got a job, haven't you, and I should imagine one school's pretty much the same as another. And it'll get you away from that awful Walsh woman. Surely that's a relief? I think I'd have murdered her before now if I'd been in your shoes.' Julie, throughout the whole of the trauma about Marcus and his wife's suicide bid, and the death of Frances's mother, had remained philosophical and unflappable. Frances had found her composure very reassuring. Julie was a couple of years younger than Frances, but had already developed a much more rational way of looking at things than Frances was able to manage. Was it because she had not yet fallen in love, Frances wondered. Love tended to make things look all cock-eyed, and Frances, twice already, had been in that state. Or had she only imagined she was in love? She wished she knew.

'What you should do now,' Julie continued, 'is to get yourself away on a damn good holiday. You've been through a heck of a lot and you need a change.'

'I can't,' replied Frances. 'I'm teaching, aren't I? We don't break up till nearly the end of July. I know Miss Walsh has said she refuses to go on teaching with me, but she's got to put up with me till then.'

'I don't mean right this minute, you fathead!' said Julie. 'I mean at the end of term. And for goodness' sake shut up about that rotten old Walsh woman. I'm sick of hearing her name.'

Frances smiled. 'Sorry . . . OK, I'll try. But it hurt me when Miss Reynolds told me that. I've never done Miss Walsh any harm; I've never meant to, anyway. I don't know why she should hate me so much.'

'Jealousy, love. You're young and pretty, and she's probably never had a fellow.'

'Thanks, Julie.' Frances gave a wry smile. 'Sometimes I wish I hadn't either. They're nothing but trouble . . . It's a good idea of yours, though, about a holiday. I could go to Auntie Alice's, I suppose, but I don't really want to. She'd be too nosy.' She was thoughtful for a moment.

'I've just been thinking,' she went on. 'When Marcus and I—' She stopped at Julie's look of exasperation. 'All right, all right, you don't need to look at me like that. I was only going to say that when we were at night school they were talking about a trip to France. And I thought how nice it would be to go.' She had had dreams – impossible, reckless dreams – of going with Marcus, but she didn't tell Julie this. 'I wonder if there are any places left? I could find out, I suppose. You wouldn't consider coming with me, would you, Julie?'

'Me? I can't speak French. Well, I can just about manage *La plume de ma tante est rouge*, or whatever rubbish they used to teach us, but that wouldn't be much use, would it? Anyway, I wasn't at the classes. It'll be just for the students.'

'We don't know that for sure. Would you consider it, please, if there are any vacancies?'

Julie agreed that she would. Like Frances, she had never been abroad, and both girls were delighted when, after contacting Mrs Beecham, the French teacher, they discovered there were just two places left on the trip. It was perfectly in order for Frances to bring a friend, she said. Several of the students were bringing their husbands and wives, or a friend along.

All the planning – getting a passport, sorting out her wardrobe, brushing up on her conversational French – helped to take Frances's mind away from the heartache she had suffered. She missed her mother dreadfully. No matter how disagreeable and difficult Iris might have been these last couple of years her passing left a void too vast to be filled, Frances's desolation being exacerbated by the memory of their last calamitous meeting. Eliza was still living in the bungalow, but would shortly be moving back to her own little house. When the will was read it was found that Iris's assets – from the sale of the house and a quite substantial sum of money – was to be divided between Josie, Frances and their brother, Bertie, after a goodly bequest to Eliza.

Frances had received a very nice letter from Adrian when her mother died. She had not written to tell him about Iris's death, but obviously someone had. She wondered what else he might have been told. She even wondered if she should write to him and confess all; tell him she was sorry she had ended their engagement so unceremoniously, that she had been too hasty, that she had been having second thoughts . . .

She had thought about Adrian a lot recently. The celluloid doll, with the feather in its head, that he had won for her at the Pleasure Beach, now sitting on her dressing table, was a constant reminder. So was a blue leather-backed hynm book – to use when she sang in the choir – that he had given her for her birthday, and, more frivolously, the large golden box with the red ribbon which had contained her favourite chocolates and now held her handkerchiefs.

It had occurred to her that not once during their relationship had Marcus ever given her so much as a packet of sweets. He had been quite generous in paying for drinks, but there had been none of the homely, inconsequential little gifts which might have shown her that he really cared for her.

She had not written to Adrian, however. What right had she to intrude in the new life he was making, she chided herself, a life she had already told him she did not wish to share. For all she knew he might have another young lady by now, might even be engaged again. And the problems would still be the same; she had not wanted to be a clergy wife nor go to live in Birmingham. So why should she imagine, because she was feeling lonely and sorry for herself, that things would be any different? They had had some good times together, though, and she realised – much too late – that she was missing him.

Her departure from Wyre Bank School was uncere-monious. She did not expect, nor did she get, a leaving present although most of the staff wished her luck. Marjorie seemed quite tearful, but Frances promised she would keep in touch; her friend lived only about ten minutes' walk away from the flat. Miss Reynolds said she was sorry to see her go and wished her well; so, surprisingly, did Miss Cameron. Only Miss Walsh, to the end, remained unrelent-ing in her antipathy towards Frances. She had not spoken one word or exchanged a glance with her since the furore about Marcus. And for that reason alone Frances felt glad she was leaving.

Mid-August found Frances and Julie enjoying the pleasures of the French capital; and for the first time since her bereavement and her unhappy love affair Frances was beginning to feel that she was, at last, casting off much of her sorrow, her shame and bewilderment.

It had been a long journey to France, including an overnight Channel crossing and coach journey. They were travel-stained and weary when they arrived at their small hotel near the Tuileries, but after a quick wash and brush-up they were raring to go again. And the delights to be found in the world's most romantic city soon made up for the inconveniences of the journey.

The two days they spent there were crammed full of new sights and sounds and impressions. They climbed the steep cobbled streets of Montmartre to the white-domed Sacré-Coeur. They took a boat trip on the Seine, and explored the markets and bookstalls of the left bank. The elegance of the Rue de Rivoli; the mile-long vista of the Champs-Elysées viewed through the Arc de Triomphe; the Louvre, where one just had to go and stare at the Mona Lisa; the panoramic view from the Eiffel Tower – they delighted in every new experience. Not least, the bitter taste of the red wine, the long loaves of crusty bread and onion soup they enjoyed at a little bistro near the Notre-Dame. And not once did Frances pause to wish that she might be enjoying it all with someone other than Julie.

The healing process that began in the French capital continued in the Loire Valley, where the group spent the larger part of their holiday. They stayed in the city of Tours, and from there they visited the various châteaux, soaring above the river and the forests where, once, the kings and nobles of France had hunted. Each one seemed more memorable than the one before. Chinon; Blois; the terraced gardens of Villandry; the heraldic banners, bright with fleur-de-lys, flying from the battlements of Amboise; and Chenonceaux, with its poignant memories of the ill-fated Mary Stuart who had stayed there when she was Queen of France.

The weather was hot and the tourist sites were crowded, as was only to be expected in August, but Frances still felt, if she closed her eyes, that she could imagine the kings and queens and noblemen of old gazing through the windows of the châteaux, or riding off to the crusades across the bridges that spanned the moats.

'Well, do you think your French has improved?' asked Julie on the last evening. 'That was the idea of coming, wasn't it, to talk to the people in their own langugage?'

Frances laughed. 'They're so much better at it than we are, aren't they? If you speak to them in French they answer in English, so why bother? I've enjoyed it though, haven't you? Well, I know you have. Thanks for coming with me, Julie.'

'I wouldn't have missed it for anything,' said Julie. 'And you're looking tons better, Fran. You're starting to put it all behind you, aren't you?' she ventured to ask. 'Marcus . . . and everything.'

'Marcus who?' replied Frances with an easy laugh. But she knew that the pain was still there whenever she heard his name unexpectedly, or when stray thoughts of him still lingered – although it was mainly the memory of the hurt she had caused to others and the realisation of what an utter fool she had been that grieved her now, rather than the ending of their relationship.

'You're not thinking of buying a posh new house and leaving me, are you, now you've come into your fortune?' asked Julie, soon after they returned home.

'Hardly a fortune,' Frances replied, 'although I suppose I'm worth a bob or two now, as Mum would have said. No, I'm happy enough here in the flat, and you and I seem to jog along very well together, don't we? I did think, though, that I might buy a car. Not a Jag or a Bentley – nothing wildly expensive,' she added, at Julie's look of amazement. 'I thought of getting one of those little Mini-Minors. A red one, I think.' She did not say it had been Marcus who had first suggested it. 'I won't be able to walk to my new school like I could to Wyre Bank. I know there are buses, but I think I'd like to be independent.'

'You'll have to learn to drive,' Julie pointed out. 'Perhaps your brother-in-law could teach you.'

'No, I don't think so,' said Frances. She was loath to do anything to disturb the uneasy truce that now existed between her and Josie. 'I'll book a course of lessons. Nothing easier . . .'

She enrolled the following week with a driving school and by the time she started at Park Gates School in September she had already had a couple of driving lessons. By the end of the term she hoped not only to have her own car, but to be driving it as well.

She called on Megan the week before the autumn term started, at her home near Victoria Hospital, after phoning first to see if it was convenient. Megan might well be at the clinic with baby Maria; even though she was a trained nurse with considerable experience with young children she had told Frances that she visited the baby clinic frequently. Frances guessed she was lonely and craved the company of other young women in similar circumstances. Or Bernard might be at home, and Frances did not want to encounter him if she could help it. Megan seemed very inhibited and much less willing to chat when her husband was there.

Frances had not seen her much lately, hardly at all since Iris's death. She had never taken Megan into her confidence regarding Marcus, knowing how judgemental her friend might be, and with good reason, too. Now, however, after she had admired Maria – six months old, already trying to sit up and possessing three teeth, her proud mother boasted – she found herself confessing everything to her friend, every shameful detail of her affair with Marcus. There was no need for her to have done so. She and Megan did not move in the same circles and it was doubtful that her friend would have heard any rumours – nor had she – but Frances had a desire to come clean. She knew that Megan regarded her, Frances, as her best friend; and best friends should have no secrets from one another.

Megan did not seem shocked, or all that surprised. 'I don't stand in judgement any more, not like I used to,' she told Frances. 'I admit, at one time, I was a self-righteous little prig, but I've grown up since those days. I've had to grow up since I married Bernard. Things are not always just as they seem; I realise that now. You thought this Marcus really loved you, didn't you? And I can't blame you for that. That's what I thought, too . . . about Bernard.'

'You mean . . .?' Frances was disturbed at the look of sad resignation in Megan's eyes. 'But Bernard does love you, Megan, surely? I know you found him, er, rather demanding when you first got married – you told me, remember? – but you've no reason to doubt his love for you, have you?'

'Oh, no. I know Bernard loves me, in his own way. He's very good to me, especially with material things. You can see that, can't you?' Their home, indeed, was the last word in perfection; deep-pile carpets, plush armchairs and sofas, every modern convenience in the kitchen, though all with an unlived-in, sterile appearance. 'But I can't always give him all that he wants. He's a very virile man . . . if you understand me. I didn't realise that until I married him. I can't always . . . satisfy him.' Megan's pale blue eyes, for an instant, looked stricken. 'But I know there are others, perhaps, who may be able to do so.'

'You mean he's got somebody else?' Frances, forgetting for a moment that she, only recently, had been the 'somebody else' in an abortive affair, was horrified. 'But that's dreadful, Megan!'

'I don't know for sure,' said Megan, calmly; much too calmly, Frances thought. 'I have my suspicions. He comes home late and I know he's not always been working at the hospital. I've never really liked it, Frances, that side of marriage, so I suppose you can't blame him entirely. I know he would never, ever leave me. He loves me, you see, I know he does. And he loves Maria, too, now he's got over the disappointment of not having a son. And now that he knows . . . I must tell you, Frances – I'm going to have another!' Megan's eyes were shining again, just as though she had never uttered the startling revelations that had so appalled her friend.

'What?' Frances was more alarmed than ever. 'You're having another baby?'

'Yes! Isn't it wonderful?'

'But I thought you'd been told, when you had Maria, that it might be—'

'Dangerous?' Megan finished the sentence with the word that Frances had been unwilling to voice. 'There's always a certain amount of danger when you have a baby, Frances. But I came through it safely the first time, and there's no reason why I shouldn't do so again. That's what Bernard says. He says I'll have to be extra careful and I'll go into hospital a few weeks before, like I did with Maria. I'll be all right, Fran, really I will. Bernard so badly wants a son . . . and so do I, to complete our family.'

At one time Megan had said she wanted at least two of each, thought Frances, and there was no guarantee that this one would be a boy. She felt very frightened for her friend, but she knew she must not show it.

'That's fine then,' she said. 'I'm . . . really pleased for you. You're very tolerant, though, Megan, I must say, after what you've just told me about Bernard.'

'Oh, I don't know anything for sure,' said Megan, hastily. 'You won't repeat it, will you, Frances? I don't know why I told you. I haven't told anyone else. And I might be . . . mistaken.'

Frances felt sure she was not mistaken, and that Megan had told her because she could not keep the awful knowledge to herself any longer.

'No, of course not. My lips are sealed,' Frances assured her. 'When's the baby due?'

'The end of February. The same time of year as I had Maria. We've decided on Bernard Joseph for his name, but we'll call him Joe.' Megan smiled beatifically, but Frances, trying to smile back at her, could feel nothing but a dreadful unease.

Chapter 23

Park Gates Junior School was vastly different, in outward appearance at least, from the schools on the Wyre Bank estate. Wyre Bank School was surrounded by large areas of grass, and the trees, mere saplings at first when the school was built twelve years ago, had now grown into quite tall specimens which enhanced the surroundings. There were flowerbeds, too, a riot of colour in the summertime, which were well tended by gardeners employed by the Parks Department of Blackpool Corporation.

Park Gates, by contrast, stood in the centre of a vast area of concrete. Not a blade of grass was to be seen, the only greenery being a few scrubby bushes growing in the hard dry patches of earth at the side of the iron railings. These railings, which must, somehow, have escaped the salvage campaign in the early years of the Second World War, were some seven feet high, spiky and menacing, giving the place the appearance of a prison. The building itself was two storeys high and constructed of shiny red Accrington brick, a favourite building material in Blackpool, with huge doors, like those of a fortress, at each corner.

They all appeared to be locked and bolted and Frances had hammered on each of them in turn on her preliminary visit to the school, during the last week in August. At last one of them was opened, very reluctantly, by the caretaker. 'What is it? What d'yer want?' he asked, peering at her suspiciously. 'School doesn't start for another week. There's only me here, and the headmaster, of course, Mr Knighton.'

'Yes, it's him I've come to see,' Frances explained, rather timidly. The fellow wasn't making her feel exactly welcome.

'I'm Miss Goodwin, the new teacher. He's arranged to see me today.'

'Oh well, I suppose it'll be orlright then.' He scratched his head dubiously. 'I can't remember him saying owt to me, though, and he usually does. I'm that busy, though, I might've forgotten. You'd best come in, miss, and I'll take you to his office.'

The interior of the building, at first sight, seemed just as forbidding as the outside. The walls of the long corridor were covered, to shoulder height, with dark green tiles, the top row edged with a floral notif, reminding Frances of a huge public lavatory. This had been the fashion, she recalled, in the late Victorian era from which the school dated. The hall they passed through on the way to the headmaster's study was enormous, the immensely high ceiling, another feature of Victorian buildings, being supported by iron girders. She noticed there was a stage at one end, however, obviously of fairly recent construction, and she wondered if this school, maybe, was one that put on performances from time to time. If that was the case then at least she would have something to look forward to. She knew that her work in the dramatic field usually brought out the best in the children she taught.

She also noticed that the school was spotlessly clean. The tiled walls gleamed, as did the high mullioned windows and the polished wooden floor of the hall. There was a pleasant aroma of wax polish and disinfectant and she guessed that the caretaker had been hard at work when she had disturbed him.

'Here y'are, miss.' He knocked on the door of a room just beyond the hall. 'I'll just see if Mr Knighton's expecting you.'

I've already told you he is, thought Frances, although she said nothing. Goodness, if she was going to be intimidated by the caretaker, heaven knows what effect the headmaster might have on her.

'Mr Knighton, excuse me, but there's a young woman here, says she's got an appointment with you,' the caretaker, still sounding very sceptical, called through the half-open door. 'Shall I let her come in?' He turned to Frances. 'What did you say yer name was?'

'Miss Goodwin.'

'Says she's called Miss Goodwin.'

'Yes, yes, of course, Mr Walters,' the headmaster's voice came back. 'I've been expecting her. Thank you very much. You can get back to your work now.'

A small man, not much taller than Frances herself, with a shock of dark hair springing from a high forehead, had jumped up from behind the desk and bounded across the room. 'How do you do, Miss Goodwin? I'm delighted to meet you.' She found herself looking into a pair of shrewd grey eyes, which held a humorous glint.

'How do you do, Mr Knighton?' she replied. 'I'm very pleased to meet you, too.'

He closed the door firmly behind them. 'Take no notice of Mr Walters. Gave you the third degree, did he?'

Frances gave a little laugh. 'Not exactly, but he didn't seem to know who I was.'

'He knows all right. I'd told him you were coming, but he likes to exert his authority. He's been here longer than me, you see, and he looks upon the place as "his" school. Not that I'm saying a word against him, you understand.' He paused to draw out a chair near the desk. 'Do sit down, Miss Goodwin. No, Mr Walters is a first-class caretaker; a real treasure. He couldn't look after this place any better if it were Buckingham Palace. We're very lucky to have him.'

'Yes, I noticed how clean it all is,' replied Frances. 'It all looks very nice. Our caretaker, the one at Wyre Bank, is very good, too.' She remembered that she was no longer at Wyre Bank, but at Park Gates, and she was not really here to discuss caretakers and their merits.

'Yes . . . Wyre Bank,' said Mr Knighton, sitting down in the chair behind the large desk and observing her appraisingly. 'You may find the regime here rather different at first, Miss Goodwin. And this is a Junior school, of course, whereas you have been used to teaching Infants, but I'm sure you'll soon settle in. And you can be sure that the staff will do all they can to make you feel welcome. That's what I found when I came here.

'Oh yes,' he went on, at Frances's questioning glance. 'I'm very much the "new boy" here, you know. I've been here two years, that's all, whereas some of the staff have spent almost a lifetime in the place. Some are more ready than others to adapt to changes – and I've made quite a few – but I must say I've found them all quite amenable. It's a happy school, Miss Goodwin, and I hope you will be happy here, as well.'

And Frances, suddenly, had the feeling that she would be; very happy. She felt apprehensive no longer. She had been aware on entering the building, after she had become used to the dingy outmoded décor, that there was, nevertheless, an ambience about the place, an impression that the generations of children and teachers who had spent their days here over the last seventy, eighty years had been happy here, on the whole, and had left behind some of their feelings of contentment. Or was that too fanciful? Frances only knew that she had not experienced anything like that at Wyre Bank, a much newer building that had not had time to gather to itself any sense of history, of timelessness.

'Yes, I'm sure I will be happy here,' she said now. 'Thank you for . . . for finding a place for me. I'm very grateful.'

Mr Knighton continued to look steadily at her and Frances, somewhat discomfited, lowered her eyes. 'I'm not going to pretend I don't know anything about the reason for you coming to teach here,' he said after a few seconds, not sounding at all condemning. 'I wouldn't insult your intelligence by dissembling. I have been told about your little spot of trouble, and I have also been told, by Miss Reynolds, that you were not to blame; that you had been . . . misled. I am sorry for what has happened, but I hope you will be able to put it all behind you now and start afresh.'

'Thank you,' said Frances quietly. 'And the rest of the staff – do they know?'

'Some of them,' replied Mr Knighton. 'It doesn't really concern them, and you can rest assured they won't ever mention it. Now, this is your class list. There are thirty children – that's not too bad, is it, in the present climate? And your class will be called 1F. That's because we already have another First Year teacher whose name begins with G, Mrs Goodall; so, as your first name is Frances we thought that would be in order . . .

'Come along now, Miss Goodwin.' He leaped to his feet like a Jack-in-the-box. 'I'll show you your classroom. You can have a look round and get acquainted with the place.' Frances had almost to run to keep up with the headmaster as he strode along the corridor, calling out staccato comments to her over his shoulder. 'When you're ready come back to my office and we'll have a cup of tea. I'll have to make it myself today.' He gave a wry grin. 'The school secretary usually does that, but she doesn't come in during the holidays. The rest of the staff will be in on Friday, just before term starts, so if you come along then you'll be able to meet them. Here you are – this is your classroom. Just let me know if there's anything else you think you might need . . .'

Frances settled into her new surroundings and the new routine very quickly. The children were of mixed ability, some much brighter, others decidedly less so, than the ones she had taught at Wyre Bank. Mr Knighton did not believe in 'streaming'; grouping children according to their ability, as was practised in some schools. Miss Reynolds had not believed in it either, but the academic differences in the children became more apparent as they got older. They adapted easily to their new teacher, as she did to them. They were all new, she explained to them; they were just 'up' from the Infants, and she had come from another school, so they would have to help one another.

The staff, too, all twelve of them, were most supportive and friendly, and Frances noticed none of the bitterness and backbiting that had been all too apparent, at times, in the staffroom at Wyre Bank. Probably it was as Marjorie had once told her, that a goodly percentage of men on the staff did help to make a more relaxed atmosphere than was the case in an all-women workplace. There were five men, six including Mr Knighton, and seven women, a not-too-uneven ratio considering that more women than men entered the profession, especially to teach the younger age groups.

'I'm surprised they've let you loose in a staffroom full of men,' Julie observed jokingly soon after Frances went to Park Gates, 'considering your track record.'

Frances laughed. She was finding she could laugh much more easily now about what had happened. Julie knew this, too; she was a considerate girl and she would never have made a joke about it had she not known that her friend was now more at ease with herself. 'You haven't seen them, kid, the men on the staff,' she replied. 'There's no danger of me running off with any of them I can assure you. Forty-five if they're a day, most of 'em; in fact, that goes for the women as well. Some of them are quite elderly; well, you know – fifty plus. The head's the youngest . . .'

Philip Knighton was round about forty years of age, Frances guessed, and this was his first headship. He had moved here, as Miss Reynolds had done, from one of the Lancashire inland towns – Burnley, she had been informed by Mrs Goodall, who had another class of First Year children.

Mavis Goodall was just such another as Marjorie Aspinall; kindly, plump, middle-aged and given to chattering, though not in a malicious way, and Frances felt straight away that she would get on well with her.

'The boss is something of a new broom,' she told Frances. 'Not that you can blame him for that. We had all got rather set in our ways. Our previous headmaster was well turned sixty-five when he retired, and he had let things slide more than a little. So we needed stirring up, you might say. You'll like Mr Knighton. We've all taken to him – you can't help it; he's such a nice, thoughtful man. Philip, he likes us to call him, but not all of us do. We're not used to such informality, you see. He's a great character, though, and he's revolutionised this place.'

Frances could see, soon after the term started, that the

school was not the dark forbidding place she had first imagined. The gloomy corridors, which did not get much light, were brightened up considerably by huge murals, each class being responsible for one section. This was just one innovation of the new head. Frances chose a favourite poem, 'The Owl and the Pussy-Cat', for the first contribution of her class, and she was gratified by the compliments of her colleagues, especially as she knew that art work was not really her strongest point.

The staff seemed pleased that she was keen on music and drama. Not all of them were, but they had to feign a certain amount of enthusiasm, like it or not, because the new head was fanatical about concerts. Harvest, Christmas, the end of each term – any excuse, it seemed, to get the children singing or dancing or acting on the stage. Mr Knighton believed that it developed their self-confidence. It was what Frances, also, had always believed and she looked forward to using her talents in this direction. She decided, though, that it would not be in a pushy sort of way, remembering only too well her clashes with Miss Walsh; but none of the staff here seemed resentful or awkward in any way. They were only too glad that someone younger, with tons of enthusiasm – first Philip Knighton, now Frances – had come along to shake them out of their complacency.

'I would have thought that some of the teachers might have looked for another post,' Frances observed, 'when Mr Knighton came. New ideas and all that; they don't go down well with everyone.'

'Why should we, dear?' said Mavis Goodall. 'We're all very happy here. That's why we've stayed, because we're contented. In my opinion the schools where the staff keeps chopping and changing can't be happy places. Oh, I know some folks want promotion, but most of us here think we're all right as we are. We jog along quite nicely in our own little ways.'

And that was evident when you took a look in the staffroom where they all congregated at playtimes and lunchtimes. Apathetic, some might call them, but Frances soon realised that that was not strictly true. All the teachers worked hard in their own way, in their own classrooms, most of them following Philip Knighton's lead in his various projects and enthusiasms without demur, though some more willingly than others. They were not slaves to the job, however, and made full use of their leisure time.

Mr Burgess read the *Daily Mail* from cover to cover each lunchtime; Mr Dalton, who was in charge of PE and games, and dressed habitually in a tracksuit, did his football pools; and Mr Sanderson buried his head in a spy story. Two of the women teachers racked their brains over the crossword in the *Daily Express*; Mrs Goodall got on with her knitting – a matinée jacket for her latest grandchild; whilst most of the others just chatted, occasionally taking time to mark a pile of exercise books.

'It's all so free and easy,' Frances explained to Julie. 'And yet they seem to get through the work just as well as the ones who dash around as though their tails were on fire. It's like Marjorie once said; there's a tendency amongst some teachers to take it all too seriously, to forget there's a whole world outside the classroom walls. You do need outside interests.'

'Speaking of which,' said Julie. 'Rehearsals start next week for *Carousel*. You're coming with me, aren't you?'

'Oh!' said Frances, rather taken aback. 'I don't know . . . I hadn't really thought about it.'

'Then you'd better start thinking pretty sharpish,' said her friend, 'because I won't take no for an answer this year. Two years ago it was Adrian and all the work you were doing for the church, then it was . . . night school. In fact, you've only been in one production, haven't you? What's your excuse this time, or can't you think of one? You'd better not,' she added in a menacing tone.

'No, I won't,' replied Frances, smiling. 'No excuses this time, Julie. I'll come with you. That is, if they'll have me back. Like you say, I've only been in it once.'

'What? A smashing singer and dancer like you are! Of course they'll have you. You'd have been taking the lead by

370

now if you'd stuck with it. Not like me; I'm still in the blooming chorus!'

'And that's where I'll be, with you,' replied Frances. 'That will suit me just fine. I wonder if all the same people will still be there?'

Julie grinned. 'If you mean Jonathan Russell, yes, I'm sure he will. He's been in it every year up to now.'

'Why should I mean him?' said Frances, with a show of nonchalance which was not entirely assumed. 'I've not seen him since . . . goodness knows when.'

Jonathan had, in truth, come into her mind just then, but before that she had not given him a thought for ages. So much had happened. She had not seen a great deal of Dennis since he moved to the Junior School, apart from the time Marcus had asked her to have a word with him . . . She hoped he was not in any more trouble. And now she was no longer at Wyre Bank. Russell's Garden Centre was not all that far away from where she lived, but their paths never seemed to cross.

'Hey, you're miles away.' Julie waved a hand in front of her face. 'I know you always liked him . . . didn't you?' she added coyly.

'I liked him . . . yes,' answered Frances evenly. 'But I never got to know him, did I, except as Dennis's father?'

'I guess that was your fault, not Jonathan's,' said Julie. 'But it's never too late, is it? I don't think anything came of it with that girl he was friendly with, did it?'

'Glenys Mortimer? I don't know,' replied Frances. 'How should I know . . . or care? Honestly, Julie, I'm not bothered. Don't start matchmaking, please. I've had quite enough problems with fellows. If I come along to *Carousel* – and I will – it will be just to enjoy being in the show. So don't start getting any daft ideas.'

And Julie, looking at her friend's serious face, realised that she meant every word of it. She decided not to go on teasing her. 'OK,' she said. 'I get the message . . . but I'm really glad you've decided to come along. *Carousel* is a fantastic musical.'

* * *

It was just as well, Frances decided, that she had made up her mind not to start having any silly ideas about Jonathan Russell, because as soon as rehearsals started it became obvious that he was not the slightest bit interested in her.

Admittedly he said, 'Hello, Frances; nice to see you again,' and smiled in quite a friendly way, but she was aware at once of a certain edginess in his manner. She enquired about Dennis. His father said he was getting along very nicely, thank you, settling well into his new class and he liked his new teacher. He was nearly ten years old now and in the Third Year Juniors.

'Please give him my love,' said Frances. Then, realising that might have sounded a bit silly – boys of ten didn't like all that soppy stuff, and Jonathan wasn't answering – she amended it. 'Well . . . tell him I was asking about him, won't you? I'm not at Wyre Bank now, so I don't see him,' she added.

'Yes, I had heard,' said Jonathan, quite indifferently. 'I'll tell him you were asking about him. I must go, Frances. They're getting ready to start. See you around.' He waved his hand casually as he went across to talk to a group of men at the other side of the room.

She felt stunned for a moment – not that she was bothered about him – but he had never treated her in this offhand way before. Then she realised that the gossip about her and Marcus must have reached his ears. No doubt it had reached everyone's ears at the time, but she hoped it might have died down by now. Besides, she would have thought that Jonathan Russell was not the sort of man who would listen to gossip or let it affect his judgement. But then he didn't know the whole story, did he, both sides of it? If she could explain to him how it had really been, how Marcus had told her all sorts of lies . . . Why should she bother though? Jonathan had obviously weighed her in the balance and found her wanting.

She decided that she did not care. She was beginning to put the past and all its mistakes behind her. She had a new job, one in which she was very contented; the sadness following her mother's death was gradually waning; and her relationship with Josie seemed to be on an even keel. She had come along to the Starlight Players again to put a bit of variety back into her life. 'When I marry Mister Snow . . .' and 'What's the use of wondrin' if he's good or if he's bad . . .' she hummed as she tidied her classroom at the end of the day, or ironed her blouse to wear the next morning. She was determined to enjoy *Carousel* to the full, and they were such lovely songs. If only they weren't all so poignant . . .

Jonathan had been dismayed when he had heard the rumours about Frances and that teacher from the Junior School; Mr Avery, who happened to be Dennis's teacher that year. Dennis had liked the fellow very much, pronouncing him a good sort who was always ready to have a laugh and a joke with you. Jonathan, also, when he had met him at an open evening had been quite impressed. He seemed to have the children's welfare at heart and had been most understanding about Dennis's little problem.

Jonathan had been horrified when he had received the letter from the headmaster saying that Dennis had been caught stealing from the newsagent's shop. He had been at a loss as to how to deal with it. He had lost his temper, ranting and raving at the boy more than he should have done, he recalled. He had shaken him hard and had been tempted to give him a good hiding . . . but he hadn't. He had sent him to bed early and deprived him of sweets and a visit to the football match. What else could a parent do, apart from going on loving the child and letting him know that you did?

Mr Avery had said he believed it was just an isolated incident, and that he and Miss Goodwin, Dennis's teacher from the Infant School, had both had a serious talk with Dennis. Jonathan had been grateful for Frances's part in this, although he had never seen her to say thank you. Dennis's behaviour had, indeed, improved at that point, for a time. At any rate, he had done no more stealing.

So the two of them, Frances and that Avery fellow, must have been friendly even then, thought Jonathan. Come to think of it, they had been quite a talking point at that school concert, gazing at one another all starry-eyed when they sang those duets; but Jonathan, who had taken part in stage shows himself, had dismissed it as play-acting. Besides, Frances had been engaged to that young minister at the time.

He remembered how this friendship had come as a bitter disappointment to him. He had been about to pluck up courage and ask Frances Goodwin to come out with him for an evening; to the cinema, maybe, and a meal afterwards. He had wrestled with his conscience for a while, the still-painful memories of Jean telling him that it was too soon to be thinking of another romance. Then he had decided that life must go on; he was still young and Jean would not have wanted him to mourn for ever . . . only to discover that the young teacher he so admired had become friendly with the Methodist minister.

He could have put up some opposition, he supposed, but he had not done so, realising that the two of them looked very happy together, very well suited, and that maybe Frances Goodwin was not the girl for him after all. Instead he had taken out Sylvia Bowland for a while, an old family friend. He had known all along, though, that this would come to nothing. She had been too close to Jean; besides, she had a man friend who had been pursuing her for years. It had come as no surprise when Sylvia got engaged.

And so he had turned to Glenys. She was young and pretty and lively, and made him feel at least ten years younger. She was good at her job, too. The garden centre had thrived since she came on the scene; and he had had an idea, for a while, that they might make a go of it, not just with the business, but marriage as well. He had never taken her into his bed, however, although he guessed she would have been more than willing. There was Dennis to consider; he wouldn't have wanted the boy to overhear anything or to find her still there in the morning.

It was Dennis, in fact, who had put the kibosh on that little affair. Jonathan had been aware that his son had never cared for Glenys. The boy's bouts of bad temper, even the stealing episode, had coincided with their friendship; but Jonathan had decided, nevertheless, that he could not allow Dennis to rule his life. Then it became obvious that the antipathy was mutual. Glenys hardly ever spoke to his son, and Jonathan gradually began to realise – he had probably known it all along – that she could never be a mother figure to him. Besides, she had a very possessive streak. She never liked him going to the Starlight Players, or even to visit his parents, which he did sometimes at the weekend. Strangely enough, he had never felt he wanted to introduce her to his mother and father. And so, little by little, their relationship had fallen apart, ending in a blazing row when Glenys stormed out of the garden centre, saying she would work for him no longer, nor did she ever want to see him again. It was just as well; it had never been right. But in the meantime Frances had become engaged to her minister friend, only to let the fellow down badly when she got herself entangled with that Avery bloke.

That was what Jonathan had heard, and although at first he had tried to defend her it seemed as though there must be a good deal of truth in the stories that were going around. After all, Mrs Avery had tried to commit suicide, and Frances had been transferred to another school. Jonathan had always prided himself on being a good judge of character. He had summed up Frances Goodwin as an honest high-principled girl, full of integrity and common sense – in addition to the fact that he found her charming and pretty and easy to get on with – and he was dismayed now to realise that she must, after all, be fickle and shallow, guilty of duplicity and dishonesty. Because what was it but dishonest to take another woman's husband? He made up his mind to forget about her.

Megan's pregnancy was proceeding much more smoothly than might have been expected. Frances had seen her from time to time and was relieved at how well she looked. She did not appear so bloated and heavy as she had when she was carrying Maria. The baby was sitting much more comfortably this time, Megan explained, her ankles had not swollen and there seemed to be no sign of the high blood pressure that had occurred before. She would, however, be going into hospital a few weeks before the baby was due, as a precaution. Because it had been a difficult birth last time, they were taking no chances. That was at Bernard's insistence, Megan told her. Frances was pleased to see that he had his wife's best interests at heart. His own, too, no doubt, because he wanted to make sure that his precious son – if, indeed, it was a son – arrived safely.

Megan had made no further reference to Bernard's unfaithfulness, which had so disturbed Frances. Maybe her friend had imagined it, Frances thought now, or had decided it would be best not to mention it again. Frances could scarcely believe it anyway; though she had never liked Bernard Conway she would never have thought he could be guilty of that. For one thing, how would it square with his Catholic conscience?

She visited Megan in hospital in February, about a fortnight before the baby was due and found her friend, still, in quite good health and the best of spirits. Baby Maria was in the safe hands of her parents, so all Megan had to do was rest and wait and try to keep calm. That was what Bernard had told her and he assured her that everything was going to be all right.

'It looks as though she's going to be OK, doesn't it?' Frances observed on the way out to Megan's friend, Shirley, who was still on the same ward. 'You remember, you told me last time it could be dangerous.'

'The danger is still there,' said Shirley, quite unemotionally, 'but she's much calmer this time, and that helps. She's not strong, though, and she's very tiny. But she's in excellent hands with Dr Templeton. All we can do is keep our fingers crossed, or touch wood.' She tapped the edge of the table. 'Or say our prayers, if you believe in that sort of thing. Megan does.'

'So do I,' replied Frances. 'At least, I try to believe. It's hard sometimes. But I know she's got a good doctor and nurses and that's the main thing, isn't it? And Bernard, of course . . . I know he has a strong faith – like Megan – as well as being a good doctor.' She was determined not to say anything wrong about him; he did seem to be doing his utmost for Megan.

'Him? Goodness knows what he believes,' said Shirley forcefully. Then, almost in a whisper, 'I only know he's a right bastard.'

'Why? What do you mean?' asked Frances, startled at Shirley's outburst. 'He seems to be dancing attendance on Megan now. She speaks very well of him.'

'And well he might, after all he's done.'

'What do you mean?' asked Frances again.

'Nothing . . . I shouldn't have said anything. Forget it,' said Shirley. 'It's just me and my big mouth, but I never could stand him.'

Frances decided not to enquire any further. It would not be right to gossip about Megan although she could guess what Shirley was referring to. 'The important thing is that Megan gets through the birth safely,' she said. 'I'm sure Mrs Ashcroft will phone me when there's some news. She did last time.

'Shirley,' she said, as an afterthought, 'I'll give you my phone number – well, the school one; we're not on the phone at the flat. I know you're busy, but if there's anything you think I should know could you give me a ring, please?'

Shirley promised that she would do so.

The phone call came sooner than Frances had expected. It was one lunchtime the following week when the school secretary came to find Frances in the staffroom.

'Miss Goodwin, there's a young lady on the phone who would like to speak to you. She says she's ringing from Victoria Hospital.'

Frances jumped up in great excitement. 'Oh, it'll be about my friend, Megan. She's having a baby. It must have arrived early. Thank you, Mrs Williams.'

'I'll leave you to talk in private,' said Mrs Williams. 'I'll come back when you've finished.'

Frances seized the phone. 'Hello, Frances here. Is that you, Shirley? I guessed it would be you. Any news?'

'Yes . . . yes, it's me,' replied Shirley. There was a gravity in her voice, even in those first few words, that alarmed Frances. 'I'm afraid I . . . Are you sitting down, Frances? I think you'd better. I'm sorry, I have some very sad news.'

'What?' Although Frances knew at once what it must be. 'Megan . . .? She's not . . .?'

There was a deep sigh at the other end of the phone. 'I'm sorry, Frances. Megan died . . . this morning. It was a difficult birth . . . like we always knew it would be. It was . . . too much for her.'

'Oh . . . that's dreadful.' Frances could scarcely take it in. At the moment she was too stunned to shed any tears. 'I . . . can't believe it. What about the baby?'

'The baby is all right,' said Shirley in a quiet voice. 'It's . . . a boy.'

Frances's first thought was that Bernard had got his desire – at the cost of his wife's life. 'Were – were you there?' she asked. 'At the birth?'

'No. No, I wasn't there. And perhaps – after all – I'm glad,' said Shirley. 'It all happened early this morning. I only came on duty an hour ago. I know Dr Templeton did all he could to save her, but it was no use.'

'And Bernard? Was he there?'

'I . . . I believe so,' said Shirley faintly. 'I haven't seen him. He's gone to tell Megan's parents. Oh, Frances, I'm sorry to tell you such awful news, but you did say to let you know.'

'Yes . . . thank you, Shirley. Thank you for ringing . . . Goodbye.'

Frances put down the phone. She still could not take it in. She sat there stupefied, staring into space, and that is how Mrs Williams found her several minutes later. Only when the kindly secretary put an arm round her, asking if it was bad news, did the tears finally come. And then it seemed as though they would never stop.

Frances felt far more grief-stricken at the funeral of her friend than she had when her mother was buried. Iris's death had not been entirely unexpected, but neither, if she were honest with herself, had Megan's. Frances had pushed to the back of her mind her knowledge of the danger her friend was in, believing with the skill of the doctors, combined with the power of prayer, that it would – it must – be all right. It was as though the tears Frances had shed this last week – copious tears, accompanied by racking sobs and cries of, 'Why? Why has God let it happen?' – were an accumulation of the grief about all that had happened to her recently.

She was dry-eyed at the funeral, however, her weeping, for the moment, over. She observed, as though watching from afar, Megan's tiny oak coffin surrounded by masses of flowers, a long wreath of white chrysanthemums in the shape of a cross lying on the top. Megan may not have had a lot of close friends, but she was liked and respected by many people. Her nursing colleagues and several former patients had come to say their farewells and the Catholic church was half full. It seemed only a short while, to Frances, since Megan and Bernard had stood at those same chancel steps exchanging their marriage vows. Now Megan's coffin lay there. As there had been at the wedding, there was a celebration of the Mass, a Requiem Mass this time, only those who were of 'the faith' being allowed to partake of the Host. It still seemed alien to Frances and she found herself wishing, not for the first time, that Adrian was at her side.

Megan's parents were very brave throughout the service and the burial, later, in Layton Cemetery, Mr Ashcroft supporting his wife with his arm around her shoulders the whole time. What a dreadful tragedy it was for them both, especially as Megan was their only child. Frances hoped that the grandchildren, little Maria, still not quite one year old, and baby Joe – as Megan had said he would be called – might be some comfort to the couple and that Bernard would not try to keep them all to himself. Surely he would be obliged to ask for their help; with his responsible work at the hospital he would not be able to cope otherwise? Frances realised, however, that it was none of her business and it was unlikely she would see very much of Megan's children. It was all so very, very sad.

There was a small gathering afterwards of relatives and close friends at a town centre café. Frances and Shirley were both invited, but left as soon as it was expedient for them to do so, after saying goodbye and expressing their condolences, once again, to Bernard and Megan's parents.

Bernard, for once, was subdued; suitably grave and dignified, as one would expect him to be, but Frances did not think that even Bernard could have feigned the look of bewilderment and sadness in his eyes.

'He looks very shaken,' she said to Shirley as they walked through the town centre to the bus station. 'More than I thought he might be, although I suppose he did love Megan.'

'Yes . . . maybe he did, in his own way,' replied Shirley. 'He wanted her; there was no doubt about that – probably because she was such a contrast to himself and to some of the other nurses. That's what the rest of us thought. She was so fragile and dainty and . . . pure. Not like any of the others.'

She turned to look at Frances. 'He had others, you know. Before and after. There are some girls who are like that. Nurses who are quite willing to be of assistance to the doctor, not only in the ward.'

'Yes, I think Megan knew,' said Frances. 'At least, she hinted that she did.'

'She knew?' Shirley sounded amazed.

'Yes. She wasn't all that naïve, not about some things. Why didn't the rest of you warn her before she married him, if you knew what he was like?'

'I'm not sure. We didn't know her well enough, I suppose. It was hard to get close to her. Anyway, it's too late now. Poor Megan.'

'Yes . . . poor Megan. It's such a tragedy. But he's got his son, hasn't he?' Frances had found herself wishing, at times, that it had been another girl, but she knew that was vindictive. 'You don't suppose – Bernard – he wouldn't have told them to save the baby rather than Megan?'

'I wasn't there,' said Shirley, quite curtly. 'No . . . I'm sure they did all they could, all of them, to save Megan.' And from the tone of her voice Frances knew it was useless to pursue the matter. Shirley may have disliked Bernard Conway, but he was a doctor, she was a nurse, and Frances understood that, as members of the medical profession, they would stick together.

Chapter 24

It would be good to see Adrian again. When she had written to him Frances had not anticipated that he might come to see her. She had written to tell him of Megan's death because she knew he had always been fond of the young woman, and because she had to try to come to terms with it herself. She had hoped that talking and writing about it might help to ease the pain that she still felt, but the depression that had settled on her since she lost her friend was, if anything, getting worse rather than better.

Now, Adrian's letter told her he was coming to see her on Saturday afternoon. She wondered whether, all along, though so deeply hidden that she was not even aware of it, this may well have been her intention when she wrote to him: to make the first tentative overtures towards inviting him back into her life. Whether this was so or not she knew she was looking forward to seeing him more than she had looked forward to anything for quite some time.

'It's good to see you again, Frances.' He kissed her lightly on the cheek before following her into the flat. Julie, tactfully, had gone out for the day, although she had not shown much enthusiasm at the idea of Adrian coming to see her friend again. Frances knew that Julie was one of the few people who had not thought she was out of her mind when she ended her engagement.

'I was so sorry, so dreadfully sorry to hear about Megan,' Adrian said, taking off his duffel coat and sitting down; making himself at home straight away, Frances was pleased to see. 'It's shaken you very badly, hasn't it?' He looked at her searchingly, his clear grey eyes full of compassion. Affection, too? Frances was looking for a sign of it, but she wasn't sure. 'That's why I've come, really, because I could sense that you were terribly distressed. And I'm still your friend, Frances, in spite of . . . everything that has happened. I felt that you might want to just talk about it. Talking helps, sometimes, doesn't it?' He smiled at her questioningly.

'Yes . . . it might,' she answered. 'I have talked to people; to Julie, and to my friend Marjorie – you remember Marjorie, from Wyre Bank? – but not . . . not in any great depth. I don't think they would want to enter into a deep discussion. I don't understand it, Adrian. Why? I keep asking myself why. She was so young. She had everything to live for. I know she wasn't all that happy with Bernard, but she would have coped, and she was very happy with her little girl . . . and she was looking forward so much to the next one. It all seems so unfair.' She looked at him pleadingly. 'And don't try to tell me it's God's will.'

'I won't,' said Adrian gently, 'because I can't believe that it was.'

'It was his fault – Bernard's, I mean,' Frances went on, speaking quickly. 'And that's something I can't come to terms with. He knew; he knew all along that she shouldn't be having another baby, and yet he was willing to put her life at risk, just because he wanted a son. And there's something else that's troubling me, Adrian. I can't get it out of my mind.'

'What's that, Frances?' he asked, very calmly.

'I know it's a terrible thought,' she began, 'but do you suppose . . . if Bernard had to choose between his son being stillborn and his wife dying . . . did he choose to let Megan die? I remember hearing, you see, that to Catholics the life of the baby is more important, and I know he so desperately wanted a son. He was there at the birth, you know. I mentioned it to Shirley, Megan's nurse friend, but she shut up like a clam.'

'Well, she would, wouldn't she?' Adrian observed. 'The medical profession close ranks, and they're not the only ones. Teachers do as well, don't they, to protect their own?'

'They might,' said Frances, 'sometimes . . .' She was

thinking that she knew of certain teachers who had been only too ready to condemn, not to protect.

'And even the clergy have been known to close ranks, too,' said Adrian, 'in certain circumstances. It wouldn't do you any good to know, Frances,' he continued quietly, 'and you'll only make yourself ill if you carry on fretting about it. You're not going to find out, and do you really want to? Personally, I think you are wrong. I think that the doctors and nurses in this day and age will do everything in their power to save both the mother and the baby. But in Megan's case, sadly, it proved impossible. I think Bernard may have been wrong to put her into that danger, but Megan knew the risk as well. It was a risk they both wanted to take. I remember telling you once before, the Catholic point of view can be very different from ours, and we may not understand it, but we have to try and respect it.'

'You're still as tolerant as ever, Adrian.' Frances smiled at him. 'But what I can't understand is this; some might say it was God's will that Megan died, and yet, if she had lived, then we would be saying how good He was to have let her pull through, as though that was His will. How can they both be? It doesn't make sense.'

'Nothing does if you try to analyse it too much,' said Adrian. 'Just try to believe that God is there, somehow, in the middle of it all. He's there for you, Frances,' he added gently.

'Tell me, how are things at the church?' he went on, in a much more down-to-earth manner. 'A few people write to me, but I don't enquire too much. The new minister has to find his own feet and I don't want to appear to be nosing.'

'To be quite honest, Adrian, I don't know,' replied Frances. 'You see . . . I don't go any more. So much has happened. There was all that . . . trouble at school. I know you must have heard about it?' She looked at him, a trifle apprehensively, but he just gave a brief noncommittal nod. 'And then I had to change schools, and I felt that people might be . . . well . . . gossiping, so I kept away, and I've never gone back.'

'I see.' He smiled at her. 'Well . . . I can't say I blame

you. People do gossip for a time, maybe – it's only human nature – but the talk dies down after a while, you know.'

'When they find somebody else to talk about,' added Frances wryly.

'True enough.' Adrian smiled. 'My mum always says when they're talking about you they're leaving somebody else alone. If you don't feel like going back to the Methodist Church you could always try the Church of England. You used to be C of E, didn't you?'

Frances nodded, rather impatiently. Couldn't he see, at the moment, that she didn't feel like going anywhere?

He obviously could, as his reply showed. 'Not that it's anything to do with me, Frances. I haven't come here to preach at you, only to help . . . if I can. And because I thought it would be nice to see you again.'

She didn't answer, continuing to stare moodily at the carpet. Maybe it had not been such a good idea after all for Adrian to come here. She had been looking forward so much to seeing him, but now all the feelings of guilt were returning about how badly she had let him down. Combined with the guilt she still felt about Geraldine Avery, and about her mother's death, it all seemed too much to bear. She had thought she was beginning to pick up the pieces; now she felt overwhelmed by it all again. Adrian's presence seemed to be oppressing her further, rather than lightening her load. It was good to see him, but she kept remembering how happy they had been together at one time . . . and how she had hurt him so badly.

'Whose is that car outside?' asked Adrian suddenly. 'That red Mini-Minor?' She knew he was trying to introduce some levity into the conversation, to help to lift her low spirits, and that for his sake as well as her own she must make an effort to repond. 'Is it yours?'

'Yes . . . yes, it's mine,' she replied.

'Well, fancy that. I didn't know you could drive.'

'I can't. Well, I'm learning, but I haven't taken my test yet. I bought it soon after I moved to Park Gates, but it' taking me rather longer than I thought to learn to drive

And since . . . well . . . these last few weeks, I seem to have lost heart.'

'They're grand little cars,' said Adrian. 'Possibly not quite big enough for my purposes, though. I find myself acting as chauffeur to some of the old folk who find it difficult to get about. I've still got my old banger, you can see . . . Frances, you mustn't give up.' He leaned forward, looking at her intently. 'Not with your driving, not with anything. You've got such a lot to look forward to, I'm sure. Tell me about your new school.'

And so she did. She told him about Philip Knighton and his various enthusiasms; for concerts and for school visits to all the places of interest in the Fylde, and for projects to widen the children's experiences, the latest one being to create a colourful garden area out of the wilderness of concrete and dried up earth that edged the school. She told Adrian, too, how she had gone back to the Starlight Players to take part in their next production, *Carousel*. They would be performing it in a few weeks' time, but she had missed a couple of rehearsals recently, so upset had she been over Megan's death.

Little by little as she talked with him she could feel her sadness, her sense of despair, evaporating. He had always had that effect, she recalled, on her and on others. It was one of his greatest gifts as a minister, this ability he had to listen, to draw people out of themselves, to make them believe that life, after all, was worth living.

It had been arranged that he would stay for a meal and, to her surprise, he followed her into the kitchen, asking if he could be of any assistance in setting the table or – wonder of wonders! – peeling the potatoes. No, she assured him; the casserole, a Lancashire hotpot, was already simmering gently in the oven, but he could set out the knives and forks and open a tin of fruit salad, if he wished. (Her culinary skills still did not run to preparing a pudding as well as a main course!)

She had always believed, when she was engaged to him, that he thought it was the woman's job, single-handedly, to see to the cooking, as his mother had always done. Had he changed his view, she wondered, or was he just making a special effort today? He was, of course, quite capable of looking after himself and making the odd meal. He had no option in his bachelor existence, although she guessed he would quite often be invited to dine at the homes of parishioners. Anyone in particular? she wondered, although it was really none of her business.

'Tell me about Birmingham,' she said, when the meal had been dished out and they were seated at the table. She was pleased to see the casserole had turned out well, the potatoes well browned on the top and the lamb chops tender, just as they should be, the whole dish almost as good as her mother used to make. 'Are you still enjoying it down there?' Or maybe 'enjoying' was not really the right word. Adrian was not there primarily for enjoyment, but because he felt it was his calling. 'I mean . . . you still feel it was the right move to make? Let me see, how long have you been there now? It must be . . . nearly two years.'

'Two years in August,' he replied. 'Yes, I'm sure it was the right thing to do. There are all sorts of problems down there. Homeless people, drug addicts, alcoholics; they're becoming more prevalent, unfortunately. We've opened a centre for them. There was a rundown old house near to the church; it used to be a doctor's surgery at one time and they were going to pull it down, so we managed to buy it quite cheaply, and we've made it into a centre for all these folk who need help. We have a rota of people who come in to dish out soup, or medical supplies, or just . . . to listen.'

As Frances listened to him she realised again what a selfless, dedicated man he was. He made her feel quite ashamed, so inadequate. What had she ever done to help anyone, she asked herself. She had not wanted to share in Adrian's work. Because of her own selfish desires she had opted to stay here, in Blackpool, and what a load of trouble that decision had led her into. She felt now, at this moment, if Adrian were to ask her, again, to share her life with him then she would agree . . . even though she knew, deep down and to her shame, that dealing with vagrants and drunkards would not be to her liking at all.

'I shall probably spend another couple of years in Birmingham,' he told her, 'and then I think I shall look for a living in the East End of London. There's a lot of work to be done down there, I believe, but the same is true of all the big cities. Of course, it's not entirely up to me, is it?' he added with a grin. 'It all depends on Him up there, what He wants me to do.'

Frances now realised that he was not going to suggest that they might try again, and that she would not be much use to him if he did. He would want a wife who would share his work and his ideals wholeheartedly. She was not that person. She tried to tell him what was in her mind.

'Adrian, I want to say I'm sorry for the way I treated you. It was unfair of me. No; it was much more than that, I was being downright selfish. I must admit . . . just recently . . . I thought I might have made a big mistake in letting you go. I even imagined we might start again. But I know now that we couldn't. It just wouldn't work. I could never share in what you are doing. I could never be so completely self-sacrificing. In fact,' she added, dispiritedly, 'I sometimes wonder what good I am at all, to anybody.'

'Frances,' he cried, 'you mustn't talk like that. It just isn't true. I know that you and I – that it wouldn't have worked out. I loved you so much, Frances. I still care very deeply about you, but it wouldn't be fair of me to expect you to share my life. It just isn't you. But don't you realise you have other talents? Has nobody ever told you what a very good teacher you are?'

She smiled ruefully. 'Yes, Miss Reynolds, but she had to let me go, didn't she? She had no choice. And I think Mr Knighton thinks I'm OK. I do enjoy it. I like the work. I like the kids.'

'And they love you, Frances. At least I know they did at Wyre Bank and I should imagine it's the same at this new place.'

'But I never imagined I would make a lifetime career of it. You know, working up the promotion ladder; deputy headship, headship, retirement at sixty-five.' She gave a shudder. 'The prospect of that does not thrill me. So maybe

I'm not such a dedicated teacher, like some of them are.'

'I wasn't suggesting that teaching should be the only thing in your life,' said Adrian with a gleam in his eye. 'With your looks, Frances, I should imagine that's very unlikely.'

'It doesn't matter what I look like, does it?' she replied pensively. 'It's what I'm like inside that counts. And I don't think I'm very nice. Men seem to be giving me a wide berth at the moment, anyway,' she added, thinking of one man in particular. 'I've not got a very good record, have I?'

'Try to put it behind you, Frances.' Adrian gave a sad smile. 'Yes . . . I did know about your little spot of bother at Wyre Bank School. I knew about . . . Marcus Avery. Pointless to tell you now that I never liked him, isn't it? But I'm sorry, Frances, really sorry, my dear, that you have been hurt so badly. I'm not going to tell you who told me about it. A well meaning person – or we'll try to think so – wrote to me, thinking I "ought to know". Suffice it to say that there are always those, even within the church – maybe more so, within the church –' he gave a mirthless grin, 'who are not averse to passing on a bit of gossip.'

Frances was not surprised to learn that he knew; in fact she was glad. She wanted him to know the full extent of her wickedness, but she knew she could never have found the words to tell him herself. 'I've been a fool,' she said. 'No, more than that. I behaved shamefully . . . and that's how I feel now, ashamed. I feel as though no decent man will ever want to bother with me.'

'Nonsense,' said Adrian. 'I'm sure you don't really mean that. You're feeling sorry for yourself, and I never thought you would be guilty of that. There will be somebody for you, just round the corner. I'm sure of it.'

'That's more than I am,' replied Frances. 'At the moment, though, I have no wish to enter into any sort of . . . relationship. I've had my fingers burned rather badly, Adrian, though I know it was my own fault. All I want to do is to carry on with my life again, peacefully, happily, if I can. I thought I was beginning to, until Megan died, then I began to feel worse than ever.'

Adrian nodded understandingly, but did not reply. He was letting her do the talking, but she could tell he was listening with a sympathetic ear.

'If only I could shake off this despondency that has settled on me. Maybe I will when the spring comes. I always feel worse in the winter; the darkness depresses me. But it has helped immensely talking to you, Adrian. I'm so glad you came.'

'You'll never walk alone,' he said suddenly. 'Isn't that one of the songs in *Carousel*?'

'Yes, it is,' she answered. 'The words are almost too heart-rending to sing. That's one of the reasons I haven't been to the practice for a week or two. I thought I might break down. All the songs have that effect on me.' She laughed. 'I'm hopelessly sentimental at times, but all that stuff about a golden sky at the end of the storm, I just couldn't take it the way I was feeling. I hope it's true, though,' she added. 'You just have to go on hoping, don't you, that things will get better?'

'They will,' said Adrian. 'I can assure you, they will. And you know, don't you, that what the song says is true? We never need to walk alone, none of us. It really means "Him up there",' he said again with a smile, 'but I have a feeling you won't be alone for very much longer. You're a very lovely girl, Frances, and you mustn't be so hard on yourself. I happen to believe you're just as nice on the inside and I'm sure I'm not the only one who thinks so.'

Frances said goodbye to him without any regrets on her part. She knew that their lives must diverge along very different paths. Nevertheless, it had been good to see Adrian. Already she felt calmer, more at peace with herself, ready to face life without that awful feeling of foreboding that had engulfed her recently.

Obeying a sudden impulse – or maybe it was Adrian who had planted the idea in her mind – she decided to go to church the next morning. Julie confessed she was not much of a churchgoer, so she had a lie-in while Frances went on her own. Not to the Methodist church, however, Adrian's former place – she didn't think she could face that, especially as she now knew for certain that there had been gossip about her – but to St Christopher's which was also on the Wyre Bank estate.

It was a fairly new building, only some ten years old, having been opened soon after the estate came into being, but Frances found that the service was very traditional, containing much of the ritual and conformity that she associated with the Church of England in whose precepts she had been brought up as a little girl. It was Church Parade Sunday when all the uniformed organisations of the district – the Cubs and Scouts, the Brownies and Girl Guides, and members of the Girls' Friendly Society – paraded with their flags and banners, carrying them up the aisle at the beginning of the service and collecting them from the vicar's hands at the end.

Frances was pleased to recognise a few familiar faces. There was Linda, the fussy little girl who had been in her first class at Wyre Bank, carrying the Brownie flag. She smiled proudly as she passed Frances's seat. Frances was not surprised she had been chosen for that honour; she had always been a self-possessed child. She did not know the boy who was carrying the Cub flag, but she was delighted to see that one of the escorts who walked with him was Dennis Russell. Dennis saw her and his eyes glanced momentarily in her direction with a flicker of pleasure, but he did not smile. He was taking his duty very seriously as she remembered, from her days in the Girl Guides, one was supposed to do. One was not expected to smile or wave at mums and dads and friends when on parade.

Frances wondered if Jonathan might have come along to support his son, but there was no sign of him. She recalled him saying he did not go to church, that he had lost all inclination to do so after his wife died, but that was a long time ago.

'Good to have you with us,' said the vicar, shaking hands with her at the door. 'I hope you will come again.'

Frances felt that she might. He did not know her, but he was trying to make her welcome, and a few people, recognising her, had smiled and said hello. That was all she wanted at the moment. A degree of anonymity; the ability to come and go as she pleased without too much involvement.

'Miss . . . Miss Goodwin.' She turned as she heard a voice on the path behind her, and there was Dennis racing towards her. 'I saw you, Miss Goodwin, in the church, but I couldn't let on. We're not supposed to grin at people, see. It's dead nice to see you again, though. We've missed you at Wyre Bank,' he added, a little self-consciously.

'And I've missed you,' replied Frances. 'You and Barry.' The two boys, after transferring to the Juniors, had occasionally popped back to the Infant school to see their favourite teacher. Without letting on to their mates, she realised, who might have thought it 'soppy'. 'Barry's not here this morning?' she asked.

'Oh no, he's not in Cubs, miss. He's OK, though. We're still friends. I'll tell him I've seen you.'

'Yes, you do that, Dennis.' Frances smiled at him, noticing how much he had matured since she last saw him. He had filled out, both in his face and body, and he no longer had that hangdog expression he had worn at times, especially when he had been caught out in wrongdoing. She guessed that this was now a thing of the past. His brown eyes were bright and alert and full of enthusiasm. He wore his uniform with pride; the dark green jersey, blue and white striped neckerchief which showed to which pack he belonged, and the little peaked cap which perched jauntily on top of his flame-coloured hair. She noticed he had an array of badges stitched on his sleeve, which showed that he was a keen member of the pack.

'Akela says I can carry the flag next time it's Church Parade,' he told her. He paused before adding, shyly, 'D'you think . . .? Would you like to come and watch me, Miss Goodwin?'

'I most certainly will, Dennis,' she assured him. 'It's the first time I've been to this church – well, for quite a while – but . . . yes, I'll come again. Don't forget to tell Barry you've seen me. Bye, Dennis. Be seeing you.'

Miss Goodwin was just great, thought Dennis as he walked back towards his home. He had always thought so and he'd thump anyone who said anything wrong about her. A few kids had been saying she'd been carrying on with Mr Avery and that his wife had found out and there'd been a lot of bother – their mums had told them – but Barry Cartwright had soon shut 'em up. Barry liked her as well, but she'd left now and nobody talked about her any more. Which was just as well because Dennis knew he wasn't really much of a fighter.

Miss Goodwin had helped him a lot, a heck of a lot. He had always known it was wrong to steal and he had never really known why he did it, except that he was all in a muddle. Miss Goodwin had understood though, and after she had come and talked to him that time he had known he must never, ever do it again.

She had told him off, though, about saying he would like her to marry his dad. Perhaps it had been a potty sort of thing to say, but he had thought it would be dead good if it happened. He still thought so, but his dad never mentioned her now. Glenys had gone, though, which couldn't be bad, and he had his dad all to himself now . . . but he couldn't help wishing and wondering.

He saw her again a few weeks later when he went with his gran and granddad to watch his dad in *Carousel*. There she was in the chorus, singing and dancing and looking real pretty in a pink and white checked dress with her hair all loose. And there was her name in the programme, Frances Goodwin. He leaned forward in his seat – they were on the next to the front row – smiling up at her, but he didn't think she could see him. His dad had told him it looked all dark from the stage when you looked into the auditorium.

'Dad,' he said at breakfast time the next morning. 'You didn't tell me Miss Goodwin was in the show.'

'Didn't I?' said his dad, in a casual voice as though he couldn't care less. 'Oh well, it must have slipped my mind. I didn't think it was important, son. You don't see her any more, do you, now she's not teaching at Wyre Bank?'

'I have—' began Dennis, then he stopped. He had been about to say, 'I have seen her – I saw her at church,' then he thought better of it. Because he had just thought of a plan. It was a jolly good idea and it might work. 'I mean . . . no, I haven't seen her . . . not till last night. I thought it was good, seeing her again. She's dead nice, Miss Goodwin.' He glanced warily at his dad, but Jonathan was hidden behind the pages of the *Daily Express*.

'Uh-huh,' he replied.

'Dad,' said Dennis again, a few minutes later, so that his dad couldn't make any connection, 'you will come and watch me on Sunday, won't you, when I carry the flag? You did promise.'

'I said I might,' replied his dad, regarding him seriously. 'I didn't actually promise. You know I'm not much of a churchgoer, but . . . all right then, I'll come, just this once. I know it's important to you, Den, and I'm very proud of you lately. I've got to say you've been a different boy since you joined the Cubs.'

Yipee! thought Dennis. What his dad didn't realise was that he had been a different boy since that Glenys woman had slung her hook.

'Thanks, Dad,' he said. All he had to do now was to make sure Miss Goodwin was there as well. She had said she would be, but he wanted to make sure. He would write her a little note to remind her. He knew where she lived and there couldn't be any harm in that, could there? She wouldn't suspect anything.

It did not occur to him that his dad had been seeing Frances Goodwin regularly at rehearsals of *Carousel*, and that if he had wanted to get friendly with her, then he would already have done so.

'Where's your friend?' Jonathan had asked Julie Forrester, after Frances was missing for the second time at rehearsal. 'Is she ill?'

'No, she's not exactly ill,' Julie replied, 'but she's very low – depressed, you know. A friend of hers died recently –

she was only young, the same age as Frances, and she died having a baby – and she's dreadfully upset about it. I thought it might cheer her up to come to rehearsal, but I couldn't persuade her. She's really down in the dumps at the moment.'

'Oh dear, I'm sorry to hear that,' said Jonathan. He was tempted to say, Tell her we've missed her, but decided against it. 'She'll be back in time for the show, won't she? It's only four weeks off.'

'Yes, I'm sure she will. She seemed a bit brighter this morning because she had a letter from Adrian – you know, the fellow she used to be engaged to.'

'The minister?'

'Yes, that's the one. He's coming to see her on Saturday.'

'Oh . . .' A faint alarm-bell sounded in Jonathan's head. 'So . . . do you think it's going to be on again with her and . . . what was he called?'

'Adrian Glover. I hope not. No, I don't think that would be a good idea at all.'

'Didn't you like him?'

'Yes, I suppose I liked him well enough. Everybody liked Adrian, he was such a thoroughly decent sort of chap. Should be, of course, being a minister. But I was one of the few who never thought he was right for Frances. He would have submerged her, or tried to. And Frances is the sort of person who has to have a life of her own.'

'Yes, I should imagine she is,' said Jonathan. Julie looked at him keenly, aware of a trace of bitterness in his voice.

'Don't be too hard on her,' she said. 'Frances has had a rough time recently and she feels it very much when she thinks people are avoiding her.'

'Meaning me?'

'I didn't say that,' replied Julie, 'but, yes, I suppose you have been rather cool towards her lately, haven't you?'

'I may have been,' said Jonathan. 'Frances and I – we don't seem to have got off to a very good start. In fact, we never really started at all. I would like to have been friendly with her – very much so – then she got engaged to that minister fellow. And after that . . . well, I must admit I changed my opinion of her somewhat.'

'You shouldn't listen to rumours.'

'I don't, but they were rather more than that, weren't they? Damn it all, my lad was in his class. I couldn't help hearing.'

'It wasn't her fault. She's had a rough time.'

'So you keep telling me.' Jonathan gave an eloquent grin. 'What are you trying to do anyway? A spot of matchmaking?'

'Good heavens, no!' replied Julie. 'Frances would kill me if she knew I was talking to you like this. She's off men at the moment, believe me. She's had her fingers burned.'

'That's what happens when you play with fire . . . Sorry,' Jonathan added, at a baleful look from Julie. 'I didn't mean to sound so condemning. Why are we having this conversation anyway?' He realised it was the first time he had ever exchanged more than a few words with this bonny, dark-haired friend of Frances.

'Because you asked me where Frances was. You started it.'

'So I did.' He nodded thoughtfully. 'My lad, Dennis, always liked her. She was very good to him when he was in a spot of bother. Julie, listen. You'll let me know, will you, if anything comes of this visit of . . . Adrian Glover?'

'Why should I?' Julie answered pertly. 'If you want to make it up with Frances then why don't you go round and see her? Don't be expecting me to do your courting for you, like kids in the playground – "Johnny Jones says he loves yer," and all that. I've told you, I'm not matchmaking. It seems to me that neither of you knows what you want,' she added, starting to walk away.

'You could be right,' said Jonathan. 'Thanks anyway, Julie.'

'What for?'

'For putting me in the picture. For helping me to sort things out a bit.'

'Have you?'

'I might have done.'

Julie gave an exasperated tut as she went to join the

chorus of girls lining up for the 'Real Nice Clambake' song. She hoped, more than anything, that Frances and Jonathan would get together eventually, but her friend would be very cross if she thought she was interfering. Though she might have managed to give him a push in the right direction.

At the next rehearsal, which Frances had finally decided she must attend, Jonathan had raised his eyebrows questioningly at Julie and she had given a slight shake of her head. Just to make sure he had got the message she whispered to him in the queue for tea, 'It was no go with the Reverend Adrian, thank goodness, so it's up to you now, mate.' She had told him she wouldn't help, but if anybody needed a shove it was that pair of fatheads. After a couple of weeks had gone by, however, the situation was still the same. Jonathan, whom she would have expected to be such a forceful person, ready to go all out for what he wanted, was still dithering around, while Frances was behaving as though he were the invisible man.

And then it was the week of the show. 'A resounding success . . . The best ever . . . First-rate singing and dancing . . . Heart-rendingly poignant', were some of the comments in Blackpool's *Evening Gazette*.

'You're going to the party, are you?' Jonathan asked Julie on the Friday night.

'Yes, of course.'

'And Frances?'

'Yes, she'll be there. But why don't you ask her yourself?'

'Because she's still avoiding me.'

'Can you blame her?'

'No, I suppose not.'

Julie cast her eyes heavenwards, despairing of them both.

But Jonathan was not at the party, which took place after the last performance, neither was he at the performance itself.

'Jonathan Russell doesn't seem to be here,' Frances observed as she looked along the chorus line of men, ready for the opening song.

'No, haven't you heard?' said the girl next to her. 'I just

heard Joe Markland telling some of the fellows. His son's had an accident. He's in hospital and Jonathan's dashed off to be with him. There's no mother, you know. He's a widower.'

Then they were straight into 'June is Busting Out All Over', with Frances finding it almost impossible to concentrate on her singing or dancing. They found out later in the evening that Dennis had had a fall on a Cub outing to Nicky Nook, a local beauty spot near Garstang. He was concussed, with a broken arm and was in Victoria Hospital.

'Poor little lad,' said Frances. 'That's terrrible. And I only had that letter from him this morning reminding me about the Church parade. As if I'd forget. I'd promised him I'd go and watch. He will be so disappointed to miss carrying the flag.'

'You can go and see him in hospital,' said Julie.

'Do you think I should?'

'Why not?'

'Well, they're rather strict about visiting at the Vic, and I'm not a relation, am I? Besides, Jonathan'll be there.'

'So what?'

'So . . . nothing. But we're not exactly hitting it off, are we? I can but try, though, to see Dennis, I mean. Poor little lad. I do hope he's come round . . .'

It was early on Sunday morning when Dennis opened his eyes. Jonathan had never been so relieved about anything in his life. He had panicked for a while, fearing he was going to lose him, but the doctor had assured him that Dennis would come round fairly soon from his concussion and they had already set his broken arm.

'Dad . . .' he said, unsurely. His brown eyes were puzzled, looking like deep dark pools in his white face. 'What . . . what's happened?' He glanced down at the plaster encasing his arm. 'Where am I?'

'You're in hospital, Den,' said Jonathan gently. 'You're a silly chump, aren't you, going and falling like that?'

'What . . . when?'

'When you went to Nicky Nook with the Cubs. Akela said you took a tumble on the path. You knocked yourself out, and not content with that you had to go and break your arm as well.'

The shale path had been steep and slippery after a spell of dry weather. Dennis had lost his footing and catapulted to the little stream below, banging his head on a rock. Luckily they were not too far from civilisation and an ambulance was quickly summoned to the nearby village of Scorton. It was fortunate, too, that Blackpool's Victoria Hospital was almost as near as the one at Preston, so they had decided to take him there.

Dennis shook his head confusedly. Then, 'The flag . . .' he said, raising his head and trying to sit up. 'I'm carrying the flag . . .'

Jonathan gently pushed him back on to the pillows. 'Steady on, old chap. You mustn't try to sit up, not yet. Just take it easy now.'

'But I can't, Dad. I can't stay here. What day is it?'

'It's Sunday. Sunday morning. You've been here since Saturday afternoon.'

'But I'm carrying the flag on Sunday, for the Cubs. Don't you remember? I've got to be there.' He tried to sit up again.

Once more Jonathan restrained him. 'Yes, I know all about that, Den. But it doesn't matter. Somebody else will do it, and you can have your turn next time. OK? And I'll come and watch you, like I promised.'

'But you don't understand, Dad.' Dennis looked at him so pleadingly. 'I've asked somebody else to come as well. She'll be there, in church, and she'll wonder where I am. And . . . and I wanted you to be there, too.'

'Who have you asked, Dennis?' But Jonathan already knew the answer.

'Miss Goodwin. I saw her there last time, see. And I asked her if she'd like to come when I was carrying the flag. And she said she would.' Dennis's head flopped sideways on the pillow, exhausted with all his explaining. There was just the trace of a tear glistening in the corner of his eye. 'I do like her, Dad. I've always liked her. And I thought—'

'You little devil!' Jonathan tenderly brushed away the tear from his son's cheek then he took hold of his hand. 'I know what you thought. And it was a very kind thought, too. But you really ought to let grown-ups do their own thinking, you know.'

Dennis looked at his father with an understanding that was far beyond his years. 'But grown-ups don't always know what they really want, do they?'

Jonathan burst out laughing. 'You could be right, son. Yes . . . I'm sure you're right.'

'But what about Miss Goodwin, Dad? She'll wonder where I am.'

'You're all in a muddle, son.' Jonathan gently touched the bandages that swathed his head. 'She'll already know about it, won't she? Have you forgotten? She's in *Carousel*. She would know last night when I didn't turn up for the show. And if I know Frances Goodwin she'll be here to see you before very long.'

Dennis's eyes lit up like stars. 'D'you think so, Dad?'

'I'm sure of it,' said Jonathan. 'Oh look, here's nurse. She'll be telling me off for getting you all excited. Listen, Den, I'll go home and have a little rest, get myself some dinner, then I'll be back this afternoon. OK?'

'OK, Dad.' Dennis grinned at him in a conspiratorial way. 'You're sure she'll come then?'

Jonathan winked. 'I'd stake my life on it.'

Jonathan's thoughts, as he prepared his simple lunch of eggs on toast, were as much of Frances Goodwin as of Dennis. For the time being his anxiety about his son had driven all other considerations out of his mind. Now he knew that Dennis was going to be all right he had time to ponder, and he was realising what a fool he had been not to make up this silly misunderstanding ages ago.

The little devil, though! Jonathan grinned to himself at the thought of his son trying his hand at matchmaking. And maybe it was not such a bad idea at that. He had long been attracted to Frances. He could not, however, say that he loved her because he didn't know her well enough. He had not yet had a chance to let his feelings develop, other matters having intruded upon their relationship. But develop they would; he felt sure of that.

She was such a lovely girl and beauty such as hers – inward as well as outward, he was now beginning to realise – could not help but attract admirers. And who could blame the girl for being swept off her feet by a dollop of masculine charm. That Avery fellow had possessed charm in abundance. Even Jonathan, a mere male, could see that. He suspected, now, that Frances had plunged headlong into that affair in all innocence, no doubt being conned by a pack of lies. But what did it matter? That was all history and he was determined to make it up with the young woman. He would ask her to go out with him, for a meal or to the cinema – maybe both – as he had intended doing at the party. It would be a start at least and then who could tell? He hoped desperately that what he had said to his son would prove to be true, that Frances would be at the hospital that afternoon.

Frances found there was no problem getting into Dennis's ward. When she arrived at two o'clock laden with comics, chocolate bars and a big bag of fruit, she was surprised, though somewhat relieved, to see she was the only visitor.

'The others'll be coming soon, I 'spect,' said Dennis. 'My dad and my gran and granddad.' He looked very pale and small in the big bed, his head swathed in bandages and his arm in plaster, but his eyes were bright with excitement. 'You'll stay, miss, won't you? My dad said he thought you'd come.'

'Oh . . . did he? I wonder why he said that, Dennis?'

'Because I told him about you coming to watch me carrying the flag. You got my letter, didn't you?'

'Yes, of course I did. But I wouldn't have forgotten, you know.'

'I know. Perhaps Akela'll let me do it next time.'

'I'm sure she will, Dennis.'

'And you'll come and watch?'

'Yes, I'll be there.'

He nodded contentedly then closed his eyes. Frances glanced round uneasily. Perhaps she had better slip away while Dennis was asleep, before Jonathan came. In spite of what Dennis said, he might think she had no business to be there. She was no longer the boy's teacher – she wasn't even at the same school any more – although she hoped she might be considered a friend, of Dennis if not of his father. But it was too late. Jonathan was already coming into the ward.

She stood up as he approached. 'Jonathan . . . I hope you don't mind me being here. They told me last night. I just had to come.' She looked away hurriedly, reaching out and touching Dennis's hand. 'He's just dropped off again.'

'Mmm. It'll be the effect of the concussion, poor little chap. But they've said he's going to be fine. You thought I would mind you being here? Why on earth should I mind?' He was speaking in a loud whisper. 'I'm delighted to see you. Frances . . .' He took hold of her arm. 'I'm sorry. We seem to have been at cross-purposes lately, you and I. I can't understand why.'

'Can't you?' She looked at him steadily. 'I think I know why. And I'm sorry, too.'

'Sorry? What have you to be sorry for?'

'Because I know you thought badly of me. And because of – oh, just . . . everything.'

'Let's start again, shall we?' Jonathan smiled at her. 'That is, if you would like to?'

Frances nodded. 'Yes, I think I would.'

'I was going to see you at the party. I had made up my mind. I was going to ask you to come for a meal with me, sometime next week. Now, of course, we'll have to see how Dennis goes on.'

'And I was going to ask you to come and help us at school,' said Frances. 'We're doing a gardening project and we need some help. I've already mentioned your name to the head. You'll get paid, of course.'

'Of course.' He laughed. 'But that's the least of my

worries. I'd be delighted to help.'

'It was just an excuse, really, to see you again.' Frances smiled at him, then looked away, a shade embarrassed. 'I've always felt I would like to get to know you but, somehow, it never happened.'

'No, other things got in our way.'

'And other people, too . . .'

'But it's never too late, Frances . . .'

'Hiya, Dad.' Dennis had opened his eyes again. 'You said Miss Goodwin'd come, didn't you? You were right. She's been here ages, haven't you, miss?'

Frances grinned at the boy. 'Dennis, do you think you could try to call me Frances? You know I've always hated being called "miss", and Miss Goodwin is such a mouthful. And we're friends, aren't we? I'm not your teacher any more.'

'OK, miss – I mean, Frances. Yes, I think that'd be dead good. Oh look, Dad. Here's Gran and Granddad coming.'

Jonathan rose to his feet as the middle-aged couple hesitantly entered at the far end of the ward, glancing uncertainly at each bed. Frances got up too. 'I'd better be going now, Jonathan. They don't like too many visitors. Besides, you'll want to talk to your mum and dad.'

Jonathan gently pushed her back into the chair. 'You'll stay just where you are. If the nurse complains, then we'll do something about it. But I'd like you to meet them.' He smiled encouragingly at her. 'I won't be a minute.' Then he dashed off to greet his parents.

'Er . . . Frances?' said Dennis.

'Yes, Dennis, what is it?'

'D'you remember, I said something to you, ages ago, something about me dad . . . and you said it was a silly idea?'

'Yes . . . I think I remember,' said Frances guardedly.

'Well, miss – I mean, Frances – d'you still think it's a silly idea?'

Frances burst out laughing. 'I'll tell you what I think. I think you'll soon be out of that bed and racing around again. And I also think you're too cheeky by far!' she added

404

in a reproving tone, but still smiling at him. Playfully she pinched his cheek. 'But it may not be such a silly idea after all.' She half closed her eye in a confiding wink. 'Let's just see how it goes, shall we?'

Jonathan re-entered the ward at that moment with his mother and father.

'Frances,' he smiled encouragingly at her. 'I'd like you to meet my parents.' He held out his hand and when she rose to her feet he continued to hold her hand. 'Mum, Dad. This is Frances Goodwin, a very special friend of mine.

She smiled, exchanging 'How do you dos?' as she shook hands with the middle-aged couple, aware of their interest in her and their slight surprise, but also of their friendliness and warmth. She felt she would like them as she grew to know them better.

'Frances used to be our Dennis's teacher,' said Jonathan. 'His very favourite teacher, but now she's our friend, his and mine. Anyway he'll tell you all about her, I've no doubt. The nurses get fidgety when there are more than two round the bed, so we'll leave you with Dennis for a little while. See you soon.'

'OK, son,' replied his father. 'That's a good idea. You don't know how relieved we are that this little lad's on the mend.'

'We promise we won't overtire him,' added his mother.

Jonathan put his arm round Frances's waist as they went out of the ward and into a visitors' small waiting room.

'Just an excuse really.' Jonathan grinned at her as he closed the door behind them. 'I'm glad the room's empty, but I don't suppose it will be for very long.' He held her gently by the shoulders, then, bending his head to hers, he kissed her softly on the lips. 'And that, I'm afraid, will have to be all for the moment.'

'I can wait, Jonathan,' she said, smiling up at him.

'But not too long?'

'No, not too long, I hope.'

What a strange place it was to be starting their courtship, a hospital waiting room. However, as she looked into

Jonathan's warm brown eyes she hardly noticed the bare green walls, the dark varnished paintwork, the functional wooden chairs and table and the faintly antiseptic smell that pervaded the room. She felt, beyond any doubt, that this was the start of something good.

She knew that Jonathan was a good man, just as good, in his own way, as Adrian. Maybe not so completely altruistic, so determined to lead a life of selfless service; but Adrian's goodness would have been well-nigh impossible to emulate. Jonathan was more like herself, resourceful, ready to face a challenge, and independent. She knew that she would need a degree of independence and Jonathan would allow her that.

He was not without a few faults, however, and that was all to the good. She knew he was inclined to be hasty-tempered – that, she recalled, had been how she first met him, when he had sprung to the defence of his son – and maybe too quick to make judgements. He had been right, though, to disapprove of her conduct with Marcus Avery. Even now the memory of her perfidy had the power to make her shudder. But it only served to show what an honourable sort of man Jonathan Russell was. She knew he was a man she could trust implicitly, and as she recognised, for the first time, the look of wonderment, of barely suppressed ardour in his eyes, she knew, too, that this was a man she could grow to love.

As Time Goes By

Harry Bowling

Carter Lane is an ordinary backstreet in Bermondsey and, for Dolly and Mick Flynn, it is home. When Dolly's boys volunteer for the armed forces and her daughter Sadie seems determined to throw her life away on a married man, Dolly's neighbour, Liz Kenny, is there to offer words of advice and a shoulder to cry on.

But when a bomb uncovers a skeleton in the yard of Gleeson's leather factory, their own lives are thrown into turmoil. As the Blitz takes its toll and the inhabitants of Carter Lane endure the sorrows and the partings which they had dreaded above all else, they find comfort in one another and solace in the knowledge that their wounds will heal – as time goes by.

'The king of Cockney sagas packs close-knit community good-heartedness into East End epics' *Daily Mail*

0 7472 5882 1

HEADLINE

At The Toss of a Sixpence

Lynda Page

At eleven years of age, Albertina Listerman loses her parents in a terrible accident. Approaching her twenty-first birthday, she experiences further tragedy: her half-brother commits suicide, having squandered the family fortune, and Ally is no longer acceptable in the elegant Victorian society of her childhood.

Robbed of her very last penny, Ally is thrust into a world of hardship for which she is ill-prepared. Her only salvation comes from meeting Jack Fossett during one of the worst rainstorms in Leicestershire's history. Jack is a kind, caring young lad who takes pity on the beautiful, bedraggled girl, and he and his younger brother and sister welcome Ally into their hearts.

But Jack's mother, Flo, is deeply resentful of all gentlefolk. And time must pass and secrets must be revealed before Ally and Flo can see eye to eye — particularly when they discover that Ally is in fact not as destitute as she thought . . .

0 7472 5504 0

HEADLINE